MERCIER ET CAMIER

DU MEME AUTEUR

Romans et nouvelles

Murphy
Watt
Premier amour
Mercier et Camier
Molloy
Malone meurt
L'innommable
Nouvelles (L'expulsé, Le calmant, La fin) et textes
    pour rien
Comment c'est
Têtes-mortes (D'un ouvrage abandonné, Assez,
    Imagination morte imaginez, Bing)

Théâtre, télévision et radio

En attendant Godot
Fin de partie, *suivi de* Acte sans paroles I
Tous ceux qui tombent
La dernière bande, *suivi de* Cendres
Oh les beaux jours
Comédie et actes divers (Va et vient, Cascando,
    Paroles et musique, Dis Joe, Acte sans paroles II)

SAMUEL BECKETT

MERCIER ET CAMIER

LES ÉDITIONS DE MINUIT

IL A ÉTÉ TIRÉ DE CET OUVRAGE
QUATRE-VINGT-DIX-NEUF EXEMPLAI-
RES SUR PUR FIL LAFUMA, NUMÉ-
ROTÉS DE 1 A 99 PLUS SEPT
EXEMPLAIRES HORS-COMMERCE NU-
MÉROTÉS DE H.-C. I A H.-C. VII
ET 201 EXEMPLAIRES SUR BOUFFANT
SÉLECT NUMÉROTÉS DE 100 A 300

IL A ÉTÉ TIRÉ EN OUTRE QUATRE-
VINGT-DOUZE EXEMPLAIRES SUR
BOUFFANT SELECT MARQUÉS « 92 »
NUMÉROTÉS DE 1 A 92 ET RÉSER-
VÉS A LA LIBRAIRIE DES ÉDITIONS
DE MINUIT

I

Le voyage de Mercier et Camier, je peux le raconter si je veux, car j'étais avec eux tout le temps.

Ce fut un voyage matériellement assez facile, sans mers ni frontières à franchir, à travers des régions peu accidentées, quoique désertiques par endroits. Ils restèrent chez eux, Mercier et Camier, ils eurent cette chance inestimable. Ils n'eurent pas à affronter, avec plus ou moins de bonheur, des mœurs étrangères, une langue, un code, un climat et une cuisine bizarres, dans un décor n'ayant que peu de rapport, au point de vue de la ressemblance, avec celui auquel l'âge tendre d'abord, ensuite l'âge mûr, les avaient endurcis. Le temps, quoique souvent inclément (mais ils en avaient l'habitude), ne sortit jamais des limites du tempéré, c'est-à-dire de ce que peut supporter, sans danger sinon sans désagrément, un homme de chez eux convenablement vêtu et chaussé. Quant à l'argent, s'ils n'en avaient pas assez pour voyager en première classe et pour descendre dans les palaces, ils en avaient assez pour aller et venir, sans tendre la main. On peut donc affirmer qu'à ce point de vue les conditions leur étaient favorables, modérément. Ils eurent à lutter, mais moins que beaucoup de gens, moins peut-être que la plupart des gens qui s'en vont, poussés par un besoin tantôt clair, tantôt obscur.

Ils s'étaient longuement consultés avant d'entreprendre ce voyage, pesant avec tout le calme dont ils étaient capables les avantages et désavantages qui pouvaient en résulter, pour eux. Le noir, le rose, ils les soutenaient à tour de rôle. La seule certitude qu'ils tiraient de ces débats était celle de ne pas se lancer à la légère dans l'aventure.

Camier arriva le premier au rendez-vous. C'est-à-dire qu'à son arrivée Mercier n'y était pas. En réalité, Mercier l'avait devancé de dix bonnes minutes. Ce fut donc Mercier, et non Camier, qui arriva le premier au rendez-vous. Ayant patienté pendant cinq minutes, en scrutant les diverses voies d'accès que pouvait emprunter son ami, Mercier partit faire un tour qui devait durer un quart d'heure. Camier à son tour, ne voyant pas Mercier venir, partit au bout de cinq minutes faire un petit tour. Revenu au rendez-vous un quart d'heure plus tard, ce fut en vain qu'il chercha Mercier des yeux. Et cela se comprend. Car Mercier, ayant patienté encore cinq minutes à l'endroit convenu, était reparti se dérouiller les jambes, pour employer une expression qui lui était chère. Camier donc, après cinq minutes d'une attente hébétée, s'en alla de nouveau, en se disant, Peut-être tomberai-je sur lui dans les rues avoisinantes. C'est à cet instant que Mercier, de retour de sa petite promenade, qui cette fois-ci ne s'était pas prolongée au-delà de dix minutes, vit s'éloigner une silhouette qui dans les brumes du matin ressemblait vaguement à celle de Camier, et qui l'était en effet. Malheureusement elle disparut, comme engloutie par le pavé, et Mercier reprit sa station. Mais après les cinq minutes en voie apparemment de devenir réglementaires il l'abandonna, ayant besoin de mouve-

9

ment. Leur joie fut donc pendant un instant extrême, celle de Mercier et celle de Camier, lorsque après cinq et dix minutes respectivement d'inquiète musardise, débouchant simultanément sur la place, ils se trouvèrent face à face, pour la première fois depuis la veille au soir. Il était neuf heures cinquante. Soit :

	Arr.	Dép.	Arr.	Dép.	Arr.	Dép.	Arr.
Mercier ..	9.05	9.10	9.25	9.30	9.40	9.45	9.50
Camier ..	9.15	9.20	9.35	9.40	9.50		

Que cela pue l'artifice.

Pendant qu'ils s'embrassaient la pluie se mit à tomber, avec une soudaineté toute orientale. Ils se précipitèrent donc dans l'abri en forme de pagode que l'on avait construit à cet endroit, pour servir d'abri contre la pluie et autres intempéries, contre le temps quoi. Sombre et abondant en coins et alcôves, il convenait également aux amoureux et aux personnes âgées, hommes et femmes. En même temps que nos deux pigeons un chien s'y engouffra, suivi peu après d'un autre. Mercier et Camier se regardèrent, irrésolus. Ils ne s'étaient pas embrassés jusqu'au

10

bout et pourtant cela les gênait de recommencer. Quant aux chiens, ils faisaient déjà l'amour, avec un naturel parfait.

L'endroit où ils se trouvaient, l'endroit où, non sans peine, ils étaient tombés d'accord pour se donner rendez-vous, n'était pas à proprement parler une place, mais plutôt un petit square enclavé dans un fouillis de rues et de ruelles. Ce square était garni des plantations, carrés de fleurs, bassins, fontaines, statues, pelouses et bancs habituels, avec une telle densité qu'il en semblait étranglé. Il tenait du dédale, le petit square, on y circulait avec gêne, et il fallait bien le connaître pour en pouvoir sortir à la première tentative. On y entrait naturellement le plus facilement du monde. Au centre, ou à peu près, s'élevait un hêtre pourpre immense et luisant, planté, à en croire l'enseigne grossièrement clouée au tronc, par un maréchal de France du nom paisible de Saint-Ruth, plusieurs siècles auparavant. A peine l'eut-il planté, d'après l'inscription, qu'il fut tué — le maréchal — par un boulet de canon, toujours au service de la même cause désespérée, sur un champ de bataille n'ayant que très peu de rapport, au point

11

de vue du paysage, avec ceux où il avait fait ses preuves, comme brigadier et ensuite comme lieutenant, si c'est bien dans cet ordre qu'on fait ses preuves, sur les champs de bataille. C'est sans doute à cet arbre que le square devait d'exister, conséquence dont le maréchal ne devait guère se douter, alors qu'à l'écart des quinconces, devant une société élégante et repue, il soutenait, dans le trou gras de rosée vespérale, le frêle sauvageon. Mais pour en finir avec cet arbre, et pour ne plus avoir à en parler, c'est de lui que le square tirait le peu qu'il lui restait de charme, ainsi que, bien entendu, son nom, à savoir Square Saint-Ruth. Le géant étouffé touchait au terme de sa carrière et ne s'arrêterait plus de dépérir jusqu'au jour où l'on l'enlèverait, par morcellement. Ensuite, pendant un petit moment, dans le square au nom mystérieux, on respirerait mieux.

Mercier et Camier ne connaissaient pas cet endroit. C'est ce qui les amena sans doute à s'y donner rendez-vous. Certaines choses, nous ne les saurons jamais avec certitude.

A travers la vitre orangée la pluie leur

semblait d'or, ce qui les fit penser, conformément au hasard de leurs excursions, l'un à Rome, l'autre à Naples, mais sans se l'avouer l'un à l'autre, et avec un sentiment voisin de la honte. Cela aurait dû leur faire du bien, cette intrusion d'une lointaine époque, où ils étaient jeunes, et avaient chaud, et aimaient la peinture, et raillaient le mariage. Mais cela ne leur fit pas de bien. Ils ne se connaissaient pas alors, mais depuis qu'ils se connaissaient ils en avaient parlé, de cette époque, trop parlé, par bribes, suivant leur coutume.

Rentrons, dit Camier.

Pourquoi ? dit Mercier.

Ça ne s'arrêtera pas de la journée, dit Camier.

C'est une averse, plus ou moins prolongée, dit Mercier.

Je ne peux pas rester debout, sans rien faire, dit Camier.

Asseyons-nous, dit Mercier.

C'est pire, dit Camier.

Alors marchons de long en large, dit Mercier. Donnons-nous le bras et faisons les cent pas. L'espace est réduit, mais il pourrait l'être davantage. Pose là notre

13

parapluie, aide-moi à me débarrasser de notre sac, voilà, merci, et en avant.

Camier se laissa faire.

Un deux un deux, dit Mercier.

Un deux, dit Camier.

Par moments le ciel s'éclaircissait et la pluie tombait moins fort. Alors ils s'arrêtaient devant la porte. Mais aussitôt le ciel s'assombrissait de nouveau et la pluie redoublait de violence.

Ne regarde pas, dit Mercier.

Entendre me suffit, dit Camier.

Cela est vrai, dit Mercier.

Patience et courage, dit Camier.

Les chiens ne te gênent pas ? dit Mercier.

Pourquoi ne se retire-t-il pas ? dit Camier.

Il ne peut pas, dit Mercier.

Pourquoi ? dit Camier.

Un dispositif quelconque, dit Mercier, sans doute pour assurer l'insémination.

Ils commencent à la chevauchée, dit Camier, et ils finissent cul-à-cul.

Que veux-tu ? dit Mercier. L'extase est terminée, ils voudraient se quitter, aller pisser contre une borne ou manger un morceau de merde, mais ils ne peuvent pas.

14

Alors ils se tournent le dos. Tu en ferais autant, à leur place.

La délicatesse m'en empêcherait, dit Camier.

Et que ferais-tu ? dit Mercier.

Je ferais semblant, dit Camier, de regretter de ne pas pouvoir remettre ça tout de suite, tant ç'avait été bon.

Après un moment de silence Camier dit :

Si on s'assoyait, cela m'a vidé.

Tu veux dire s'asseyait, dit Mercier.

Je veux dire s'assoyait, dit Camier.

Assoyons-nous, dit Mercier.

De toutes parts déjà les gens vaquaient à leurs affaires. L'air se remplissait de cris de contentement et de mécontentement, ainsi que des tons posés de ceux pour qui la vie avait épuisé ses surprises, aussi bien du côté négatif que du côté positif. Les choses elles aussi se mettaient lourdement en branle, et notamment les véhicules lourds, tels camions, charrettes et transports en commun. La pluie avait beau faire rage, tout recommençait avec autant d'ardeur apparemment que si le ciel avait été d'azur.

Tu m'as fait attendre, dit Mercier.

15

Au contraire, dit Camier, c'est toi qui m'as fait attendre.

Je suis arrivé à neuf heures cinq, dit Mercier.

Moi à neuf heures quinze, dit Camier.

Tu vois bien que tu m'as fait attendre, dit Mercier.

On n'attend ni ne fait attendre, dit Camier, qu'à partir d'un moment convenu d'avance.

Et le rendez-vous était pour quelle heure, selon toi ? dit Mercier.

Pour le quart de neuf heures, dit Camier.

Je ne comprends pas, dit Mercier.

Que ne comprends-tu pas ? dit Camier.

Ce que ça veut dire, le quart de neuf heures, dit Mercier.

Ça veut dire neuf heures quinze minutes, dit Camier.

Alors tu te trompes lourdement, dit Mercier.

C'est-à-dire ? dit Camier.

Ne finiras-tu jamais de m'étonner ? dit Mercier.

Explique-toi, dit Camier.

Je ferme les yeux et je revois la scène, dit Mercier, ta main dans la mienne, les

16

larmes qui me montent aux yeux et ma voix mal affermie qui disait, Ainsi soit-il, à demain, neuf heures. Une femme ivre est passée, chantant une chanson obscène et relevant sa jupe.

Elle t'a troublé les esprits, dit Camier. Il sortit un calepin de sa poche, le feuilleta et lut : Lundi deux, Saint-Macaire, Mercier, quart de neuf, square Saint-Ruth. Cherche parapluie chez Hélène.

Et qu'est-ce que ça prouve ? dit Mercier.

Ma bonne foi, dit Camier.

Cela est vrai, dit Mercier.

Nous ne saurons jamais, dit Camier, à quelle heure nous nous sommes donné rendez-vous, aujourd'hui. Ne cherchons donc plus.

Une seule chose est certaine, dans cette histoire, dit Mercier, c'est que nous nous sommes retrouvés à dix heures moins dix, en même temps que les aiguilles.

Soyons-en reconnaissants, dit Camier.

Il ne pleuvait pas encore, dit Mercier.

L'élan matinal était intact, dit Camier.

Ne perds pas notre calepin, dit Mercier.

Alors jaillit le premier d'une longue série d'êtres malfaisants. Son uniforme, vert d'un

17

vert détrempé et copieusement garni, à l'endroit réglementaire, d'insignes héroïques et de rubans, lui allait bien, très bien. Fort de l'exemple du grand Sarsfield, il avait failli crever dans la défense d'un territoire qui en lui-même devait certainement le laisser indifférent et qui considéré comme symbole ne l'excitait pas beaucoup non plus probablement. Il tenait une canne à la fois élégante et massive, il s'appuyait même dessus, par moments. Il avait très mal à la hanche, la douleur par moments lui zébrait la fesse et entrait dans le trou, d'où elle envoyait des signaux de détresse par tout le système intestinal et jusqu'à la valvule pylorique, avec prolongements urétro-scrotaux, bien entendu, et envie d'uriner quasi incessante. Invalide à quinze pour cent, ce qui le faisait déconsidérer par la grande majorité de ceux, et de celles, avec qui son métier et ses vestiges de bonhomie le mettaient quotidiennement en contact, il lui semblait parfois qu'il aurait mieux fait, pendant la grande tourmente, de se consacrer aux escarmouches domestiques, à la langue gaélique, au raffermissement de sa foi et aux trésors d'un folklore unique au monde. Le danger corporel eût été moindre et les bénéfices plus certains. Mais cette pensée, après en avoir dégusté toute l'amertume, il avait coutume de la bannir, comme indigne de lui. Sa moustache, qui se voulait raide, et qui l'avait été, ne l'était plus. De temps en temps, d'en dessous, quand il y pensait, il y envoyait un jet d'haleine fétide, mêlée de salive. Cela la redressait momentanément. Immobile au pied des marches de la pagode, sa cape entrouverte, ruisselant de pluie, ses regards allaient et venaient, de Mercier et Camier aux chiens, des chiens à Mercier et Camier.

A qui est cette bicyclette ? dit-il.

Mercier et Camier se regardèrent.

Nous n'avions pas besoin de ça, dit Camier.

Enlevez-la, dit le gardien.

Ça serait peut-être une petite distraction, dit Mercier.

A qui sont ces chiens ? dit le gardien.

Pour moi, dit Camier, nous allons être obligés de nous éloigner.

Serait-ce le coup de fouet dont nous avions besoin, pour nous mettre en route ? dit Mercier.

M'obligerez-vous à appeler un agent ? dit le gardien.

On dirait qu'il sent mauvais, par dessus le marché, dit Camier.

Préférez-vous que j'appelle un serrurier, dit le gardien, pour qu'il fracture le cadenas ? Ou que je l'enlève moi-même à coups de pied dans les rayons ?

Comprends-tu quelque chose à ces propos incohérents ? dit Camier.

Ma vue a beaucoup baissé, dit Mercier. Il est question, je crois, d'une bicyclette.

Et alors ? dit Camier.

Sa présence ici, dit Mercier, serait contraire à la loi.

Alors, qu'il l'enlève, dit Camier.

Il ne peut pas, dit Mercier. Un système de sûreté quelconque, tel un cadenas, ou un câble, l'attache, à un arbre sans doute, ou à une statue. Telle est du moins mon interprétation.

Elle est plausible, dit Mercier.

Malheureusement il n'y a pas que la bicyclette, si j'ai bien compris, dit Mercier. Il y a aussi les chiens.

Que font-ils de mal ? dit Camier.

Ils contreviennent à l'arrêté, dit Mercier, au même titre que la petite reine.

Mais eux ils ne sont attachés à rien, dit Camier, sinon l'un à l'autre, par le coït.

Cela est vrai, dit Mercier.

Alors, qu'il fasse son devoir, dit Camier, qu'il nous les enlève immédiatement.

Je suis de ton avis, dit Mercier.

Les chiens peuvent attendre, dit le gardien.

Haha ! dit Camier.

Pourquoi ris-tu de si bon cœur ? dit Mercier.

Ils peuvent attendre ! dit Camier.

Je vous en foutrai, des rires, dit le gardien.

Mon père me disait toujours, dit Mercier, d'ôter ma pipe de la bouche avant de m'adresser à un étranger, quelque humble que fût sa condition.

Quelque humble, dit Camier, que cela sonne drôlement.

Le gardien monta les marches de l'abri et s'immobilisa dans l'encadrement de la porte. L'air s'assombrit aussitôt, et devint plus jaune.

Je crois qu'il va nous attaquer, dit Camier.

21

A toi les couilles, comme d'habitude, dit Mercier.

Cher sergent, dit Camier, que nous voulez-vous exactement ?

Vous voyez cette bicyclette ? dit le gardien.

Je ne vois rien, dit Camier. Mercier, vois-tu une bicyclette ?

Est-elle à vous ? dit le gardien.

Une chose que nous ne voyons pas, dit Camier, dont l'existence ressort uniquement de vos assertions, comment pouvons-nous savoir si elle est à nous, ou à autrui ?

Pourquoi serait-elle à nous ? dit Mercier. Ces chiens sont-ils à nous ? Non. Nous les voyons aujourd'hui pour la première fois. Et vous voulez que la bicyclette, si bicyclette il y a, soit à nous. Pourtant les chiens ne sont pas à nous.

Je m'en fous de vos chiens, dit le gardien.

Mais comme pour se démentir il se précipita sur eux et les expulsa, à coups de pied et de canne, et avec force jurons, hors de la pagode. Attachés qu'ils étaient toujours, l'un à l'autre, leur retraite fut difficile. Car les efforts qu'ils faisaient pour se

sauver, s'exerçant en sens contraire, ne lais-
saient pas de s'annuler. Ils durent beaucoup
souffrir.

Sales bêtes, dit le gardien.

Il s'est maintenant foutu des chiens, dit
Mercier.

Il les a chassés de l'abri, dit Camier, c'est
incontestable, mais point du square.

La pluie ne tardera pas à défaire leurs
liens, dit Mercier. Abrutis par l'amour ils
n'y avaient pas pensé.

En somme, il leur a rendu un service, dit
Camier.

Soyons un peu gentils avec lui, dit Mercier, c'est un héros de la grande guerre.
Pendant que nous, bien au chaud, nous
nous masturbions à pleins tubes, sans crainte
d'interruption, lui il rampait dans la boue
flamande, en chiant dans ses bottes.

Ne déduisez rien de ces paroles en l'air,
Mercier et Camier furent vieux jeunes.

C'est une idée, dit Camier.

Regarde-moi ce plâtras de décorations,
dit Mercier. Tu te rends compte de ce que
ça représente comme coliques ?

Faiblement, dit Camier, j'ai toujours été
bouché.

Admettons que cette soi-disant bicyclette soit à nous, dit Mercier. Où est le mal ?

Soyons francs, dit Camier, elle est à nous.

Je vous donne cinq minutes pour l'enlever, dit le gardien. Puis j'appelle un agent.

C'est aujourd'hui enfin, dit Mercier, après des années de tergiversations, que nous partons, vers une destination inconnue, et dont nous ne reviendrons peut-être pas vivants. Nous attendons simplement que le temps se lève, pour nous élancer. Essayez de comprendre.

Ça ne me regarde pas, dit le gardien.

En plus, dit Mercier, il nous reste certaines choses à mettre au point, avant qu'il ne soit trop tard.

A mettre au point ? dit Camier.

C'est ce que j'ai dit, dit Mercier.

Je croyais que tout était au point, dit Camier.

Tout ne l'est pas, dit Mercier.

L'enlevez-vous ou ne l'enlevez-vous pas, dit le gardien.

Peut-on acheter votre complaisance, dit Mercier, puisque vous êtes insensible à la raison.

Certainement, dit le gardien.

Donne-lui un shilling, dit Mercier, C'est malheureux quand même, que notre premier débours soit sous le signe d'un vil chantage.

Assassins, dit le gardien. Puis il disparut.

Que les gens sont d'un bloc, dit Mercier.

Maitenant il va rôder autour, dit Camier.

Qu'est-ce que ça peut nous faire ? dit Mercier.

Je n'aime pas qu'on me rôde autour, dit Camier.

Tu veux dire rôde autour de moi, dit Mercier.

Je veux dire me rôde autour, dit Camier.

Ce petit jeu-là ne durera pas longtemps.

Il ne devait pas être loin de midi.

Maintenant, à nous, dit Mercier.

A nous ? dit Camier.

Parfaitement, dit Mercier, à nous, aux choses sérieuses.

Si on mangeait un morceau, dit Camier.

Mettons d'abord les choses au point, dit Mercier. Après nous nous restaurerons.

S'ensuivit un long débat, entrecoupé de longs silences, pendant lesquels la méditation s'effectuait. Il arrivait alors, tantôt à Mercier, tantôt à Camier, de s'abîmer si avant

25

dans ses pensées que la voix de l'autre, repre-
nant son argumentation, était impuissante à
l'en tirer, ou ne se faisait pas entendre. Ou,
arrivés simultanément à des conclusions souvent contraires, ils se mettaient simultanément à les exprimer. Il n'était pas rare non
plus que l'un tombât en syncope avant que
l'autre eût achevé son exposé. Et de temps
en temps ils se regardaient, incapables de
prononcer un mot, et l'esprit vide. C'est à
l'issu d'une de ces torpeurs qu'ils renoncè-
rent à pousser leur enquête plus loin, pour
l'instant. L'après-midi était fort avancé, la
pluie tombait toujours, la courte journée
d'hiver inclinait vers sa fin.

C'est toi qui as les provisions, dit Mercier.

Au contraire, c'est toi, dit Camier.

C'est vrai, dit Mercier.

Je n'ai plus faim, dit Camier.

Il faut manger, dit Mercier.

Je n'en vois pas l'utilité, dit Camier.

Le chemin qu'il nous reste à faire est long
et difficile, dit Mercier.

Plus vite on crèvera, mieux ça vaudra, dit
Camier.

Cela est vrai, dit Mercier.

La tête du gardien parut à la porte. C'était

invraisemblable, ou ne voyait que sa tête.

Si vous désirez passer la nuit, dit-il, ce sera une demi-couronne.

Les choses sont-elles maintenant au point ? dit Camier.

Non, dit Mercier.

Le seront-elles jamais ? dit Camier.

Je le crois, dit Mercier. Oui, je crois, pas fermement, mais je crois, que le jour viendra où les choses seront au point, enfin.

Ce sera charmant, dit Camier.

Espérons, dit Mercier.

Ils se regardèrent longuement. Camier se disait, Même lui, je ne le vois pas. Une pensée analogue agitait son vis-à-vis.

Deux points semblaient pourtant acquis, à la suite de cet entretien.

1. Mercier partirait seul, à bicyclette, avec l'imperméable. Il ferait le nécessaire, arrivé à l'étape, pour que tout soit prêt pour recevoir Camier, qui se mettrait en route dès que le temps le permettrait. Camier garderait le parapluie.

2. Il se trouvait que c'était Mercier, jusqu'à présent, qui avait fait preuve d'allant, et Camier de mollesse. L'inverse était à prévoir d'un moment à l'autre. Qu'au moins

27

faible le plus faible toujours s'en remette, pour la marche à suivre. Ils pouvaient être vaillants en même temps. Ce serait merveilleux. Ou ils pouvaient accuser simultanément une grosse défaillance. Qu'en ce cas ils ne s'abandonnent pas au désespoir, mais qu'ils attendent, avec confiance, que le mauvais moment soit passé. Malgré le vague de ces termes ils se comprenaient, à peu près.

Je détourne les yeux, dit Camier, ne sachant plus à quoi penser.

On dirait l'éclaircie, dit Mercier.

Le soleil sort enfin, dit Camier, afin qu'on admire sa chute, à l'horizon.

Ce long instant de clarté, dit Mercier, aux mille couleurs, il me touche toujours.

La journée de labeur est terminée, dit Camier. Une sorte d'encre surgit à l'orient et inonde le ciel.

La cloche sonna, annonçant la fermeture.

Je garde l'impression, dit Camier, de formes vagues et cotonneuses. Elles vont et viennent, en criant sourdement.

En effet, dit Mercier, je crois que nous avons des témoins, depuis ce matin.

Serions-nous seuls, à présent ? dit Camier.

Je ne vois personne, dit Mercier.

Partons ensemble, puisque c'est ainsi, dit Camier.

Ils sortirent de l'abri.

Le sac, dit Mercier.

Le parapluie, dit Camier.

L'imperméable, dit Mercier.

Je l'ai, dit Camier.

Il n'y a rien d'autre ? dit Mercier.

Je ne vois rien d'autre, dit Camier.

J'irai les chercher, dit Mercier, occupe-toi de la bicyclette.

C'était une bicyclette de femme, sans roue libre malheureusement. Pour freiner on pédalait en sens inverse.

Le gardien, sa trousse de clefs à la main, les regarda s'éloigner. Mercier tenait le guidon, Camier la selle.

Assassins, dit-il.

II

Des vitrines s'éclairaient, d'autres s'éteignaient, cela dépendait de la vitrine. Les rues glissantes s'emplissaient de gens se pressant apparemment vers un but déterminé. L'air s'imprégnait d'une sorte de bien-être courroucé et las. En fermant les yeux on n'entendait pas une voix, seulement l'immense halètement des pas. Dans ce silence de horde ils avançaient, comme ils pouvaient. Ils se tenaient sur le bord extérieur du trottoir, Mercier devant, la main sur le guidon, Camier derrière, la main sur la selle, et la bicyclette glissait dans la rigole, à leur côté.

Te me gênes plus que tu ne m'aides, dit Mercier.

Je ne cherche pas à t'aider, dit Camier, je cherche à m'aider moi.

Alors tout est bien, dit Mercier.

J'ai froid, dit Camier.

Il faisait froid, en effet.

Il fait froid, en effet, dit Mercier.

Où allons-nous, de ce pas mal assuré ? dit Camier.

Nous nous dirigeons je crois vers le canal, dit Mercier.

Déjà ? dit Camier.

Il se peut que ça nous fasse plaisir, dit Mercier, d'enfiler le chemin de halage et de le suivre, jusqu'à ce qu'ennui s'ensuive. Devant nous, nous appelant, sans que nous ayons à lever les yeux, les couleurs mourantes que nous aimons tant.

Parle pour toi, dit Camier.

L'eau également sera livide, dit Mercier, pendant un bon moment, ce qui n'est pas à dédaigner non plus. Et, qui sait, il nous poussera peut-être l'envie de nous y jeter.

Les petits ponts s'espacent de plus en plus, dit Camier. Penchés sur les sas nous essayons de comprendre. Des chalands amarrés contre la berge s'envolent les voix des mariniers, nous souhaitant le bonsoir. Leur journée est terminée, ils fument la dernière pipe, avant de se mettre au lit.

Les sas ? dit Mercier.

Les sas, dit Camier, S-A-S, sas.

Chacun pour soi, dit Mercier, et Dieu pour tous.

La ville est loin derrière nous, dit Camier. Peu à peu la nuit nous rattrape, bleue-noire. Les étoiles sont voilées, par les nuages. La lune ne se lèvera que vers quatre heures du matin. Il fait de plus en plus froid. Nous pataugeons dans les flaques d'eau que la pluie a laissées. Il n'y a plus moyen d'avancer. Reculer est également hors de question.

Il ajouta, quelques moments plus tard :

A quoi rêves-tu, Mercier ?

A l'horreur de l'existence, confusément, dit Mercier.

Si on allait boire un coup ? dit Camier.

Je nous croyais d'accord, dit Mercier, pour ne plus boire qu'en cas d'accident, ou d'indisposition. Cela ne figure-t-il pas parmi nos nombreuses conventions ?

Il ne s'agit pas de boire, dit Camier, il s'agit de prendre un petit verre, en vitesse, pour nous donner du cœur au ventre.

Ils s'arrêtèrent au premier bar.

Pas de vélos ici, dit le patron.

Réflexion faite, ce n'était peut-être qu'un employé.

Lui, il l'appelle un vélo, dit Camier.

Sortons, dit Mercier.

Fumiers, dit le barman.

Et maintenant ? dit Camier.

Si on l'attachait à un bec de gaz ? dit Mercier.

On serait plus libre, de ses mouvements, dit Camier.

Ils se décidèrent finalement pour une grille. Cela revenait au même.

Et maintenant ? dit Mercier.

On retourne chez monsieur Vélo ? dit Camier.

Jamais, dit Mercier.

Ne dis jamais ça, dit Camier.

Ils allèrent donc au bar d'en face.

Assis au comptoir ils devisèrent de choses et d'autres, à bâtons rompus, suivant leur habitude. Ils parlaient, se taisaient, s'écoutaient, ne s'écoutaient plus, chacun à son gré, et suivant son rythme à soi. Il y avait des moments, des minutes entières, où Camier n'avait pas la force de porter son verre à sa bouche. Quant à Mercier, il était sujet à la même défaillance. Alors le plus fort donnait à boire au plus faible, en lui insérant entre les lèvres le bord de son

33

verre. Des masses ténébreuses et comme en peluche se pressaient autour d'eux, de plus en plus serrées à mesure que l'heure avançait. Il ressortait néanmoins de cet entretien, entre autres choses, ce qui suit.

1. Il serait inutile, et même téméraire, d'aller plus loin, pour l'instant.

2. Ils n'avaient qu'à demander à Hélène de les loger pour la nuit.

3. Rien ne les empêcherait de se mettre en route le lendemain, à la première heure, et par n'importe quel temps.

4. Ils n'avaient pas de reproches à s'adresser.

5. Ce qu'ils cherchaient existait-il ?

6. Que cherchaient-ils ?

7. Rien ne pressait.

8. Tous leurs jugements relatifs à cette expédition étaient à revoir, à tête reposée.

9. Une seule chose comptait : partir.

10. Et puis merde.

A nouveau dans la rue ils se prirent le bras. Après quelques centaines de mètres Mercier fit remarquer à Camier qu'ils n'étaient pas au pas.

Tu as ton rythme, dit Camier, moi j'ai le mien.

Je ne nous fais pas de reproches, dit Mercier. Mais c'est fatigant. On avance par saccades.

J'aimerais mieux, dit Camier, que tu me demandes carrément et sans ambages, soit de lâcher ton bras et de m'éloigner, soit de me plier à tes titubations.

Camier, Camier, dit Mercier, en lui serrant le bras.

Arrivés à un carrefour ils s'arrêtèrent.

Par où faut-il qu'on se trascine, à présent ? dit Camier.

Notre situation est bizarre, dit Mercier, je veux dire par rapport à la maison d'Hélène, si je me suis bien repéré. Car ces diverses voies que tu vois, elles y conduisent toutes avec une égale félicité.

Alors rebroussons chemin, dit Camier.

Cela nous en éloignerait sensiblement, dit Mercier.

On ne peut cependant rester plantés là toute la nuit, dit Camier, comme deux cons.

Lançons notre parapluie en l'air, dit Mercier. Il retombera d'une certaine manière, suivant des lois que nous ignorons. Nous n'aurons plus qu'à nous élancer dans l'axe indiqué.

Le parapluie répondit, A gauche. Il avait l'air d'un grand oiseau blessé, un grand oiseau de malheur que des chasseurs venaient d'abattre et qui haletant attendait le coup de grâce. La ressemblance était frappante. Camier le ramassa et le pendit à sa poche.

Il n'est pas cassé, j'espère, dit Mercier.

Leur attention fut attirée, à ce moment, par une figure étrange, celle d'un monsieur vêtu, malgré la fraîcheur de l'air, d'un simple frac et chapeau haut-de-forme. Il semblait suivre, pour le moment, le même chemin qu'eux, car ils le voyaient de dos. Ses mains, d'un geste coquettement dément, soulevaient, tout en les écartant, les basques de son habit. Il marchait avec précaution, les jambes raides et écartées.

As-tu envie de chanter ? dit Camier.

Pas à ma connaissance, dit Mercier.

Il recommençait à pleuvoir. Mais la pluie avait-elle jamais cessé ?

Dépêchons-nous, dit Camier.

Pourquoi me demandes-tu ça ? dit Mercier.

Camier ne semblait pas pressé de répondre. Enfin il dit :

J'entends chanter.

Ils s'arrêtèrent, afin de mieux écouter.

Je n'entends rien, dit Mercier.

Tu as pourtant une bonne ouïe, je pense, dit Camier.

Très convenable, dit Mercier.

Etrange, dit Camier.

Tu l'entends toujours ? dit Mercier.

On dirait un chœur mixte, dit Camier.

C'est peut-être une illusion, dit Mercier.

C'est possible, dit Camier.

Si on courait, dit Mercier.

Ils coururent pendant un bon moment, par les rues sombres, humides et désertes. Quand ils eurent fini de courir, Camier dit :

Nous allons arriver chez Hélène dans un bel état, mouillés jusqu'aux os.

Nous nous déshabillerons aussitôt, dit Camier. Nous mettrons nos vêtements à sécher, devant le feu, ou dans l'armoire à linge, où passent les tuyaux d'eau chaude.

Au fait, dit Mercier, pourquoi ne s'est-on pas servi de notre parapluie ?

Camier regarda le parapluie qu'il tenait maintenant à la main. Il l'y avait mis pour pouvoir courir plus librement.

On aurait pu, dit-il.

A quoi sert-il de s'encombrer d'un parapluie, dit Mercier, si on ne l'ouvre pas en
temps voulu ?

Je suis de ton avis, dit Camier.

Ouvre-le, nom de Dieu, dit Mercier.

Mais Camier ne put l'ouvrir.

Je ne peux pas, dit-il.

Donne, dit Mercier.

Mais Mercier non plus ne put l'ouvrir.

A ce moment la pluie, agent complaisant
de la malignité universelle, se convertit en
véritable déluge.

Il est coincé, dit Camier. Ne le force pas,
surtout.

Charogne, dit Mercier.

C'est pour moi ? dit Camier.

C'est pour le parapluie, dit Mercier. Il le
leva, en se servant des deux mains, haut au-
dessus de sa tête et le jeta avec violence par
terre. Enculé, va, dit-il. Il ajouta, en présen-
tant au ciel une face convulsée et ruisselante,
et en levant et serrant les poings, Quant à
toi, je t'emmerde.

La douleur de Mercier, héroïquement con-
tenue depuis le matin, se donnait maintenant libre carrière, cela ne faisait pas de
doute.

C'est à notre petit omni-omni que tu tiens ce langage ? dit Camier. Tu as tort. C'est lui au contraire qui t'emmerde toi. Lui est inemmerdable. Omni-omni, l'inemmerdable.

Je te prie de laisser le nom de madame Mercier en dehors de cette discussion, dit Mercier.

C'est le délire, dit Camier.

La boue serait un peu plus profonde à cet endroit, dit Mercier, que je m'y roulerais jusqu'au matin.

Chez Hélène on remarquait tout de suite le tapis.

Regarde-moi cette moquette, dit Camier.

Mercier la regarda.

C'est un gentil tapis, dit-il.

Inouï, dit Camier.

On dirait que tu le vois pour la première fois, dit Mercier. Tu t'y es pourtant assez vautré.

Je le vois pour la première fois, dit Camier. Je ne l'oublierai jamais.

On dit ça, dit Mercier.

Si on voyait surtout le tapis, ce soir-là, on ne voyait pas que lui. Car on voyait l'ara aussi. Sur son bâton, suspendu à un angle du plafond, et qu'agitaient confusément des propensions oscillatoires et tourbillonnantes, il se tenait en équilibre inquiet. Il ne dormait pas, malgré l'heure tardive. Sa poitrine allait faiblement se bombant et se creusant, avec une arythmie oppressée. D'imperceptibles frissons soulevaient le duvet, à chaque expiration. De temps en temps le bec s'ouvrait et restait pendant quelques secondes ouvert. On aurait dit un poisson. Alors on voyait la langue noire et fuselée qui remuait. Les yeux, légèrement détournés de la lumière, remplis d'une angoisse et d'un égarement indicibles, semblaient aux écoutes. Des rides anxieuses couraient sur le plumage, flambant d'un éclat ironique. Au-dessous de lui, sur le tapis, s'étalait un grand journal déplié.

Il y a mon lit et il y a le divan, dit Hélène.

Débrouillez-vous, dit Mercier, moi je ne coucherai avec personne.

Un gentil petit pompier, pas trop prolongé, dit Camier, je veux bien, mais pas plus.

C'est fini, les gentils petits pompiers pas plus, dit Hélène.

Je me coucherai par terre, dit Mercier, et j'attendrai l'aube. Devant mes yeux ouverts défileront des scènes et des visages. La pluie sur la verrière fera son bruit de griffes et la nuit me contera ses couleurs. L'envie me viendra de me jeter par la fenêtre, mais je la dominerai. Il répéta, dans un rugissement, Je la dominerai !

A nouveau dans la rue ils se demandèrent ce qu'ils avaient fait de la bicyclette. Le sac également avait disparu.

Tu as vu le perroquet ? dit Mercier.

Il est joli, dit Camier.

Il a gémi dans la nuit, dit Mercier. Je ne savais pas que les perroquets gémissaient, et cependant il a gémi, assez souvent même.

C'était peut-être une souris, dit Camier.

Je le verrai jusqu'au jour de ma mort, dit Mercier.

Je ne savais pas qu'elle avait un perroquet, dit Camier. Mais c'est surtout la moquette qui m'a donné un coup.

Moi non plus, dit Mercier. Elle dit qu'elle l'a depuis des années.

Elle ment naturellement, dit Camier.

Il pleuvait toujours. Ils se réfugièrent sous une porte cochère, ne sachant pas où aller.

41

A quel moment précis as-tu constaté l'absence de notre sac ? dit Mercier.

Ce matin, dit Camier, en voulant avaler quelques sulfamides.

Ces détails ne m'intéressent pas, dit Mercier.

Tu te rappelles les événements d'hier soir ? dit Camier.

Je me les rappelle, grosso modo, dit Mercier. Mais nous étions dans un quartier que je connais peu.

Comment tu te sens, aujourd'hui ? dit Camier.

Je me sens faible, mais décidé, dit Mercier. Et toi ?

Ça va plutôt un peu mieux qu'hier, dit Camier.

Je ne vois pas le parapluie, dit Mercier.

Camier s'inspecta, en baissant la tête et en écartant les bras, comme s'il s'agissait d'un bouton.

Nous avons dû l'oublier chez Hélène, dit-il.

J'ai l'impression, dit Mercier, que si nous ne quittons pas cette ville aujourd'hui, nous ne la quitterons jamais. Réfléchissons donc bien, avant de nous lancer à la poursuite de ces objets.

42

Qu'est-ce qu'il y avait dans le sac, au juste ? dit Camier.

Des objets de toilette, dit Mercier.

Luxe inutile, dit Camier.

Quelques paires de chaussettes et un caleçon, dit Mercier.

Tu te rends compte, dit Camier.

Et des provisions de bouche, dit Mercier.

Juste bonnes à jeter, dit Camier.

A condition de les récupérer, dit Mercier.

Prenons le premier express en partance vers le sud ! s'écria Camier. Il ajouta, Comme ça on ne sera pas tenté de descendre à la première station.

Et pourquoi vers le sud, dit Mercier, plutôt que vers le nord, ou vers l'est, ou vers l'ouest ?

J'aime mieux le sud, dit Camier.

Est-ce une raison ? dit Mercier.

C'est la gare la plus proche, dit Camier.

Je n'avais pas pensé à ça, dit Mercier. Il sortit dans la rue et regarda le ciel. Le ciel était gris et bas, de quelque côté qu'il regardât.

Le ciel est uniformément pisseux, dit-il, en rentrant sous la voûte. Nous allons nous faire saucer comme des rats, sans notre parapluie.

Tu veux dire comme des chiens, dit Camier.

Je veux dire comme des rats, dit Mercier.

On aurait le parapluie, dit Camier, qu'on serait dans l'impossibilité d'en profiter. Il est cassé.

Que me racontes-tu là ? dit Mercier.

Nous l'avons cassé hier soir, dit Camier, en le consultant. C'était ton idée.

Mercier se prit la tête entre les mains. Peu à peu la scène lui revint. Il se redressa, fièrement.

Allons, dit-il, pas de regrets inutiles.

Nous mettrons l'imperméable tour à tour, dit Camier.

Nous serons dans le train, dit Mercier, fonçant vers le sud.

A travers les vitres ruisselantes, dit Camier, nous essayons de compter les vaches. Elles frissonnent tristement, à l'abri imparfait des haies. Des corbeaux s'envolent, tout mouillés et dépenaillés. Mais peu à peu le temps s'améliore. Et nous débarquons sous le soleil éclatant d'un bel après-midi d'hiver. On se croit à Monaco.

Je ne me souviens d'avoir rien mangé, depuis vingt-quatre heures, dit Mercier.

Moi j'ai mangé une soupe aux oignons, vers quatre heures du matin, dit Camier. Tu as dû m'entendre.

Et pourtant je n'ai pas faim, dit Mercier.

Il faut manger, dit Camier. Sinon l'estomac s'étale et s'aplatit, comme un pseudo-kyste.

Comment va ton kyste, au fait ? dit Mercier.

Il est torpide, dit Camier. Mais un désastre se prépare, sous la surface.

Et que comptes-tu faire, à ce moment-là ? dit Mercier.

Je n'ose pas y penser, dit Camier.

Je mangerais bien un gâteau à la crème, dit Mercier. Je n'y tiens pas, mais je le mangerais.

Aux fraises, dit Camier.

Mercier réfléchit.

Aux prunes, plutôt, dit-il.

Je m'en vais te le chercher, dit Camier. Attends-moi là.

Non, non ! s'écria Mercier, ne me quitte pas, ne nous quittons pas !

Calme-toi, dit Camier. C'est moi qui ai

45

l'imperméable, pour le moment. A moi donc d'y aller. J'en ai pour deux minutes. Il sortit dans la rue et se mit à la traverser.

Camier ! s'écria Mercier.

Camier se retourna.

Un massepain ! s'écria Mercier.

Quoi ? s'écria Camier.

Un massepain ! s'écria Mercier.

Camier rentra précipitamment sous la voûte.

Tu veux me faire écraser, dit-il. Qu'est-ce que tu veux ?

Un massepain, dit Mercier.

Un massepain, un massepain, dit Camier. Qu'est-ce que c'est, un massepain ?

Mercier le lui dit.

Et à la crème, dit Camier.

Mais naturellement, à la crème ! s'écria Mercier. Allez, file.

Camier ne bougea pas.

Mais qu'est-ce que tu attends ? dit Mercier.

J'étais en train de me consulter, dit Camier. Je me disais, Camier, faut-il, ou ne faut-il pas, nous fâcher ?

Consulte-toi ailleurs, dit Mercier.

Tout autre se fâcherait, à ma place, dit

46

Camier. Moi non, toutes choses considérées.
Car je me dis, L'heure est grave et Mercier
n'est pas dans son assiette. Il s'approcha de
Mercier qui recula vivement. J'allais seulement t'embrasser, dit Camier. Je le ferai
une autre fois, quand tu seras mieux, si j'y
pense. Il sortit sous la pluie et disparut.

Seul, Mercier se mit à marcher de long
en large, sous la voûte, plongé dans des
réflexions amères. C'était leur première sé-
paration, depuis l'avant-veille au soir. Levant
brusquement les yeux, comme pour fuir une
vision devenue insupportable, il vit deux
enfants, un petit garçon et une petite fille,
qui le regardaient. Ils portaient des petits
cirés noirs à capuchon en tous points pareils
et le garçon portait sur le dos un petit sac.
Ils se tenaient par la main.

Papa, dirent-ils, presque ensemble.

Bonsoir, mes enfants, dit Mercier, maintenant allez-vous-en.

Mais ils ne s'en allèrent point. Les mains
jointes allaient et venaient, avec un petit
mouvement de balançoire. Enfin la fillette
se dégagea et avança vers celui qu'ils avaient
traité de papa. Elle tendit les bras vers lui,
comme pour solliciter un baiser, ou tout au

moins une caresse. Le garçon la suivit, visiblement inquiet. Mercier leva son pied et le fit sonner avec violence contre le pavé. Allez-vous-en ! s'écria-t-il. Il marcha sur eux, gesticulant et grimaçant. Les enfants reculèrent jusqu'au trottoir, où ils s'immobilisèrent à nouveau. Foutez-moi le camp ! hurla Mercier. Il fit un bond furieux en avant et les enfants s'enfuirent. Mercier sortit sous la pluie et les regarda qui s'éloignaient en courant. Mais bientôt ils s'arrêtèrent et regardèrent en arrière. Ce qu'ils virent alors dut les impressionner, car ils reprirent leur fuite et s'engouffrèrent dans la première rue latérale. Quant à l'infortuné Mercier, jugeant après quelques minutes de guet rageur que la menace était passée, il rentra tout trempé sous la voûte et reprit ses réflexions, sinon au point où elles venaient d'être interrompues, du moins à un point voisin. Les réflexions de Mercier avaient ceci de particulier qu'elles palpitaient partout d'une houle pareille, et rejetaient invariablement sur le même récif, à quelque point qu'on s'y engageât. C'était peut-être moins des réflexions qu'une rêverie tumultueuse et grise, où passé et avenir se confondaient d'une façon peu agréable et où le présent tenait le rôle ingrat de noyé éternel. Enfin.

Voilà, dit Camier, j'espère que tu ne t'es pas inquiété.

Mercier défit le papier et sortit le gâteau sur la paume de sa main. Il y porta son nez, et ses yeux, en s'inclinant profondément. Il regarda Camier, sans se redresser, d'un petit regard de côté, plein de méfiance.

C'est un baba, dit Camier. C'est tout ce que j'ai pu trouver.

Mercier, toujours plié en deux, alla se mettre dans l'embrasure de la porte, afin de voir plus clair, et examina le gâteau à nouveau.

Il est plein de rhum, dit Camier.

Mercier ferma lentement la main et le gâteau jaillit d'entre ses doigts. Ses yeux écarquillés s'emplirent de larmes. Camier s'approcha pour mieux voir. Les larmes coulaient, expulsées par les suivantes, tout le long des joues et disparaissaient dans la barbe. Le visage restait calme. Les yeux, débordant toujours, et sans doute aveuglés, semblaient suivre avec attention un objet se déplaçant sur le sol.

Si tu n'en voulais pas, dit Camier, tu n'avais qu'à le donner à un chien, ou à un gosse.

Je pleure, dit Mercier, ne me dérange pas.

Quand Mercier eut fini de pleurer, Camier dit :

Prends notre mouchoir.

Il y a des jours, dit Mercier, où l'on naît à chaque instant. Alors partout il y a plein de petits Mercier merdeux. C'est effarant. On ne crèvera jamais.

Assez, dit Camier. Tu te tiens comme un S majuscule. On te donnerait quatre-vingt-dix ans.

Ce serait un beau cadeau, dit Mercier. Il s'essuya la main sur le fond de son pantalon. Je sens que je vais me mettre à quatre pattes, dit-il.

Je m'en vais, dit Camier.

Tu m'abandonnes, dit Mercier. Je le savais.

Tu connais mon caractère, dit Camier.

Non, dit Mercier, mais je comptais sur ton affection pour m'aider à purger ma peine.

Je peux t'aider, je ne peux pas te ressusciter, dit Camier.

Prends-moi par la main, dit Mercier, et emmène-moi loin d'ici. Je trottinerai bien sagement à tes côtés, comme un petit chiot, ou un enfant en bas âge. Et le jour viendra —.

Un terrible bruit de freins déchira l'air, suivi d'un hurlement et d'un choc retentissant. Mercier et Camier se précipitèrent (après une brève hésitation) dehors et purent voir, avant que l'attroupement s'interposât, une grosse femme, d'un âge qui paraissait avancé, s'agitant faiblement par terre. Le désordre de ses vêtements laissait voir des dessous blanchâtres et moutonnants d'une densité extraordinaire. Son sang, issu d'une ou de plusieurs blessures, gagnait déjà la rigole.

Ah, dit Mercier, voilà ce dont j'avais besoin. Je me sens tout ragaillardi. Il avait en effet l'air transformé.

Que cela nous serve de leçon, dit Camier.

C'est-à-dire ? dit Mercier.

Qu'il ne faut jamais désespérer, dit Camier. Faisons confiance à la vie.

A la bonne heure, dit Mercier. Je craignais de t'avoir mal compris.

Chemin faisant ils croisèrent une voiture

ambulance qui fonçait vers le théâtre de l'accident.

Plaît-il ? dit Camier.

Une honte, dit Mercier.

Je ne suis pas, dit Camier.

Une V-8, dit Mercier.

Et alors ? dit Camier.

Et on nous parle d'une pénurie de carburant, dit Mercier.

Il y a peut-être plusieurs victimes, dit Camier.

Ce serait un bébé qu'ils ne feraient pas autrement, dit Mercier.

La pluie tombait avec douceur, comme d'une pomme d'arrosoir très fine. Mercier marchait la tête renversée. De temps en temps, de sa main libre, il se frottait le visage. Il ne s'était pas lavé depuis quelque temps.

III

Résumé
des deux chapitres précédents

I

Mise en marche.
Rencontre difficile de Mercier et Camier.
Le square Saint-Ruth.
Le hêtre pourpre.
La pluie.
L'abri.
Les chiens.
Dépression de Camier.
Le gardien.
La bicyclette.
Dispute avec le gardien.
Mercier et Camier confèrent.
Résultat de cette conférence.
Eclaircie vespérale.
La cloche.
Mercier et Camier s'en vont.

II

La ville au crépuscule.
Mercier et Camier se dirigent vers le canal.
Evocation du canal.
Colère d'un barman.
Premier bar.
Mercier et Camier confèrent.
Résultats de cette conférence.
Mercier et Camier se dirigent vers l'appartement d'Hélène.
Doutes au sujet du chemin.
Le parapluie.
L'homme au frac.
La pluie.
Camier entend chanter.
Mercier et Camier courent.
Le parapluie.
Le déluge.
Douleur de Mercier.
Chez Hélène.
Le tapis.
L'ara.
Le deuxième jour.
La pluie.
Disparition du sac, de la bicyclette, du parapluie.

Mercier et Camier confèrent.
Résultats de cette conférence.
Camier s'en va.
Douleur de Mercier.
Mercier et les enfants.
Réflexions de Mercier.
Camier revient.
Le baba.
Faiblesse de Mercier.
L'accident.
Mercier et Camier s'en vont.
Pluie sur le visage de Mercier.

IV

Enfant j'espère unique, je suis né à P —.
Mes parents étaient originaires de Q —.
C'est d'eux que je reçus, avec le tréponème
pâle, le grand nez dont vous voyez les débris.
Ils étaient sévères avec moi, mais justes. Au
moindre écart de conduite mon père me battait, avec son cuir à rasoir solide, jusqu'au
sang. Mais il ne manquait jamais d'en avertir
maman, pour qu'elle me pansât avec de
la teinture d'iode, ou du permanganate.
Voilà qui explique sans doute mon caractère cachottier et renfermé. Peu apte aux
exercices de l'esprit, je fus retiré de l'école
à l'âge de treize ans et mis chez des fermiers
des environs. Le ciel, pour parler comme
eux, n'ayant pas voulu qu'ils eussent des
enfants, ils se rabattirent sur moi, avec un
acharnement tout naturel. Et lorsque mes
parents moururent, dans un providentiel

accident de chemin de fer, ils m'adoptèrent, avec toutes les formes voulues par la loi. Mais, débile de corps autant que d'esprit, je fus pour eux l'occasion de bien des déceptions. Mener la charrue, manier la faux, patauger dans les betteraves, etc., c'était là des travaux qui dépassaient mes forces et qui me terrassaient littéralement sur place pour peu qu'on m'y obligeât. Même comme berger, comme vacher et comme chevrier, j'avais beau m'évertuer, je n'arrivais pas à donner satisfaction. Car les bêtes erraient, sans que j'y prisse garde, dans les terres des voisins, et s'y empiffraient de fleurs, de fruits et de légumes. Je ne parle pas des combats de taureaux, de boucs et de béliers, qui m'effrayaient à tel point que je courais à toutes jambes me cacher dans la grange. En plus, l'impossibilité où j'étais de compter au-delà de dix faisait que le troupeau ne rentrait presque jamais au complet, ce qui naturellement m'attirait des reproches. Les seules branches où je puisse me vanter d'avoir, je ne dirais pas excellé, mais du moins réussi, c'est l'abattage des petits agneaux, bouvillons et chevreaux et l'émasculation des petits taureaux, béliers et boucs, à condition tou-

tefois qu'ils fussent bien tendres et innocents. C'est donc dans cette spécialité que
je me suis cantonné, dès l'âge de quinze ans.
J'ai encore chez moi de mignonnes petites,
enfin relativement petites, couilles de bélier,
provenant de cette heureuse période. Dans
la basse-cour aussi je savais sévir avec beaucoup de chic et de précision. J'avais une
façon d'étouffer les oies qui n'était qu'à moi
et qui forçait l'admiration générale. Oh, je
sais que vous ne m'écoutez que d'une oreille
distraite, et même agacée, mais cela m'est
égal. Car je suis vieux et le seul plaisir qui
me reste, c'est de rappeler, à voix haute et
dans le style noble que je hais, les beaux
jours qui ne risquent heureusement pas de
revenir. A vingt ans, ou peut-être dix-neuf,
ayant eu la maladresse d'engrosser une lai-
tière, je me sauvai, sous le couvert de la nuit,
car on me surveillait de très près. Je profitai
de cette occasion pour mettre le feu aux
granges, greniers et écuries. Mais ces incen-
dies, à peine partis, furent étouffés par une
forte averse que personne n'aurait pu prévoir, tant était pur le ciel au moment de
l'attentat. La pluie, c'est la ruine de ce
malheureux pays. Il y a cinquante ans de

cela, autant dire cinq cents. Il brandit son
bâton et en frappa violemment la banquette
d'où sortit aussitôt un nuage de poussière
ténu et éphémère. Cinq cents, vociféra-t-il.

Le train ralentit. Mercier et Camier se
regardèrent. Le train s'arrêta.

Malheur, dit Mercier, nous sommes dans
un omnibus.

C'est peut-être une chance, dit Camier.

Vous parlez d'une chance, dit le vieillard.

Le train s'ébranla de nouveau.

Nous aurions pu descendre, dit Camier.
Maintenant il est trop tard.

Vous descendrez avec moi, à la prochaine,
dit le vieillard.

Ça change tout, dit Mercier.

Garçon boucher, dit le vieillard, garçon
épicier, garçon maquignon, croque-mort,
sacristain, et j'en passe, toujours dans les
cadavres, voilà ma vie. Je survivais en par-
lant, tous les jours un peu plus, tous les
jours un peu mieux. Il faut dire que j'avais
de qui tenir, mon père étant sorti, on devine
avec quelle précipitation, des entrailles d'un
curé de campagne, tout le monde le savait.
On ne voyait que moi, dans les caboulots
et claques de banlieue. Camarades, que je

59

leur disais, moi qui ne savais pas écrire, camarades, Homère nous apprend, Iliade chant trois, vers quatre-vingt cinq et suivants, en quoi consiste le bonheur sur terre, c'est-à-dire le bonheur. Oh, je ne les épargnais pas. Potopompos scroton évohé, que je leur disais. J'avais suivi des cours, voyez-vous. Il poussa un rire strident et sauvage. Des cours gratuits généreusement destinés aux pouilleux affamés de veilleuses. Potopompos scroton, bander mou et boire sec. Sortez d'ici, que je leur disais, la queue basse et la tête haute, et revenez demain. La bourgeoise, au pilon, qu'elle se démerde. Des fois je me faisais attraper. Je me relevais tout ensanglanté et les vêtements en charpie. Les enfants, que je leur disais, c'est la scorie de l'amour. Dieu aussi, il en prenait pour son grade. Mais on finit pas s'habituer. Je me mettais sur mon trente-et-un et j'allais dans les noces, les enterrements, les bals, les veillées, les baptêmes. J'étais le bienvenu. On m'aimait presque. Je leur en racontais de toutes les couleurs, sur l'hymen, la vaseline, l'aube de la poisse, la fin des soucis. Toujours dans les cadavres, voilà ma vie. Jusqu'au jour où la ferme m'échut.

Que dis-je, la ferme, les fermes, car il y
en avait deux. Ils m'aimaient toujours, les
pauvres. Ça tombait bien, car mon pif commençait à s'effriter. On vous aime moins,
lorsque votre pif commence à s'effriter. On
arrive.

Mercier et Camier rentrèrent leurs jambes,
pour le laisser passer.

Vous ne descendez pas ? dit le vieillard.
Vous avez raison. Il n'y a que les damnés
qui descendent ici.

Il portait des guêtres, un chapeau melon
jaune et une sorte de redingote qui lui des-
cendait jusqu'aux genoux. Il descendit avec
raideur sur le quai, se retourna, claqua la
portière et leva vers eux son hideux visage.

Moi, voyez-vous, dit-il, je choisis mon
compartiment, j'attends que le train
s'ébranle, puis je monte. On se croit tranquille, bien à l'abri des fâcheux, mais pardon. Car voilà le vieux Madden qui s'amène,
au dernier moment. Le train prend de la
vitesse, on est enfermé avec lui, rien à faire.

Le train s'ébranla de nouveau.

Adieu adieu, cria monsieur Madden. Ils
m'aimaient toujours, ils m'aimaient —.

Mercier, qui avait le dos tourné au sens

61

de la marche, le vit, indifférent aux gens qui affluaient vers la sortie, poser sa tête sur ses mains qui, elles, s'appuyaient sur la pomme du bâton.

On parle beaucoup du ciel, les yeux s'y portent souvent, ils se détachent, histoire de se reposer, des masses permises et voulues, pour s'offrir à ce monceau de déserts transparents, c'est un fait. Qu'ils sont contents alors d'aller fouiller à nouveau dans les ombres et papilloter parmi les présences. Voilà où nous en sommes.

Tout, dit Mercier, ça change tout.

Camier essuya la vitre du revers de sa manche, dont il tenait le bord de ses doigts recourbés.

C'est une véritable catastrophe, dit Mercier. J'en suis —. Il réfléchit. J'en suis effondré, dit-il.

Visibilité nulle, dit Camier.

Tu restes étrangement calme, dit Mercier. Aurais-tu profité de mon état pour substituer, au rapide convenu, cet abominable tacot ?

Je te dois des esplications, dit Camier. Camier disait toujours esplications. Presque toujours.

Je ne te demande pas d'eSplications, dit Mercier, je te demande de répondre oui ou non à ma question.

Ce n'est pas le moment de couper les ponts, dit Camier, ni de brûler les étapes.

C'est un aveu, dit Mercier. Je le savais. J'ai été dupé, de façon honteuse. Si je ne me précipite pas par la portière, c'est que je ne tiens pas spécialement à me fouler la cheville.

Je t'espliquerai tout, dit Camier.

Tu ne m'eSpliqueras rien du tout, dit Mercier. Tu as profité de ma faiblesse pour me faire accroire que je montais dans un rapide, alors que ——. Son visage se décomposa. Il avait beaucoup de facilité, pour se décomposer, le visage de Mercier. Les paroles me manquent, dit-il, pour exprimer ce que je ressens.

C'est précisément ton état de faiblesse, dit Camier, qui m'a inspiré ce subterfuge.

Explique-toi, dit Mercier.

Etant donné ta condition, dit Camier, il fallait partir, sans partir.

Tu es vulgaire, dit Mercier.

Nous allons descendre à la prochaine station, dit Camier. Nous irons manger un morceau et nous nous mettrons d'accord sur la marche à suivre. Si nous nous décidons à aller de l'avant, nous irons de l'avant. Nous aurons perdu deux heures. Qu'est-ce que c'est, deux heures ?

Je ne sais pas, dit Mercier.

Si, par contre, dit Camier, nous jugeons préférable de retourner à la ville —.

A la ville ? dit Mercier.

A la ville, dit Camier, nous retournerons à la ville. Nous disposons d'un choix de transports rapides et confortables, je parle naturellement du tram, de l'autobus et du chemin de fer.

Mais nous venons de la ville, dit Mercier, et maintenant tu parles d'y retourner.

Quand nous avons quitté la ville, dit Camier, il fallait quitter la ville. Nous l'avons donc quittée, avec juste raison. Mais nous ne sommes pas des enfants. Si la nécessité, changeant de visage, s'exerce maintenant à nous refouler, nous n'allons pas nous mettre à gigoter, j'espère.

La seule nécessité que je ressente, dit Mercier, c'est de m'éloigner de cet enfer le plus vite possible.

C'est ce qu'il faut examiner, dit Camier.

Ne te fie jamais au vent qui gonfle tes voiles, il est toujours périmé.

Mercier se retint.

Il est possible enfin, dit Camier, car il faut tout prévoir, que nous prenions l'héroïque résolution de rester sur place. En ce cas j'ai ce qu'il nous faut.

Un village qui n'était qu'une rue, mais une longue rue, où tout s'alignait, maisons d'habitation, boutiques, bars, les deux églises, gare, station d'essence, cimetière, etc. Un détroit.

Prends l'imperméable, dit Camier.

Bah, je ne suis pas en sucre, dit Mercier.

Ils entrèrent dans l'auberge.

Vous faites erreur, dit l'homme. C'est ici la Maison Clappe et Fils, expéditeurs en gros de fruits et de légumes.

Et qu'est-ce qui vous fait supposer, dit Camier, que nous n'avons pas affaire au père Clappe, ou à l'un de ces déchets ?

Ils ressortirent dans la rue.

Est-ce ici l'auberge, dit Camier, ou est-ce la halle au poisson ?

Cette fois-ci l'homme s'écarta, en se trémoussant.

Passez messieurs, entrez messieurs, dit-il.

65

Ce n'est pas le Savoy, mais c'est — comment dirais-je ? Il les toisa d'un regard rapide et sournois. Comment dirais-je ? dit-il.

Dites-le, dit Camier. Ne nous faites pas languir.

C'est... cosy, dit l'homme. Voilà. C'est cosy. Vous allez voir. Patrice ! cria-t-il. Il ajouta, d'une voix basse et comme tâtonnante. C'est... gemütlich.

Il nous prend pour des touristes, dit Mercier.

Ah, dit l'homme, en se frottant les mains, c'est que je m'y connais, en physionomies. Ce n'est pas tous les jours que j'ai l'honneur —. Il hésita. Que j'ai l'honneur, dit-il. Patrice !

Pour ma part, dit Mercier, je suis heureux de faire votre connaissance, enfin. Il y a longtemps que votre personne me hante.

Ah, dit l'homme.

Mais oui, dit Mercier. Vous vous tenez généralement sur un seuil, ou à une fenêtre. Derrière vous un torrent de lumière et de joie, qui devrait normalement réduire vos traits à néant. Mais il n'en est rien. Vous souriez. Vous ne devez pas me voir, car je suis de l'autre côté de la ruelle, enveloppé

66

dans d'épaisses ténèbres. Moi aussi je souris, et je passe mon chemin. Vous vous appelez Gall. Me voyez-vous, dans mes songes, monsieur Gall ?

Débarrassez-vous, dit l'homme.

De toute façon je suis content de vous retrouver, dit Mercier, dans des conditions tellement meilleures.

Débarrassons-nous de quoi ? dit Camier.

Enfin, de vos manteaux, dit l'homme, de vos chapeaux, que sais-je. Patrice !

Mais regardez-nous, dit Camier. Avons-nous vraiment l'air de porter des chapeaux ? Serions-nous gantés, à notre insu ? Voyons un peu.

Qu'attendez-vous pour faire monter nos malles ? dit Mercier.

Patrice ! cria l'homme.

Vengeance ! Vengeance ! dit Mercier. Il s'approcha de l'homme. Ne voyez-vous pas, dit-il, que je dégouline de toutes mes guenilles ? Donnez-nous à manger.

C'était un jour de foire. La salle était pleine de fermiers, marchands de bestiaux et assimilés. Les bêtes, elles, étaient déjà loin, elles s'égrenaient sur les routes bourbeuses du large, aux cris des bouviers. Les unes rentraient chez elles, les autres allaient elles ne savaient où. Derrière les brebis aux toisons ruisselantes bringuebalaient les charrettes à claire-voie. C'est à travers l'étoffe de leurs poches que les bouviers tenaient l'aiguillon.

Mercier s'accouda au comptoir. Camier, au contraire, s'y appuya du dos.

Ils gardent leurs chapeaux en mangeant, dit-il.

Où est-il, à présent ? dit Mercier.

Il est près de la porte, dit Camier, en train de nous surveiller sans en avoir l'air.

Voit-on ses dents ? dit Mercier.

Il cache sa bouche derrière sa main, dit Camier.

Je ne demande pas s'il cache sa bouche, dit Mercier. Je demande si on voit ses dents.

On ne voit pas ses dents d'ici, dit Camier, à cause de sa main qui les cache.

Que faisons-nous ici ? dit Mercier.

Nous allons d'abord nous restaurer, dit Camier. Barman, qu'est-ce que vous avez de bon, aujourd'hui, à manger ?

La barman avait beaucoup de bonnes choses. Il les nomma. Mercier n'écoutait pas.

Je voudrais une salade d'oursin, dit Mercier, avec de la sauce bouglé.

Connais pas, dit le barman.

Alors donnez-moi un sandwich à la ploutre, dit Mercier.

Terminé, dit le barman. Il avait entendu dire qu'il ne fallait pas les contrarier.

Ne faites pas l'insolent, dit Mercier. Il se tourna vers Camier. Qu'est-ce que c'est, cette gargote ? dit-il. C'est ça, notre voyage ?

A ce moment-là le voyage de Mercier et Camier semblait sérieusement compromis, en effet. S'il ne tourna pas court, ce fut sans doute grâce à Camier, dont on ne saurait trop admirer l'esprit d'initiative et la grandeur d'âme.

Mercier, dit-il, repose-toi sur moi.

Mais fais quelque chose, fais quelque chose, dit Mercier. Faut-il que ce soit toujours moi qui prenne les devants ?

Appelez votre patron, dit Camier.

Le barman ne semblait pas y tenir.

Appelez-le, dit Mercier, appelez-le, mon ami, puisqu'on vous le demande. Faites le petit bruit qu'il connaît, entre mille, et qu'il entendrait au plus fort de la tempête.

69

Ou faites le petit signe de tête que lui seul perçoit et auquel tous les fléaux de la nature réunis ne l'empêcheraient pas de se rendre.

Mais celui que Mercier avait appelé monsieur Gall était déjà à côté d'eux.

Ai-je l'honneur de m'adresser au propriétaire ? dit Camier.

Je suis le gérant, dit le gérant, puisqu'il s'agit du gérant.

Il paraît qu'il n'y a plus de ploutre, dit Mercier. Vous avez une drôle de façon de gérer, pour un gérant. Qu'avez-vous fait de vos dents ? C'est ça que vous appelez gemütlich ?

Le gérant paraissait réfléchir. Il n'aimait pas les scandales. Les bouts de sa moustache grise et tombante semblaient vouloir se rejoindre. Le barman le regardait. Mercier fut frappé par les rares cheveux gris, fins comme ceux d'un bébé, qu'une coquetterie pitoyable ramenait soigneusement en avant, à partir de l'occiput. Il n'avait jamais vu monsieur Gall ainsi, mais toujours droit et souriant et radieux.

Allons, allons, dit Mercier, n'en parlons plus. Au fond c'est une lacune très pardonnable.

Vous n'auriez pas une chambre, dit Camier, où mon ami pourrait se reposer, un petit moment. Il est mort de fatigue. Il se pencha vers le gérant et lui dit quelque chose à l'oreille.

Sa mère ? dit le gérant.

Ma mère ? dit Mercier. Elle est morte en me perpétrant, la vache. Elle n'osait pas me regarder en face. Qu'est-ce qui te prend, toi ? dit-il à Camier. Tu ne peux jamais laisser ma famille tranquille ?

J'aurais bien une chambre, dit le gérant, seulement —.

Pour que mon ami puisse se reposer, un petit moment, dit Camier. Il ne tient plus debout.

Allez, vieux copain de cauchemar, dit Mercier, tu ne peux pas me refuser ça.

Ce serait naturellement au prix de la journée, dit le gérant.

Dans les étages supérieurs, autant que possible, dit Mercier, de façon à ce que je puisse me jeter par la fenêtre, sans crainte, le cas échéant.

Vous resterez avec lui ? dit le gérant.

Bien entendu, dit Camier. Vous nous ferez monter une petite collation. Il est d'ailleurs possible que nous passions la nuit.

Peu probable, dit Mercier.

Patrice ! cria le gérant. Où est Patrice ? dit-il au barman.

Il est malade, dit le barman.

Comment, malade ? dit le gérant. Je l'ai vu hier soir. Il me semble même l'avoir aperçu tout à l'heure.

Il est malade, dit le barman. On dit même qu'il va y passer.

Que c'est ennuyeux, dit le gérant. Qu'est-ce qu'il a qui ne va pas ?

Je ne sais pas, dit le barman.

Et pourquoi ne m'a-t-on pas informé ? dit le gérant.

On devait croire que vous étiez au courant, dit le barman.

Et qui a dit que c'était grave ? dit le gérant.

C'est un bruit qui court, dit le barman.

Et où est-il ? dit le gérant. Chez lui ou —.

Mais foutez-nous la paix avec votre Patrice, dit Mercier. Vous voulez donc m'achever ?

Montez avec ces messieurs, dit le gérant. Prends leur commande et reviens en vitesse.

Le cinq ? dit le barman.

Ou le sept, dit le gérant. A la convenance de ces messieurs.

Il les regarda s'éloigner. Il se versa à boire et but d'un trait.

Tiens, bonjour, monsieur Graves, dit-il. Qu'est-ce que je peux vous servir ?

Drôles d'oiseaux, dit monsieur Graves.

C'est rien, dit le gérant, j'ai l'habitude.

Et où auriez-vous pris l'habitude ? dit monsieur Graves, de sa voix basse et grasse de patriarche pastoral débutant. Pas chez nous autres, je pense.

Où j'ai pris l'habitude ? dit le gérant. Il ferma les yeux, pour mieux voir ce qui malgré tout lui tenait encore un peu à cœur. Chez mes maîtres, dit-il.

Je suis heureux de vous l'entendre dire, dit monsieur Graves. Je vous souhaite le bonjour.

Au plaisir, monsieur Graves, dit le gérant.

Son regard las erra à travers la salle, où les honorables culs-terreux se mettaient en branle. Monsieur Graves avait donné le signal du départ, ils ne tarderaient pas à suivre un exemple de tant de poids.

Voilà, monsieur Gast, dit le barman.

Monsieur Gast ne répondit pas tout de

suite, étant tout entier à la scène qui, devant ses yeux ouverts, s'estompait peu à peu sous la netteté grandissante d'une petite place moyenâgeuse et grise, où des formes passaient emmitouflées jusqu'aux yeux et muettes, à grandes enjambées laborieuses, à travers la neige profonde.

Ils ont pris les deux chambres, dit le barman.

Monsieur Gast se retourna.

Ils ont commandé une bouteille de whiskey, dit le barman.

Rien à manger ? dit monsieur Gast.

Non, dit le barman.

Ils ont payé ? dit monsieur Gast.

Oui, dit le barman.

C'est tout ce qui m'intéresse, dit monsieur Gast.

Ils ne me disent rien qui vaille, dit le barman. Surtout le grand barbu. Le petit gros, ça va encore.

Ne t'occupe pas de ça, dit monsieur Gast.

Il alla se poster près de la porte, pour l'échange des dernières civilités avec ses clients, dont le départ imminent, en troupeau, ne faisait plus de doute. Ils montaient pour la plupart dans de vieilles Ford hautes sur roue. D'aucuns s'éparpillaient par le village, à la recherche d'occasions. D'autres enfin se mettaient à causer par petits groupes, sous la pluie, dont ils ne semblaient nullement gênés. Qui sait, ils étaient peut-être si contents, pour des raisons techniques, de la voir tomber qu'ils étaient contents de la sentir qui tombait sur eux et les mouillait. On ne sait jamais avec ces gens-là. Bientôt ils seraient loin, dispersés par les chemins qu'efface avidement déjà le crépuscule du jour avare. Chacun se hâte vers son petit royaume, vers sa femme qui attend, vers ses bêtes bien au chaud, vers ses chiens à l'affût du moteur du maître.

Monsieur Gast rentra dans la salle.

Tu les as servis ? dit-il.

Oui, dit le barman.

Ils n'ont rien dit ? dit monsieur Gast.

Seulement qu'on les laisse tranquilles, dit le barman, car ils n'ont plus besoin de rien.

Où est Patrice ? dit monsieur Gast. Chez lui ou à l'hôpital ?

Je crois qu'il est chez lui, dit le barman, mais je n'en suis pas sûr.

Tu n'as pas l'air de savoir grand-chose, dit monsieur Gast.

Je m'occupe de mon travail, dit le barman. Il fixa monsieur Gast dans les yeux. De mes devoirs et de mes droits, dit-il.

Tu fais bien, dit monsieur Gast. C'est de cette façon qu'on arrive aux suprêmes honneurs.

Avec les Gast et consorts on n'a pas besoin de savoir, on peut toujours deviner.

Si on me demande, dit monsieur Gast, je suis sorti et serai bientôt de retour.

Il sortit et revint en effet peu de temps après.

Il est mort, dit-il.

Le barman s'essuya précipitamment les mains et se signa.

Ses dernières paroles, dit monsieur Gast, avant de rendre l'âme, furent inintelligibles. Les avant-dernières, à titre de curiosité, furent celles-ci : A boire, Jésus, à boire.

Qu'est-ce qu'il avait, au juste ? dit le barman.

Je ne suis pas arrivé à le savoir, dit monsieur Gast. On lui devait combien de jours ?

Il a touché samedi comme tout le monde, dit le barman.

Alors pas la peine d'en parler, dit monsieur Gast. J'enverrai une croix.

C'était un bon copain, dit le barman.

Monsieur Gast haussa les épaules.

Où est Thérèse ? dit-il, Aurait-elle succombé, à son tour ? Thérèse ! cria-t-il.

Elle est aux cabinets, dit le barman.

Tu es bien informé, dit monsieur Gast.

J'arrive ! s'écria Thérèse.

C'était une jeune et forte femme et elle portait sous le bras un grand plateau et un torchon à la main.

Regarde-moi cette écurie, dit monsieur Gast.

Un homme entra dans la salle. Il portait une casquette, un trench-coat bardé de pattes et de poches, une culotte de cheval et des chaussures d'alpiniste. Ses épaules encore vaillantes pliaient sous le poids d'un sac plein à craquer et il tenait à la main un immense bâton. Il traversa la salle d'un pas incertain, en traînant bruyamment ses semelles cloutées.

Il est des personnages dont il convient de parler dès le début, car ils peuvent disparaître d'un moment à l'autre, et ne jamais revenir.

Mon parquet, dit monsieur Gast.

De l'eau, de l'eau, dit monsieur Conaire (autant le dire tout de suite).

Monsieur Gast ne broncha pas, le barman non plus. Si monsieur Gast avait bronché, le barman aurait sans doute bronché lui aussi. Mais, monsieur Gast ne bronchant pas, le paysan ne broncha pas non plus.

Eau d'abord, dit monsieur Conaire, flots d'alcool ensuite. Merci. Encore. Merci. Assez.

Il fit tomber son sac avec des tortillements convulsifs des épaules et des reins.

Du gin, dit-il.

Il enleva sa casquette et la secoua avec violence dans tous sens. Puis il la remit sur son crâne pointu et luisant.

Vous voyez devant vous, messieurs, dit-il, un homme. Profitez-en. Je suis venu à pied du plus profond du four à gaz métropolitain, sans m'arrêter une seule fois, sauf pour —. Il regarda autour de lui, vit Thérèse (il l'avait déjà vue mais il fallait qu'il la vît avec ostentation), se pencha par-dessus le comptoir et acheva sa phrase à voix basse. Ses yeux allaient de monsieur Gast à Georges (le barman s'appelle maintenant Georges), de Georges à monsieur Gast, comme pour s'assurer que ses paroles avaient produit l'effet escompté. Puis se redressant il dit d'une voix sonore, Peu et souvent, peu et souvent, et lentement, lentement, voilà où j'en suis. Il lança un coup d'œil vers Thérèse et partit d'un rire strident. Il avait réussi une plaisanterie entre hommes. Où est votre lieu d'aisance, au fait ? dit-il. Aisance ! ajouta-t-il. On appelle ça aisance !

Monsieur Gast décrivit le chemin qui y menait.

Que c'est compliqué, dit monsieur Conaire. Toujours cette abominable latence de bon ton. A Francfort, lorsqu'on descend du train, que voit-on, en lettres de feu géantes ? Un seul mot : HIER. C'est la ruée. A Perpignan aussi ils ont compris. Je pense au Café de la Poste. A boire.

Vous le préférez sec ? dit monsieur Gast.

Monsieur Conaire recula et prit une pose avantageuse.

Quel âge me donneriez-vous ? dit-il. Il enleva sa casquette. Bas les masques, dit-il. Il tourna lentement sur lui-même. Allez-y, dit-il, ne me ménagez pas.

Monsieur Gast nomma un chiffre.

Merde, dit monsieur Conaire, en plein dans le mille.

C'est la calvitie qui trompe, dit monsieur Gast.

Pas un mot de plus, dit monsieur Conaire. Dans la cour, vous dites ?

Au fond et à gauche, dit monsieur Gast.

Et pour pénétrer jusque-là ? dit monsieur Conaire.

Monsieur Gast répéta ses indications.

C'est bon, dit monsieur Conaire, je vais y jeter un coup d'œil, histoire de ne pas me laisser déborder. En sortant il entreprit Thérèse.

Bonjour, ma jolie, dit-il.

Thérèse le regarda.

Monsieur, dit-elle.

Qu'elle est mignonne, dit monsieur Conaire. A la porte il se retourna. Et accorte, dit-il, c'est fou. Il sortit.

Monsieur Gast et Georges se regardèrent.

Sors ton ardoise, dit monsieur Gast. Il s'adressa ensuite à Thérèse. Tu ne peux pas être un peu plus aimable ? dit-il.

C'est un vieux dégoûtant, dit Thérèse.

Il ne s'agit pas de rouler par terre, dit monsieur Gast. Il se mit à marcher de long en large, puis s'arrêta, ayant pris son parti.

Arrêtez tout, dit-il, et recueillez-vous. Je

vais vous parler de l'hôte, cet animal aimable
et sauvage. C'est dommage que Patrice ne
soit pas là pour m'entendre.

Il leva la tête, mit les mains derrière le
dos et parla de l'hôte. Il voyait, tout en choi-
sissant avec soin ses termes et en calculant
ses effets, une petite fenêtre ouverte sur un
paysage plat, net et vide. C'est une lande, et
un chemin étroit, sans bordure ni ombre, y
déroule à perte de vue ses douces courbes
alternantes. L'air gris pâle est sans un souf-
fle. On voit au loin, entre terre et ciel, une
sorte de commissure qui laisse passer par
endroits comme le trop-plein d'un monde
ensoleillé. On dirait un après-midi d'automne, début novembre probablement. La
petite masse sombre qui approche si lentement, on finit quand même par savoir ce que
c'est. C'est une voiture bâchée tirée par un
cheval noir. Il la tire avec aisance et comme
en flânant. Le conducteur marche devant, en
balançant son fouet. Il porte un manteau
ample, lourd et clair, qui lui tombe jusqu'aux pieds. Il est peut-être heureux, car il
chante, par bribes. De temps en temps il se
retourne, sans doute pour regarder dans
l'intérieur de la voiture. Maintenant on dis-

81

tingue ses traits. Il a l'air jeune, il lève la tête et sourit.

Ce sera tout pour aujourd'hui, dit monsieur Gast. Pénétrez-vous bien de cette façon de voir. Réfléchissez-y, tout en travaillant. C'est le fruit d'une éternité de courbettes publiques et de ricanements privés. Je vous en fais cadeau. Si on me demande, je suis sorti. Thérèse, tu me réveilleras à six heures, comme d'habitude. Il sortit.

Il y a du vrai dans ce qu'il dit, dit Georges.

Ah, les hommes, les hommes, dit Thérèse, ils n'ont pas d'idéal.

Monsieur Conaire revint, tout content d'en avoir fini si vite.

J'ai eu du mal, dit-il, mais j'y suis arrivé. Du gin.

Du mal, se dit Georges, mais il y est arrivé.

Ce qu'il fait froid ici, dit monsieur Conaire. Qu'est-ce que vous prenez ? Profitez, je sens le gouffre qui m'appelle, de nouveau.

Georges profita.

A votre santé, monsieur, dit-il.

Buvez-y, buvez-y, dit monsieur Conaire,

elle mérite qu'on s'y intéresse. Et cette ravissante jeune fille, dit-il, daignerait-elle trinquer avec nous ?

Elle est mariée, dit Georges, et mère de trois enfants.

Fi donc ! s'écria monsieur Conaire. Comment peut-on dire des choses pareilles !

On t'offre le porto, dit Georges.

Thérèse vint se mettre derrière le comptoir.

Les chairs meurtries que cela représente, dit monsieur Conaire. Le joli entre-jambes en charpie ! Les cris ! Le sang ! La glaire ! L'arrière-faix ! Il mit la main devant les yeux. L'arrière-faix ! gémit-il.

A la bonne vôtre, dit Thérèse.

Buvez, buvez, dit monsieur Conaire, ne faites pas attention à moi. Quelle horreur ! Quelle horreur !

Il écarta la main et les vit qui lui souriaient, comme à un enfant.

Excusez-moi, dit-il. Quand je pense aux femmes je pense aux vierges, c'est plus fort que moi. Il ajouta, Elles n'ont pas de poils et ne font jamais pipi ni caca.

C'est tout naturel, dit Georges.

Je vous prenais pour une vierge, dit monsieur Conaire. Ce n'est pas pour vous flatter, mais sincèrement je vous prenais pour une vierge. Un peu forte, si vous voulez, bien rondelette, bien gironde, des seins, comme ça, des fesses, des cuisses —. Il s'interrompit. Inutile, dit-il, d'une voix altérée, je ne banderai pas aujourd'hui. Du gin.

Thérèse retourna à son travail.

J'en viens maintenant à l'objet de ma visite, dit monsieur Conaire, nullement abattu apparemment. Connaîtriez-vous un nommé Camier ?

Non, dit Georges.

Il m'a pourtant donné rendez-vous, ici même, pour le début de l'après-midi, dit monsieur Conaire. Voici sa carte.

Georges lut :

FRANCIS XAVIER CAMIER
Enquêtes et Filatures
Discrétion assurée

Connais pas, dit-il.

Un petit gros, dit monsieur Conaire. Rougeaud, cheveux rares, multiples mentons, ventre en poire, jambes torses, petits yeux de cochon.

Il y a deux types là-haut, dit Georges, qui sont arrivés tout à l'heure.

84

Comment est l'autre ? dit monsieur Conaire.

Un grand maigre barbu, dit Georges, qui tient à peine debout. Il a l'air méchant comme une teigne.

C'est lui, c'est eux, s'écria monsieur Conaire. Allez le prévenir immédiatement. Dites-lui que monsieur Conaire est arrivé et l'attend en bas.

Comment vous dites ? dit Georges.

Co-naire, dit monsieur Conaire. Conaire.

C'est qu'ils ont dit de ne pas les déranger, dit Georges. Ils ne sont pas commodes, vous savez.

Ecoutez, dit monsieur Conaire.

Georges écouta.

Je veux bien aller voir, dit-il.

Allez-y, allez-y, dit monsieur Conaire.

Georges sortit et revint quelques minutes plus tard.

Ils dorment, dit-il.

Il faut les réveiller, dit monsieur Conaire.

La bouteille est vide, dit Georges, et ils sont là —.

Quelle bouteille ? dit monieur Conaire.

Ils ont fait monter une bouteille de J. J., dit Georges.

Oh les cochons, dit monsieur Conaire.

Ils sont allongés tout habillés par terre, côte à côte, dit Georges. La main dans la main.

Oh les cochons, dit monsieur Conaire.

V

Le champ s'étendait devant eux. Rien n'y poussait, rien d'utile aux hommes c'est-à-dire. On ne voyait pas très bien non plus en quoi ce champ pouvait intéresser les animaux. Les oiseaux devaient y trouver des lombrics. Il était de forme fort irrégulière et entourée de haies malingres, composées de vieilles souches d'arbres et de fourrés de ronces. Il y avait peut-être quelques mûres sauvages en automne. Une herbe bleue et aigre disputait le sol aux chardons et aux orties. Ces dernières auraient pu servir de fourrage, à la rigueur. Au-delà des haies d'autres champs, d'aspect semblable, entourés d'autres haies, d'aspect non moins semblable. Comment passait-on d'un champ à l'autre ? A travers les haies peut-être. Une chèvre s'intéressait capricieusement aux ronces. Dressée sur ses pattes de derrière, celles de devant appuyées sur une souche, elle cherchait les épines les plus tendres. Elle s'en détournait avec pétulance, faisait quelques pas furieux et s'immobilisait. De temps en temps elle faisait un petit bond, droit en l'air. Puis elle se mettait de nouveau dans la haie. Ferait-elle ainsi le tour du champ ? Ou se lasserait-elle avant ?

On finirait bien par comprendre. Des maisons s'élèveraient. Ou un prêtre viendrait, avec son goupillon, et ce serait un cimetière. Quand la prospérité reviendrait.

Camier lisait dans son calepin. Les feuilles lues, il les arrachait, les froissait et les jetait. En voici une, à titre d'échantillon :

20.10. Joly, Lise, 14, quitte dom. 14 à 8 comme d'hab. pr. éc. Cartable, tête nue, jambes id., sandales, sans mant., robe bleue. Mince, blonde, jol., conf. Pas vue en classe. Phot. réc. *Parents purée.* 25. Att. hausse.

5.11. Hamilton, Gertrude, 68, pet., forte corp., chev. bl. Boîte. Toque russe. Voile. Robe noire. Paillettes. Canne éb. Cyanose. Vit ch. fille mar. Trompe surv. nuit 29-30 ult. Purée prob. Boucles ém. Phot. à 65. Dipso. coutumière fugues. Attention ! Peut rentrer crise finie. *Grosse fort.* 100 + frais.

10.11. Gérard, Gérald, 50, ag. change, 7 enf., bonne sit. Fort temp. (qu'elle dit). Dep. 6 mois se dérobe au dev. conj. Découche jam. Mat. à la B. Déj. club. PM bureau. Dîne mais. Soir joue avec enf. Sort jam. Sports néant. Aime lire ! 50-75 selon + frais.

N.B. — 12.11. Vu G.G. Arrangé. 80 + tuy.

Il me regarde faire, sans un mot, se dit Camier. Il sortit une grande enveloppe de sa poche, en sortit et jeta les objets suivants : plusieurs boutons, deux échantillons de cheveux ou de poils, un mouchoir brodé, plusieurs lacets (sa spécialité), une brosse à dents, un morceau de caoutchouc, une jarretière, des bouts d'étoffe divers. L'enveloppe aussi, il la jeta, quand il eut fini de la vider. C'est comme si je me curais le nez, se dit-il. Il se leva, mû par des scrupules qui lui faisaient honneur, et ramassa les feuilles froissées de son calepin, c'est-à-dire celles que le petit vent du matin n'avait pas chassées au loin, ou cachées dans un pli du sol, ou derrière une touffe de chardons. Les feuilles ainsi récupérées, il les déchira en petits morceaux, qu'il jeta. Il retourna vers Mercier.

Voilà, dit-il, je me sens plus léger.

Je vois un trou à ta chaussette, dit Mercier.

Je me sens plus léger, dit Camier. Les photos, je les garde pour l'instant. Il tâta sa poche. Tu n'es pas assis sur l'herbe humide, au moins ? dit-il.

Je suis assis sur ma moitié de notre perméable, dit Mercier. On est divinement bien ainsi.

Il fait beau trop tôt, dit Camier. C'est mauvais signe.

Quel temps fait-il, au fait ? dit Mercier.

Mais regarde, dit Camier.

J'aimerais bien que tu me le dises, dit Mercier. Après je te dirai si je suis de ton avis.

Une tache pâle et sans chaleur, dit Camier, a paru dans le ciel. Ça doit être le soleil. On ne le voit heureusement que par moments, à cause des nuages tout souillés et effrangés chassant de l'ouest devant sa face. Il y en a qu'on dirait mangés aux mites. Il fait froid, mais il ne pleut pas encore.

Rassieds-toi, dit Mercier. Tu sens le froid moins que moi, c'est entendu, mais profite du talus quand même. Ne présume pas trop de tes forces, Camier. Je serais bien emmerdé si tu attrapais une pneumonie.

Camier se rassit.

Gagne vers moi, dit Mercier, on aura plus chaud. Encore. Maintenant fais comme moi, rabats le bord de ton côté sur tes jambes. Voilà. Il ne manque plus que l'œuf dur et la bouteille de limonade.

Je sens l'humidité qui me rentre dans la raie, dit Camier.

Du moment qu'il n'en sort pas, dit Mercier.

C'est que je crains pour mon kyste, dit Camier.

Ce qu'il te manque à toi, dit Mercier, c'est le sens de la proportion.

Je ne vois pas le rapport, dit Camier.

Voilà, dit Mercier, tu ne vois jamais le rapport. Quant tu crains pour ton kyste, songe aux fistules. Et quand tu trembles pour ta fistule, réfléchis un peu aux chancres. C'est un système qui vaut également pour ce que d'aucuns appellent encore le bonheur. Prends un type par exemple qui ne souffre de rien, ni au corps ni à l'autre truc. Comment va-t-il s'en sortir ? C'est simple. En pensant au néant. Ainsi dans

91

chaque situation la nature nous convie-t-elle au sourire, sinon au rire.

Encore, dit Camier.

Merci, dit Mercier. Et maintenant envisageons calmement les choses.

Après un moment de silence Camier se mit à rire. Mercier lui aussi finit par trouver cela drôle. Ils rirent donc ensemble pendant un bon moment, en se tenant par les épaules, afin de ne pas s'effondrer.

Quelle franche gaîté, dit Camier, enfin. On dirait du Vauvenargues.

Enfin tu comprends ce que je veux dire, dit Mercier.

Comment te sens-tu aujourd'hui ? dit Camier. Je ne te l'ai pas encore demandé.

Je me sens débile, dit Mercier, mais plus résolu que jamais. Et toi ?

Pour le moment ça va, dit Camier. M'être débarrassé de toute cette saleté m'a fait du bien. Je me sens plus léger. Il écouta. Je dis que je me sens plus léger, dit-il. Mais décidément cette phrase laissait Mercier indifférent. Dire que je me sens d'attaque, non, dit Camier. Il me serait impossible par exemple de repasser par où je suis passé hier.

Qu'avons-nous décidé au juste ? dit Mercier. Je me rappelle que nous nous sommes mis d'accord, comme toujours d'ailleurs, mais je ne sais plus sur quoi. Mais toi tu dois le savoir, puisque en somme c'est ton projet que nous sommes en train de réaliser, n'est-ce pas ?

Pour moi aussi, dit Camier, certains détails sont devenus obscurs, sans parler de certaines finesses de raisonnement. Je te dirai donc plutôt ce que nous allons faire que pourquoi nous allons le faire. Encore mieux, ce que nous allons essayer de faire.

Je suis prêt à tout essayer, dit Mercier, à condition de savoir quoi.

Nous allons donc rentrer bien gentiment, et sans nous dépêcher, en ville, dit Camier, et y rester le temps qu'il faudra.

Le temps qu'il faudra pour quoi faire ? dit Mercier.

Pour récupérer les objets que nous avons égarés, dit Camier, ou pour y renoncer.

Il a dû en effet être riche en finesses, dit Mercier, le raisonnement capable de nous amener à une décision pareille.

Il me semble, dit Camier, quoique je ne puisse le certifier, que le sac est le nœud de

93

toute cette affaire. Nous avons décidé, je crois, qu'il s'y trouve, ou s'y trouvait, un ou plusieurs objets dont nous pouvons difficilement nous passer.

Mais nous avons déjà passé en revue tout ce qu'il contenait, dit Mercier, et jugé qu'il n'y avait là que du superflu.

Je ne le nie pas, dit Camier, et il est peu probable que notre conception du superflu se soit modifiée, depuis hier matin. D'où vient donc notre trouble ? Voilà la question que nous avons dû nous poser.

Et d'où vient-il ? dit Mercier.

Il viendrait, d'après nous, dit Camier, si j'ai bonne mémoire, de l'intuition que ce sac contient, ou contenait, un ou plusieurs objets indispensables à notre salut.

Mais nous savons que ce n'est pas vrai, dit Mercier.

La petite voix implorante, dit Camier, qui nous parle parfois de vies antérieures, la connais-tu ?

Je la confonds de plus en plus, dit Mercier, avec celle qui veut me faire croire que je ne suis pas encore mort. Mais je vois ce que tu veux dire.

Ce serait un organe analogue, dit Camier,

qui depuis vingt-quatre heures va chucho-
tant, Le sac ! Votre sac ! Notre conférence
d'hier soir, au cours de laquelle nous avons
comparé nos impressions, n'a laissé subsister aucun doute à ce sujet, si j'ai bon sou-
venir.

Je ne me rappelle rien de tel, dit Mercier.

Nous aurions donc affirmé, dit Camier, la
nécessité, sinon de trouver, tout au moins de
chercher, notre sac, et de là s'ensuit irrésisti-
blement le reste de notre programme. Car la
recherche du sac entraîne, d'une manière
fatale, celle de la bicyclette et du parapluie.

Je ne vois pas du tout pourquoi, dit Mercier. Pourquoi pas nous occuper simplement
du sac, sans nous occuper de la bicyclette
et du parapluie, puisque c'est du sac qu'il
s'agit, et non de la bicyclette ni du parapluie,
mais du — ?

J'ai compris, j'ai compris, dit Camier.

Alors ? dit Mercier. Pourquoi pas
nous — ?

Ne recommence pas ! hurla Camier.

Alors ? dit Mercier.

Moi non plus je ne vois pas très bien pourquoi, dit Camier. Je sais seulement qu'hier
soir nous avons très bien vu pourquoi. Tu

ne voudrais pas tout remettre en question, j'espère ?

Lorsque les causes m'échappent, dit Mercier, je ne suis pas à mon aise.

Cette fois-ci Camier fut seul à mouiller son pantalon. Suivons-les attentivement, Mercier et Camier, ne nous en éloignons jamais plus que de la hauteur d'un escalier, ou de l'épaisseur d'un mur. Qu'aucun souci d'ordonnance, ou d'harmonie, ne nous en détourne jamais, pour l'instant.

Mercier ne rit pas avec Camier ? dit Camier, dès qu'il put parler.

Pas cette fois-ci, dit Mercier.

Pour moi nous avons dû tenir le raisonnement que voici, dit Camier, ou quelque chose d'approchant. Les choses (je mets les choses au pire), quelles qu'elles soient, dont nous croyons avoir besoin, afin de pouvoir poursuivre notre voyage —.

Notre voyage, dit Mercier. Quel voyage ?

Notre voyage, dit Camier, avec le maximum de chances de succès, nous les avions et ne les avons plus. Nous les plaçons donc dans le sac, comme dans la chose qui contient. Mais à bien y réfléchir rien ne nous prouve qu'elles ne sont pas dans le parapluie, ou attachées à quelque partie de la bicyclette, avec de la ficelle peut-être. Tout ce que nous savons, c'est que nous les avions et que nous ne les avons plus. Et même de cela nous n'avons aucune certitude.

Pour des prémisses, c'est des prémisses, dit Mercier.

Qu'est-ce que tu veux, dit Camier.

Et ta petite voix qui chuchote, Le sac ! Notre sac !, qu'est-ce que tu en fais ? dit Mercier.

Mais elle est contaminée bien avant de nous parvenir, dit Camier. Ne sois pas puéril, Mercier. Pense un peu aux miasmes qu'elle a dû traverser.

J'ai fait un rêve étrange cette nuit, dit Mercier. Maintenant ça me revient.

Il s'agit donc, dit Camier, d'inconnus qui non seulement ne sont pas forcément dans le sac, mais qu'aucun sac à dos peut-être ne saurait contenir, la bicyclette elle-même par exemple, ou le parapluie, ou tous les deux. La vérité, à quoi la reconnaîtrons-nous ? A une sensation de bien-être soudainement accrue ? Je ne le pense pas.

J'étais dans un bois, avec ma grand'mère, dit Mercier. Je ne —.

97

Ça m'étonnerait, dit Camier. Non, ce que je vois, c'est un soulagement graduel de longue haleine atteignant son paroxysme d'ici quinze jours ou trois semaines si tout va bien, sans que nous sachions exactement à quoi l'attribuer. Ce sera la joie dans l'ignorance (combinaison fréquente, entre parenthèses), la joie d'avoir récupéré un bien essentiel, dans l'ignorance de sa nature. Ce qui est certain, c'est l'obligation que nous impose notre état présent et à venir d'essayer, par tous les moyens, de rentrer en possession de notre équipement initial, avant de prendre notre essor proprement dit. Nous échouerons peut-être. Mais nous aurons fait notre devoir. Voilà à peu près à mon avis les arguments que nous avons dû employer. Ils sont frappants, en effet.

Elle portait ses seins à la main, dit Mercier, elle les tenait par le téton, entre pouce et index. Mais, je ne —.

Camier s'emporta, c'est-à-dire qu'il fit semblant de s'emporter, car contre Mercier Camier était incapable de s'emporter réellement. La bouche de Mercier restait entrouverte. Dans la barbe désordonnée et grise brillaient des gouttes venues apparemment

98

de nulle part. Un peu plus haut les doigts couraient sur l'immense nez osseux à la peau rouge tendue, se glissaient furtivement dans les grands trous noirs, s'écartaient pour suivre les creux des joues, recommençaient. Les yeux gris pâle regardaient fixement devant eux, comme avec effroi. Le front, large et bas, barré de rides profondes en forme d'ailes, rides dues, plus qu'à la réflexion, à cet étonnement chronique qui lève les sourcils d'abord et ouvre les yeux ensuite, le front était quand même ce que cette tête avait de moins grotesque. Il était couronné d'une masse invraisemblablement emmêlée de cheveux crasseux, où tous les tons étaient représentés, du blondasse au blanc. Quant aux oreilles, n'en parlons pas.

Mercier se défendit mollement.

Tu me demandes des esplications, dit Camier. Je te les fournis. Tu ne m'écoutes pas.

C'est que mon rêve m'avait repris, dit Mercier.

Oui, dit Camier, au lieu de m'écouter tu ne penses qu'à me raconter ton rêve. Tu n'ignores pas cependant ce que nous avons arrêté à ce sujet : pas de récits de rêve, sous aucun prétexte. Une convention analogue nous interdit les citations.

Lo bello stilo che m'ha fatto onore, dit Mercier, est-ce une citation ?

Lo bello quoi ? dit Camier.

Lo bello stilo che m'ha fatto onore, dit Mercier.

Comment veux-tu que je sache ? dit Camier. Ça m'en a tout l'air. Pourquoi ?

Ce sont des mots qui me bruissent dans la tête depuis hier, dit Mercier, et me brûlent les lèvres.

Tu me dégoûtes, Mercier, dit Camier. Nous prenons certaines précautions afin d'être le mieux possible, le moins mal possible, et c'est exactement comme si on fonçait à l'aveuglette, tête baissée. Il se leva. Te sens-tu la force de bouger ? dit-il.

Non, dit Mercier.

Evidemment, dit Camier. Je m'en vais te chercher à manger.

Va-t'en, dit Mercier.

Les petites jambes fortes et torses le portèrent rapidement jusqu'au village. Les épaules dansaient, les bras allaient et venaient devant la poitrine, de la comédie. Mercier, resté à l'abri du talus, ne savait, encore une fois, à laquelle se laisser aller, des deux pentes habituelles. Puisqu'elles se rejoignaient. Finalement il se dit, Je suis Mercier, seul, malade, dans le froid, dans l'humidité, vieux, à moitié fou, empêtré dans une histoire sans issue. Il regarda un instant, avec nostalgie, le ciel hideux, la terre affreuse. A ton âge, se dit-il. Et ainsi de suite. Comédie aussi. Alors peu importe.

J'allais partir, dit monsieur Conaire, en désespoir de cause.

Georges, dit Camier, je veux cinq sandwichs, dont quatre dans un papier et un à part. Vous voyez, dit-il, en se tournant aimablement vers monsieur Conaire, je pense à tout. Car celui que je mangerai ici me prêtera la force nécessaire pour arriver avec les quatre autres.

Raisonnement de clerc, dit monsieur Conaire. Vous partez avec vos cinq sandwichs, dans un papier, vous vous sentez subitement défaillir, vous ouvrez le paquet, vous en sortez un sandwich, vous le mangez, vous récupérez, vous repartez avec les quatre autres.

Là-dessus je vous répondrai simplement ceci, dit Camier, en vous priant de vous mêler de ce qui vous regarde, que j'envisage de boire une pinte de stout, ce qui ne se fait pas à jeûn. Je ne dis pas que je le ferai, je dis que je le ferai peut-être. Je suis donc obligé de manger un sandwich immédiatement. Il l'entama. En voulez-vous un ? dit-il.

Vous le soignez, dit monsieur Conaire. Hier des gâteaux, aujourd'hui des sandwichs, demain du pain sec et jeudi des pierres.

De la moutarde, dit Camier.

Avant de me quitter hier, dit monsieur Conaire, pour votre affaire de vie ou de mort, vous m'avez donné rendez-vous, ici même, pour l'après-midi. J'arrive, vous demanderez à Georges dans quel état, avec ma ponctualité habituelle. J'attends. Vous me direz que j'ai l'habitude. C'est possible. Des doutes commencent à m'assaillir. Me serais-je trompé d'endroit ? De jour ? Je m'en ouvre au barman. J'apprends que vous êtes quelque part dans les étages, avec votre baron, et cela depuis un bon moment, plongés tous les deux dans une stupeur crapuleuse. Je demande qu'on vous réveille, en faisant valoir combien mon affaire est urgente. Mais non. Il ne faut pas vous déranger, sous aucun prétexte. Vous m'attirez dans cette maison, soi-disant pour qu'on puisse causer tranquillement, et à peine j'arrive que vous prenez des dispositions pour empêcher que je vous voie. Je reçois des conseils. Attendez, ils ne tarderont pas à descendre. Faible, j'attends. Descendez-vous ? Bah ! Je reviens à la charge. Réveillez-le, dites-lui que monsieur Conaire est en bas. Allez vous faire foutre. Les vœux de l'hôte sont sacrés, voilà ce qu'on m'oppose. Je menace, on me rit au nez. Je veux passer outre. Par la violence. On me barre le chemin. Par la ruse, en profitant d'un instant d'inattention pour me glisser dans l'escalier. On me rattrape. J'implore, c'est la rigolade. On m'excite à boire, à rester dîner, à passer la nuit. Je vous verrai demain. On me fera signe dès que vous descendrez. La salle s'emplit. Des manœuvres, quelques voyageurs. Je suis pris dans le tourbillon. Je me réveille sur un canapé. Il est sept heures. Vous êtes partis. Pourquoi ne m'a-t-on pas prévenu ? On ne savait pas. A quelle heure sont-ils partis ? On ne sait pas. Vont-ils revenir ? On ne sait pas.

Camier leva une chope imaginaire, on voyait cela à ses doigts recourbés. La réelle, il la vida lentement d'un trait. Il paya, prit son paquet et alla à la porte. A la porte il s'arrêta.

Monsieur Conaire, dit-il, je vous présente mes excuses. Hier j'ai beaucoup pensé à vous, pendant un moment. Puis je n'ai plus pensé à vous, mais pas du tout, pas un instant. C'était comme si vous n'aviez jamais existé, monsieur Conaire. Non, je me trompe, c'était comme si vous aviez cessé d'exister. Non, ce n'est pas ça, c'était comme si vous existiez à mon insu. Ce que je vous dis là, monsieur Conaire, ne le prenez pas en mauvaise part. Ce n'est pas pour vous offenser, monsieur Conaire. C'est que j'avais compris, ou plutôt décidé, que mon travail était fini, je veux dire le travail qu'on me connaît, et que j'avais eu tort en pensant que vous pourriez vous joindre à nous, même pour un jour ou deux. Je renouvelle mes excuses, monsieur Conaire, et je vous dis adieu.

Et ma chienne ! s'écria monsieur Conaire.

Vous la connaissez, dit Camier. Elle vous manque. Vous donneriez cher, enfin, ce qu'on appelle cher, pour la retrouver. Rendez-vous compte de votre bonheur. Il sortit.

Monsieur Conaire faillit le suivre. Mais il se retenait depuis quelque temps déjà et au fond il était content que l'entretien eût pris fin. En revenant de la cour il jeta un coup d'œil dans la rue. Puis il rentra dans la salle, où une telle tristesse s'empara de lui qu'il se remit au gin.

Ma chienne, gémit-il.

Allons, allons, dit Georges, on vous en trouvera une autre.

Marquise ! gémit monsieur Conaire. Elle souriait !

En voilà un autre de liquidé, sauf malheur.

On ne voyait pas monsieur Gast, et pour cause, car il cherchait des perce-neige pour Patrice, dans un petit bois. A quelque chose malheur est bon.

On ne voyait pas Thérèse non plus, et c'est sans regret qu'on ne la voyait pas.

Pour les autres, patience.

Mercier ne voulut rien manger. Camier l'y obligea pourtant.

Tu es vert, dit Camier.

Je crois que je vais rendre, dit Mercier.

Il ne se trompait pas. Camier le soutint.

Ça te fera du bien, dit Camier.

Petit à petit Mercier se sentait mieux, en

effet, mieux c'est-à-dire qu'avant d'avoir rendu.

J'ai roulé de si tristes pensées, dit-il, depuis ton départ. Je me demandais si tu allais revenir.

En te laissant l'imperméable ? dit Camier.

Il y a de quoi m'abandonner, je le sais, dit Mercier. Il réfléchit un instant. Il faut être Camier pour ne pas abandonner Mercier, dit-il.

Peux-tu marcher ? dit Camier.

Je marcherai, n'aie pas peur, dit Mercier. Il se leva et fit quelques pas. Regarde comme je marche bien, dit-il.

Si on jetait l'imperméable ? dit Camier. A quoi nous sert-il ?

Il retarde l'action de la pluie, dit Mercier.

C'est un linceul, dit Camier.

N'exagérons rien, dit Mercier.

Veux-tu que je te dise toute ma pensée ? dit Camier. Celui qui le porte est gêné, au physique comme au moral, au même titre que celui qui ne le porte pas.

Il y a du vrai dans ce que tu dis, dit Mercier.

Ils regardèrent l'imperméable. Il s'étalait au pied du talus. Il avait l'air écorché. Des

106

lambeaux d'une doublure à carreaux, aux tons charmants d'extinction, adhéraient aux épaules. Un jaune plus clair marquait les endroits où l'humidité n'avait pas encore traversé.

Si je l'apostrophais ? dit Mercier.

On a le temps, dit Camier.

Mercier réfléchit.

Adieu, vieille gabardine, dit-il.

Le silence se prolongeant, Camier dit :

C'est ça ton apostrophe ?

Oui, dit Mercier.

Allons-nous-en, dit Camier.

Alors on ne le jette pas ? dit Mercier.

On le laisse là, dit Camier. Pas la peine de se fatiguer.

J'aurais voulu le lancer, dit Mercier.

Laissons-le là, dit Camier. Peu à peu les traces de nos corps s'effaceront. Sous l'effet du soleil il se repliera, comme une feuille morte.

Et si on l'enterrait ? dit Mercier.

Ce serait de la sensiblerie, dit Camier.

Pour pas qu'un autre le prenne, dit Mercier, un vermineux quelconque.

Qu'est-ce que ça peut nous faire ? dit Camier.

Evidemment, dit Mercier, mais ça nous fait quelque chose.

Moi je m'en vais, dit Camier.

Il s'éloigna. Mercier le rejoignit bientôt.

Tu peux t'appuyer sur moi, dit Camier.

Plus tard, plus tard, dit Mercier, avec irritation.

Qu'est-ce que tu as à regarder tout le temps en arrière ? dit Camier.

Il a bougé, dit Mercier.

Qui ? dit Camier. Ah oui, je sais. Il agite son mouchoir.

On n'a rien laissé dans les poches, au moins ? dit Mercier.

Des billets poinçonnés de toutes sortes, dit Camier, des allumettes usées, sur des bouts de marge de journal des traces oblitérées de rendez-vous irrévocables, le classique dernier dixième d'un crayon épointé, quelques feuilles crasseuses de papier cul, quelques capotes d'étanchéité douteuse, enfin de la poussière. Toute une vie, quoi.

Rien dont nous ayons besoin ? dit Mercier.

Puisque je te dis toute une vie, dit Camier.

Ils marchèrent pendant quelque temps

sans parler, comme cela leur arrivait quelquefois.

Nous y mettrons dix jours s'il le faut,
dit Camier.

On ne se fait pas véhiculer ? dit Mercier.

Ce que nous cherchons n'est pas néces-
sairement à l'autre bout de l'île, dit Camier.
Que notre devise soit donc —.

Ce que nous cherchons, dit Mercier

Nous ne voyageons pas pour le plaisir de
voyager, que je sache, dit Camier. Nous sommes cons, mais pas à ce point. Il observa
Mercier avec curiosité. On dirait que tu
suffoques, dit-il. Si tu as quelque chose à
dire, dis-le.

J'allais en effet dire quelque chose, dit
Mercier. Mais, réflexion faite, je le garde.

Pas sur l'estomac, j'espère ? dit Camier.

Continue, dit Mercier.

Où en étais-je ? dit Camier.

Que notre devise soit donc, dit Mercier.

Ah oui, dit Camier. Que notre devise
soit donc lenteur et circonspection, avec des
embardées à droite et à gauche et de brusques retours en arrière, selon les dards obscurs de l'intuition. N'ayons pas peur non
plus de nous arrêter pendant des jours en-

tiers, et même des semaines. Nous avons toute la vie devant nous, enfin tout le solde.

Quel temps fait-il, à présent ? dit Mercier.

Pour qui me prends-tu ? dit Camier. Pour Manto ?

Je suis tout entier à mes équilibres, dit Mercier.

Il fait le même temps que toujours, dit Camier, avec cette petite différence, qu'on commence à s'y habituer.

Il me semblait sentir des gouttes, sur ma figure, dit Mercier.

Courage, dit Camier, c'est bientôt la station des damnés. Je vois le clocher.

C'est bien, dit Mercier. Nous allons pouvoir nous reposer.

VI

Résumé des deux chapitres précédents

IV

Le train.
Hors-d'œuvre Madden, 1.
L'omnibus.
Hors-d'œuvre Madden, fin.
Le village.
L'auberge.
Monsieur Gast.
Les bêtes sur les routes.
Les fermiers.
Rêve de Mercier.
Le voyage compromis.
Sang-froid de Camier.
Maladie de Patrice.

Mercier et Camier montent.
Monsieur Graves.
Départ des fermiers.
Mort de Patrice.
Ses avant-dernières paroles.
Hors-d'œuvre Conaire, 1.
Monsieur Gast parle de l'hôte.
Vision de monsieur Gast.
Hors-d'œuvre Conaire, 2.
Mercier et Camier dorment.

v

Le lendemain.
Le champ.
La chèvre.
L'aurore.
Rire de Mercier et Camier.
Conférence (avec rire de Camier seul et
   visage de Mercier).
Rêve de Mercier.
Départ de Camier.
Mercier seul.
L'auberge.
Hors-d'œuvre Conaire, fin.
Les perce-neige.

Mercier mange.
Mercier vomit.
L'imperméable.
Ils s'en vont.
Clocher des damnés.

VII

Enfin un jour ce fut la ville, d'abord les
faubourgs, ensuite le centre. Ils avaient perdu la notion du temps, mais l'aspect des
rues, l'aspect des gens et les bruits dont
s'emplissait l'air, tout leur parlait du repos
hebdomadaire. La nuit tombait. Ils tournèrent un peu autour du centre, ne sachant
où aller. A la fin, sur la proposition de Mercier (dont ce devait être au tour de mener),
ils allèrent chez Hélène. Elle était au lit,
un peu souffrante. Elle se leva cependant et
les fit entrer, non sans avoir crié, à travers
la porte, Qui est là ? Ils la mirent au courant, de leurs déboires, de leurs espoirs. Ils
lui racontèrent l'histoire du taureau qui les
avait chassés. Elle sortit et revint avec le
parapluie. Camier le manœuvra pendant un

bon moment. Mais il marche très bien, dit-il, très très bien. Je l'ai réparé, dit Hélène. On dirait même qu'il marche mieux qu'avant, dit Camier. C'est possible, dit Hélène. Il s'ouvre en souplesse, dit Camier, et quand j'appuie, toc ! sur la détente, il s'affaisse tout seul. J'ouvre, je ferme, et d'un, et de deux, et d'un, et de deux, toc ! plouf ! toc ! —. Assez, dit Mercier, tu vas nous le casser encore. Je suis un peu souffrante, dit Hélène. C'est de bon augure, dit Camier. Mais le sac n'y était pas. Je ne vois pas le perroquet, dit Mercier. Je l'ai mis à la campagne, dit Hélène. La nuit s'écoula paisiblement, pour eux, sans stupre d'aucune sorte. Le lendemain ils restèrent à la maison. Le temps leur semblant long, ils se touchèrent un peu, mais sans se fatiguer. Devant un bon feu, à la lumière mêlée de la lampe et du jour plombé, ils se tordaient doucement sur le tapis, les corps nus entremêlés, se touchant avec langueur, avec des gestes d'arrangeuse de fleurs, pendant que la pluie battait les vitres. Que cela devait être bon ! Vers le soir Hélène fit monter quelques bonnes bouteilles, et ils s'assoupirent pleins de contentement. Des hommes moins tenaces auraient pu céder à la tentation d'en rester là. Mais le lendemain après-midi les vit à nouveau dans la rue, tout tendus vers le but qu'ils s'étaient assigné. Ils n'avaient devant eux que quelques heures d'un jour lugubre, avant la nuit, l'avant-nuit. Il fallait donc faire vite. Et cependant l'obscurité, que les becs de gaz empêcheraient d'être totale, ne saurait les gêner, tout compte fait, dans leurs recherches. Au contraire, elle ne pourrait que leur être d'un précieux secours. Car le quartier où ils se proposaient de se rendre, et dont ils connaissaient mal les approches, ils s'y rendraient plus facilement la nuit que le jour, puisque la seule fois qu'ils s'y étaient rendus il ne faisait pas jour, mais nuit, ou presque. Ils entrèrent donc dans un bar, car c'est dans les bars que les Mercier et Camier attendent la nuit avec le moins de désagrément. Ils avaient d'ailleurs pour cela une raison moins sérieuse, à savoir l'intérêt qu'ils avaient, sur le plan intellectuel aussi, à s'envelopper autant que possible de la même atmosphère que celle qui avait rendu si incertains leurs premiers pas. C'est à quoi ils s'employèrent, sans plus tarder. L'enjeu est trop gros, dit Camier, pour qu'on

116

néglige les précautions élémentaires. Ainsi d'une seule pierre ils firent deux coups, et même trois. Car ils profitèrent du répit pour causer de choses et d'autres, avec un grand profit, pour eux. Car c'est dans les bars que les Mercier et Camier de ce corps céleste parlent avec le plus de liberté, le plus de profit. Il se fit dans leurs idées peu à peu une grande clarté. En furent notamment inondées les notions suivantes :

1. Le manque d'argent est un mal. Mais il peut devenir un bien.

2. Ce qui est perdu est perdu.

3. La bicyclette est un grand bien. Mais mal utilisée elle devient dangereuse.

4. Etre complètement à la côte, cela donne à réfléchir.

5. Il y a deux besoins : celui que l'on a, et celui de l'avoir.

6. L'intuition fait faire bien des folies.

7. N'est jamais perdu ce que l'âme vomit.

8. Sentir ses poches qui chaque jour se vident des suprêmes ressources, voilà de quoi briser les résolutions les mieux trempées.

9. Le pantalon mâle s'est enlisé dans une ornière, spécialement la braguette, qu'il faudrait reporter à l'entre-jambes, sous forme de pièce à bascule par où, indépendamment de toute question sordide de miction, les bourses pourraient sortir prendre le frais, tout en restant cachées aux curieux. Le caleçon serait naturellement à corriger dans le même sens.

10. Contrairement à une opinion répandue, il y a des endroits dans la nature d'où Dieu paraît absent.

11. Que ferions-nous sans les femmes ? Nous prendrions un autre pli.

12. Ame a trois lettres et une ou une et demie et même jusqu'à deux syllabes.

13. Que peut-on dire sur la vie que l'on n'ait pas dit déjà ? Beaucoup de choses. Qu'elle vise mal du cul, par exemple.

Ils ne perdaient pas pour si peu de vue le but qu'ils s'étaient assigné. Seulement il leur paraissait, avec de plus en plus d'évidence à mesure que l'heure avançait, un but à poursuivre dans le calme, et le froid du sang. Et, étant encore assez calmes pour savoir qu'ils ne l'étaient plus, ils purent

prendre l'heureuse décision de remettre toute action jusqu'au lendemain, et, au besoin,
jusqu'au surlendemain. Ils regagnèrent donc
de fort bonne humeur l'appartement d'Hélène et s'endormirent sans cérémonie aucune. Et même le lendemain ils se refusèrent
aux jolis passe-temps des matinées de pluie,
tant ils désiraient rester frais et dispos pour
les épreuves à venir.

Midi sonnait comme ils sortaient de l'im-
meuble. Ils s'arrêtèrent sous le porche.

Oh le joli arc-en-ciel, dit Camier.

Le parapluie, dit Mercier.

Ils se regardèrent. Camier rentra dans l'escalier. Quand il revint, portant le parapluie,
Mercier dit :

Tu as été long.

Oh tu sais, dit Camier, on fait ce qu'on
peut. Faut-il l'ouvrir ?

Mercier regarda longuement le ciel.

Qu'est-ce que tu en penses ? dit-il.

Camier sortit sur le trottoir et soumit
le ciel à une inspection minutieuse, en se
tournant successivement vers le nord, l'est,
le sud, l'ouest.

Alors ? dit Mercier.

Attends, attends, dit Camier. Il s'avança

jusqu'au milieu de la chaussée, afin de dimi-
nuer les risques d'erreur. Enfin il rentra
sous le porche.

A notre place, dit-il, je ne l'ouvrirais pas.

Et peut-on savoir pour quelle raison ?
dit Mercier. Il pleut ferme, à ce qu'il me
semble. Tu es même tout mouillé.

Toi, tu serais d'avis de l'ouvrir ? dit Camier.

Je ne dis pas ça, dit Mercier. Je me demande seulement quand nous l'ouvrirons si
nous ne l'ouvrons pas maintenant.

C'était à bien le regarder plutôt une om-
brelle qu'un parapluie. Au repos, la distance
entre la pointe et l'extrémité des tiges ne
représentait guère plus d'un quart de la lon-
gueur totale. Le manche se terminait en
boule d'ambre, garnie de glands. L'étoffe
était rouge, ou l'avait été, et l'était même
toujours par endroits. Quelques franges en
ornaient encore le périmètre, à des inter-
valles peu réguliers.

Regarde-le bien, dit Camier. Tiens,
prends-le. Mais prends-le, il ne va pas te
mordre.

Arrière ! s'écria Mercier.

D'où sort-il ? dit Camier.

Je l'ai acheté chez Khan, dit Mercier, sachant que nous n'avions qu'un seul manteau à nous deux. Il m'en a demandé un shilling, je l'ai eu pour neuf pence. J'ai cru qu'il allait m'embrasser.

Il a dû faire ses débuts vers 1900, dit Camier. C'était je crois l'année de Ladysmith, sur le Klip. T'en souviens-tu ? Un temps splendide. Des garden-parties tous les jours. La vie s'ouvrait devant nous, radieuse. Tous les espoirs permis. On jouait aux assiégés. On mourait comme des mouches. De faim. De soif. Pan ! Pan ! les dernières cartouches. Rendez-vous ! Jamais ! On mangeait les cadavres. On buvait son pipi. Pan ! Pan ! encore deux qu'on avait égarées. Qu'entend-on ? Un cri du mirador. Poussière à l'horizon ! C'est la colonne ! On a la langue noire. Hourra quand même ! Ra ! Ra ! On dirait des corbeaux. Un maréchal des logis meurt de joie. Nous sommes sauvés. Le siècle avait deux mois.

Regarde-le maintenant, dit Mercier.

Comment te sens-tu ? dit Camier. J'oublie toujours de te le demander.

Je me sentais bien en descendant l'escalier, dit Mercier. Maintenant ça va moins bien. Gonflé, si tu veux, mais pas à bloc. Et toi ?

Un bouchon, dit Camier, au milieu de l'océan déchaîné.

C'est le moment de frapper, dit Mercier.

Quant à cet abri portatif, dit Camier, je crois qu'on ferait bien de le réserver pour les journées de grande chaleur. D'un ciel d'un bleu impitoyable le soleil darde ses rayons ardents. Nous n'avons pas un seul chapeau.

Autant le jeter tout de suite, dit Mercier.

Je veux bien, dit Camier.

Nous serons allongés à l'ombre des ifs, dit Mercier, du matin jusqu'au soir.

Quels ifs ? dit Camier.

N'importe lesquels, dit Mercier.

Et s'il n'y a pas d'ifs ? dit Camier.

Nous en trouverons bien, dit Mercier.

Il y a des départements entiers, dans ce malheureux pays, dit Camier, où, sans parler d'ifs, nul arbre ne pousse, de quelque essence que ce soit, et où le buisson le plus hardi ne dépasse pas un mètre de haut.

Nous les éviterons pendant la canicule, dit Mercier.

Tu as réponse à tout, dit Camier.

Ce ne sont pas des réponses, dit Mercier.

Alors, on le jette ? dit Camier.

Nous hésitons, dit Mercier.

Nous hésitons à le jeter, dit Camier. Nos raisons ?

J'en vois deux, dit Mercier. Mais sont-elles viables ? Voilà ce qu'il faut décider.

Je nous le dirai, dit Camier, quand je les connaîtrai.

Tout parasol qu'il semble être, dit Mercier, il peut nous protéger contre la pluie, pendant un certain temps. Je veux dire que nous serons peut-être moins mouillés avec que sans, pendant un certain temps.

Et l'autre ? dit Camier.

L'autre quoi ? dit Mercier.

L'autre raison, dit Camier.

Voilà, dit Mercier. Elle est peut-être un peu plus difficile à saisir.

Nous la saisirons, dit Camier.

Ose-t-on jeter froidement une chose, dit Mercier, qui peut s'avérer par la suite précisément celle dont nous avions besoin, celle dont la perte nous a arrêtés en plein élan et obligés à revenir sur nos pas, la queue entre les jambes ?

Nous ne le jetterons jamais, dit Camier.

Ne dis pas ça, dit Mercier. Mais il sera peut-être temps de le jeter quand il ne pourra plus nous servir d'abri, à cause de l'usure, ou que nous aurons acquis la certitude qu'entre lui et notre détresse présente il n'a jamais existé le moindre rapport.

Très bien, dit Camier. Mais il ne suffit pas de savoir qu'on ne le jette pas, il faut savoir également s'il faut l'ouvrir.

Puisque c'est en partie afin de l'ouvrir que ne nous le jetons pas, dit Mercier.

Je sais, je sais, dit Camier. Mais faut-il l'ouvrir dès maintenant ou attendre que le temps se caractérise davantage ?

Mercier scruta le ciel impénétrable.

Va jeter un coup d'œil, dit-il. Dis-moi ce que tu en penses.

Camier sortit dans la rue. Il poussa même jusqu'au coin, de sorte que Mercier le perdit de vue. Revenu, il dit :

Il y a peut-être des trouées dans le bas. Veux-tu que je monte sur le toit ?

Mercier se concentra. Enfin il dit, impulsivement :

Ouvrons-le, et à la grâce de Dieu.

Mais Camier ne put l'ouvrir.

Donne, dit Mercier.

Mais Mercier ne fut pas plus heureux. Il le brandit. Mais il se maîtrisa à temps. Proverbe.

Qu'avons-nous fait à Dieu ? dit-il.

Nous l'avons renié, dit Camier.

Tu ne me feras pas croire qu'il est rancunier à ce point, dit Mercier.

Je vais le montrer à Hélène, dit Camier. Elle nous arrangera ça en moins de deux. Il prit le parapluie et disparut dans l'escalier. Quand il revint Mercier dit :

Tu appelles ça moins de deux ?

C'est toujours un peu plus long la deuxième fois, dit Camier.

Le parapluie ? dit Mercier.

Elle en a pour une demi-heure, dit Camier, et nous n'avons pas de temps à perdre.

Cela nous oblige à revenir, dit Mercier.

Mais de toute façon —, dit Camier.

De toute façon rien, dit Mercier. Moi je veux qu'on soit fixés d'ici la nuit et qu'on s'en aille.

Où ? dit Camier.

Loin d'ici, dit Mercier.

Alors ? dit Camier.

De deux choses l'une, dit Mercier.

Hélas ! dit Camier.

Ou bien nous attendons qu'il soit prêt, dit Mercier, ou bien —.

Mais je lui ai dit que ça ne pressait pas, dit Camier, qu'elle avait jusqu'à demain matin pour le faire.

Ou bien l'un de nous reste ici, dit Mercier, jusqu'à ce que le parapluie soit prêt, pendant que l'autre s'occupe du sac et de la bicyclette. Ça nous fera gagner du temps. Et on se retrouve quelque part à une heure qui reste à déterminer.

Ils continuent à l'appeler le parapluie, que c'est drôle.

Mais elle ne peut pas le faire tout de suite, dit Camier.

Voici ce qu'on va faire, dit Mercier, incontestablement en grande forme. Tu vas expliquer à Hélène de quelle manière les choses se présentent. Tu lui demanderas d'arranger le parapluie tout de suite. Elle te dira oui ou non, n'est-ce pas ?

Elle me dira non, dit Camier.

Si elle te dit non, dit Mercier, tu prends le parapluie tel quel et tu descends. Je serai ici et nous partirons ensemble. Si au contraire elle te dit oui, tu attends que le travail soit fait et tu me rejoins à l'endroit et à l'heu-

re que je t'indiquerai, ou que tu m'indique-
ras, ça n'a aucune importance.

Et si tu restais, dit Camier, et que moi
je m'en aille ? Moi j'ai l'habitude des recherches.

Ce que tu dis est raisonnable, dit Mercier.
Mais fais-moi ce plaisir. Ça fait du bien,
de temps en temps, de s'arracher à son rôle.

Alors, où et quand ? dit Camier.

Que tout cela est lamentable.

Dès qu'il fut seul Mercier s'en alla. Son
chemin croisa, à un moment donné, celui
d'un vieillard d'aspect excentrique et misé-
rable qui portait sous le bras une sorte de
planchette pliée en deux. Il semblait à Mercier qu'il l'avait déjà vu quelque part et tout
en poursuivant son chemin il se demandait
où cela avait pu être. Le vieillard lui aussi,
à qui par extraordinaire le passage de Mercier n'avait pas échappé, gardait l'impression
d'un grotesque déjà vu et il s'employa pendant quelque temps à chercher dans quelles
circonstances. Ainsi en vain ils pensaient
l'un à l'autre, pendant qu'à pas lents l'inter-
valle grandissait. Mais les Mercier, un rien
les arrête, un murmure qui monte, s'enfle,
se décompose, une voix qui dit que c'est

127

étrange, l'automne du jour, quelle que soit la saison. Il y a un recommencement, mais le cœur ne semble pas y être, et comment y serait-il ? Cela se sent surtout à la ville, mais à la campagne aussi cela se sent, là où il y a des vaches et des oiseaux. A travers d'immenses étendues vides les paysans errent lentement, on se demande comment ils vont pouvoir rentrer chez eux avant la nuit, à la ferme qu'on ne voit pas, au village qu'on ne voit pas. Il n'y a plus assez de temps et pourtant Dieu sait s'il y en a. Même les fleurs ont quelque chose de fermé et une sorte d'affolement gagne les ailes. Toujours l'épervier fonce trop tôt, les corbeaux en plein jour quittent les guérets et se dépêchent vers le lieu de rassemblement, où ils ne feront plus que croasser et se chamailler jusqu'à la nuit. A ce moment-là des velléités de sortie les agitent, mais c'est trop tard. C'est un fait, la journée est finie longtemps avant de finir et les hommes tombent de fatigue bien avant l'heure du repos. Mais motus, les dernières heures du jour sont pleines de fièvre, on court à droite et à gauche et rien ne se fait. L'heure du danger, on la laisse passer, parce qu'il n'y a pas de danger, et ensuite on est sans armes. Les gens dans la rue vont cernés de catastrophes en marche. Trop court pour que ce soit la peine de commencer, trop long pour qu'on ne commence pas quand même, voilà leur temps, cage de la Balue des heures. Demandez l'heure à un passant, il vous dira n'importe quoi, au jugé, par-dessus son épaule, en s'éloignant. Mais soyez tranquille, il ne s'est pas trompé de beaucoup, lui qui consulte sa montre tous les quarts d'heure, la règle sur les horloges astronomiques publiques, fait ses calculs, se demande comment il va faire, pour faire tout ce qu'il a à faire, avant la fin du jour interminable. Ou il traduit, d'un geste furieux et las, l'étrange impression dont il souffre, à savoir qu'il est l'heure qu'il a toujours été et sera toujours, celle qui unit aux beautés du trop tard les charmes du prématuré, l'heure du Jamais ! sans plus d'un plus terrible corbeau. D'ailleurs c'est toute la journée ainsi, depuis le premier tic jusqu'au dernier tac, ou mettons depuis le troisième jusqu'à l'antépénultième, car il met du temps quand même, le tam-tam thoracique, à nous rappeler au rêve, et il met du temps aussi à nous en congédier. Mais les

129

autres on les entend, chaque grain de millet on l'entend, on se retourne et on se voit, chaque fois un peu plus près, toute la vie un peu plus près. La joie par cuillerées à sel, comme l'eau aux grands déshydratés, et une gentille petite agonie à doses homéopathiques, qu'est-ce qu'il vous faut encore ? Un cœur à la place du cœur ? Allons, allons. Mais demandez par contre à un passant de vous montrer votre chemin et il vous prend la main et vous conduit, par mille détours délicieux, à pied d'œuvre. C'est une grande bâtisse grise, elle n'est pas achevée, elle ne sera jamais achevée, elle a deux portes, l'une pour ceux qui rentrent, l'autre pour ceux qui sortent, et aux fenêtres il y a des visages qui regardent. Vous n'aviez qu'à ne rien demander.

La main de Mercier lâcha le barreau de la grille auquel l'avait cloué ces renvois, supportés avec courage, d'époques révolues, comme on dit. Oui, il les avait supportés avec courage, car il savait qu'ils cesseraient à la fin dans une lente chute vers le murmure et puis le silence, ce silence qui est aussi un murmure, mais inarticulé. La porte se ferme, ou la trappe, dans l'oubliette ce sont toujours les mêmes propos, mais dans la prison proprement dite le calme est revenu. Mais son chemin ne tarda pas à croiser celui d'un vieillard hirsute et déguenillé, qui marchait à côté d'un âne. L'âne, qui n'avait pas de bride, suivait à petits pas fastidieux et braves le bord du trottoir et ne s'en écartait que pour contourner une voiture en station ou des gamins jouant aux billes, accroupis dans le ruisseau. L'âne portait deux paniers, dont l'un était plein de coquillages et l'autre de sable. L'homme marchait dans la rue, entre le flanc gris rebondi et les voitures hostiles. Ils ne levaient les yeux, l'âne et l'homme, que de loin en loin, pour mesurer un danger. Mercier se dit, Ce n'est pas le monde extérieur qui compromettra cette harmonie. Il n'a pas fini de nous décevoir, ce Mercier. Il avait peut-être présumé de ses forces, en quittant Camier à une heure si sombre. Certes il fallait de la force pour rester avec Camier, comme il en fallait pour rester avec Mercier, mais moins qu'il n'en fallait pour la bataille du soliloque. Pourtant le voilà reparti, les voix se sont tues, l'âne et le vieillard ont failli le terrasser mais il s'est ressaisi, le brouillard bienfaisant qui

131

est ce qu'il a de mieux s'est répandu à nouveau dans ses œuvres vives, il peut encore aller loin. Il avance presque invisible en rasant la grille, à l'ombre d'on ne sait quels arbres soi-disant verts, des houx peut-être, ruisselants de pluie, si l'on peut appeler ombre un jour à peine plus plombé que celui des tourbières proches. Le col de son veston est relevé, sa main droite est dans sa manche gauche, et inversement, elles se ballotent sur son ventre dans un vrai geste de vieux, et il entrevoit par moments, comme à travers des algues mouvantes, un pied qui traîne sur une dalle. De lourdes chaînes, suspendues entre de petits piliers en fer, festonnent de leurs chutes de guirlande le trottoir du côté de la chaussée. Lorsqu'on les remue elles se balancent longuement, calmement ou avec des tortillements de serpent qui peu à peu se résorbent. Mercier venait jouer ici, quand il était petit. Courant le long du trottoir, il mettait les chaînes en branle, l'une après l'autre, avec un bâton. Arrivé au bout, il se retournait pour les voir. Le trottoir tressaillait, d'un bout à l'autre, de lourdes secousses, longues à s'apaiser.

VIII

La place de Camier était près de la porte.
La petite table devant lui était rouge et son
dessus était couvert d'un verre épais. A sa
gauche des inconnus parlaient d'inconnus et
à sa droite il était question, à voix basse,
de l'intérêt que portent les jésuites à la chose
publique. On citait à ce propos, ou à un
autre voisin, un article paru dans une revue
ecclésiastique sur la fécondation artificielle.
La conclusion de cet article semblait être
qu'il y avait péché toutes les fois que le
sperme était de provenance non maritale.
La discussion s'engagea là-dessus. Plusieurs
voix y participaient.

Parlez d'autre chose, dit Camier, si vous
ne voulez pas que j'aille tout raconter à
l'archevêque. Vous me troublez.

Il distinguait mal ce qui se passait devant

lui, tant tout était flou et enfumé. Ne crevaient le brouillard que quelques effets de manche avec pipe à la clef, çà et là un chapeau pointu et des fragments de membres inférieurs, notamment des pieds, dont les attitudes tendues et tourmentées changeaient à chaque instant, comme si l'âme y avait son siège. Mais derrière lui il y avait le gros bon mur tout simple et net, il le sentait dans son dos, il y frottait son occiput. Quand Mercier viendra, se dit-il, car il viendra, je le connais, où va-t-il se mettre ? Ici, à cette table ? Ce problème l'absorba pendant un bon moment. Il décida finalement que non, qu'il ne le fallait pas, que lui Camier ne le supporterait pas, il ne savait pas pourquoi. Que se passerait-il alors ? Afin de mieux envisager ce qui se passerait alors, puisqu'il ne fallait pas que Mercier vînt le rejoindre dans son coin, Camier sortit les mains de ses poches, les disposa devant lui dans un petit tas douillet et accueillant et y blottit son visage, d'abord doucement et puis de tout le poids du crâne. Et Camier ne tarda pas à voir, à se voir qui voit Mercier avant que Mercier le voie, à se voir qui se lève et court à la porte. Te

voilà enfin, s'écrie-t-il, je croyais que tu
m'avais abandonné, et il l'entraîne vers le
comptoir, ou dans la salle du fond, ou ils
sortent ensemble, quoique cela ne soit guère
probable, car Mercier est las, il a envie de
s'asseoir, de se rafraîchir, avant d'aller plus
loin, et il a des choses à raconter qui peuvent
difficilement attendre, et Camier lui aussi a
des choses à raconter, oui, ils ont des choses
importantes à se dire et ils sont las, et puis
il y a longtemps qu'ils ne se sont pas vus, et
il faut que tout cela se calme et s'éclair-
cisse, et qu'ils sachent à peu près à quoi s'en
tenir, et si l'avenir s'annonce bon ou mauvais
ou tout simplement quelconque, comme c'est
le cas si souvent, et s'il existe un côté plutôt qu'un autre où ils auraient intérêt à se
diriger, enfin bref où ils en sont, avant de
pouvoir se précipiter, dans un accès de luci-
dité souriante, vers l'un des nombreux buts
qu'équipolle un jugement indulgent, ou que
souriants (facultatif) ils fassent justice de
cet élan en les admirant de loin, car ils
sont loin, l'un après l'autre. C'est alors
qu'on entrevoit ce qu'on aurait pu être, s'il
n'avait pas fallu être ce qu'on est, et ce n'est
pas tous les jours qu'il est donné de couper

135

en quatre un cheveu de cette qualité. Car du moment que l'on vit, bernique. L'ordre mis ainsi dans l'avenir immédiat, Camier leva la tête et vit en face de lui un être qu'il mit quelque temps à reconnaître, tant c'était Mercier, d'où un tissage de réflexions qui ne devait s'apaiser que le surlendemain (mais quel apaisement alors) dans la douce conclusion que ce qu'il avait tant redouté, au point de juger la chose insupportable, ce n'était point de sentir son ami à ses côtés, mais de le voir pousser la porte et achever de franchir le grand espace qui les séparait depuis le matin. A la ligne.

L'entrée de Mercier avait jeté un certain trouble dans la salle, une sorte de froid embarrassé. C'était pourtant des dockers et des marins pour la plupart, avec quelques employés des douanes, des gens qui en général ne s'émeuvent pas facilement, devant des dehors qui sortent de l'ordinaire. N'empêche qu'il se produisit comme un reflux des voix, les gestes se suspendirent, les chopes tremblèrent sur le bord des lèvres, les visages se tournèrent tous du même côté. Un observateur, s'il y en avait eu, mais il n'y en avait pas, aurait pensé peut-être à un troupeau de moutons, ou de bufles, mis en émoi par un danger obscur. Les corps figés, les visages tendus et irrités qu'aimante la menace, ils sont un instant plus immobiles que la nature qui les emprisonne. Puis c'est la fuite éperdue, ou l'assaut donné à l'intrus (s'il est faible), ou la reprise des occupations, de la paissance, de la rumination, de l'amour, des gambades. Ou il aurait pensé à ces malades ambulants dont le passage arrête les conversations, fait oublier le corps et emplit l'âme de crainte, de pitié, de colère, de rire et de dégoût. Oui, lorsqu'on insulte à la nature il faut faire très attention, si l'on ne veut entendre le hallali, ou subir les secours de quelque main répugnante. Un instant il sembla à Camier que les choses allaient mal tourner, et sous la table ses jarrets se tendirent. Mais peu à peu se développa une sorte d'immense soupir, une exhalation qui monta, monta, comme une vague cavalant vers la grève et dont enfin la furie s'abolit, en gouttes et en fracas, aux rires des enfants.

Qu'est-ce qui t'est arrivé ? dit Camier.

Mercier leva la tête, sans toutefois fixer Camier des yeux, ni même le mur. Que

pouvait-il bien regarder avec une telle inten-
sité ? On se le demande.

Quelle tête tu fais, dit Camier. On dirait
que tu sors des enfers. Qu'est-ce que tu dis ?
En effet les lèvres de Mercier avaient bougé.
On peut porter la barbe, dit Camier, sans
marmotter dedans.

Je n'en connais qu'un, dit Mercier.

On ne t'a pas battu ? dit Camier.

Il tomba sur eux l'ombre d'un homme
géant. Son tablier s'arrêtait à mi-cuisse. Camier le regarda, lui regarda Mercier et Mercier se mit à regarder Camier. Ainsi, sans
que les regards se croisassent, fut-il engendré
des images d'une grande complexité, chacun jouissant de soi-même en trois versions
distinctes et simultanées et en même temps,
quoique plus obscurément, des trois versions de soi dont jouissaient les deux autres,
soit au total neuf images difficilement con-
ciliables, sans parler des excitations nombreuses et confuses se bousculant dans les
marges du champ. Cela faisait un mélange
plutôt pénible, mais instructif, instructif.
Ajoutez-y les multiples regards dont les trois
étaient l'objet, au milieu d'un nouveau silence, et vous aurez une faible idée de ce à

138

quoi on s'expose en voulant faire le malin, je veux dire en quittant l'enceinte vide, sombre et close où tous les quelques âges, le temps d'une seconde, rougeoie la lointaine lueur, l'inoffensive folie de se sentir être, avoir été.

Qu'est-ce que je vous sers ? dit le garçon.

Quand on aura besoin de vous on vous appellera, dit Camier.

Qu'est-ce que je vous sers ? dit le garçon.

La même chose, dit Mercier.

Vous n'avez encore rien consommé, dit le garçon.

La même chose que monsieur, dit Mercier.

Le garçon regarda le verre de Camier. Il était vide.

Je ne me rappelle plus ce que je vous ai servi, dit-il.

Moi non plus, dit Camier.

Quant à moi, dit Mercier, je ne l'ai jamais su.

Faites un effort, dit Camier.

Vous nous intimidez, dit Mercier. Bravo.

Nous crânons, dit Camier, tout en faisant sous nous. Allez vite chercher de la sciure, mon ami.

Et ainsi de suite, chacun disant des choses qu'il n'aurait pas dû dire, jusqu'à ce
qu'une sorte d'accord intervînt, scellé par
quelques sourires acajou et aigres amabilités.
Le brouhaha reprit.

A nous, dit Camier.

Mercier leva son verre.

Je ne pensais pas à ça, dit Camier.

Mercier posa son verre.

Mais pourquoi pas, après tout ? dit
Camier.

Ils levèrent donc leurs verres et burent
à la santé l'un de l'autre, chacun disant, A
la tienne, au même instant, ou presque.
Camier ajouta, Et au succès de notre —.
Mais ce vœu, il ne put l'achever. Aide-moi,
dit-il.

Je ne connais pas le mot, dit Mercier,
ni même la phrase, capable d'exprimer ce
que nous croyons être en train de vouloir
faire.

Ta main, dit Camier, tes deux mains.

Pour quoi faire ? dit Mercier.

Pour les serrer dans les miennes, dit Camier.

Les mains se cherchèrent sous la table,
parmi les jambes, se trouvèrent, se serrèrent,

une petite entre deux grandes, une grande entre deux petites.

Oui, dit Mercier.

Comment oui ? dit Camier.

Plaît-il ? dit Mercier.

Tu as dit oui, dit Camier. A quoi acquiesces-tu ?

A quoi à qui est-ce ? dit Mercier. Tu perds le nord, Camier.

Tu as dit oui, dit Camier. Veux-tu me dire à quel propos ?

J'ai dit oui ? dit Mercier. Impossible. La dernière fois que j'ai employé ce terme, c'était le jour de mon mariage. Avec Toffana. La mère de mes enfants. *Mes* enfants. Inaliénables. Tu ne la connais pas. Elle vit encore. Un entonnoir. On croyait baiser une fondrière. Quand je pense que c'est pour cet hectolitre de merde que j'ai renoncé à mon rêve le plus cher. Il se tut, avec coquetterie. Mais Camier n'avait pas envie de jouer. De sorte que Mercier dut dire, Tu n'oses pas me demander lequel ? Eh bien, je m'en vais te le confier. Celui de me retrancher du cocotier de l'espèce.

Moi j'aurais chéri un enfant de couleur, dit Mercier.

Depuis, j'emploie l'autre forme, dit Mercier. On fait ce qu'on peut, mais on ne peut rien. On se tortille, se tortille, et le soir vous retrouve à la même place que le matin. Mais ! En voilà un vocable de valeur, si je ne me trompe. Tout est *vox inanis* sauf, certains jours, certaines conjonctions, voilà la contribution de Mercier à la querelle des universaux. Tu es rouge comme un coq, Camier, un de ces jours tu vas éclater.

Où sont nos affaires ? dit Camier.

Où est notre parapluie ? dit Mercier.

En voulant aider Hélène, dit Camier, j'ai eu un mouvement malencontreux.

Pas un mot de plus, dit Mercier.

Je l'ai jeté dans le bassin, dit Camier.

Sortons d'ici, dit Mercier.

Pour aller où ? dit Camier.

Obliquement devant nous, dit Mercier.

Nos affaires ? dit Camier.

N'en parlons plus, dit Mercier.

Tu me feras damner, dit Camier.

Tu veux des détails ? dit Mercier.

Camier ne répondit rien. Les mots lui manquent, se dit Mercier.

Tu te souviens de notre bicyclette ? dit Mercier.

Oui, dit Camier.

Parle plus fort, dit Mercier, je n'entends rien.

Je me souviens de notre bicyclette, dit Camier.

Il en subsiste, dit Mercier, solidement enchaîné à une grille, ce qui peut raisonnablement subsister, après plus de huit jours de pluie incessante, d'une bicyclette à laquelle on a soustrait les deux roues, la selle, le timbre et le porte-bagages. Et le réflecteur, ajouta-t-il, j'allais l'oublier. Quelle tête j'ai.

Et la pompe, naturellement, dit Camier.

Tu me croiras ou tu ne me croiras pas, dit Mercier, ça m'est égal, mais on nous a laissé notre pompe.

Elle était cependant bonne, dit Camier. Où est-elle ?

J'ai pensé qu'il s'agissait peut-être d'un simple oubli, dit Mercier. Alors je l'ai laissée. J'ai cru bien faire. Que gonflerions-nous, à présent ? Je l'ai invertie, par exemple. Je ne sais pourquoi.

Elle tient aussi bien comme ça ? dit Camier.

Oh, tout aussi bien, dit Mercier.

Ils sortirent. Il faisait du vent.

Pleut-il toujours ? dit Mercier.

Pas pour l'instant, à ce qu'il me semble, dit Camier.

L'air est pourtant humide, dit Mercier.

Si nous n'avons rien à nous dire, dit Camier, ne nous disons rien.

Nous avons des choses à nous dire, dit Mercier.

Alors pourquoi ne nous les disons-nous pas ? dit Camier.

C'est que nous ne savons pas, dit Mercier.

Alors taisons-nous, dit Camier.

Mais nous essayons, dit Mercier.

Nous sommes sortis sans encombre, et indemnes, dit Camier.

Tu vois, dit Mercier. Continue.

Nous avançons péniblement —.

Péniblement ! s'écria Mercier.

Malaisément... malaisément par des rues sombres et relativement abandonnées, à cause de l'heure sans doute, et du temps incertain, sans savoir qui mène, ni qui suit.

Au coin du feu, bien au chaud, on s'assoupit, dit Mercier. Le livre tombe des mains, et la tête sur la poitrine. Les flammes baissent, la braise pâlit, le rêve sourd et se coule vers sa pâture. Mais le guetteur veille, on se

144

réveille et on va se coucher, en remerciant
Dieu de la situation, durement gagnée, qui
procure de telles joies, entre tant d'autres,
une telle paix, pendant que le vent cingle les
vitres, et la pluie, et que la pensée erre, pur
esprit, parmi ceux qui n'ont pas de gîte, les
maladroits, les damnés, les faibles, les infor-
tunés.

Sait-on seulement ce que l'autre a fait, dit
Camier, depuis le temps ?

Plaît-il ? dit Mercier.

Camier répéta son observation.

Même ensemble, dit Mercier, comme
maintenant, les bras collés l'un contre l'autre, la main dans la main, les jambes à
l'unisson, il se passe à chaque instant plus
de choses que n'en pourrait contenir un gros
livre, deux gros livres, le tien et le mien.
C'est sans doute à cette exubérance que l'on
doit la bienfaisante sensation qu'il n'y a
rien, rien à faire, rien à dire. Car l'homme se
lasse, à la fin, de vouloir se désaltérer à la
lance du pompier et de voir fondre, l'une
après l'autre, les quelques chandelles qu'il
lui reste, au chalumeau oxhydrique. Alors il
se voue, une fois pour toutes, à la soif et
aux ténèbres. C'est moins énervant. Mais

145

pardonne-moi, il y a des jours où l'eau et le feu envahissent mes pensées, et partant ma conversation, dans la mesure où il existe un rapport entre les deux.

Je voudrais te poser quelques simples questions, dit Camier.

Simples questions ? dit Mercier. Tu m'étonnes, Camier.

La forme en sera de la plus grande simplicité, dit Camier. Tu n'auras qu'à y répondre, sans réfléchir.

S'il y a une chose que je déteste, dit Mercier, c'est causer en marchant.

Notre situation est désespérée, dit Camier.

Petit présompteux, va, dit Mercier. Crois-tu que c'est à cause du vent qu'il ne pleut plus, s'il ne pleut plus ?

Je n'en sais rien, dit Camier.

Ça nous change, dit Mercier, c'est certain. Mais il semble augmenter à chaque instant, voilà ce qui me chiffonne. On ne pourra bientôt plus converser qu'en hurlant.

Deux petites questions de rien du tout, dit Camier. Après, tu reprendras ta rhapsodie.

Ecoute, dit Mercier. Je ne connais plus de

réponses, j'aime autant te le dire tout de suite. J'en ai connu, dans le temps, et des meilleures, c'était ma seule compagnie. J'inventais même des phrases à l'interrogatif pour aller avec. Mais il y a longtemps que j'ai rendu la liberté à toute cette engeance.

Il ne s'agit pas de celles-là, dit Camier.

Et desquelles donc ? dit Mercier. Ceci devient intéressant.

Tu vas voir, dit Camier. D'abord, quelles sont les nouvelles du sac ?

Je n'entends rien, dit Mercier.

Le sac, s'écria Camier. Où est le sac ?

Prenons par ici, dit Mercier. Nous serons plus à l'abri.

Ils s'engagèrent dans une rue étroite bordée de maisons hautes et vieilles.

Je t'écoute, dit Mercier.

Où est le sac ? dit Camier.

Quelle idée de revenir là-dessus, dit Mercier.

Tu ne m'as encore rien dit, dit Camier.

Mercier s'arrêta, ce qui obligea Camier à s'arrêter aussi. Si Mercier ne s'était pas arrêté Camier ne se serait pas arrêté non plus. Mais Mercier s'étant arrêté Camier dut s'arrêter aussi.

147

Je ne t'ai rien dit ? dit Mercier.

Rigoureusement rien, dit Camier.

Qu'y a-t-il à dire, dit Mercier, à supposer que je ne t'aie rien dit ?

Enfin si tu l'as trouvé, comment ça s'est passé, et ainsi de suite, dit Camier.

Mercier dit, Reprenons notre ——. Perplexe, de sa main libre il indiqua vaguement ses jambes, et celles de son ami.

J'ai compris, dit Camier.

Ils la reprirent donc, cette chose indescriptible, qui n'était pas sans rapport avec leurs jambes.

Tu disais ? dit Mercier.

Le sac, dit Camier.

Est-ce que je l'ai ? dit Mercier.

On ne dirait pas, dit Camier.

Alors ? dit Mercier.

C'est maigre, dit Camier.

A qui le dis-tu, dit Mercier.

Il a pu se passer tant de choses, dit Camier. Tu as pu le chercher, mais en vain, le trouver et le reperdre ou même le jeter, te dire, Ce n'est pas la peine que je m'en occupe, ou, Assez pour ce soir, demain nous verrons, que sais-je ?

Je l'ai cherché en vain, dit Mercier, lon-

148

guement, patiemment, avec soin et sans succès.

Il exagérait.

Est-ce que je te demande comment tu as fait, exactement, pour casser le parapluie ? dit Mercier. Ou dans quelles transes tu as vécu avant de le jeter ? Moi, j'ai inspecté un grand nombre d'endroits, j'ai interrogé de nombreuses personnes, j'ai fait la part de l'invisibilité des choses, des transformations qu'opère le temps, du penchant des gens, dont moi, à la fable et au mensonge, à l'envie de faire plaisir et à celle de blesser, et j'aurais aussi bien fait, tout aussi bien, de me tenir tranquille, n'importe où car cela n'a pas d'importance, et de chercher encore contre l'approche sans fin, les pantoufles traînantes et le tintement des clefs, un meilleur remède que les cris, les enjambées, l'essoufflement, les holà.

Quelle limpidité, dit Camier.

Mercier poursuivit :

Pourquoi insistons-nous, Camier, toi et moi par exemple, t'es-tu jamais posé cette question, toi qui en poses tellement ? Va-t-on jeter le peu de nous qu'il nous reste dans l'ennui des fuites et les rêves d'élargissement ? N'entrevois-tu pas, comme moi, le moyen de t'accommoder de cette absurde peine, d'attendre le bourreau avec placidité, comme l'entérinement d'un état de fait ?

Non, dit Camier.

Il m'est souvent arrivé, dit Mercier, au concert, de regretter que la musique se tût, car elle me plaisait assez, mais de me laisser aller sans façons au sommeil, tant j'étais fatigué.

Ils se retinrent au bord d'un grand espace ouvert, une place peut-être, plein de tumulte, de lueurs bringuebalantes, d'ombres se tordant.

Rebroussons chemin, dit Mercier. Cette rue est charmante. Elle sent le bordel.

Ils entreprirent la rue dans l'autre sens. Cela la changeait, malgré l'obscurité. Mais, eux, cela les changeait à peine.

Je vois de lointaines contrées —, dit Mercier.

Un instant, dit Camier.

Quel poison, dit Mercier.

Où allons-nous ? dit Camier.

Te sèmerai-je jamais ? dit Mercier.

Tu ne sais pas où nous allons ? dit Camier.

Qu'est-ce que ça peut nous faire, dit Mercier, où nous allons ? Nous allons, c'est suffisant.

Ne crie pas, dit Camier.

Nous allons par là où on va avec le minimum d'horripilation, dit Mercier. Nous profitons de ce que la merde est moindre dans certaines voies pour nous y faufiler, ni vu ni connu je t'embrouille. Nous tombons sur une petite rue formidable, nous n'avons plus qu'à l'arpenter jusqu'à ce qu'elle se montre sous ses vraies couleurs, et tu veux savoir où nous allons. Où as-tu les nerfs ce soir, Camier ?

Je résume, dit Camier. Nous avons décidé, à tort ou à travers, qu'il —.

A tort ou à raison, dit Mercier.

A tort ou à travers, dit Camier, qu'il fallait quitter cette ville. Nous l'avons donc quittée. Ce n'était pas facile. Cette gloire durera autant que nous, quoi qu'il advienne. Mais à peine l'avions-nous quittée que nous nous sommes trouvés dans l'obligation d'y retourner, sans perdre un instant. C'était soi-disant pour récupérer certaines choses à nous qui y étaient restées. Quoi qu'on puisse dire de ce motif, c'est à lui seul que nous

151

avons obéi, en maugréant mais avec courage, et nul autre que lui n'a été invoqué, pour justifier notre volte-face. Nous étions d'accord pour quitter la ville à nouveau dès que cela nous serait possible, c'est-à-dire dès que nous aurions récupéré, ou renoncé à récupérer, l'ensemble ou une partie de nos affaires. Il ne nous reste donc plus qu'à choisir, enfin qu'à nommer, notre chemin de sortie. As-tu une préférence ? Quel mode de transport te semble le plus indiqué ? Veux-tu qu'on y aille tout de suite ou préfères-tu attendre l'aube ? Je veux qu'on soit fixé avant la nuit, et qu'on s'en aille, c'est toi qui l'as dit. Et si on doit passer la nuit ici, où doit-on la passer ? Ou se peut-il que nous soyons d'ores et déjà en butte à des forces nouvelles, ne se faisant encore qu'obscurément sentir, s'opposant sourdement à ce que notre programme se poursuive et appelant une nouvelle mise au point ? Voilà ce que je propose à ta considération. Si pour une raison ou pour une autre tu ne peux pas y penser, ou y répondre, n'y pense pas, ou n'y réponds pas, rien ne t'y oblige. J'y penserai pour nous, et j'y répondrai.

Ils firent à nouveau demi-tour, de concert.

Nous parlons trop, dit Mercier. Je n'ai jamais tant dit ni entendu d'inepties depuis que je te suis.

C'est moi qui suis, dit Camier.

N'ergotons pas, dit Mercier.

Peut-être n'est-il pas loin, dit Camier, le jour où nous ne pourrons plus rien nous dire. Réfléchissons donc, avant de nous retenir. Car ce jour-là tu te tourneras vers moi en vain, je ne serai pas là, mais ailleurs, dans un état identique, ou similaire.

Que vas-tu chercher là ? dit Mercier.

A telle enseigne, dit Camier, que je me demande souvent, assez souvent, si nous ne ferions pas mieux de nous quitter sans plus tarder.

Tu ne m'auras pas par les sentiments, dit Mercier.

Aujourd'hui même, par exemple, dit Camier, j'ai failli ne pas me rendre au rendez-vous.

Que c'est curieux, dit Mercier, j'ai dû terrasser un ange analogue.

L'un de nous finira par se laisser faire, dit Camier.

En effet, dit Mercier, on n'aurait pas besoin de succomber tous les deux à la fois.

Ce ne serait pas forcément un abandon, dit Camier.

Loin de là, dit Mercier, loin de là.

Je veux dire un désistement, dit Camier.

C'est ainsi que je l'entends, dit Mercier.

Mais il y a des chances, dit Camier.

Des chances de quoi ? dit Mercier.

Pour que ça en soit un, dit Camier.

Evidemment, dit Mercier, continuer tout seul, que ce soit le lâcheur ou le lâché... Tu permets que je n'aille pas au bout de ma pensée ?

Ils firent quelques pas en silence. Puis Camier partit d'un rire spontané.

Couillon, va, dit-il, un enfant te ferait marcher.

Mercier fit entendre une sorte de stridulation.

Elle est bien bonne, dit-il. Tu croyais me posséder et c'est ton froc qui prenait.

J'avais plutôt chaud, en effet, dit Camier.

Je n'en menais pas large non plus, dit Mercier.

Blague à part, dit Camier, ceci mérite qu'on y mette un peu le nez.

Nous conférerons, dit Mercier, nous ferons un large tour d'horizon.

Avant de nous engager plus avant, dit Camier.

Voilà, dit Mercier.

Pour cela il faut être en pleine possession de toutes nos nombreuses facultés, dit Camier.

Ça vaudrait mieux, dit Mercier.

Or, le sommes-nous ? dit Camier.

Sommes-nous quoi ? dit Mercier.

En pleine possession de nos facultés, dit Camier.

J'espère que non, dit Mercier.

Nous avons besoin de dormir, dit Camier.

Voilà, dit Mercier.

Si on allait chez Hélène ? dit Camier.

Je n'y tiens pas, dit Mercier.

Moi non plus, dit Camier.

Il doit y avoir des claques par ici, dit Mercier.

Tout est sombre, dit Camier. Pas une lumière. Aucun numéro.

Demandons à ce brave agent, dit Mercier.

Ils abordèrent l'agent.

Pardon, dit Mercier, connaîtriez-vous, par hasard, dans les parages, une maison, comment dirai-je, une maison de tolérance ?

L'agent les dévisagea.

Ne nous regardez pas comme ça, dit Mercier. Avec des garanties hygiéniques, autant que possible. Nous avons horreur de la syphilis, mon ami et moi.

Vous n'avez pas honte, à votre âge ? dit l'agent.

De quoi vous mêlez-vous ? dit Camier.

Honte ? dit Mercier. As-tu honte, Camier, à ton âge ?

Passez votre chemin, dit l'agent.

Je relève votre numéro, dit Camier.

Veux-tu mon crayon ? dit Mercier.

Seize cent soixante-cinq, dit Camier. L'année de la pestilence. Facile à retenir.

Voyez-vous, dit Mercier, renoncer à l'amour, à cause d'un simple ralentissement de la spermatogenèse, voilà ce qui serait puéril, à mon avis. Vous ne voudriez pas qu'on vécût sans amour, inspecteur, ne fût-ce qu'une fois par mois, la nuit du premier samedi, par exemple ?

Et voilà où vont nos contributions directes, dit Camier.

Je vous arrête, dit l'agent.

Pour quel motif ? dit Camier.

L'amour vénal est le seul qu'il nous reste,

dit Mercier. A vous autres gaillards la passion et les bonnes fortunes.

Et la jouissance solitaire, dit Camier.

L'agent saisit le bras de Camier et le tordit.

A moi, Mercier, dit Camier.

Lâchez-le, s'il vous plaît, dit Mercier.

Aïe ! dit Camier.

Maintenant d'une seule main, grande comme deux mains ordinaires, rouge vif et couverte de poils, le bras de Camier, l'agent lui appliqua de l'autre une gifle violente. Cela commençait à l'intéresser. Ce n'était pas tous les jours qu'un divertissement de cette qualité venait rompre la monotonie de sa faction. Le métier avait du bon, il l'avait toujours dit. Il sortit son bâton. Allez hop, dit-il, et pas d'histoires. De la main qui tenait le bâton il prit un sifflet dans sa poche et se le mit aux lèvres, car il n'était pas moins adroit que vigoureux. Mais il ne prenait pas Mercier suffisamment au sérieux (qui l'en blâmera ?), et ce fut sa perte, car Mercier leva son pied droit (qui aurait pu s'y attendre ?) et l'envoya maladroitement mais avec sécheresse dans les testicules (appelons les choses par leur nom) de l'adversaire (pas moyen de les rater). L'agent lâcha tout et tomba avec des hurlements de douleur et d'écœurement. Mercier lui-même en perdit l'équilibre et fit une chute qui lui fit très mal à la hanche. Mais Camier, fou d'indignation, ramassa prestement le bâton, écarta le casque d'un coup de pied et frappa le crâne de toutes ses forces, plusieurs fois, en tenant le bâton des deux mains. Les cris s'arrêtèrent. Mercier se releva. Aide-moi ! hurla Camier. Il tira furieusement sur le capuchon, qui se trouvait coincé entre la tête et les pavés. Qu'est-ce que tu veux faire ? dit Mercier. Lui couvrir la gueule, dit Camier. Ils dégagèrent le capuchon et le rabattirent sur le visage. Puis Camier se remit à frapper. Assez, dit Mercier, donne-moi ce contondant. Camier lâcha le bâton et se sauva en courant. Attends, dit Mercier. Camier s'arrêta. Dépêche-toi, dit Camier. Mercier ramassa le bâton et en frappa le crâne couvert d'un coup modéré et attentif, d'un seul. On dirait un œuf dur, dit-il. Qui sait, songea-t-il, c'est peut-être celui-là qui l'achève. Il jeta le bâton et rejoignit Camier, qu'il prit par le bras. Allons-y franchement, dit Mercier. Camier tremblait, mais pas pour long-

158

temps. Arrivés au bord de la place ils durent s'arrêter, devant la violence des rafales. Puis lentement, tête baissée, titubant, s'agrippant l'un à l'autre, ils avancèrent dans un déchaînement d'ombres et de rumeurs, trébuchant sur les pavés où des branches noires traînaient déjà, avec un bruit râcleur, ou faisaient de brusques bonds, comme sur des ressorts. A l'autre bout s'amorçait une petite rue tranquille, comme celle qu'ils venaient de quitter. Il y régnait un calme extraordinaire, mais qui allait peu à peu s'amoindrissant.

Il ne t'a pas fait trop mal, j'espère ? dit Mercier.

Quel salaud, dit Camier. Tu as vu cette gueule ?

Voilà qui simplifie bien des choses, je crois, dit Mercier.

Ils appellent ça garder la paix, dit Camier.

On n'aurait jamais trouvé tout seuls, dit Mercier.

Je crois que le plus simple maintenant serait d'aller chez Hélène, dit Camier.

Incontestablement, dit Mercier.

Tu es sûr qu'on ne nous a pas vus ? dit Camier.

Le hasard fait bien les choses, dit Mercier. Au fond je n'ai jamais compté que sur lui.

Heureusement que ce n'est pas loin, dit Camier.

Te rends-tu compte de ce que ça signifie pour nous ? dit Mercier.

Je ne vois pas que ça change grand-chose, pour le moment, dit Camier.

Ça ne devrait rien changer, dit Mercier, mais ça changera tout.

Ça devrait tout changer, dit Camier, mais ça ne changera rien.

Tu vas voir, dit Mercier. Les fleurs sont dans le vase, et les moutons sont rentrés au parc.

Je ne comprends pas, dit Camier.

Le peu de chemin qu'il leur restait à faire, ils en firent la plus grande partie en silence, tantôt exposés à la pleine fureur des vents, tantôt par des zones calmes. Mercier essayait d'embrasser dans leur plénitude les conséquences pour eux de ce qui s'était produit, et Camier essayait de trouver un sens à la phrase qu'il venait d'entendre. Mais ils n'arrivaient pas, Mercier à concevoir leur bonheur, Camier à mener son exégèse à bien, car ils étaient fatigués, ils avaient besoin de dormir, le vent les faisait chanceler et, pour comble de désagrément, il pleuvait dans leurs têtes des coups insatiables.

IX

Résumé des deux chapitres précédents

VII

Soir de la huitième (?) journée.
Chez Hélène.
Le parapluie.
Lendemain chez Hélène.
Passe-temps.
Lendemain après-midi, dans la rue.
Le bar.
Mercier et Camier confèrent.
Résultats de cette conférence.
Chez Hélène.
Lendemain à midi, devant chez Hélène.
Le parapluie.
Regards vers le ciel.
Le parapluie.
Nouveaux regards vers le ciel.

Ladysmith.
Le parapluie.
Nouveaux regards sur le ciel.
Le parapluie.
Mercier s'en va.
Rencontres de Mercier.
Cerveau de Mercier.
Les chaînes.

VIII

Même jour.
Le cul et la chemise, avec graphiques (passage entièrement supprimé).
Avant-dernier bar.
Mère l'Eglise et l'insémination artificielle.
Mercier arrive.
Le garçon géant.
Contribution de Mercier à la querelle des universaux.
Le parapluie, fin.
La bicyclette, fin.
Dans la rue.
Le vent.
Le coin du feu.
La lance et le chalumeau.

Le vent.
Les formes catéchétiques.
La rue fatale.
Le sac.
La musique et le sommeil.
Le gouffre.
La rue fatale.
Lointaines contrées.
La rue fatale.
L'agent.
Mort de l'agent.
Le gouffre.
« Les fleurs sont dans le vase. »
Le vent.
Les coups endocraniens.

X

Un chemin encore carrossable traverse la haute lande. C'est l'ancien chemin des armées. Il coupe à travers de vastes tourbières, à cinq cents mètres d'altitude, mille si vous aimez mieux. Il ne dessert plus rien. Quelques forts en ruines, quelques maisons en ruines. La mer n'est pas loin, les vallées qui descendent vers l'est permettent de la voir, elle n'a guère plus de couleur que le ciel qui n'en a guère, elle est comme une cimaise. Dans les plis de la lande des lacs sont cachés, il faut quitter la route pour les voir, de petits sentiers y mènent, de hautes falaises les surplombent. Tout semble plat,

ou en pentes douces, et cependant on passe
tout près de hautes falaises, sans en soup-
çonner l'existence. De granit, par-dessus le
marché. Etrange pays. C'est à l'Ouest que
la chaîne atteint son maximum, ses pics
font lever les yeux aux plus moroses, ces
pics d'où l'on voit la plaine sans horizon, les célèbres pâturages, la vallée d'or.
Devant eux la route serpente à perte de vue,
vers le sud. Elle monte, mais on ne le dirait
pas. Personne ne passe plus par ici, sinon
les maniaques du pittoresque, ou de la marche à pied. Déguisée par la brande la tourbière attire, avec une attirance à laquelle les
mortels ont du mal à résister. Puis elle les
engloutit, ou le brouillard descend. La ville
non plus n'est pas loin, il est des endroits
d'où l'on voit ses lumières la nuit, sa lumière
plutôt, et le jour sa fumée. On distingue
même, par temps très clair, les môles du
port, des deux ports, ils avancent bras mi-
nuscules dans la mer vitreuse, on les sait à
plat mais on les voit levés. On voit les îles
et les promontoires, il s'agit seulement de
se retourner au bon endroit, et la nuit bien
entendu les phares, à feux fixes et tournants.
Le ciel même bleu semble plus bas, vu de

ce plateau, on a beau se raisonner, l'impression demeure. C'est là qu'on voudrait se coucher, dans un creux bien tapissé de bruyère sèche, et s'endormir, une dernière fois, un après-midi. Il ferait du soleil, la tête serait parmi la vie minutieuse des tiges et des corolles, on s'endormirait vite, on quitterait vite des choses charmantes. C'est un ciel sans oiseaux, quelques oiseaux de proie tout au plus, pas d'oiseaux-oiseaux. Fin du passage descriptif.

Quelle est cette croix ? dit Camier.

Les revoilà.

En pleine tourbière, non loin de la route, mais trop loin pour qu'on pût en lire l'inscription, une croix fort simple s'élevait.

Je l'ai su, dit Mercier, mais je l'ai oublié.

Moi aussi je l'ai su, dit Camier, j'en suis presque sûr.

Mais il n'en était pas absolument sûr.

C'était la tombe d'un patriote, amené par l'ennemi à cet endroit, la nuit, et exécuté. Ou peut-être n'y avaient-ils amené que son cadavre, pour l'y déposer. On l'enterra beaucoup plus tard, avec une certaine cérémonie. Il s'appelait Masse. On n'en faisait plus grand cas, dans les milieux nationalistes. Il

167

avait plutôt mal travaillé, en effet. Mais il avait toujours ce monument. Tout cela, ils l'avaient su, Mercier et Camier, et sans doute bien d'autres choses encore, mais ils avaient tout oublié.

C'est vexant, dit Camier.

Veux-tu qu'on aille voir ? dit Mercier.

Et toi ? dit Camier.

Si tu veux, dit Mercier.

Ils s'étaient taillé des bâtons, dans les derniers bosquets. Ils avançaient d'un bon pas, pour des vieux.

Comment Mercier se sent-il aujourd'hui ? dit Camier.

Ma foi, dit Mercier, je me suis senti plus mal. Et Camier ?

Je m'abstiens de me plaindre, dit Camier.

Ils se demandaient lequel s'écroulerait le premier. Ils firent un bon kilomètre en silence. Ils ne se tenaient plus par le bras. Chacun marchait librement de son côté de la route, si bien qu'il y avait entre eux presque toute la largeur de celle-ci. Ils se mirent à parler simultanément. Mercier dit, N'as-tu pas quelquefois l'impression — ? et Camier, Y a-t-il des vers — ?

Pardon, dit Camier, tu disais ?

Non non, dit Mercier, à toi.

Mais non, dit Camier, c'était sans intérêt.

Ça ne fait rien, dit Mercier, vas-y.

Je t'assure, dit Camier.

Je t'en prie, dit Mercier.

Après toi, dit Camier.

Je t'ai interrompu, dit Mercier.

C'est moi qui t'ai interrompu, dit Camier.

Mais non, dit Mercier.

Mais si, dit Camier.

Le silence se rétablit. Mercier le rompit, ou plutôt Camier.

Tu as attrapé froid ? dit Mercier.

Camier avait toussé, en effet.

Il est un peu trop tôt pour le savoir, dit Camier.

J'espère que ce n'est rien, dit Mercier.

Quel beau temps, dit Camier.

N'est-ce pas ? dit Mercier.

Que la lande est belle, dit Camier.

Très belle, dit Mercier.

Regarde-moi cette bruyère, dit Camier.

Mercier regarda avec ostentation la bruyère. Il siffla.

En dessous il y a la tourbe, dit Camier.

On ne dirait jamais, dit Mercier.

Camier toussa.

Tu tousses comme un perdu, dit Mercier.

Crois-tu qu'il y a des vers, dit Camier, comme dans la terre ?

La tourbe possède des vertus remarquables, dit Mercier.

Ah, dit Camier.

Elle conserve, dit Mercier.

Mais est-ce qu'il y a des vers`? dit Camier.

Veux-tu qu'on creuse un peu, pour voir ? dit Mercier.

Penses-tu, dit Camier, quelle idée. Il toussa.

Il faisait beau, en effet, enfin ce qu'on appelle beau, dans ce pays, mais frais, et la nuit n'était pas loin.

Où va-t-on passer la nuit ? dit Camier. As-tu pensé à ça ?

C'est drôle, dit Mercier, j'ai souvent l'impression que nous ne sommes pas seuls. Toi non ?

Je ne sais pas si je comprends, dit Camier.

Tantôt vif, tantôt lent, voilà Camier.

Comme la présence d'un tiers, dit Mercier. Elle nous enveloppe. Je l'ai senti depuis le premier jour. Je ne suis pourtant rien moins que spirite.

Ça te gêne ? dit Camier.

Dans les premiers temps, non, dit Mercier.

Et maintenant ? dit Camier.

Ça commence à me gêner un peu, dit Mercier.

Oui, la nuit n'était pas loin, et c'était une bonne chose pour eux, sans peut-être qu'ils se l'avouassent encore, que la nuit ne fût pas loin.

Enfin, qui es-tu, Camier ? dit Mercier.

Moi ? dit Camier. Je suis Camier, Francis Xavier.

C'est maigre, dit Mercier.

A qui le dis-tu, dit Camier.

Je pourrais me poser la même question, dit Mercier.

Où compte-on passer la nuit ? dit Camier. A la belle étoile ?

Ça ne nous ferait pas de mal, dit Mercier, après je ne sais combien de nuits consécutives chez Hélène. L'as-tu encore enculée ?

J'ai essayé, dit Camier, mais je n'avais pas la tête à ça.

Tu fais trop l'amour, depuis quelque temps, dit Mercier. Tu n'as pas honte, à ton âge ? Tu vas attraper un échauffement.

J'ai le gland en feu, en effet, dit Camier.
C'est un cercle vicieux.

Il faut te mettre de la pommade, dit Mercier.

Je n'ose pas y toucher, dit Camier.

Et ton kyste ? dit Mercier.

Ne m'en parle pas, dit Camier.

Il ne t'est pas rentré dans le trou, au moins, dit Mercier, comme tu le craignais à un moment ?

Il en garde l'entrée toujours, dit Camier. Il grandit tous les jours, et cependant il n'est pas plus près du trou qu'il y a vingt ans. Essaie d'y comprendre quelque chose.

L'eau de tourbe est très bonne pour ces trucs-là, dit Mercier. Tu n'as qu'à t'asseoir dedans. Et ça pourrait te rafraîchir le canal en même temps.

Pas le moindre arbre, est-il besoin de le dire ? C'est plus prudent. Ici l'oasis est de fougères.

Nous aurons froid, dit Camier, et l'humidité nous pénétrera jusqu'aux moelles.

Il y a des ruines, dit Mercier. Ou bien nous marcherons, jusqu'à l'épuisement. Rien de tel pour combattre les intempéries.

A quelque distance de là ils arrivèrent

devant les ruines d'une maison, sinon d'un fort. Elles devaient avoir un demi-siècle à peu près. Il n'y en aurait plus d'autres avant longtemps. Il faisait presque nuit.

Maintenant il faut choisir, dit Mercier.

Choisir entre quoi ? dit Camier.

Entre les ruines et l'épuisement, dit Mercier.

N'y aurait-il pas moyen de les combiner ? dit Camier.

Nous n'atteindrons jamais les prochaines, dit Mercier.

C'est simple, dit Camier.

On dit ça, dit Mercier.

Nous n'avons qu'à marcher encore un peu, dit Camier, jusqu'à ce que nous estimions qu'il nous reste juste assez de forces pour revenir ici. Puis nous ferons demi-tour et nous reviendrons ici, devant les ruines, complètement épuisés.

C'est dangereux, dit Mercier.

Vois-tu quelque chose de mieux ? dit Camier.

On pourrait peut-être danser un peu ici, dit Mercier, enfin, se livrer à des mouvements violents quelconques. De cette façon on ne risquerait rien. On serait sûr de pouvoir s'effondrer, à l'abri des décombres, dès qu'on aurait son compte.

Je peux me traîner sur la route encore quelque temps, dit Camier, mais je serais incapable du moindre bond.

Alors, faisons simplement les cent pas, dit Mercier.

La tentation de nous coucher prématurément, de vouloir en finir, avant la fin, serait plus forte que nous, dit Camier.

Ton plan est pourtant plein d'embûches, dit Mercier. La fatigue est une chose étrange, surtout dans ses derniers stades, une progression mixte jusqu'à la folie, et dont on ignore tout des causes. Sans parler de la nuit qui tombe et qui peut nous entraîner parmi les fondrières.

Sois sérieux, dit Camier. Qu'est-ce qu'on risque, après tout ?

Evidemment, dit Mercier.

Ils se remirent donc en marche, si l'on peut appeler cela en marche.

Il y a des fois, dit Camier, où c'est un véritable plaisir de causer avec toi.

Je ne suis pas méchant, au fond, dit Mercier.

Au bout d'un certain temps Mercier dit :

Je ne crois pas que je puisse aller beaucoup plus loin.

Déjà ? dit Camier. C'est les jambes ? Les pieds ?

C'est plutôt la tête, dit Mercier.

Il faisait nuit, la route disparaissait à quelques mètres. Il était trop tôt pour que les étoiles pussent éclairer. La lune ne se lèverait que beaucoup plus tard. C'était au fond l'heure la plus sombre. Ils s'étaient arrêtés. Ils se voyaient à peine, à travers la route. Camier s'approcha de Mercier.

Nous allons retourner, dit Camier. Appuie-toi sur moi.

C'est dans la tête, je te dis, dit Mercier.

Tu vois des formes qui n'existent pas, dit Camier. Des bouquets d'arbres, par exemple, là où il n'y en a point. Ou d'étranges animaux surgissent, vaches et chevaux géants, aux vives couleurs, ils surgissent des ténèbres, pour peu que tu lèves la tête, de hautes granges aussi et des meules immenses. Tout ça de plus en plus flou et cotonneux, comme si à vue d'œil on devenait aveugle, haha, à vue d'œil aveugle.

Tu peux me prendre la main, si tu veux, dit Mercier.

Ainsi la main dans la main ils s'en retournèrent, et c'était la grande dans la petite.

Tu as la main moite, dit Mercier, et tu tousses. Tu as peut-être la tuberculose des vieillards.

A peine l'eut-il dit qu'il se mit à le regretter, en tremblant. Que craignait-il ? Que regrettait-il ? Il craignait que cette balle, Camier ne la lui renvoyât, l'obligeant ainsi à comprendre, et à répondre, ou à un silence inconvenant, et il regrettait de s'être exposé à un tel dilemme. Bêtises, regrets, excuses, craintes, blâmes, excuses, et puis quelquefois, rarement mais quelquefois, la grande paix de la faute impunie, car Camier restait muet, c'était à se demander s'il avait entendu. Il était peut-être bien plus fatigué qu'il ne voulait l'avouer, aussi près que Mercier de la limite de ses forces. Ce qui donne, don précieux entre tous, de la vraisemblance à cette façon de voir, c'est qu'à peu de temps de là Mercier fut obligé de répéter une même phrase deux ou trois fois de suite avant que Camier en tînt compte. Soit :

J'espère qu'on n'a pas dépassé la masure, dit Mercier.

Camier ne répondit pas.

J'espère qu'on n'a pas dépassé la masure, dit Mercier.

Quoi ? dit Camier.

Je dis que j'espère que nous n'avons pas dépassé la masure, dit Mercier.

Camier ne répondit pas tout de suite. La vie a de ces occasions où les mots les plus simples et limpides mettent quelque temps à dégager tout leur bouquet. Et masure prêtait à confusion. Mais enfin il arrêta brusquement leur marche, ce petit homme épuisé qui avait pris soi-disant la direction des opérations.

Elle est un peu à l'écart de la route, dit Mercier. Nous avons pu passer devant sans la voir, tellement cette nuit est noire, du moins je le suppose.

On aurait vu l'espèce de sentier, dit Camier.

Il me semble, dit Mercier. Quant à moi, franchement, je ne vois plus rien, ni le chemin, ni mes pieds habituels, ni mes jambes, ni ma poitrine (il est vrai qu'elle est creuse). Un bout de barbe peut-être, soyons francs, de temps en temps, elle est assez blanche pour ça. On serait passé devant la

177

Scala, un soir de gala, que je n'aurais rien remarqué. C'est une épave, mon cher Camier, que tu es en train de remorquer, avec ta bonté habituelle.

Et moi, j'ai été distrait, dit Camier. C'est impardonnable.

Tu as toutes les excuses, dit Mercier, toutes les excuses, sans exception. Ne me lâche pas la main surtout. La gymnastique du désespoir, ne t'en prive pas, ça fait du bien, sur le moment, mais ne me lâche pas la main.

Des mouvements désordonnés agitaient Camier, en effet.

Tu es crevé, mon pauvre Camier, dit Mercier. Avoue-le.

Tu vas voir si je suis crevé, dit Camier.

Tu as mal à ton petit cul, dit Mercier, et à ton petit pénis.

Nous ne retournerons plus en arrière, dit Camier, quoi qu'il advienne.

A la bonne heure, dit Mercier. J'en ai marre de nos gigotements de papillon dégoûté. Mais où est-ce que je puise la force de parler ? Veux-tu me le dire ?

Camier faillit dire, En avant, mais il se retint à temps. Car puisqu'ils étaient d'accord pour ne pas retourner en arrière, et que la nature du terrain interdisait toute déviation aussi bien à gauche qu'à droite, sous peine de désastre, où pouvaient-ils aller, sous peine de désastre, sinon en avant ? Il se contenta donc d'avancer, en tirant Mercier après lui.

Essaie de te tenir à ma hauteur, dit Camier, nom de Dieu.

Estime-toi heureux, dit Mercier, que tu ne sois pas obligé de me porter. Appuie-toi sur moi, c'est toi qui l'as dit.

C'est vrai, dit Camier.

Je décline, dit Mercier, pour ne pas t'être trop à charge. Et quand je traîne un peu tu pousses les hauts cris. Qu'est-ce que c'est que ces façons ?

Bientôt ils n'avancèrent plus qu'en titubant. On avance très bien en titubant, moins bien évidemment qu'en ne titubant pas, moins vite surtout, mais on avance. Ils débordaient sur la tourbière, ce qui aurait pu avoir de graves conséquences, pour eux, mais rien à faire. Les chutes commençaient, tantôt c'était Mercier qui entraînait Camier (dans sa chute), tantôt c'était le contraire, et tantôt ils s'effondraient tous les deux en même temps, comme un seul homme, sans s'être concertés et dans une parfaite indépendance l'un de l'autre. Ils ne se relevaient pas toujours tout de suite, jeunes ils avaient fait de la boxe, mais ils se relevaient toujours, rien à faire. Et dans les pires moments les mains restaient fidèles, les mains dont on n'aurait plus su dire laquelle donnait, laquelle recevait l'étreinte, tant tout était devenu confus. Leur inquiétude (au sujet des ruines) y était sans doute pour quelque chose, et c'était dommage, car elle était mal fondée. Car ils y arrivèrent à la fin, devant ces ruines qu'ils craignaient dépassées, ils eurent même la force de gagner ce qu'elles avaient de plus secret, jusqu'à en être entourés de toutes parts, et comme ensevelis. Ce fut seulement alors, à l'abri enfin d'un froid qu'ils ne sentaient plus, d'une humidité qui ne les gênait point, qu'ils acceptèrent le repos, ou plutôt le sommeil, et que les mains furent libres, rendues aux vieux offices.

La nuit aussi les glaces reflètent, celle-là, celles-ci, celle-là dans celles-ci, en multipliant des perspectives innombrables et vaines. Ils dorment côte à côte, le profond somme des vieux. Ils se parleront encore, mais ce sera

par l'effet du hasard, comme on dit. Mais
se sont-ils jamais parlé autrement ? D'ailleurs on ne sait plus rien avec certitude,
dorénavant. Ce serait le moment de finir.
Après tout c'est fini. Mais il y a encore le
jour, tous les jours, et toute la vie la vie,
on les connaît trop bien, les longs glisse-
ments posthumes, le gris trouble qui s'apai-
se, les clartés d'un instant, la poussière de
l'achevé, se soulevant, tourbillonnant, se
posant, parachevant. Cela se défend aussi.
Laissons-le donc se réveiller, Mercier, Camier, peu importe, Camier, il se réveille,
il fait nuit, toujours nuit, il ignore l'heure,
nous aussi, peu importe, il fait nuit, il se
lève et s'éloigne dans l'obscurité, il se cou-
che un peu plus loin, toujours dans les ruines, inutile de le faire remarquer, elles ont
de l'étendue. Pourquoi ? Impossible de le
savoir. Plus moyen de savoir ces choses-là.
Les raisons ne manquent jamais pour changer de place. Elles doivent êtres bonnes, car
voilà que la même chose arrive à Mercier,
à peu près en même temps sans doute. Toute la question de priorité, si lumineuse jusqu'à présent, cesse ici complètement de
l'être. Les voilà donc couchés, ou peut-être

seulement accroupis, à une distance relativement respectable l'un de l'autre, au regard
c'est-à-dire des adhérences habituelles. Ils
s'assoupissent à nouveau (curieux ce soudain temps présent), ou peut-être ne font-ils
que réfléchir. Réflexion faite, ils doivent
s'assoupir, tout porte à le croire. Toujours
est-il qu'avant l'aube, bien avant l'aube, l'un
d'eux se relève, mettons Mercier, chacun à
son tour, et va voir si Camier est toujours
là, c'est-à-dire à l'endroit où il croit l'avoir
laissé, c'est-à-dire à l'endroit où ils s'étaient
laissés tomber en premier lieu, l'un à côté
de l'autre. Est-ce clair ? Dommage qu'il n'y
ait pas un troisième larron quelque part,
avec la subodeur d'un Christ un peu plus
loin, canant devant le calice, très trop humai-
nement. Mais Camier n'y est plus, car comment y serait-il ? Alors Mercier se dit, Tiens,
il a pris les devants, sacré Camier, se fraye
un chemin à travers les décombres, les yeux
écarquillés (afin de ne rien perdre de la
lumière), les bras bougeant comme des anten-
nes, les pieds méfiants, gagne et grimpe (les
ruines sont en contre-bas, cela ne se sent-il
pas ?) le sentier qui mène à la route. Au
même moment presque, pas exactement,

cela ne marcherait pas, mais presque, un
peu plus tôt, un peu plus tard, cela n'a pas
d'importance, ou si peu, Camier se livre au
même manège. La vache, se dit-il, il m'a
brûlé la politesse, et il se glisse, avec mille
précautions, la vie est si précieuse, la douleur si redoutable, la vieille peau si peu
réparable, hors de ce chaos ami, on dirait
du Mantegna, sans un mot sans un mouvement de remerciements. On ne rend pas grâce aux pierres, on a tort. Enfin c'est à peu
près de cette façon que les choses durent
se passer. Les voilà donc sur la route, sensiblement rafraîchis quand même, et chacun sait l'autre proche, le sent, le croit, le
craint, l'espère, le nie et n'y peut rien. De
temps en temps ils s'arrêtent, l'oreille dressée vers le bruit des pas, des pas reconnais-
sables entre tous les pas, et ils sont nombreux, qui vont doucement foulant les
chemins de la terre, jour et nuit. Mais la
nuit on voit ce qui n'est pas, entend ce qui
n'est pas, c'est un fait certain, on se fait des
illusions, ce n'est vraiment pas la peine de
faire attention. Et pourtant on fait attention,
Dieu le sait. De sorte qu'il peut arriver que
l'un des deux s'arrête, s'assied au bord de

la route, presque dans la tourbière, pour se reposer, ou pour mieux réfléchir, ou pour ne plus réfléchir, les raisons ne manquent jamais pour s'arrêter, et que l'autre arrive, celui qui était derrière, et voit cette sorte d'ombre de Sordel, mais sans y croire, enfin sans y croire assez pour pouvoir se jeter dans ses bras, ou lui flanquer un coup de pied à l'envoyer cul par dessus tête dans les fondrières. L'assis aussi, il voit, à moins qu'il n'ait fermé les yeux, de toute façon il entend, à moins qu'il ne dorme, et se traite d'halluciné, mais sans conviction. Puis un peu plus loin c'est l'assis qui se lève, et l'autre qui s'assied, et ainsi de suite, vous voyez le truc, ils peuvent aller ainsi jusqu'à la ville, s'infirmant, s'affirmant, à blanc. Car c'est bien entendu vers la ville qu'ils vont, comme à chaque fois qu'ils la quittent, comme après de longs calculs vains la tête retombe parmi les données. Mais au fond des vallées dégringolant vers l'est le ciel change, c'est ce vieux cochon de soleil qui rapplique, ponctuel comme un bourreau. Attention, on va revoir les splendeurs terrestres, on va se revoir, ce qui est encore plus drôle, la nuit n'aura rien changé, ce n'est que le revers de la pansper-

184

moconnerie, heureusement qu'elle en a un, d'accord, les frères sont là pour l'attester (au cas où il y aurait doute), tous les frères, et les hauts de cœur et tout le bataclan des saisisse-ments chenus. Alors ils se voient, que voulez-vous, ils n'avaient qu'à partir plus tôt, mais sait-on jamais ? A qui le tour, à Camier, alors retourne-toi canaille, et regarde bien. Tu n'en crois pas tes yeux, cela ne fait rien, tu vas les en croire, car c'est bien lui, ton joli cœur barbu, ossu, fourbu, foutu, à jet de pierre, mais ne la jette pas, pense au bon vieux temps, où vous rouliez dans la merde ensemble. Mercier également se rend à l'évi-dence, c'est une habitude qu'on prend, par-mi les axiomes, Camier lève la main, c'est sans risque, c'est élégant, c'est galant, cela n'engage à rien. L'instant que Mercier hésite, avant de rendre ce salut, inattendu pour en dire le moins, Camier en profite pour repren-dre son chemin. On ne s'en sort plus, de ce présent. Mais même les morts on peut bien les saluer, rien ne s'y oppose, c'est même bien vu, ils n'en profitent pas mais cela fait plaisir aux croque-morts, cela les aide à cro-quer, et aux amis et aux parents, et aux che-vaux, cela les aide à se croire en survie, à celui qui salue cela fait du bien aussi, c'est vivifiant. Mercier ne se laisse pas démonter, que non, il lève la main à son tour, la bonne, l'hétérologue, dans ce geste large et complaisamment désintéressé qu'ont les prélats, dédiant à Dieu des portions de matière favorisées. Que je suis bon, dit Mercier, meilleur que s'il me voyait. Mais pour en finir avec ces délires, arrivé à la première fourche (finie la lande) Camier s'arrêta (enfin un petit passé), et son cœur battait (encore un) plus fort à la pensée de ce qu'il allait mettre dans ce suprême salut gravide à en péter de délicatesse sans précédent. C'était la vraie campagne déjà, haies vives (vives !), boue, purin, mares, rochers, bouses, taudis, et de loin en loin un être indubitablement humain, un véritable anthropopseudomorphe, grattant son lopin depuis les premières croûtes de l'aube, ou changeant son fumier de place, avec une bêche, car il a perdu sa pelle, et sa fourche est cassée. Un arbre géant, fouillis de branches noires, occupe l'angle de la fourche. Des deux branches la gauche mène tout droit à la ville, enfin ce qu'on appelle tout droit dans ce pays, tandis que l'autre n'y aboutit qu'après avoir traîné à travers une éruption de hameaux pestilentiels, dont seul le feu aurait pu faire justice, et qu'on s'acharnait à conserver par tous les moyens, dont cette caricature de chemin, en prévision sans doute du jour glorieux où la ville, sous peine de crever, viendrait les rejoindre. Arrivé donc à cette jonction, Camier s'arrêta et se retourna, ce qui fit que Mercier s'arrêta aussi et se retourna à moitié, prêt à s'enfuir, est-il besoin de le dire deux fois ? Mais il avait tort de s'inquiéter, car Camier leva simplement la main, dans un salut semblable en tous points à celui dont il s'était déjà si obligeamment fendu, tendit l'autre, raide et sans doute vibrante, vers la branche droite et s'y engouffra avec une héroïque vivacité. Il aurait eu à se précipiter dans une maison en flammes, d'où trois générations de sa famille attendaient d'être retirées, qu'il ne s'y serait pas pris autrement. Rassuré, mais pas complètement, Mercier avança précautionneusement jusqu'à la fourche. Il regarda à droite. Camier avait disparu. Il s'engagea dans la branche gauche, d'un pas accéléré. Décrochés ! C'est à peu près ainsi que les choses durent se passer. La terre se traînait vers la lumière, la brève trop longue lumière.

XI

Et voilà. On met du temps à savoir à peu
près ce qui s'est passé. C'est la seule excuse,
la meilleure en tout cas. Il y a même là de
quoi vivre, mais sérieusement, de quoi se
lever, s'habiller (très important), se nourrir,
excréter, se promener quand il fait beau, se
déshabiller, se coucher et faire les autres choses, et subir les autres choses, qu'il serait plutôt fastidieux d'énumérer, oui, plutôt fastidieux. Puis il y a le huit, chiffre fatidique
(mais lequel ne l'est pas ?), deux pour chaque pied, deux pour chaque main, et pour les
amputés six, quatre, deux ou point, cela
dépend de l'amputé. L'intérêt ne risque pas
de faiblir, dans ces conditions. On cultive sa
mémoire, elle finit par être passable, un tré-
sor, on se balade dans sa crypte, sans chan-
delle, on revisite les lieux, on se remémore
les bruits (très important), on finit par les

savoir par cœur, on ne sait plus où donner de
la tête, du nez, des yeux, des oreilles, sur
quelle dépouille se pencher, elles sentent
toutes aussi bon les unes que les autres, quel
disque se jouer. Ah le joli outre-tombe ! Et
puis il peut vous arriver encore de ces choses ; De ces aventures ! Mais oui, mais oui.
Vous croyez en avoir fini et puis un bon
jour, pan, en plein dans l'œil. Ou dans le
cul, ou dans les couilles, ou dans le con, les
cibles ne manquent pas, surtout au-dessous
de la ceinture. Dire qu'avec cela il y a des
cadavres qui s'ennuient ! Quelle insensibi-
lité ! Vengeance ! Vengeance !

C'est fatigant, évidemment, c'est absor-
bant, le temps manque peut-être pour pom-
mader l'âme, mais on ne peut pas tout avoir,
le corps en bouillie, la conscience à vif et
l'archée comme au temps de l'innocence,
avant la chute, sans filet, oui, c'est un fait,
le temps manque, pour l'éternité.

Il est cependant une sorte de spleen difficilement conjurable. C'est l'attente de la
nuit qui portera conseil, car ce n'est pas
toutes les nuits qui possèdent cette pro-
priété. Cela peut durer des mois. C'est
l'entre-deux, la longue, la mièvre, la lassante

mêlée des regrets, des derniers avec les réso-
lus, on y est passé mille fois, c'est tordant
mais on n'arrive pas à se tordre, à se dissou-
dre dans le sourire mille fois souri. C'est la
fin, l'avant-fin du jour et les cachets ne vous
font plus rien. Heureusement que ce n'est
pas toujours éternel, en général cela ne dure
que quelques mois, quelques années, on a
même vu des fins brusques, dans les pays
chauds par exemple. Et puis ce n'est pas
forcément sans intermission, les divertissements ne sont pas formellement interdits,
mais non, certains vous apportent même une
véritable illusion de vie, tant qu'ils durent,
de jour en cours, de non-foutu. Et même
sans aller jusque-là ils vous soulagent, un
peu, les divertissements, certains, ceux qui
sont permis, tant qu'ils durent.

Il y a aussi les jolies couleurs, verts et
citrons expirants, restons dans le vague,
elles pâlissent encore mais c'est pour mieux
vous embrocher, s'éteindront-elles jamais,
oui, mais oui, elles s'éteindront.

Et avec ça ? Ce sera tout, merci.

Vue de l'extérieur c'était une maison comme tant d'autres. Vue de l'intérieur aussi.
Camier en sortit. Il se promenait encore, un

peu, quand il faisait beau. C'était l'été. On aurait préféré l'automne, fin octobre, début novembre, mais c'était l'été, rien à faire. Le soleil se couchait, les archets s'accordaient (on se demande pourquoi) avant d'attaquer le vieil enueg. Légèrement vêtu Camier avançait, la tête sur le sternum. Il se redressait de temps en temps, d'un mouvement brusque et aussitôt annulé, histoire de s'orienter. Il ne se sentait pas trop mal, il était dans un bon jour. Les passants le bousculaient, mais pas exprès, non, pas exprès, ils auraient préféré ne pas toucher. Il faisait un tour, il ne faisait qu'un tour, il ne tarderait pas à être fatigué, très fatigué. Alors s'arrêtant il ouvrirait grands ouverts les petits yeux bleu-rouge et les promènerait autour de lui, le temps de faire le point. Les forces, pour rentrer, c'était souvent juste, ce qui l'obligeait à entrer dans le premier bar venu, pour s'en redonner, et pour se donner confiance, confiance et courage, vis-à-vis du chemin de retour, dont il n'avait souvent qu'une notion confuse. Il s'aidait d'une canne, dont il frappait le sol à chaque pas, non pas à tous les deux pas, à chaque pas. Une main se rabattit sur son épaule. Camier s'immobilisa, se fit tout petit, mais ne leva pas la tête. Cela lui était égal, c'était même mieux ainsi, plus simple, mais ce n'était pas une raison pour quitter la terre des yeux. Il entendit dire, Le monde est petit. Des doigts lui soulevèrent le menton. Il vit un homme de haute stature, fort sordidement mis. Inutile de le détailler. Il semblait âgé. Il sentait mauvais, l'odeur des vieillards plus celle du non-lavé, enfin il sentait fort. Camier le huma en amateur averti.

Tu connais mon ami Mercier, dit l'homme.

Camier chercha des yeux en vain.

Derrière toi, dit l'homme.

Camier se retourna. Mercier, qui semblait tout entier à une vitrine de chapelier, se présentait de profil.

Vous permettez, dit l'homme. Mercier, Camier, Camier, Mercier.

On aurait dit deux aveugles à qui rien ne manque, sinon la vue, pour se faire une idée l'un de l'autre, ni le désir, ni la disposition des corps.

Je vois que vous vous connaissez, dit l'homme. J'en étais sûr. Ne vous saluez pas surtout.

Je ne vous connais pas, monsieur, dit Camier.

Je suis Watt, dit Watt. Je suis méconnaissable, en effet.

Watt ? dit Camier. Ce nom ne me dit rien.

Je suis peu connu, c'est exact, dit Watt, mais je le serai, un jour. Je ne dis pas universellement, il y a peu de chances par exemple que ma notoriété pénètre jusqu'aux habitants de Londres ou de Cuq-Toulza.

Où avez-vous fait ma connaissance ? dit Camier. Vous excuserez ce peu de mémoire. Je n'ai pas encore eu le temps de tout démêler.

Volontiers, dit Watt. Au berceau.

Vous avouerez qu'en ce cas il m'est difficile de vous démentir, dit Camier.

Personne ne te demande de me démentir, dit Watt. Il m'est vraiment pénible d'entendre, par deux fois, dans un si court laps de temps, les mêmes sottises.

Vous m'êtes parfaitement étranger, dit Camier. Au berceau, vous dites ?

Dans ton moïse, dit Watt. Tu n'as pas changé.

En ce cas vous avez connu ma mère, dit Camier.

Une sainte femme, dit Watt. Elle te changeait toutes les deux heures, jusqu'à l'âge de cinq ans. Il se tourna vers Mercier. Tandis que la tienne, dit-il, je ne l'ai connue qu'inanimée.

J'ai connu un nommé Murphy, dit Mercier, qui vous ressemblait un peu, en beaucoup plus jeune. Mais il est mort, il y a dix ans, dans des circonstances assez mystérieuses. On n'a jamais retrouvé son corps, figurez-vous.

Vous ne le connaissez donc pas non plus ? dit Camier.

Voyons, voyons, dit Watt, retutoyez-vous, mes enfants. Ne vous gênez pas devant moi. Je suis la discrétion même. Un tombeau.

Messieurs, dit Camier, vous permettrez que je vous quitte.

Si je n'étais pas sans désirs, dit Mercier, je m'achèterais un de ces chapeaux, pour mettre sur ma tête.

Je vous offre la tournée, dit Watt. Il ajouta, Les gars, avec un sourire sans méchanceté, tendre presque.

Vraiment —, dit Camier.

Le marron, là, sur la forme, dit Mercier.

Watt s'empara du bras droit de Mercier, du bras gauche (après une courte lutte) de Camier, et les entraîna.

Où allons-nous encore ? dit Camier.

Mercier aperçut au loin les chaînes de son enfance, celles qui lui avaient servi de jouet. Watt lui dit :

Si tu levais les pieds tu avancerais mieux. Je ne t'emmène pas chez le dentiste, aujourd'hui.

Ils marchaient face au couchant (on ne peut pas tout se refuser) dont les flammèches jaillissaient plus haut que les hautes maisons.

Dommage que Dumas Père ne puisse nous voir, dit Watt.

Ou l'un des évangélistes, dit Camier.

Mercier et Camier, c'était tout de même une autre qualité.

Mercier dit, d'une voix de fausset chevrotante, Je l'aurais ôté au passage des corbillards.

Mes forces sont limitées, dit Camier, si les vôtres ne le sont pas.

Nous arrivons, dit Watt.

Un agent leur barra le chemin.

Ceci est un trottoir, dit-il, pas une piste de cirque.

C'était un agent prédestiné à une promotion rapide, cela se voyait.

De quoi vous mêlez-vous ? dit Camier.

Foutez-nous la paix, dit Mercier.

Doucement, doucement, dit Watt. Il se pencha vers l'agent. Inspecteur, dit-il, ne vous fâchez pas. Ils sont un peu — il se tapota le front — mais ils ne feraient pas de mal à une mouche. Le grand se croit saint Jean-Baptiste, dont vous avez certainement entendu parler, tandis que le petit hésite entre Jules César et Toussaint Louverture. Quant à moi, je me résigne à rester dans le rôle que la naissance m'a collé, il est spacieux, et m'ordonne, entre autres, de promener ces messieurs, lorsque le temps le permet. Doucement, doucement. Dans ces conditions vous m'accorderez qu'il nous est difficile de nous disposer en file indienne, comme le veut la bienséance.

Allez vous promener à la campagne, dit l'agent.

Nous l'avons essayé, dit Watt, à plusieurs reprises. Mais ils deviennent complètement enragés à la seule vue d'un champ. N'est-ce pas curieux ? Tandis que les vitrines, le béton, le ciment, l'asphalte, la foule, les néons, les pickpockets, les agents, les bordels, toute l'agitation du Bondy métropolitain, cela les calme et les prédispose à une nuit réparatrice.

Vous ne pouvez pas accaparer le trottoir, dit l'agent.

Attention, dit Watt. Vous voyez, ils commencent à s'agiter. Je me demande si je vais pouvoir les contenir.

Vous empêchez les honnêtes gens de passer, dit l'agent. Ça ne peut pas durer.

Bien sûr, dit Watt. On va vous arranger ça. Vous allez voir. Il leur lâcha les bras et leur entoura les tailles, en les serrant contre lui. Avancez, mes jolis, dit-il. Ils repartirent, titubant, les jambes entremêlées. L'agent les regarda s'éloigner. Fumiers, dit-il.

Vous vous foutez de nous, dit Camier. Lâchez-moi.

Mais on est bien ainsi, dit Watt. Nous sentons la décomposition à plein nez, tous les trois. Vous avez vu sa tête ? Il se contenait pour ne pas se moucher. C'est pour ça qu'il nous a laissés partir.

Ils s'effondrèrent dans un bar, pêle-mêle, Camier et Mercier tiraient vers le comptoir, mais Watt les fit asseoir, à une table, et commanda trois doubles d'une voix retentissante.

Vous me direz sans doute que vous n'avez jamais mis les pieds dans cet endroit, dit-il. A votre aise. Je n'ose pas commander de la bière, on nous mettrait à la porte.

Le whiskey arriva.

Moi aussi, j'ai cherché, dit Watt, tout seul, seulement moi je croyais savoir quoi. Vous vous rendez compte ! Il leva les mains et les passa sur son visage, elles descendirent lentement le long des épaules, de la poitrine, et se rejoignirent sur ses genoux. Incroyable mais vrai, dit-il.

Des membres discontinus s'agitaient dans l'air gris. D'infimes silences de mort ponctuaient le brouhaha.

Il naîtra, il est né de nous, dit Watt, celui qui n'ayant rien ne voudra rien, sinon qu'on lui laisse le rien qu'il a.

Mercier et Camier ne prêtaient à ces propos qu'une attention distraite. Ils commençaient à se dévisager avec quelque chose du vieux regard.

J'ai failli me livrer, dit Camier.

Tu es retourné à l'endroit ? dit Mercier.

Watt se frottait les mains.

Vous me faites plaisir, dit-il, vous me faites réellement plaisir. Vous me réconfortez presque.

Puis je me suis dit —, dit Camier.

Puissiez-vous ressentir, un jour, dit Watt, ce que je ressens, en ce moment. Cela ne vous empêchera pas d'avoir vécu en vain, mais ce sera, comment dirai-je — ?

Puis je me suis dit, dit Camier, que tu aurais peut-être la même idée. Alors tu comprends. Ce n'était pas ma seule raison, seulement la première qui me soit venue à l'esprit.

Tu n'es pas retourné à l'endroit ? dit Mercier.

Un peu de chaleur pour le vieux cœur, dit Watt, voilà, un petit peu de chaleur pour le pauvre vieux cœur.

J'y serais bien retourné, dit Camier, jeter un coup d'œil, mais j'avais peur de tomber sur toi. Ce whiskey n'est pas mauvais.

Watt frappa la table avec force, ce qui amena dans la salle un silence impressionnant. C'était sans doute ce qu'il voulait, car il lança, d'une voix que faisait craquer la véhémence :

La vie au poteau !

Des murmures indignés se firent entendre. Le gérant s'approcha, à moins que ce ne fût le patron. Il était mis avec soin. D'aucuns eussent sans doute préféré, étant donné le pantalon perle, des chaussures noires à la place des jaunes qu'il portait. Mais après tout il était chez lui. Comme boutonnière il avait choisi une tulipe. Sortez, dit-il.

D'où ? dit Camier. D'ici ?

Foutez le camp, dit le gérant. Cela devait être un gérant. Mais combien différent de monsieur Gast !

Il vient de perdre son unique enfant, dit Camier, unique au monde.

Un bijumeau, dit Mercier.

Sa douleur éclate, dit Camier, quoi de plus naturel ?

Sa femme est à l'agonie, dit Mercier.

Nous ne le quittons pas d'une semelle, dit Camier.

Encore un petit double, dit Mercier, si nous arrivons à le lui faire avaler il est sauvé.

Personne mieux que lui, dit Camier,

n'aime la vie, l'humble existence de tous les jours, les innocents plaisirs et jusqu'aux peines qui nous permettent de parachever le rachat. Dites-le bien à ces messieurs. Un cri de révolte lui est echappé. Son deuil est si récent ! Demain, devant son porridge, il en aura honte.

Il s'essuiera la bouche, dit Mercier, il glissera la serviette dans le rond, il joindra les deux mains et il s'écriera, Heureux les morts qui meurent !

S'il avait cassé un verre, dit Camier, nous serions les premiers à le blâmer. Mais ce n'est pas le cas.

Oubliez cet incident, dit Mercier. Il ne se renouvellera pas. Pas vrai, Toto ?

Passez l'éponge, dit Camier, selon saint Mathieu.

Et faites-nous servir la même chose, dit Mercier. Votre whiskey est succulent.

Il y a longtemps que je n'en ai goûté d'aussi bon, dit Camier.

Un bigarreau ? dit le gérant.

Un bijumeau, dit Camier.

Oui, dit Mercier, tout en double sauf le cul. On l'enterre après-demain. Pas vrai, Toto ?

201

C'est l'organisateur qui s'est foutu dedans, dit Camier.

L'organisateur ? dit le gérant.

Chaque œuf a son petit boute-en-train, dit Mercier. L'ignoriez-vous ? Il lui arrive de perdre le nord. Ça vous étonne ?

Calmez-le, dit le gérant. Ne m'obligez pas à sévir. Il se retira. Il avait été ferme sans raideur, humain avec dignité, il saurait se justifier auprès de ses habitués, bouchers pour la plupart, que la mort de l'agneau avait rendus un peu intolérants.

On leur apporta la deuxième tournée. La monnaie de la première était restée sur la table. Payez-vous, mon ami, dit Camier.

Le gérant passait de groupe en groupe. Peu à peu la salle se remettait à vivre.

Comment peut-on dire des choses pareilles ? dit Camier.

Les penser est déjà un délit, dit Mercier.

Vis-à-vis des hommes, dit Camier.

Et des bêtes, dit Mercier.

Dieu seul lui donnerait raison, dit Camier.

Celui-là, dit Mercier.

Watt semblait dormir. Il n'avait pas touché à son deuxième verre.

Un peu d'eau ? dit Camier.

Laisse-le tranquille, dit Mercier.

Mercier se leva et alla à la fenêtre. Il glissa sa tête entre le rideau et la vitre, ce qui lui permit, conformément à ses prévisions, de voir le ciel. Il y restait de la couleur. Il remarqua en même temps, ce dont il ne s'était pas douté, qu'il en tombait une pluie fine et sans doute douce. La vitre n'en était pas mouillée. Il retourna à la table et se rassit.

Tu sais à quoi je pense, souvent ? dit Camier.

Il pleut, dit Mercier.

A la chèvre, dit Camier.

Mercier regardait Watt avec perplexité.

Tu ne te rappelles pas ? dit Camier. Le jour poignait, par un temps défectueux.

Où est-ce que j'ai vu ce type ? dit Mercier. Il recula sa chaise, se baissa et visa par en dessous le visage écrasé sous le chapeau.

Le vieux Madden, lui aussi —, commença Camier.

Brusquement Watt saisit la canne de Camier, la dégagea, la souleva et en frappa avec colère la table voisine, où devant une chope bien tirée un homme aux favoris lisait le journal, en fumant sa pipe. Ce qui devait

arriver arriva, la tablette en verre vola en
éclats, la canne se cassa en deux, la chope se
renversa et l'homme aux favoris tomba à la
renverse, toujours assis sur sa chaise, la pipe
à la bouche et le journal à la main. Le morceau de la canne qui lui restait à la main,
Watt l'envoya voler vers le comptoir, où
il descendit plusieurs bouteilles et un bon
nombre de verres. Watt attendit que ces
divers fracas se fussent calmés, puis voci-
féra :

La vie aux chiottes !

Mercier et Camier, comme mûs par une
même ficelle, vidèrent précipitamment leurs
verres et coururent à la sortie. Là ils se
retournèrent. Un hurlement étouffé domina
un instant le vacarme :

Vive Quin !

Il pleut, dit Camier.

Je te l'avais dit, dit Mercier.

Alors adieu, dit Camier.

Tu ne veux pas m'accompagner un bout
de chemin ? dit Mercier.

De quel côté vas-tu ? dit Camier.

J'habite maintenant de l'autre côté du
canal, dit Mercier.

Ce n'est pas mon chemin, dit Camier.

Il y a une perspective qui en vaut la peine,
dit Mercier.

Ça m'étonnerait, dit Camier.

C'est comme tu voudras, dit Mercier.

Sans blague, dit Camier.

On prendra un dernier verre, dit Mercier.

Je n'ai pas le sou, dit Camier.

Mercier mit la main dans sa poche.

Non, dit Camier.

Moi j'en ai, dit Mercier.

Non, je te dis, dit Camier.

On dirait des fleurs arctiques, dit Mercier. Dans une demi-heure ce sera fini.

Les canaux ne me disent plus rien, dit
Camier.

Ils marchèrent en silence jusqu'au bout de
la rue.

C'est à droite ici, dit Mercier. Il s'arrêta.

Qu'est-ce que tu as ? dit Camier.

Je m'arrête, dit Mercier.

Ne fais pas le con, dit Camier.

Voilà une façon de parler, dit Mercier.

Tu m'amènes, oui ou non, dit Camier,
voir tes putains de papules ?

Ils prirent à droite, Camier sur le trottoir, Mercier dans le ruisseau.

Vive qui ? dit Camier.

J'ai entendu Quin, dit Mercier.

Ça doit être quelqu'un qui n'existe pas, dit Mercier.

Le whiskey leur avait quand même fait du bien. Ils marchaient d'un bon pas, pour des vieux. Camier regrettait sa canne.

Je regrette ma canne, dit Camier, elle appartenait à mon père.

Tu ne m'en as jamais parlé, dit Mercier.

Si tu savais, dit Camier.

Si je savais quoi ? dit Mercier.

Au fond, dit Camier, on s'est parlé de tout sauf de nous.

Nous avons mal travaillé, dit Mercier, je ne dis pas le contraire. Il réfléchit. Il prononça ce fragment de phrase, on pourrait peut-être —.

Quel coupe-gorge, dit Camier, ce n'est pas ici que nous avons perdu le sac ?

Pas loin d'ici, dit Mercier.

Entre les maisons hautes et vieilles la bande de ciel pâle paraissait encore plus étroite que la rue. Elle aurait dû au contraire paraître plus large. La nuit a de ces plaisanteries.

Ça va, à présent ? dit Mercier.

Pardon ? dit Camier.

Je te demande si ça va, à peu près, maintenant, pour toi, dit Mercier.

Non, dit Camier.

Quelques minutes plus tard des larmes lui montèrent aux yeux. Les vieux pleurent assez facilement, contrairement à ce qu'on pourrait supposer.

Et toi ? dit Camier.

Non plus, dit Mercier.

Les maisons s'espaçaient, s'écartaient, le ciel prenait de l'ampleur, ils pouvaient à nouveau se voir, ils n'avaient qu'à tourner la tête, l'un à droite, l'autre à gauche, qu'à lever la tête et la tourner. Puis soudain tout s'évasa devant eux, ce fut comme une déhiscence de l'espace, la terre abolie dans l'ombre qu'elle jette au ciel. Mais ce sont là des divertissements de courte durée et ils ne tardèrent pas à être frappés par leur situation, qui était celle de deux hommes, un grand et un petit, sur un pont. Le pont, lui, était charmant, au dire des connaisseurs. Pourquoi pas ? Il s'appelait de toute façon le pont de l'Ecluse, et à juste titre, on n'avait qu'à se pencher pour s'en assurer.

Nous y voilà, dit Mercier.

Ici ? dit Camier.

Ça a été vite, à la fin, dit Mercier.

Et ta perspective ? dit Camier.

Mais regarde, dit Mercier.

Camier interrogea les divers horizons.

Ne me bouscule pas, dit-il, je vais recommencer.

On voit mieux de la berge, dit Mercier.

Alors qu'est-ce qu'on fout ici ? dit Camier. Tu voudrais pousser quelques soupirs ?

Ils descendirent sur la berge. Un banc s'y trouvait, à dossier. Ils s'assirent.

C'est donc là, dit Camier.

La pluie tombait sans bruit dans le canal. Mercier en était chagrin. Mais bien au-dessus de l'horizon les nuages s'effrangeaient en longues effilochures ténues et noires, des cheveux de pleureuse. Elle a de ces attentions, la nature.

Je vois notre co-détenue Vénus, dit Camier, elle a l'air en perdition aux Sargosses. Pourvu que ce ne soit pas pour ça que tu m'as traîné jusqu'ici.

Plus loin, plus loin, dit Mercier.

Camier se fit d'une main une visière.

Je ne suis pourtant pas myope, dit-il.

Plus au nord, dit Mercier. Au nord, je te dis, pas au sud.

Attends, dit Camier.

Un peu plus, un peu moins.

C'est ça, tes fleurs ? dit Camier.

Tu as vu ? dit Mercier.

J'ai vu deux ou trois vagues lueurs, dit Camier.

C'est qu'il faut avoir l'habitude, dit Mercier.

J'aime autant me mettre le doigt dans l'œil, dit Camier.

C'est l'Ile Heureuse des anciens, dit Mercier.

Ils n'étaient pas difficiles, dit Camier.

Tu verras, dit Mercier, tu as mal vu, mais tu ne pourras pas oublier, tu reviendras.

Quelle est cette sinistre baraque ? dit Camier. Une usine à pain ?

C'est ici que je l'ai rencontré, dit Mercier.

Qui ? dit Camier.

Watt, dit Mercier. Il m'a dit qu'il venait souvent ici, dans le temps.

Quel est ce bâtiment ? dit Camier.

Un hôpital, dit Mercier. Pour les maladies de la peau.

C'est pour moi, dit Camier.

Et de la muqueuse, dit Mercier. Il prêta l'oreille. On ne hurle pas trop ce soir, dit-il.

C'est peut-être trop tôt, dit Camier.

Camier se leva et alla vers l'eau.

Attention, dit Mercier.

Camier revint au banc.

Tu te rappelles le perroquet ? dit Mercier.

Je me rappelle la chèvre, dit Camier.

Je crois qu'il est mort, dit Mercier.

Nous n'avons pas rencontré beaucoup d'animaux, dit Camier.

Je crois qu'il était déjà mort le jour qu'elle nous a dit qu'elle l'avait mis à la campagne, dit Mercier.

Ne t'en fais pas pour lui, dit Camier.

Il alla une seconde fois vers l'eau. Il regarda l'eau pendant quelque temps, puis il revint au banc.

Bon, je m'en vais, dit-il. Adieu, Mercier.

Bonne nuit, dit Mercier.

Seul il regarda son ciel s'éteindre, l'ombre se parfaire. L'horizon englouti, il ne le quitta pas des yeux, car il connaissait ses sursauts, par expérience. Dans le noir il entendait mieux aussi, il entendait des bruits que le long jour lui avait cachés, des murmures humains, par exemple, et la pluie sur l'eau.

XII

Résumé des deux chapitres précédents

x

La lande.
La croix.
Les ruines.
Mercier et Camier se quittent.
Le retour.

xi

La vie de survie.
Camier seul.
Mercier et Watt.
Mercier, Camier et Watt.
Le dernier agent.

Le dernier bar.
Mercier et Camier.
Le pont de l'Ecluse.
Mercier seul.
L'ombre se parfait.

(1946)

CET OUVRAGE A ÉTÉ ACHEVÉ D'IM-
PRIMER LE VINGT-SEPT AVRIL MIL
NEUF CENT SOIXANTE-DIX SUR LES
PRESSES DE L'IMPRIMERIE COR-
BIÈRE ET JUGAIN, A ALENÇON, ORNE,
ET INSCRIT DANS LES REGISTRES DE
L'ÉDITEUR SOUS LE NUMÉRO 816

Imprimé en France

A JOURNEY
TO THE CENTER
OF THE EARTH

SCHOLASTIC BOOK SERVICES

NEW YORK•TORONTO•LONDON•AUCKLAND•SYDNEY•TOKYO

21 20 19 18 17 16 15 14 13 12 11   6 7 8 9/7 0/8

Printed in the U.S.A.

Contents

1 ... *My Uncle Makes a Great Discovery*

LOOKING BACK to all that has occurred to me since that eventful day, I am scarcely able to believe in the reality of my adventures. They were truly so wonderful that even now I am bewildered when I think of them.

My uncle was a German, having married my mother's sister, an Englishwoman. Being very much attached to his fatherless nephew, he invited me to study under him in his home in the fatherland. This home was in a large town, and my uncle, a professor of philosophy, chemistry, geology, mineralogy, and many other ologies.

One day, after passing some hours in the laboratory —my uncle being absent at the time—I suddenly felt the necessity of renovating the tissues—*i.e.*, I was hungry, and was about to rouse up our old French cook, when my uncle, Professor Von Hardwigg, suddenly opened the street door, and came rushing upstairs.

Now Professor Hardwigg, my worthy uncle, is by no means a bad sort of man; he is, however, choleric and original. To bear with him means to obey; and scarcely had his heavy feet resounded within our joint domicile than he shouted for me to attend upon him.

"Harry—Harry—Harry—"

1

I hastened to obey; but before I could reach his room, jumping three steps at a time, he was stamping his right foot upon the landing.

"Harry!" he cried, in a frantic tone, "are you coming up?"

Now to tell the truth, at that moment I was far more interested in the question as to what was to constitute our dinner than in any problem of science; to me soup was more interesting than soda, an omelet more tempting than arithmetic, and an artichoke of ten times more value than any amount of asbestos.

But my uncle was not a man to be kept waiting; so adjourning therefore all minor questions, I presented myself before him.

He was a very learned man. Now most persons in this category supply themselves with information, as peddlers do with goods, for the benefit of others, and lay up stores in order to diffuse them abroad for the benefit of society in general. Not so my excellent uncle, Professor Hardwigg; he studied, he consumed the midnight oil, he pored over heavy tomes, and digested huge quartos and folios in order to keep the knowledge acquired to himself.

There was a reason, and it may be regarded as a good one, why my uncle refused to display his learning more than was absolutely necessary; he stammered; and when intent upon explaining the phenomena of the heavens, was apt to find himself at fault, and allude in such a vague way to sun, moon, and stars that few were able to comprehend his meaning. To tell the honest truth, when the right word would not come, it was generally replaced by a very powerful adjective.

In connection with the sciences there are many almost unpronounceable names—names very much resembling those of Welsh villages; and my uncle being

2

very fond of using them, his habit of stammering was not thereby improved. In fact, there were periods in his discourse when he would finally give up and swallow his discomfiture—in a glass of water.

As I said, my uncle, Professor Hardwigg, was a very learned man; and, I now add, a most kind relative. I was bound to him by the double ties of affection and interest. I took deep interest in all his doings, and hoped some day to be almost as learned myself. It was a rare thing for me to be absent from his lectures. Like him, I preferred mineralogy to all the other sciences. My anxiety was to gain *real knowledge of the earth.* Geology and mineralogy were to us the sole objects of life, and in connection with these studies many a fair specimen of stone, chalk, or metal did we break with our hammers.

Steel rods, loadstone, glass pipes, and bottles of various acids were oftener before us than our meals. My uncle Hardwigg was once known to classify six hundred different geological specimens by their weight, hardness, fusibility, sound, taste, and smell.

He corresponded with all the great, learned, and scientific men of the age. I was, therefore, in constant communication with, at all events the letters of, Sir Humphrey Davy, Captain Franklin, and other great men.

But before I state the subject on which my uncle wished to confer with me, I must say a word about his personal appearance. Alas! my readers will see a very different portrait of him at a future time, after he has gone through the fearful adventures yet to be related.

My uncle was fifty years old; tall, thin, and wiry. Large spectacles hid, to a certain extent, his vast, round, and goggle eyes, while his nose was irreverently compared to a thin file. So much indeed did it resem-

3

ble that useful article, that a compass was said in his presence to have made considerable N deviation.

The truth being told, however, the only article really attracted to my uncle's nose was tobacco.

Another peculiarity of his was that he always stepped a yard at a time, clenched his fists as if he were going to hit you, and was, when in one of his peculiar humors, very far from a pleasant companion.

It is further necessary to observe that he lived in a very nice house, in that very nice street, the König-strasse in Hamburg. Though lying in the center of a town, it was perfectly rural in its aspect—half wood, half bricks, with old-fashioned gables—one of the few old houses spared by the great fire of 1842.

When I say a nice house, I mean a handsome house —old, tottering, and not exactly comfortable to English notions: a house a little off the perpendicular and inclined to fall into the neighboring canal; exactly the house for a wandering artist to depict; all the more that you could scarcely see it for ivy and a magnificent old tree which grew over the door.

My uncle was rich; his house was his own property, and he had a considerable private income. To my notion the best part of his possessions was his god-daughter, Gretchen. And the old cook, the young lady, the Professor and I, were the sole inhabitants.

I loved mineralogy, I loved geology. To me there was nothing like pebbles—and if my uncle had been in a little less of a fury, we should have been the happiest of families. To prove the excellent Hardwigg's impatience, I solemnly declare that when the flowers in the drawing-room pots began to grow, he rose every morning at four o'clock to make them grow quicker by pulling the leaves!

Having described my uncle, I will now give an account of our interview.

4

He received me in his study; a perfect museum, containing every natural curiosity that can well be imagined—minerals, however, predominating. Every one was familiar to me, having been catalogued by my own hand. My uncle, apparently oblivious of the fact that he had summoned me to his presence, was absorbed in a book. He was particularly fond of early editions, tall copies, and unique works.

"Wonderful!" he cried, tapping his forehead. "Wonderful—wonderful!"

It was one of those yellow-leaved volumes now rarely found on stalls, and to me it appeared to possess but little value. My uncle, however, was in raptures.

He admired its binding, the clearness of its characters, the ease with which it opened in his hand, and repeated aloud, half-a-dozen times, that it was very, very old.

To my fancy he was making a great fuss about nothing, but it was not my province to say so. On the contrary, I professed considerable interest in the subject, and asked him what it was about.

"It is the Heims-Kringla of Snorre Tarleson," he said, "the celebrated Icelandic author of the twelfth century—it is a true and correct account of the Norwegian princes who reigned in Iceland."

My next question related to the language in which it was written. I hoped at all events it was translated into German. My uncle was indignant at the very thought, and declared he wouldn't give a penny for a translation. His delight was to have found the original work in the Icelandic tongue, which he declared to be one of the most magnificent and yet simple idioms in the world—while at the same time its grammatical combinations were the most varied known to students.

"About as easy as German?" was my insidious remark. My uncle shrugged his shoulders.

5

"The letters at all events," I said, "are rather difficult of comprehension."

"It is a Runic manuscript, the language of the original population of Iceland, invented by Odin himself," cried my uncle, angry at my ignorance.

I was about to venture upon some misplaced joke on the subject, when a small scrap of parchment fell out of the leaves. Like a hungry man snatching at a morsel of bread the Professor seized it. It was about five inches by three, and was scrawled over in the most extraordinary fashion.

The lines on page 8 are an exact facsimile of what was written on the venerable piece of parchment—and have wonderful importance, as they induced my uncle to undertake the most wonderful series of adventures which ever fell to the lot of human beings.

My uncle looked keenly at the document for some moments and then declared that it was Runic. The letters were similar to those in the book, but then what did they mean? This was exactly what I wanted to know.

Now as I had a strong conviction that the Runic alphabet and dialect were simply an invention to mystify poor human nature, I was delighted to find that my uncle knew as much about the matter as I did—which was nothing. At all events, the tremulous motion of his fingers made me think so.

"And yet," he muttered to himself, "it is old Icelandic; I am sure of it."

And my uncle ought to have known, for he was a perfect polyglot dictionary in himself. He did not pretend, like a certain learned pundit, to speak the two thousand languages and four thousand idioms made use of in different parts of the globe, but he did know all the more important ones.

It is a matter of great doubt to me now, to what

violent measures my uncle's impetuosity might have led him, had not the clock struck two, and our old French cook called out to let us know that dinner was on the table.

"Bother the dinner!" cried my uncle.

But as I was hungry, I sallied forth to the dining room, where I took up my usual quarters. Out of politeness I waited three minutes, but no sign of my uncle, the Professor. I was surprised. He was not usually so blind to the pleasure of a good dinner. It was the acme of German luxury—parsley soup, a ham omelet with sorrel trimmings, an oyster of veal stewed with prunes, delicious fruit, and sparkling Moselle. For the sake of poring over this musty old piece of parchment, my uncle forbore to share our meal. To satisfy my conscience, I ate for both.

The old cook and housekeeper was nearly out of her mind. After taking so much trouble, to find her master not appear at dinner was to her a sad disappointment which, as she occasionally watched the havoc I was making on the viands, became also alarm. What if my uncle were to come to table after all?

Suddenly, just as I had consumed the last apple and drunk the last glass of wine, a terrible voice was heard at no great distance. It was my uncle roaring for me to come to him. I made very nearly one leap of it, so loud, so fierce was his tone.

2 ... *The Mysterious Parchment*

```
Ж.ᛚᚱᛚᛐᛈ    ᛉᛈᛚᚦᚾᛈᛡ    ᛈᛡᛡᛡᛁᛒᛐ
ᛈᛁᛐᛈᛈᛡᛡ    ᚾᛚᛡᛡᛁᛉᚠ    ᛚᛁᛐᛒᛚᚱᛡ
ᚠᛐᛈᚾᛐᛡᛚ    ᛐᛐᛚᛐᛐᛐᛈ  ᛈᚾᚠᛒᛚᛚᛚ
ᛈᛡᛐᛚᛐᛈᛁ    ᛚᚾᛐᛡᛐᛐ    ᛈᛈᛁᛈᛈᛐ
ᛚᛐᚾᛐᛐᛚ    .ᛚᛈᛡᛚᛡ    ᛐᛐᛐᛒᛈᛐ
ᛡᛡᛒᛚᛡᛁ    ᛐᛐᚾᛐᚾᛐ    ᚠᛚᛐᛡᚾᛐ
ᛒᛐᛁᛡᛡ      ᛐᛈᛐᛁᛒᛐ    ᛡᛐᛒᛁᛁᛐ
```

"**I** DECLARE," cried my uncle, striking the table fiercely with his fist, "I declare to you it is Runic—and contains some wonderful secret, which I must get at, at any price."

I was about to reply when he stopped me.

"Sit down," he said, fiercely, "and write to my dictation."

I obeyed.

"I will substitute," he said, "a letter of our alphabet for that of the Runic: we will then see what that will produce. Now, begin and make no mistakes."

8

The dictation commenced with the following incomprehensible result:—

m.rnlls	nicdrke	.nscrc
sgtssmf	Saodrrn	eeutul
kt,samn	emtnael	oseibo
esruel	Atvaar	rrilSa
unteief	ccdrmi	ieaabs
atrateS	dt,iac	frantu
seecJde	nuaect	Kediil

Scarcely giving me time to finish, my uncle snatched the document from my hands and examined it with the most rapt and deep attention.

"I should like to know what it means," he said, after a long period.

I certainly could not tell him, nor did he expect me to, his conversation being uniformly answered by himself.

"I declare it puts me in mind of a cryptograph," he cried, "unless, indeed, the letters have been written without any real meaning; and yet, why take so much trouble? Who knows but I may be on the verge of some great discovery?"

My candid opinion was that it was all rubbish! But this opinion I kept carefully to myself, as my uncle's choler was not pleasant to bear. All this time he was comparing the book with the parchment.

"The manuscript volume and the smaller document are written in different hands," he said. "The cryptograph is of much later date than the book. There is an undoubted proof of the correctness of my surmise. [An irrefragable proof I took it to be.] The first letter is a double M, which was only added to the Icelandic language in the twelfth century—this makes the parchment 200 years posterior to the volume."

The circumstances appeared very probable and very logical, but it was all surmise to me.

"To me it appears probable that this sentence was written by some owner of the book. Now who was the owner, is the next important question. Perhaps by great good luck it may be written somewhere in the volume."

With these words, Professor Hardwigg took off his spectacles, and, taking a powerful magnifying glass, examined the book carefully.

On the fly leaf was what appeared to be a blot of ink, but on examination proved to be a line of writing almost effaced by time. This was what he sought; and, after some considerable time, he made out these letters:—

ᚾᛒᚴᚠ   ᛋᛏᛆᚾᛋᛋᛆᚠᛏ

"Arne Saknussemm!" he cried in a joyous and triumphant tone. "That is not only an Icelandic name, but of a learned professor of the sixteenth century, a celebrated alchemist."

I bowed a token of respect.

"These alchemists," he continued, "Avicena, Bacon, Lully, Paracelsus, were the true, the only learned, men of the day. They made surprising discoveries. May not this Saknussemm, nephew mine, have hidden on this bit of parchment some astounding invention? I believe the cryptograph to have a profound meaning—which I must make out."

My uncle walked about the room in a state of excitement almost impossible to describe.

"It may be so, sir," I timidly observed, "but why conceal it from posterity, if it be a useful, a worthy discovery?"

"Why—how should I know? Did not Galileo make a

secret of his discoveries in connection with Saturn? But we shall see. Until I discover the meaning of this sentence I will neither eat nor sleep."

"My dear uncle—" I began.

"Nor you neither," he added.

It was lucky I had taken double allowance that day.

"In the first place," he continued, "there must be a clue to the meaning. If we could find that, the rest would be easy enough."

I began seriously to reflect. The prospect of going without food and sleep was not a promising one; so I determined to do my best to solve the mystery. My uncle, meanwhile, went on with his soliloquy.

"The way to discover it is easy enough. In this document there are one hundred and thirty-two letters, giving seventy-nine consonants to fifty-three vowels. This is about the proportion found in most southern languages, the idioms of the north being much more rich in consonants. We may confidently predict, therefore, that we have to deal with a southern dialect."

Nothing could be more logical.

"Now," said Professor Hardwigg, "to trace the particular language."

"As Shakespeare says, 'that is the question,'" was my rather satirical reply.

"This man Saknussemm," he continued, "was a very learned man. Now as he did not write in the language of his birthplace, he probably, like most learned men of the sixteenth century, wrote in Latin. If, however, I prove wrong in this guess, we must try Spanish, French, Italian, Greek, and even Hebrew. My own opinion, though, is decidedly in favor of Latin."

This proposition startled me. Latin was my favorite study, and it seemed sacrilege to believe this gibberish to belong to the country of Virgil.

11

"Barbarous Latin, in all probability," continued my uncle, "but still Latin."

"Very probably," I replied, not to contradict him.

"Let us see into the matter," continued my uncle; "here you see we have a series of one hundred and thirty-two letters, apparently thrown pell-mell upon paper, without method or organization. There are words which are composed wholly of consonants, such as *m.rnlls,* others which are nearly all vowels, the fifth, for instance, which is *unteief,* and one of the last *oseibo.* This appears an extraordinary combination. Probably we shall find that the phrase is arranged according to some mathematical plan. No doubt a certain sentence has been written out and then jumbled up—some plan to which some figure is the clue. Now, Harry, to show your English wit—what is that figure?"

I could give him no hint. My thoughts were indeed faraway. While he was speaking I had caught sight of the portrait of my cousin Gretchen, and was wondering when she would return.

We were affianced, and loved one another very sincerely. But my uncle, who never thought even of such sublunary matters, knew nothing of this. Without noticing my abstraction, the Professor began reading the puzzling cryptograph all sorts of ways, according to some theory of his own. Presently, rousing my wandering attention, he dictated one precious attempt to me.

I mildly handed it over to him. It read as follows:—

mmessunkaSenrA.ïcefdoK.segnittamurtn
ecertserrette,rotaivsadua,ednecsedsadne
lacartniiiluJsiratracSarbmutabiledmek
meretarcsilucoIsleffenSnI.

I could scarcely keep from laughing, while my uncle,

on the contrary, got in a towering passion, struck the table with his fist, darted out of the room, out of the house, and then taking to his heels was presently lost to sight.

3 . . . *An Astounding Discovery*

"**W**HAT IS THE MATTER?**" cried the cook, entering the room. "When will master have his dinner?"

"Never."

"And, his supper?"

"I don't know. He says he will eat no more, neither shall I. My uncle has determined to fast and make me fast until he makes out this abominable inscription," I replied.

"You will be starved to death," she said.

I was very much of the same opinion, but not liking to say so, sent her away, and began some of my usual work of classification. But try as I might, nothing could keep me from thinking alternately of the stupid manuscript and of the pretty Gretchen.

Several times I thought of going out, but my uncle would have been angry at my absence. At the end of an hour, my allotted task was done. How to pass the time? I began by lighting my pipe. Like all other students, I delighted in tobacco; and, seating myself in the great armchair, I began to think.

Where was my uncle? I could easily imagine him tearing along some solitary road, gesticulating, talking to himself, cutting the air with his cane, and still thinking of the absurd bit of hieroglyphics. Would he hit upon some clue? Would he come home in better humor? While these thoughts were passing through

14

my brain, I mechanically took up the execrable puzzle and tried every imaginable way of grouping the letters. I put them together by twos, by threes, fours, and fives—in vain. Nothing intelligible came out, except that the fourteenth, fifteenth and sixteenth made *ice* in English; the eighty-fourth, eighty-fifth and eighty-sixth, the word *sir;* then at last I seemed to find the Latin words *rota, mutabile, ira, nec, atra.*

"Ha! there seems to be some truth in my uncle's notion," thought I.

Then again I seemed to find the word *luco,* which means sacred wood. Then in the third line I appeared to make out *labiled,* a perfect Hebrew word, and at the last syllables *mère, are, mer,* which were French.

It was enough to drive one mad. Four different idioms in this absurd phrase. What connection could there be between ice, sir, anger, cruel, sacred wood, changing, mother, are and sea? The first and the last might, in a sentence connected with Iceland, mean sea of ice. But what of the rest of this monstrous cryptograph?

I was, in fact, fighting against an insurmountable difficulty; my brain was almost on fire; my eyes were strained with staring at the parchment; the whole absurd collection of letters appeared to dance before my vision in a number of black little groups. My mind was possessed with temporary hallucination—I was stifling. I wanted air. Mechanically I fanned myself with the document, of which now I saw the back and then the front.

Imagine my surprise when glancing back at the wearisome puzzle, the ink having gone through, I clearly made out Latin words, and among others *craterem* and *terrestre.*

I had discovered the secret!

It came upon me like a flash of lightning. I had got the clue. All you had to do to understand the document was to read it backwards. All the ingenious ideas of the Professor were realized; he had dictated it rightly to me; by a mere accident I had discovered what he so much desired.

My delight, my emotion, may be imagined; my eyes were dazzled, and I trembled so that at first I could make nothing of it. One look, however, would tell me all I wished to know.

"Let me read," I said to myself, after drawing a long breath.

I spread it before me on the table, I passed my finger over each letter, I spelt it through, in my excitement I read it out.

What horror and stupefaction took possession of my soul. I was like a man who had received a knock-down blow. Was it possible that I really read the terrible secret, and it had really been accomplished! A man had dared to do—what?

No living being should ever know.

"Never!" cried I, jumping up. "Never shall my uncle be made aware of the dread secret. He would be quite capable of undertaking the terrible journey. Nothing would check him, nothing stop him. Worse, he would compel me to accompany him, and we should be lost forever. But no; such folly and madness cannot be allowed."

I was almost beside myself with rage and fury.

"My worthy uncle is already nearly mad," I cried aloud. "This would finish him. By some accident he may make the discovery; in which case, we are both lost. Perish the fearful secret—let the flames forever bury it in oblivion."

I snatched up book and parchment, and was about to cast them into the fire, when the door opened and my uncle entered.

I had scarcely time to put down the wretched docu-

16

ments before my uncle was by my side. He was profoundly absorbed. His thoughts were evidently bent on the terrible parchment. Some new combination had probably struck him while taking his walk.

He seated himself in his armchair, and with a pen began to make an algebraical calculation. I watched him with anxious eyes. My flesh crawled as it became probable that he would discover *the* secret.

His combinations I knew now were useless, I having discovered the one only clue. For three mortal hours he continued without speaking a word, without raising his head, scratching, rewriting, calculating over and over again. I knew that in time he must hit upon the right phrase. The letters of every alphabet have only a certain number of combinations. But then years might elapse before he would arrive at the correct solution.

Still time went on; night came, the sounds in the streets ceased, and still my uncle went on, not even answering our worthy cook when she called us to supper.

I did not dare to leave him, so waved her away, and at last fell asleep on the sofa.

When I awoke my uncle was still at work. His red eyes, his pallid countenance, his matted hair, his feverish hands, his hectically flushed cheeks, showed how terrible had been his struggle with the impossible, and what fearful fatigue he had undergone during that long sleepless night. It made me quite ill to look at him. Though he was rather severe with me, I loved him, and my heart ached at his sufferings. He was so overcome by one idea that he could not even get in a passion! All his energies were focussed on one point. And I knew that by speaking one little word all this suffering would cease. I could not speak it.

My heart was, nevertheless, inclining toward him.

17

Why, then, did I remain silent? In the interest of my uncle himself.

"Nothing shall make me speak," I muttered. "He will want to follow in the footsteps of the other! I know him well. His imagination is a perfect volcano, and to make discoveries in the interests of geology he would sacrifice his life. I wll therefore be silent and strictly keep the secret I have discovered. To reveal it would be suicidal. He would not only rush, himself, to destruction, but drag me with him."

I crossed my arms, looked another way and smoked, resolved never to speak.

When our cook wanted to go out to market, or on any other errand, she found the front door locked and the key taken away. Was this done purposely or not? Surely Professor Hardwigg did not intend the old woman and myself to become martyrs to his obstinate will. Were we to be starved to death? A frightful recollection came to my mind. Once we had fed on bits and scraps for a week while he sorted some curiosities. It gave me the cramp even to think of it!

I wanted my breakfast, and I saw no way of getting it. Still my resolution held good. I would starve rather than yield. But the cook began to take me seriously to task. What was to be done? She could not go out; and I dared not.

My uncle continued counting and writing; his imagination seemed to have transported him to the skies. He neither thought of eating nor drinking. In this way twelve o'clock came round. I was hungry, and there was nothing in the house. The cook had eaten the last bit of bread. This could not go on. It did, however, until two, when my sensations were terrible. After all, I began to think the document very absurd. Perhaps it might only be a gigantic hoax. Besides, some means would surely be found to keep my uncle back from at-

18

tempting any such absurd expedition. On the other hand, if he did attempt anything so quixotic, I should not be compelled to accompany him. Another line of reasoning partially decided me. Very likely he would make the discovery himself when I should have suffered starvation for nothing. Under the influence of hunger this reasoning appeared admirable. I determined to tell all.

The question now arose as to how it was to be done. I was still dwelling on the thought, when he rose and put on his hat.

What! go out and lock us in? Never!

"Uncle," I began.

He did not appear even to hear me.

"Professor Hardwigg," I cried.

"What," he retorted, "did you speak?"

"How about the key?"

"What key—the key of the door?"

"No, of these horrible hieroglyphics?"

He looked at me from under his spectacles, and started at the odd expression of my face. Rushing forward, he clutched me by the arm and keenly examined my countenance. His very look was an interrogation.

I simply nodded.

With an incredulous shrug of the shoulders, he turned upon his heel. Undoubtedly he thought I had gone mad.

"I have made a very important discovery."

His eyes flashed with excitement. His hand was lifted in a menacing attitude. For a moment neither of us spoke. It is hard to say which was most excited.

"You don't mean to say that you have any idea of the meaning of the scrawl?"

"I do," was my desperate reply. "Look at the sentence as dictated by you."

19

"Well, but it means nothing," was the angry answer.

"Nothing if you read from left to right, but mark, if from right to left—"

"Backwards!" cried my uncle, in wild amazement. "O most cunning Saknussemm; and I to be such a blockhead!"

He snatched up the document, gazed at it with haggard eye, and read it out as I had done.

It read as follows:—

In Sneffels yoculis craterem ken delebat.
Umbra Scartaris Julii intra calendas descende.
Audas viator, et terrestre centrum attinges,
Kod feci. Arne Saknussemm.

Which dog-Latin being translated, reads as follows:—

"Descend into the crater of Yocul of Sneffels, which the shade of Scartaris caresses, before the kalends of July, audacious traveller, and you will reach the center of the earth. I did it.

ARNE SAKNUSSEMM."

My uncle leaped three feet from the ground with joy. He looked radiant and handsome. He rushed about the room wild with delight and satisfaction. He knocked over tables and chairs. He threw his books about until at last, utterly exhausted, he fell into his armchair.

"What's o'clock?" he asked.

"About three."

"My dinner does not seem to have done me much good," he observed. "Let me have something to eat.

We can then start at once. Get my portmanteau ready."

"What for?"

"And your own," he continued. "We start at once."

My horror may be conceived. I resolved, however, to show no fear. Scientific reasons were the only ones likely to influence my uncle. Now, there were many against this terrible journey. The very idea of going down to the center of the earth was simply absurd. I determined therefore to argue the point after dinner.

My uncle's rage was now directed against the cook for having no dinner ready. My explanation, however, satisfied him, and giving her the key she soon contrived to get sufficient foods to satisfy our voracious appetites.

During the repast my uncle was rather gayer than otherwise. He made some of those peculiar jokes which belong exclusively to the learned. As soon, however, as dessert was over, he called me to his study. We each took a chair on opposite sides of the table.

"Henry," he said, in a soft and winning voice, "I have always believed you ingenious, and you have rendered me a service never to be forgotten. Without you, this great, this wondrous discovery would never have been made. It is my duty, therefore, to insist on your sharing the glory."

"He is in a good humor," thought I; "I'll soon let him know my opinion of glory."

"In the first place," he continued, "you must keep the whole affair a profound secret. There is no more envious race of men than scientific discoverers. Many would start on the same journey. At all events, we will be the first in the field."

"I doubt your having many competitors," was my reply.

"A man of real scientific acquirements would be delighted at the chance. We should find a perfect stream of pilgrims on the traces of Arne Saknussemm, if this document were once made public."

"But my dear sir, is not this paper very likely to be a hoax?" I urged.

"The book in which we find it is sufficient proof of its authenticity," he replied.

"I thoroughly allow that the celebrated Professor wrote the lines, but only, I believe, as a kind of mystification," was my answer.

Scarcely were the words out of my mouth, when I was sorry I had uttered them. My uncle looked at me with a dark and gloomy scowl, and I began to be alarmed for the results of our conversation. His mood soon changed, however, and a smile took the place of a frown.

"We shall see," he remarked, with decisive emphasis.

"But see, what is all this about Yocul, and Sneffels, and this Scartaris? I have never heard anything about them."

"The very point to which I am coming. I lately received from my friend, Augustus Peterman, of Leipzig, a map. Take down the third atlas from the second shelf, series Z, plate 4."

I rose, went to the shelf, and presently returned with the volume indicated.

"This," said my uncle, "is one of the best maps of Iceland. I believe it will settle all your doubts, difficulties and objections."

With a grim hope to the contrary, I stooped over the map.

4 . . . *We Start on a Journey*

"**Y**ou see, the whole island is composed of volcanoes," said the Professor, "and remark carefully that they all bear the name of Yokul. The word is Icelandic, and means a glacier. In most of the lofty mountains of that region the volcanic eruptions come forth from icebound caverns. Hence the name applied to every volcano on this extraordinary island."

"But what does this word Sneffels mean?"

To this question I expected no rational answer. I was mistaken.

"Follow my finger to the western coast of Iceland; there you see Reykjavik, its capital. Follow the direction of one of its innumerable fjords or arms of the sea, and what do you see below the sixty-fifth degree of latitude?"

"A peninsula—very like a thighbone in shape."

"And in the center of it—"

"A mountain."

"Well, that's Sneffels."

I had nothing to say.

"That is Sneffels—a mountain about five thousand feet in height, one of the most remarkable in the whole island, and certainly doomed to be the most celebrated in the world, for through its crater we shall reach the Center of the Earth."

"Impossible!" cried I, startled and shocked at the thought.

23

"Why impossible?" said Professor Hardwigg in his severest tones.

"Because its crater is choked with lava, by burning rocks—by infinite dangers."

"But if it be extinct?"

"That would make a difference."

"Of course it would. There are about three hundred volcanoes on the whole surface of the globe—but the greater number are extinct. Of these Sneffels is one. No eruption has occurred since 1219; in fact, it has ceased to be a volcano at all."

After this what more could I say? Yes—I thought of another objection.

"But what is all this about Scartaris and the kalends of July—?"

My uncle reflected deeply. Presently he gave forth the result of his reflections in a sententious tone.

"What appears obscure to you, to me is light. This very phrase shows how particular Saknussemm is in his directions. The Sneffels mountain has many craters. He is careful therefore to note the exact one which is the highway into the Interior of the Earth. He lets us know, for this purpose, that about the end of the month of June, the shadow of Mount Scartaris falls upon the one crater. There can be no doubt about the matter."

My uncle had an answer for everything.

"I accept all your explanations," I said, "and Saknussemm is right. He found out the entrance to the bowels of the earth; he has indicated correctly; but that he or any one else ever followed up the discovery, is madness to suppose."

"Why so, young man?"

"All scientific teaching, theoretical and practical, shows it to be impossible."

"I care nothing for theories," retorted my uncle.

"But is it not well known that heat increases one de-

gree for every seventy feet you descend into the earth?
—which gives a fine idea of the central heat. All the
matters which compose the globe are in a state of
incandescence; even gold, platinum, and the hardest
rocks are in a state of fusion. What would become of
us?"

"Don't be alarmed at the heat, my boy."

"How so?"

"Neither you nor anybody else knows anything about
the real state of the earth's interior. All modern experi-
ments tend to explode the older theories. Were any
such heat to exist, the upper crust of the earth would
be shattered to atoms, and the world would be at an
end."

A long, learned, and not uninteresting discussion followed, which ended in this way:—

"I do not believe in the dangers and difficulties
which you, Henry, seem to multiply; and the only
way to learn is, like Arne Saknussemm, to go and see."

"Well," cried I, overcome at last, "let us go and see.
Though how we can do that in the dark is another
mystery."

"Fear nothing. We shall overcome these, and many
other difficulties. Besides, as we approach the Center,
I expect to find it luminous—"

"Nothing is impossible."

"And now that we have come to a thorough understanding, not a word to any living soul. Our success depends on secrecy and despatch."

Thus ended our memorable conference, which roused
a perfect fever in me. Leaving my uncle, I went forth
like one possessed. Reaching the banks of the Elbe, I
began to think. Was all I had heard really and truly
possible? Was my uncle in his sober senses, and could
the interior of the earth be reached? Was I the victim

25

of a madman, or was he a discoverer of rare courage and grandeur of conception?

To a certain extent I was anxious to be off. I was afraid my enthusiasm would cool. I determined to pack up at once. At the end of an hour, however, on my way home, I found that my feelings had very much changed.

"I'm all abroad," I cried; " 'tis a nightmare—I must have dreamed it."

At this moment I came face to face with Gretchen, whom I warmly embraced.

"So you have come to meet me," she said; "how good of you. But what is the matter?"

Well, it was no use mincing the matter; I told her all. She listened with awe, and for some minutes she could not speak.

"Well?" I at last said, rather anxiously.

"What a magnificent journey. If I were only a man! A journey worthy of the nephew of Professor Hardwigg. I should look upon it as an honor to accompany him."

"My dear Gretchen, I thought you would be the first to cry out against this mad enterprise."

"No; on the contrary, I glory in it. It is magnificent, splendid—an idea worthy of my father. Henry Lawson, I envy you."

This was, as it were, conclusive. The final blow of all.

When we entered the house we found my uncle surrounded by workmen and porters, who were packing up. He was pulling and hauling at a bell.

"Where have you been wasting your time? Your portmanteau is not packed—my papers are not in order —the precious tailor has not brought my clothes, nor my gaiters—the key of my carpetbag is gone."

I looked at him stupefied. And still he tugged away at the bell.

26

"We are really off, then?" I said.

"Yes, of course—and yet you go out for a stroll, unfortunate boy!"

"And when do we go?"

"The day after tomorrow, at daybreak."

I heard no more; but darted off to my little bedchamber and locked myself in. There was no doubt about it now. My uncle had been hard at work all the afternoon. The garden was full of ropes, rope ladders, torches, gourds, iron clamps, crowbars, alpenstocks, and pickaxes—enough to load ten men.

I passed a terrible night. I was called early the next day, to learn that the resolution of my uncle was unchanged and irrevocable. I also found my cousin and affianced wife as warm on the subject as was her father.

Next day, at five o'clock in the morning, the post-chaise was at the door. Gretchen and the old cook received the keys of the house; and, scarcely pausing to wish any one good-bye, we started on our adventurous journey into the Center of the Earth.

5 ... *First Lessons in Climbing*

AT ALTON, a suburb of Hamburg, is the chief station
of the Kiel railway, which was to take us to the
shores of the Belt. In twenty minutes from the moment
of our departure we were in Holstein, and our carriage
entered the station. Our heavy luggage was taken out,
weighed, labelled, and placed in a huge van. We then
took our tickets, and exactly at seven o'clock were
seated opposite each other in a first-class railway carriage.

My uncle said nothing. He was too busy examining
his papers, among which of course was the famous
parchment, and some letters of introduction from the
Danish consul, which were to pave the way to an introduction to the governor of Iceland. My only amusement was looking out of the window. But as we passed
through a flat though fertile country, this occupation
was slightly monotonous. In three hours we reached
Kiel, and our baggage was at once transferred to the
steamer.

We had now a day before us, a delay of about ten
hours; which fact put my uncle in a towering passion.
We had nothing to do but to walk about the pretty
town and bay. At length, however, we went on board,
and at half past ten were steaming down the Great
Belt. It was a dark night, with a strong breeze and a
rough sea, nothing being visible but the occasional fires

on shore, with here and there a lighthouse. At seven in the morning we left Korsör, a little town on the western side of Seeland.

Here we took another railway, which in three hours brought us to the capital, Copenhagen, where, scarcely taking time for refreshment, my uncle hurried out to present one of his letters of introduction. It was to the director of the Museum of Antiquities, who, having been informed that we were tourists bound for Iceland, did all he could to assist us. One wretched hope sustained me now. Perhaps no vessel was bound for such distant parts.

Alas! a little Danish schooner, the *Valkyrie*, was to sail on the second of June for Reykjavik. The captain, M. Bjarne, was on board, and was rather surprised at the energy and cordiality with which his future passenger shook him by the hand. To him a voyage to Iceland was merely a matter of course. My uncle, on the other hand, considered the event of sublime importance. The honest sailor took advantage of the Professor's enthusiasm to double the fare.

"On Tuesday morning at seven c'lock be on board," said M. Bjarne, handing us our receip...

"Excellent! Capital! Glorious!" remarked my uncle, as we sat down to a late breakfast; "refresh yourself, my boy, and we will take a run through the town."

Our meal concluded, we went to the Kongens-Nye-Torw; to the King's magnificent palace; to the beautiful bridge over the canal near the Museum; to the immense cenotaph of Thorwaldsen, with its hideous naval groups; to the castle of Rosenberg; and to all the other lions of the place—none of which my uncle even saw, so absorbed was he in his anticipated triumphs.

But one thing struck his fancy, and that was a certain singular steeple situated on the Island of Amak, which is the southeast quarter of the city of Copenhagen. My uncle at once ordered me to turn my steps that way, and accordingly we went on board the steam ferry boat which does duty on the canal, and very soon reached the noted dockyard quay.

In the first instance we crossed some narrow streets, where we met numerous groups of galley slaves, with parti-colored trousers, gray and yellow, working under the orders and the sticks of severe taskmasters, and finally reached the Vor-Frelser's-Kirk.

This church exhibited nothing remarkable in itself; in fact, the worthy Professor had only been attracted to it by one circumstance, which was that its rather elevated steeple started from a circular platform, after which there was an exterior staircase, which wound round to the very summit.

"Let us ascend," said my uncle.

"But I never climb church towers," I cried; "I am subject to dizziness in my head."

"The very reason why you should go up. I want to cure you of a bad habit."

"But, my good sir—"

"I tell you to come. What is the use of wasting so much valuable time?"

It was impossible to dispute the dictatorial commands of my uncle. I yielded with a groan. On payment of a fee, a verger gave us the key. He, for one, was not partial to the ascent. My uncle at once showed me the way, running up the steps like a schoolboy. I followed as well as I could, though no sooner was I outside the tower, than my head began to swim. There was nothing of the eagle about me. The earth was enough for me, and no ambitious desire to soar ever entered my mind. Still, things did not go badly until I had ascended one hundred and fifty steps, and was near the platform, when I began to feel the rush of cold air. I could scarcely stand, when, clutching the

30

railings, I looked upwards. The railing was frail enough, but nothing to those which skirted the terrible winding staircase, that appeared, from where I stood, to ascend to the skies.

"Now then, Henry!"

"I can't do it!" I cried, in accents of despair.

"Are you, after all, a coward, sir?" said my uncle, in a pitiless tone. "Go up, I say!"

To this there was no reply possible. And yet the keen air acted violently on my nervous system; sky, earth, all seemed to swim round, while the steeple rocked like a ship. My legs gave way like those of a drunken man. I crawled upon my hands and knees; I hauled myself up slowly, crawling like a snake. Presently I closed my eyes, and allowed myself to be dragged upwards.

"Look around you," said my uncle, in a stern voice. "Heaven knows what profound abysses you may have to look down. This is excellent practice."

Slowly, and shivering all the while with cold, I opened my eyes. What then did I see? My first glance was upwards at the cold, fleecy clouds, which as by some optical delusion appeared to stand still, while the steeple, the weathercock, and our two selves, were carried swiftly along. Faraway on one side could be seen the grassy plain, while on the other lay the sea, bathed in translucent light. The Sund, or Sound, as we call it, could be discovered beyond the point of Elsinore, crowded with white sails, which, at that distance, looked like the wings of seagulls; while to the east could be made out the far-off coast of Sweden. The whole appeared a magic panorama.

But, faint and bewildered as I was, there was no remedy for it. Rise and stand up I must. Despite my protestations my first lesson lasted quite an hour. When, nearly two hours later, I reached the bosom of mother

31

earth, I was like a rheumatic old man bent double with pain.

"Enough for one day," said my uncle, rubbing his hands; "we will begin again tomorrow."

There was no remedy. My lessons lasted five days, and at the end of that period, I ascended blithely enough, and found myself able to look down into the depths below without even winking, and with some degree of pleasure.

6 ... *Our Voyage to Iceland*

THE HOUR OF DEPARTURE came at last. The night before, the worthy Mr. Thompson brought us the most cordial letters of introduction for Count Trampe, governor of Iceland, for M. Pictursson, coadjutor to the bishop, and for M. Finsen, mayor of the town of Reykjavik. In return, my uncle nearly crushed his hands, so warmly did he shake them.

On the second of the month, at two in the morning, our precious cargo of luggage was taken on board the good ship *Valkyrie*. We followed, and were very politely introduced by the captain to a small cabin with two standing bed places, neither very well ventilated nor very comfortable. But in the cause of science men are expected to suffer.

"Well, and have we a fair wind?" cried my uncle, in his most mellifluous accents.

"An excellent wind!" replied Captain Bjarne. "We shall leave the Sound, going free with all sails set."

A few minutes afterwards, the schooner started before the wind, under all the canvas she could carry, and entered the channel. An hour later, the capital of Denmark seemed to sink into the waves, and we were at no great distance from the coast of Elsinore. My uncle was delighted; for myself, moody and dissatisfied, I appeared almost to expect a glimpse of the ghost of Hamlet.

"Sublime madman," thought I, "you, doubtless, would approve our proceedings. You might, perhaps, even follow us to the center of the earth, there to resolve your eternal doubts."

But no ghost, or anything else, appeared upon the ancient walls. The fact is, the castle is much later than the time of the heroic prince of Denmark. It is now the residence of the keeper of the Strait of the Sound, and through that Sound more than fifteen thousand vessels of all nations pass every year.

The castle of Kronborg soon disappeared in the murky atmosphere, as well as the tower of Helsinborg, which raises its head on the Swedish bank. And here the schooner began to feel in earnest the breezes of the Cattegat. The *Valkyrie* was swift enough, but with all sailing boats there is the same uncertainty. Her cargo was coal, furniture, pottery, woolen clothing, and a load of corn. As usual, the crew was small—five Danes doing the whole of the work.

"How long will the voyage last?" asked my uncle.

"Well, I should think about ten days," replied the skipper, "unless, indeed, we meet with some northeast gales among the Faroe Islands."

"At all events, there will be no very considerable delay," cried the impatient Professor.

"No, Mr. Hardwigg," said the captain, "no fear of that. At all events, we shall get there some day."

Toward evening the schooner doubled Cape Skagen, the northernmost part of Denmark, crossed the Skager-Rak during the night, skirted the extreme point of Norway through the gut of Cape Lindness, and then reached the Northern Seas. Two days later, we were not far from the coast of Scotland, somewhere near what Danish sailors call Peterhead, and then the *Valkyrie* stretched out direct for the Faroe Islands, between Orkney and Shetland. Our vessel now felt the

34

full force of the ocean waves, and the wind shifting. We, with great difficulty, made the Faroe Isles. On the eighth day, the captain made out Myganness, the westernmost of the Isles, and from that moment headed direct for Portland, a cape on the southern shores of the singular island for which we were bound.

The voyage offered no incident worthy of record. I bore it very well, but my uncle to his great annoyance, and even shame, was remarkably seasick! This *mal de mer* troubled him the more, that it prevented him from questioning Captain Bjarne as to the subject of Sneffels, as to the means of communication, and the facilities of transport. All these explanations he had to adjourn to the period of his arrival. His time meanwhile was spent lying in bed, groaning, and dwelling anxiously on the hoped-for termination of the voyage. I didn't pity him.

On the eleventh day we sighted Cape Portland, over which towered Mount Myrdals Yokul, which, the weather being clear, we made out very readily. The Cape itself is nothing but a huge mount of granite, standing naked and alone to meet the Atlantic waves. The *Valkyrie* kept off the coast, steering to the westward. On all sides were to be seen whole "schools" of whales and sharks. After some hours we came in sight of a solitary rock in the ocean, forming a mighty vault, through which the foaming waves poured with intense fury. The islets of Westman appeared to leap from the ocean, being so low in the water as scarcely to be seen until you were right upon them. From that moment the schooner was steered to the westward in order to round Cape Reykjaness, the western point of Iceland.

My uncle, to his great disgust, was unable even to crawl on deck, so heavy a sea was on, and thus lost the first view of the Land of Promise. Forty-eight hours later, after a storm which drove us far to sea under bare poles, we came once more in sight of land, and were boarded by a pilot, who, after three hours of dangerous navigation, brought the schooner safely to an anchor in the bay of Faxa before Reykjavik.

My uncle came out of his cabin, pale, haggard, thin, but full of enthusiasm, his eyes dilated with pleasure and satisfaction. Nearly the whole population of the town was on foot to see us land. The fact was that each one of them expected some goods by the periodical vessel.

Professor Hardwigg was in haste to leave his prison, or rather as he called it, his hospital; but before he attempted to do so, he caught hold of my hand, led me to the quarter-deck of the schooner, took my arm with his left hand, and pointed inland with his right, over the northern part of the bay, to where rose a high two-peaked mountain—a double cone covered with eternal snow.

"Behold," he whispered in an awe-stricken voice, "behold—Mount Sneffels!"

Then without further remark, he put his finger to his lips, frowned darkly, and descended into the small boat which awaited us. I followed, and in a few minutes we stood upon the soil of mysterious Iceland!

Scarcely were we fairly on shore when there appeared before us a man of excellent appearance, wearing the costume of a military officer. He was, however, but a civil servant, a magistrate, the governor of the island, Baron Trampe. The Professor knew whom he had to deal with. He therefore handed him the letters from Copenhagen, and a brief conversation in Danish followed, to which I of course was a stranger, and for a very good reason, for I did not know the language in which they conversed. I afterwards heard,

36

however, that Baron Trampe placed himself entirely at the beck and call of Professor Hardwigg.

My uncle was most graciously received by M. Finsen, the mayor, who as far as costume went, was quite as military as the governor, but also, from character and occupation, quite as pacific. As for his coadjutor, M. Pictursson, he was absent on an episcopal visit to the northern portion of the diocese. We were therefore compelled to defer the pleasure of being presented to him. His absence was, however, more than compensated by the presence of M. Fridriksson, professor of natural science in the college of Reykjavik, a man of invaluable ability. This modest scholar spoke no languages save Icelandic and Latin. When, therefore, he addressed himself to me in the language of Horace, we at once came to understand one another. He was, in fact, the only person that I did thoroughly understand during the whole period of my residence in this benighted island.

Out of three rooms of which his house was composed, two were placed at our service, and in a few hours we were installed with all our baggage, the amount of which rather astonished the simple inhabitants of Reykjavik.

"Now, Harry," said my uncle, rubbing his hands, "all goes well; the worst difficulty is now over."

"How is the worst difficulty over?" I cried, in fresh amazement.

"Doubtless. Here we are in Iceland. Nothing more remains but to descend into the bowels of the earth."

"Well, sir, to a certain extent you are right. We have only to go down, but, as far as I am concerned, that is not the question. I want to know how we are to get up again."

"That is the least part of the business, and does not in any way trouble me. In the meantime, there is not

37

an hour to lose. I am about to visit the public library. Very likely I may find there some manuscripts from the hand of Saknussemm. I shall be glad to consult them."

"In the meanwhile," I replied, "I will take a walk through the town. Will you not likewise do so?"

"I feel no interest in the subject," said my uncle. "What for me is curious in this island, is not what is above the surface, but what is below."

I bowed by way of reply, put on my hat and furred cloak, and went out.

It was not an easy matter to lose oneself in the two streets of Reykjavik; I had therefore no need to ask my way. The town lies on a flat and marshy plain, between two hills. A vast field of lava skirts it on one side, falling away in terraces toward the sea. On the other hand is the large bay of Faxa, bordered on the north by the enormous glacier of Sneffels, and in which bay the *Valkyrie* was then the only vessel at anchor. Generally there was one or two English or French gunboats, to watch and protect the fisheries in the offing. They were now, however, absent on duty.

The longest of the streets of Reykjavik runs parallel to the shore. In this street the merchants and traders live in wooden huts made with beams of wood, painted red—mere log huts, such as you find in the wilds of America. The other street, situated more to the west, runs toward a little lake between the residences of the bishop and the other personages not engaged in commerce.

I had soon seen all I wanted of these weary and dismal thoroughfares. Here and there was a strip of discolored turf, like an old worn-out bit of woolen carpet; and now and then a bit of kitchen garden, in which grew potatoes, cabbage, and lettuces, almost diminutive enough to suggest the idea of Lilliput.

In the center of the new commercial street, I found the public cemetery, enclosed by an earthen wall. Though not very large, it appeared not likely to be filled for centuries. From hence I went to the house of the governor—a mere hut in comparison with the Mansion House at Hamburg, but a palace alongside the other Icelandic houses. Between the little lake and the town was the church, built in simple Protestant style, and composed of calcined stones, thrown up by volcanic action. I have not the slightest doubt that in high winds its red tiles were blown out, to the great annoyance of the pastor and congregation. Upon an eminence close at hand was the national school, in which were taught Hebrew, English, French and Danish.

In three hours my tour was complete. The general impression upon my mind was sadness. No trees, no vegetation, so to speak—on all sides volcanic peaks, the huts of turf and earth, more like roofs than houses. Thanks to the heat of these residences, grass grows on the roof; this grass is carefully cut for hay. I saw but few inhabitants during my excursion, but I met a crowd on the beach, drying, salting, and loading codfish, the principal article of exportation. The men appeared robust but heavy—fair-haired, like Germans, but of pensive mien—exiles of a higher scale in the ladder of humanity than the Eskimos, but, I thought, much more unhappy, since, with superior perceptions, they are compelled to live within the limits of the polar circle.

Sometimes they gave vent to a convulsive laugh, but by no chance did they smile. Their costume consists of a coarse capote of black wool, known in Scandinavian countries as the "vadmel," a broadbrimmed hat, trousers of red serge, and a piece of leather tied with strings for a shoe—a coarse kind of moccasin.

The women, though sad looking and mournful, had rather agreeable features, without much expression. They wear a bodice and petticoat of somber vadmel. When unmarried, they wear a little brown knitted cap over a crown of plaited hair; but when married, they cover their heads with a colored handkerchief, over which they tie a white scarf.

7 . . . Conversation and Discovery

When I returned, dinner was ready. This meal was devoured by my worthy relative with avidity and voracity. His shipboard diet had turned his interior into a perfect gulf. The repast, which was more Danish than Icelandic, was in itself nothing, but the excessive hospitality of our host made us enjoy it doubly.

The conversation turned upon scientific matters, and M. Fridriksson asked my uncle what he thought of the public library.

"Library, sir?" cried my uncle. "It appears to me to be a collection of useless odd volumes, and a beggarly amount of empty shelves."

"What!" cried M. Fridriksson. "Why, we have eight thousand volumes of most rare and valuable works, some in the Scandinavian language, besides all the new publications from Copenhagen."

"Eight thousand volumes, my dear sir; why, where are they?" cried my uncle.

"Scattered over the country, Professor Hardwigg. We are very studious, my dear sir, though we do live in Iceland. Every farmer, every laborer, every fisherman can both read and write, and we think that books, instead of being locked up in cupboards, far from the sight of students, should be distributed as widely as possible. The books of our library are therefore passed from hand to hand without returning to the library shelves perhaps for years."

"Then when foreigners visit you, there is nothing for them to see."

"Well, sir, foreigners have their own libraries, and our first consideration is that our humbler classes should be highly educated. Fortunately, the love of study is innate in the Icelandic people. In 1816 we founded a Literary Society and Mechanics' Institute; many foreign scholars of eminence are honorary members; we publish books destined to educate our people, and these books have rendered valuable services to our country. Allow me to have the honor, Professor Hardwigg, to enroll you as an honorary member."

My uncle, who already belonged to nearly every literary and scientific institution in Europe, immediately yielded to the amiable wishes of good M. Fridriksson.

"And now," he said, after many expressions of gratitude and good will, "if you will tell me what books you expected to find, perhaps I may be of some assistance to you."

I watched my uncle keenly. For a minute or two he hesitated, as if unwilling to speak; to speak openly was, perhaps, to unveil his projects. Nevertheless, after some reflection, he made up his mind.

"Well, M. Fridriksson," he said, in an easy, unconcerned kind of way, "I was desirous of ascertaining if, among other valuable works, you had any of the learned Arne Saknussemm."

"Arne Saknussemm!" cried the Professor of Reykjavik. "You speak of one of the most distinguished scholars of the sixteenth century, of the great naturalist, the great alchemist, the great traveller."

"Exactly so."

"One of the most distinguished men connected with Icelandic science and literature."

"As you say, sir—"

"A man illustrious above all."

"Yes, sir, all this is true; but his works."

"We have none of them."

"Not in Iceland?"

"There are none in Iceland or elsewhere," answered the other, sadly.

"Why so?"

"Because Arne Saknussemm was persecuted for heresy, and in 1573 his works were publicly burnt at Copenhagen, by the hands of the common hangman."

"Very good! capital!" murmured my uncle, to the great astonishment of the worthy Icelander.

"You said, sir—"

"Yes, yes, all is clear; I see the link in the chain; everything is explained, and I now understand why Arne Saknussemm, put out of court, forced to hide his magnificent discoveries, was compelled to conceal beneath the veil of an incomprehensible cryptograph the secret—"

"What secret?"

"A secret—which—" stammered my uncle.

"Have you discovered some wonderful manuscript?" cried M. Fridriksson.

"No, no; I was carried away by my enthusiasm. A mere supposition."

"Very good, sir. But, really, to turn to another subject, I hope you will not leave our island without examining into its mineralogical riches."

"Well, the fact is, I am rather late. So many learned men have been here before me."

"Yes, yes; but there is still much to be done," cried M. Fridriksson.

"You think so?" said my uncle, his eyes twinkling with hidden satisfaction.

"Yes; you have no idea how many unknown moun-

43

tains, glaciers, volcanoes there are which remain to be studied. Without moving from where we sit, I can show you one. Yonder on the edge of the horizon, you see Sneffels."

"Oh, yes, Sneffels," said my uncle.

"One of the most curious volcanoes in existence, the crater of which has been rarely visited."

"Extinct?"

"Extinct, any time these five hundred years," was the ready reply.

"Well," said my uncle, who dug his nails into his flesh, and pressed his knees tightly together to prevent himself leaping up with joy, "I have a great mind to begin my studies with an examination of the geological mysteries of this Mount Seffel—Feisel—what do you call it?"

"Sneffels, my dear sir."

This portion of the conversation took place in Latin, and I therefore understood all that had been said. I could scarcely keep my countenance when I found my uncle so cunningly concealing his delight and satisfaction. I must confess that his artful grimaces, put on to conceal his happiness, made him look like a new Mephistopheles.

"Yes, yes," he continued, "your proposition delights me. I will endeavor to climb the summit of Sneffels, and, if possible, will descend into its crater."

"I very much regret," continued M. Fridriksson, "that my occupation will entirely preclude the possibility of my accompanying you. It would have been both pleasurable and profitable if I could have spared the time."

"No, no, a thousand times no!" cried my uncle. "I do not wish to disturb the serenity of any man. I thank you, however, with all my heart. The presence of one so learned as yourself, would no doubt have been most useful, but the duties of your office and profession before everything."

In the innocence of his simple heart, our host did not perceive the irony of these remarks.

"I entirely approve your project," continued the Icelander, after some further remarks. "It is a good idea to begin by examining this volcano. You will make a harvest of curious observations. In the first place, how do you propose to get to Sneffels?"

"By sea. I shall cross the bay. Of course that is the most rapid route."

"Of course. But still it can not be done."

"Why?"

"We have not an available boat in all Reykjavik," replied the other.

"What is to be done?"

"You must go by land along the coast. It is longer, but much more interesting."

"Then I must have a guide."

"Of course; and I have your very man."

"Somebody on whom I can depend?"

"Yes; an inhabitant of the peninsula on which Sneffels is situated. He is a very shrewd and worthy man, with whom you will be well pleased. He speaks Danish like a Dane."

"When can I see him—today?"

"No, tomorrow. He will not be here before."

"Tomorrow be it," replied my uncle, with a deep sigh.

The conversation ended by compliments on both sides. During the dinner my uncle had learned much as to the history of Arne Saknussemm, the reasons for his mysterious and hieroglyphical document. He also became aware that his host would not accompany him on his adventurous expedition, and that next day we should have a guide.

45

8 . . . *The Eider-Down Hunter —Off at Last*

THAT EVENING I took a brief walk on the shore near Reykjavik, after which I returned to an early sleep on my bed of coarse planks, where I slept the sleep of the just. When I awoke I heard my uncle speaking loudly in the next room. I rose hastily and joined him. He was talking in Danish with a man of tall stature, and of perfectly Herculean build. This man appeared to be possessed of very great strength. His eyes, which started rather prominently from a very large head, the face belonging to which was simple and naïve, appeared very quick and intelligent. Very long hair, which even in England would have been accounted exceedingly red, fell over his athletic shoulders. This native of Iceland was active and supple in appearance, though he scarcely moved his arms, being in fact one of those men who despise the habit of gesticulation common to Southern people.

Everything in this man's manner revealed a calm and phlegmatic temperament. There was nothing indolent about him, but his appearance spoke of tranquillity. He was one of those who never seemed to expect anything from anybody; who liked to work when he thought proper, and whose philosophy nothing could astonish or trouble.

I began to comprehend his character, simply from the way in which he listened to the wild and impas-

46

sioned verbiage of my worthy uncle. While the excellent Professor spoke sentence after sentence, he stood with folded arms, utterly still, motionless to all my uncle's gesticulations. When he wanted to say No, he moved his head from left to right; when he acquiesced, he nodded, so slightly that you could scarcely see the undulation of his head. This economy of motion was carried to the length of avarice.

Judging from his appearance, it should have been a long time before I had suspected him to be what he was, a mighty hunter. Certainly his manner was not likely to frighten the game. How, then, did he contrive to get at his prey?

My surprise was slightly modified when I knew that this tranquil and solemn personage was only a hunter of the eider duck, the down of which is, after all, the greatest source of the Icelanders' wealth.

In the early days of summer, the female of the eider, a pretty sort of duck, builds its nest amid the rocks of the fjords—the name given to all narrow gulfs in Scandinavian countries—with which every part of the island is indented. No sooner has the eider duck made her nest than she lines the inside of it with the softest down from her breast. Then comes the hunter or trader, taking away the nest; the poor bereaved female begins her task over again, and this continues as long as any eider down is to be found.

When she can find no more, the male bird sets to work to see what he can do. As, however, his down is not so soft, and has therefore no commercial value, the hunter does not take the trouble to rob him of his nest lining. The nest is accordingly finished, the eggs are laid, the little ones are born, and next year the harvest of eider down is again collected.

Now, as the eider duck never selects steep rocks or aspects to build its nest, but rather sloping and low

47

cliffs near to the sea, the Icelandic hunter can carry on his trade operations without much difficulty. He is like a farmer who has neither to plough, to sow, nor to harrow—only to collect his harvest.

This grave, sententious, silent person, as phlegmatic as an Englishman on the French stage, was named Hans Bjelke. He had called upon us in consequence of the recommendation of M. Fridriksson. He was, in fact, our future guide. It struck me that, had I sought the world over, I could not have found a greater contradiction to my impulsive uncle.

They, however, readily understood one another. Neither of them had any thought about money; one was ready to take all that was offered him; the other ready to offer anything that was asked. It may readily be conceived, then, that an understanding was soon come to between them.

Now, the understanding was that he was to take us to the village of Stapi, situated on the southern slope of the peninsula of Sneffels, at the very foot of the volcano. Hans, the guide, told us the distance was about twenty-two miles, a journey which my uncle supposed would take about two days.

But when my uncle came to understand that they were Danish miles, of eight thousand yards each, he was obliged to be more moderate in his ideas, and, considering the horrible roads we had to follow, to allow eight or ten days for the journey.

Four horses were prepared for us, two to carry the baggage, and two to bear the important weight of myself and uncle. Hans declared that nothing ever would make him climb on the back of any animal. He knew every inch of that part of the coast, and promised to take us the very shortest way.

His engagement with my uncle was by no means to cease with our arrival at Stapi; he was further to remain in his service during the whole time required for the completion of his scientific investigations, at the fixed salary of three rix-dollars a week, being exactly fourteen shillings and twopence, minus one farthing, English currency. One stipulation, however, was made by the guide; the money was to be paid to him every Saturday night, failing which, his engagement was at an end.

The day of our departure was fixed. My uncle wished to hand the eider-down hunter an advance, but he refused in one emphatic word—

"*Efter.*"

Which, being translated from Icelandic into plain English, means—After.

The treaty concluded, our worthy guide retired without another word.

"A splendid fellow," said my uncle, "only he little suspects the marvellous part he is about to play in the history of the world."

"You mean, then," I cried, in amazement, "that he should accompany us?"

"To the Interior of the Earth, yes," replied my uncle. "Why not?"

There were yet forty-eight hours to elapse before we made our final start. To my great regret, our whole time was taken up in making preparations for our journey. All our industry and ability were devoted to packing every object in the most advantageous manner, the instruments on one side, the arms on the other, the tools here and the provisions there. There were, in fact, four distinct groups.

The instruments were of course of the best manufacture:—

1. A centigrade thermometer of Eizel, counting up to one hundred and fifty degrees, which to me did not appear half enough—or too much. Too hot by half, if

the degree of heat was to ascend so high—in which case we should certainly be cooked; not enough, if we wanted to ascertain the exact temperature of springs, or metal in a state of fusion.

2. A *manometer* worked by compressed air; an instrument used to ascertain the upper atmospheric pressure on the level of the ocean. Perhaps a common barometer would not have done as well, the atmospheric pressure being likely to increase in proportion as we descended below the surface of the earth.

3. A first-class chronometer made by Boissonnas, of Geneva, set at the meridian of Hamburg, from which Germans calculate, as the English do from Greenwich, and the French from Paris.

4. Two compasses, one for horizontal guidance, the other to ascertain the dip.

5. A night glass.

6. Two Ruhmkorf's coils, which, by means of a current of electricity, would ensure us a very excellent, easily carried, and certain means of obtaining light.

7. A voltaic battery on the newest principle.

Our arms consisted of two rifles, with two revolving six-shooters. Why these arms were provided it was impossible for me to say. I had every reason to believe that we had neither wild beasts nor savage natives to fear. My uncle, on the other hand, was quite as devoted to his arsenal as to his collection of instruments, and above all was very careful with his provision of fulminating or gun cotton, warranted to keep in any climate, and of which the expansive force was known to be greater than that of ordinary gunpowder.

Our tools consisted of two pickaxes, two crowbars, a silken ladder, three iron-shod Alpine poles, a hatchet, a hammer, a dozen wedges, some pointed pieces of iron, and a quantity of strong rope. You may conceive that the whole made a tolerable parcel, especially when

I mention that the ladder itself was three hundred feet long!

Then there came the important question of provisions. The hamper was not very large, but tolerably satisfactory, for I knew that in concentrated essence of meat and biscuit there was enough to last six months. The only liquid provided by my uncle was scheidam. Of water, not a drop. We had, however, an ample supply of gourds, and my uncle counted on finding water, and enough to fill them, as soon as we commenced our downward journey.

My remarks as to the temperature, the quality, and even as to the possibility of none being found, remained wholly without effect.

To make up the exact list of our travelling gear, for the guidance of future travellers, I will add, that we carried a medicine and surgical chest with all apparatus necessary for wounds, fractures, and blows; lint, scissors, lancets—in fact, a perfect collection of horrible-looking instruments; a number of phials containing ammonia, alcohol, ether, goulard water, aromatic vinegar—in fact, every possible and impossible drug; finally, all the materials for working the Ruhmkorf coil.

My uncle had also been careful to lay in a goodly supply of tobacco, several flasks of very fine gunpowder, boxes of tinder, besides a large belt crammed full of notes and gold. Good boots, rendered watertight, were to be found to the number of six in the tool box.

"My boy, with such clothing, with such boots, and such general equipments," said my uncle, in a state of rapturous delight, "we may hope to travel far."

It took a whole day to put all these matters in order. In the evening we dined with Baron Trampe, in company with the mayor of Reykjavik, and Doctor Hyaltalin, the great medical man of Iceland. M. Fridriksson was not present, and I was afterwards sorry to hear that he and the governor did not agree on some matters connected with the administration of the island. Unfortunately, the consequence was that I did not understand a word that was said at dinner—a kind of semiofficial reception. One thing I can say—my uncle never left off speaking.

The next day our labor came to an end. Our worthy host delighted my uncle, Professor Hardwigg, by giving him a good map of Iceland, a most important and precious document for a mineralogist.

Our last evening was spent in a long conversation with M. Fridriksson, whom I liked very much—the more that I never expected to see him or any one else again. After this agreeable way of spending an hour or so, I tried to sleep. In vain; with the exception of a few dozes, my night was miserable.

At five o'clock in the morning I was awakened from the only real half-hour's sleep of the night, by the loud neighing of horses under my window. I hastily dressed myself and went down into the street. Hans was engaged in putting the finishing stroke to our baggage, which he did in a silent, quiet way that won my admiration, and yet he did it admirably well. My uncle wasted a great deal of breath in giving him directions, but worthy Hans took not the slightest notice of his words.

At six o'clock all our preparations were completed, and M. Fridriksson shook hands heartily with us. My uncle thanked him warmly, in the Icelandic language, for his kind hospitality, speaking truly from the heart.

As for myself, I put together a few of my best Latin phrases, and paid him the highest compliments I could. This fraternal and friendly duty performed, we sallied forth and mounted our horses.

As soon as we were quite ready, M. Fridriksson advanced, and, by way of farewell, called after me in the words of Virgil—words which appeared to have been made for us, travellers starting for an uncertain destination:—

"Et quacunque viam dederit fortuna sequamur."

("And whichsoever way thou goest, may fortune follow!")

9 ... Our Start—We Meet with Adventures by the Way

THE WEATHER was overcast but settled when we commenced our adventures and perilous journey. We had neither to fear fatiguing heat nor drenching rain. It was, in fact, real tourist weather.

As there was nothing I liked better than horse exercise, the pleasure of riding through an unknown country caused the early part of our enterprise to be particularly agreeable to me.

I began to enjoy the exhilarating delight of travelling, a life of desire, gratification and liberty. The truth is that my spirits rose so rapidly that I began to be indifferent to what had once appeared to be a terrible journey.

"After all," I said to myself, "what do I risk? Simply to take a journey through a curious country, to climb a remarkable mountain, and if the worst comes to the worst, to descend into the crater of an extinct volcano."

There could be no doubt that this was all this terrible Saknussemm had done. As to the existence of a gallery, or of subterraneous passages leading into the interior of the earth, the idea was simply absurd, the hallucination of a distempered imagination. All, then, that may be required of me I will do cheerfully, and will create no difficulty.

It was just before we left Reykjavik that I came to this decision.

Hans, our extraordinary guide, went first, walking with a steady, rapid, and unvarying step. Our two horses with the luggage followed of their own accord, without requiring whip or spur. My uncle and I came behind, cutting a very tolerable figure upon our small but vigorous animals.

Iceland is one of the largest islands in Europe. It contains thirty thousand square miles of surface, and has about seventy thousand inhabitants. Geographers have divided it into four parts, and we had to cross the southwest quarter, which in the vernacular is called Sudvestr Fjordùngr.

Hans, on taking his departure from Reykjavik, had followed the line of the sea. We took our way through poor and sparse meadows, which made a desperate effort every year to show a little green. They very rarely succeed in a good show of yellow.

The rugged summits of the rocky hills were dimly visible on the edge of the horizon, through the misty fogs; every now and then some heavy flakes of snow showed conspicuous in the morning light, while certain lofty and pointed rocks were first lost in the gray low clouds, their summits clearly visible above, like jagged reefs rising from a troublous sea.

Every now and then a spur of rock came down through the arid ground, leaving us scarcely room to pass. Our horses, however, appeared not only well acquainted with the country, but, by a kind of instinct, knew which was the best road. My uncle had not even the satisfaction of urging forward his steed by whip, spur, or voice. It was utterly useless to show any signs of impatience. I could not help smiling to see him look so big on his little horse; his long legs now and then touching the ground made him look like a six-footed centaur.

"Good beast, good beast," he would cry. "I assure

55

you, Henry, that I begin to think no animal is more intelligent than an Icelandic horse. Snow, tempest, impracticable roads, rocks, icebergs—nothing stops him. He is brave; he is sober; he is safe; he never makes a false step; never glides or slips from his path. I dare to say that if any river, any fjord, has to be crossed —and I have no doubt there will be many—you will see him enter the water without hesitation like an amphibious animal, and reach the opposite side in safety. We must not, however, attempt to hurry him; we must allow him to have his own way, and I will undertake to say that between us we shall do our ten leagues a day."

"We may do so," was my reply, "but what about our worthy guide?"

"I have not the slightest anxiety about him; those sort of people go ahead without knowing even what they are about. Look at Hans. He moves so little that it is impossible for him to become fatigued. Besides, if he were to complain of weariness, he could have the loan of my horse. I should have a violent attack of the cramp if I were not to have some sort of exercise. My arms are all right—but my legs are getting a little stiff."

All this while we were advancing at a rapid pace. The country we had reached was already nearly a desert. Here and there could be seen an isolated farm, some solitary boër, or Icelandic house, built of wood, earth, fragments of lava, looking like beggars on the highway of life. These wretched and miserable huts excited in us such pity that we felt half disposed to leave alms at every door. In this country there are no roads, paths are nearly unknown, and vegetation, poor as it was, slowly as it reached perfection, soon obliterated all traces of the few travellers who passed from place to place.

Nevertheless, this division of the province, situated

only a few miles from the capital, is considered one of the best cultivated and most thickly peopled in all Iceland. What, then, must be the state of the less-known and more distant parts of the island? After travelling fully half a Danish mile, we had met neither a farmer at the door of his hut, nor even a wandering shepherd with his wild and savage flock.

A few stray cows and sheep were only seen occasionally. What, then, must we expect when we come to the upheaved regions—to the districts broken and roughened from volcanic eruptions and subterraneous commotions?

We were to learn this all in good time. I saw, however, on consulting the map, that we avoided a good deal of this rough country by following the winding and desolate shores of the sea. In reality, the great phenomena are concentrated in the interior of the island; there, horizontal layers or strata of rocks, piled one upon the other, eruptions of basaltic origin, and streams of lava have given this country a kind of supernatural reputation.

Little did I expect, however, the spectacle which awaited us when we reached the peninsula of Sneffels, where agglomerations of nature's ruins form a kind of terrible chaos.

Some two hours or more after we had left the city of Reykjavik, we reached the little town called Aoalkirkja, or the principal church. It consists simply of a few houses—not what in England or Germany we should call a hamlet.

Hans stopped here one half hour. He shared our frugal breakfast, answered *yes* and *no* to my uncle's questions as to the nature of the road, and at last, when asked where we were to pass the night, was as laconic as usual.

"Gardar!" was his one-worded reply.

I took occasion to consult the map, to see where Gardar was to be found. After looking keenly I found a small town of that name on the borders of the Hvalfjord, about four miles from Reykjavik. I pointed this out to my uncle, who made a very energetic grimace.

"Only four miles out of twenty-two? Why, it is only a little walk."

He was about to make some energetic observation to the guide, but Hans, without taking the slightest notice of him, went in front of the horses, and walked ahead with the same imperturbable phlegm he had always exhibited.

Three hours later, still travelling over those apparently interminable and sandy prairies, we were compelled to go round the Kollafjord, an easier and shorter cut than crossing the gulfs. Shortly after, we entered a place of communal jurisdiction called Ejulberg, and the clock of which would then have struck twelve, if any Icelandic church had been rich enough to possess so valuable and useful an article. These sacred edifices are, however, very much like these people, who do without watches, and never miss them.

Here the horses were allowed to take some rest and refreshment; then following a narrow strip of shore between high rocks and the sea, they took us without further halt to the "aoalkirkja" of Brantar, and after another mile to "Saurboer Annexia," a chapel of ease, situated on the southern bank of the Hvalfjord.

It was four o'clock in the evening and we had travelled four Danish miles, about equal to twenty English.

The fjord was in this place about half a mile in width. The sweeping and broken waves came rolling in upon the pointed rocks; the gulf was surrounded by rocky walls—a mighty cliff, three thousand feet in

58

height, remarkable for its brown strata, separated here and there by beds of tufa of a reddish hue. Now, whatever may have been the intelligence of our horses, I had not the slightest reliance upon them, as a means of crossing a stormy arm of the sea. To ride over salt water upon the back of a little horse seemed to me absurd.

"If they are really intelligent," I said to myself, "they will certainly not make the attempt. In any case, I shall trust rather to my own intelligence than theirs."

But my uncle was in no humor to wait. He dug his heels into the sides of his steed, and made for the shore. His horse went to the very edge of the water, sniffed at the approaching wave, and retreated.

My uncle, who was, sooth to say, quite as obstinate as the beast he bestrode, insisted on his making the desired advance. This attempt was followed by a new refusal on the part of the horse, which quietly shook his head. This demonstration of rebellion was followed by a volley of words and a stout application of whipcord; also followed by kicks on the part of the horse, which threw his head and heels upwards and tried to throw his rider. At length the sturdy little pony, spreading out his legs in a stiff and ludicrous attitude, got from under the Professor's legs, and left him standing, with both feet on a separate stone, like the Colossus of Rhodes.

"Wretched animal!" cried my uncle, suddenly transformed into a foot passenger and as angry and ashamed as a dismounted cavalry officer on the field of battle.

"*Farja*," said the guide, tapping him familiarly on the shoulder.

"What, a ferryboat!"

"*Der*," answered Hans, pointing to where lay the boat in question—("there.")

"Well," I cried, quite delighted with the information, "so it is."

"Why did you not say so before?" cried my uncle. "Why not start at once?"

"*Tidvatten*," said the guide.

"What does he say?" I asked, considerably puzzled by the delay and the dialogue.

"He says tide," replied my uncle, translating the Danish word for my information.

"Of course I understand—we must wait till the tide serves."

"*For bida?*" asked my uncle.

"*Ja*," replied Hans.

My uncle frowned, stamped his feet, and then followed the horses to where the boat lay.

I thoroughly understood and appreciated the necessity for waiting, before crossing the fjord, for that moment when the sea at its highest point is in a state of slack water. As neither the ebb nor flow can then be felt, the ferryboat was in no danger of being carried out to sea, or dashed upon the rocky coast.

The favorable moment did not come until six o'clock in the evening. Then my uncle, myself, and guide, two boatmen and the four horses got into a very awkward flat-bottom boat. Accustomed as I had been to the steam ferryboats of the Elbe, I found the long oars of the boatmen but sorry means of locomotion. We were more than an hour in crossing the fjord; but at length the passage was concluded without accident.

Half an hour later we reached Gardar.

10 ... *Travelling in Iceland* — *The Lepers*

IT OUGHT, one would have thought, to have been night, even in the sixty-fifth parallel of latitude; but still the nocturnal illumination did not surprise me. For in Iceland, during the months of June and July, the sun never sets.

The temperature, however, was very much lower than I expected. I was cold; but even that did not affect me so much as ravenous hunger. Welcome indeed, therefore, was the hut which hospitably opened its doors to us.

It was merely the house of a peasant, but in the matter of hospitality, it was worthy of being the palace of a king. As we alighted at the door the master of the house came forward, held out his hand, and without any further ceremony, signalled us to follow him.

We followed him, for to accompany him was impossible. A long, narrow, gloomy passage led into the interior of this habitation, made from beams roughly squared by the axe. This passage gave ingress to every room. The chambers were four in number: the kitchen, the workshop, where the weaving was carried on, the general sleeping chamber of the family, and the best room, to which strangers were especially invited. My uncle, whose lofty stature had not been taken into consideration when the house was built, contrived to knock his head against the beams of the roof.

We were introduced into our chamber, a kind of large room with a hard earthern floor, and lighted by a window, the panes of which were made of a sort of parchment from the intestines of sheep—very far from transparent.

The bedding was composed of dry hay thrown into two long red wooden boxes, ornamented with sentences painted in Icelandic. I really had no idea that we should be made so comfortable. There was one objection to the house, and that was, the very powerful odor of dried fish, of macerated meat, and of sour milk, which three fragrances combined, did not at all suit my olfactory nerves.

As soon as we had freed ourselves from our heavy travelling costume, the voice of our host was heard calling to us to come into the kitchen, the only room in which the Icelanders ever make any fire, no matter how cold it may be.

My uncle, nothing loth, hastened to obey this hospitable and friendly invitation. I followed.

The kitchen chimney was made on an antique model. A large stone standing in the middle of the room was the fireplace; above, in the roof, was a hole for the smoke to pass through. This apartment was kitchen, parlor and dining room all in one.

On our entrance, our worthy host, as if he had not seen us before, advanced ceremoniously, uttered a word which means "be happy," and then kissed both of us on the cheek.

His wife followed, pronounced the same word, with the same ceremonial; then the husband and wife, placing their right hands upon their hearts, bowed profoundly.

This excellent Icelandic woman was the mother of nineteen children, who, little and big, rolled, crawled, and walked about in the midst of volumes of smoke

62

arising from the angular fireplace in the middle of the room. Every now and then I could see a fresh white head, and a slightly melancholy expression of countenance, peering at me through the vapor.

Both my uncle and myself, however, were very friendly with the whole party, and before we were aware of it, there were three or four of these little ones on our shoulders, as many on our boxes, and the rest hanging about our legs. Those who could speak kept crying out *sœllvertu* in every possible and impossible key. Those who did not speak only made all the more noise.

This concert was interrupted by the announcement of supper. At this moment our worthy guide, the eider-duck hunter, came in after seeing to the feeding and stabling of the horses—which consisted of letting them loose to browse on the stunted green of the Icelandic prairies. There was little for them to eat, but moss and some very dry and innutritious grass; next day they were ready before the door, some time before we were.

"Welcome," said Hans.

Then tranquilly, with the air of an automaton, without any more expression in one kiss than another, he embraced the host and hostess and their nineteen children.

This ceremony concluded to the satisfaction of all parties, we all sat down to table, that is twenty-four of us, somewhat crowded. Those who were best off had only two juveniles on their knees.

As soon, however, as the inevitable soup was placed on the table, the natural taciturnity, common even to Icelandic babies, prevailed over all else. Our host filled our plates with a portion of *lichen* soup of Iceland moss, of by no means disagreeable flavor and an enormous lump of fish floating in sour butter. After that there came some "skyr," a kind of curds and whey, served with biscuits and juniper-berry juice. To drink, we had blanda, skimmed milk with water. I was hungry; so hungry, that by way of dessert I finished up with a basin of thick oaten porridge.

As soon as the meal was over, the children disappeared, whilst the grown people sat around the fireplace, on which was placed turf, heather, cow dung and dried fish bones. As soon as everybody was sufficiently warm, a general dispersion took place, all retiring to their respective couches. Our hostess offered to pull off our stockings and trousers, according to the custom of the country, but as we graciously declined to be so honored, she left us to our bed of dry fodder.

Next day, at five in the morning, we took our leave of these hospitable peasants. My uncle had great difficulty in making them accept a sufficient and proper remuneration.

Hans then gave the signal to start.

We had scarcely got a hundred yards from Gardar, when the character of the country changed. The soil began to be marshy and boggy, and less favorable to progress. To the right, the range of mountains was prolonged indefinitely like a great system of natural fortifications, of which we skirted the glacis. We met with numerous streams and rivulets which it was necessary to ford, and that without wetting our baggage. As we advanced, the deserted appearance increased, and yet now and then we could see human shadows flitting in the distance. When a sudden turn of the track brought us within easy reach of one of these specters, I felt a sudden impulse of disgust at the sight of a swollen head, with shining skin, utterly without hair, and whose repulsive and revolting wounds could be seen through his rags. The unhappy wretches never came forward to beg; on the contrary, they ran away;

64

not so quick, however, but that Hans was able to salute them with the universal *sœllvertu.*

"*Spetelsk,*" said he.

"A leper," explained my uncle.

The very sound of such a word caused a feeling of repulsion. The horrible affection known as leprosy, which has almost vanished before the effects of modern science, is common in Iceland. It is not contagious, but hereditary; so that marriage is strictly prohibited to these unfortunate creatures.

These poor lepers did not tend to enliven our journey, the scene of which was inexpressibly sad and lonely. The very last tufts of grassy vegetation appeared to die at our feet. Not a tree was to be seen, except a few stunted willows about as big as blackberry bushes. Now and then we watched a falcon soaring in the gray and misty air, taking his flight toward warmer and sunnier regions. I could not help feeling a sense of melancholy come over me. I sighed for my own native land, and wished to be back with Gretchen.

We were compelled to cross several little fjords, and at last came to a real gulf. The tide was at its height, and we were able to go over at once, and reached the hamlet of Alftanes, about a mile farther.

That evening, after fording the Alfa and the Heta, two rivers rich in trout and pike, we were compelled to pass the night in a deserted house, worthy of being haunted by all the fays of Scandinavian mythology. The King of Cold had taken up his residence there, and made us feel his presence all night.

The following day was remarkable by its lack of any particular incidents. Always the same damp and swampy soil; the same dreary uniformity; the same and monotonous aspect of scenery. In the evening, having accomplished the half of our projected journey, we slept at the Annexia of Krosolbt.

For a whole mile we had under our feet nothing but lava.

This disposition of the soil is called *hraun:* the crumbled lava on the surface was in some instances like ship cables stretched out horizontally, in others, coiled up in heaps; an immense field of lava came from the neighboring mountains, all extinct volcanoes, but whose remains showed what once they had been. Here and there could be made out the steam from hot water springs.

There was no time, however, for us to take more than a cursory view of these phenomena. We had to go forward with what speed we might. Soon the soft and swampy soil again appeared under the feet of our horses, while at every hundred yards we came upon one or more small lakes. Our journey was not in a westerly direction; we had, in fact, swept round the great bay of Faxa, and the twin white summits of Sneffels rose to the clouds at a distance of less than five miles.

The horses now advanced rapidly; the accidents and difficulties of the soil no longer checked them. I confess that fatigue began to tell severely upon me; but my uncle was as firm and as hard as he had been on the first day. I could not help admiring both the excellent Professor and the worthy guide; for they appeared to regard this rugged expedition as a mere walk!

On Saturday, June 20th, at six o'clock in the evening, we reached Budir, a small town picturesquely situated on the shore of the ocean; and here the guide asked for his money. My uncle settled with him immediately. It was now the family of Hans himself, that is to say, his uncles, his cousins-german, who offered us hospitality. We were exceedingly well received, and, without taking too much advantage of the goodness of these worthy people, I should have liked very much to have rested with them after the fatigues of the journey. But my uncle, who did not require rest, had no idea of anything of the kind; and, despite the fact that next day was Sunday, I was compelled once more to mount my steed.

The soil was again affected by the neighborhood of the mountains, whose granite peered out of the ground like tops of an old oak. We were skirting the enormous base of the mighty volcano. My uncle never took his eyes from off it; he could not keep from gesticulating, and looking at it with a kind of sullen defiance, as much as to say, "This is the giant I have made up my mind to conquer."

After four hours of steady travelling, the horses stopped of themselves before the door of the presbytery of Stapi.

11 ... We Reach Mount Sneffels
—The "Reykir"

STAPI IS A TOWN consisting of thirty huts, built on a large plain of lava, exposed to the rays of the sun reflected from the volcano. It stretches its humble tenements along the end of the little fjord, surrounded by a basaltic wall of the most singular character.

Basalt is a brown rock of igneous origin. It assumes regular forms which astonish by their singular appearance. Here we found Nature proceeding geometrically, and working quite after a human fashion, as if she had employed the plummet line, the compass and the rule. If elsewhere she produces grand artistic effects by piling up huge masses without order or connection, if elsewhere we see truncated cones, imperfect pyramids, with an old succession of lines, here, as if wishing to give a lesson in regularity, and preceding the architects of the early ages, she has erected a severe order of architecture, which neither the splendors of Babylon nor the marvels of Greece ever surpassed.

I had often heard of the Giant's Causeway in Ireland, the Grotto of Fingal in one of the Hebrides, but the grand spectacle of a real basaltic formation had never yet come before my eyes.

This at Stapi gave us an idea of one in all its wonderful beauty and grace.

The wall of the fjord, like nearly the whole of the peninsula, consisted of a series of vertical columns, in height about thirty feet. These upright pillars of stone, of the finest proportions, supported an archivolt of horizontal columns which formed a kind of half-vaulted roof above the sea. At certain intervals, and below this natural basin, the eye was pleased and surprised by the sight of oval openings through which the outward waves came thundering in volleys of foam. Some banks of basalt, torn from their fastenings by the fury of the waves, lay scattered on the ground like the ruins of an ancient temple—ruins eternally young, over which the storms of ages swept without producing any perceptible effect!

This was the last stage of our journey. Hans had brought us along with fidelity and intelligence, and I began to feel somewhat more comfortable when I reflected that he was to accompany us still farther on our way.

When we halted before the house of the Rector, a small and incommodious cabin, neither handsome nor more comfortable than those of his neighbors, I saw a man in the act of shoeing a horse, a hammer in his hand, and a leathern apron tied round his waist.

"Be happy," said the eider-down hunter, using his national salutation in his own language.

"*Good-dag!*" ("good day!") replied the former, in excellent Danish.

"*Kyrkoherde,*" cried Hans, turning round and introducing him to my uncle.

"The Rector," repeated the worthy Professor. "It appears, my dear Harry, that this worthy man is the Rector, and is not above doing his own work."

During the speaking of these few words the guide intimated to the Kyrkoherde what was the true state of the case. The good man, ceasing from his occupation, gave a kind of halloo, upon which a tall woman, almost a giantess, came out of the hut. She was at least six feet high, which in that region is something considerable.

My first impression was one of horror. I thought she had come to give us the Icelandic kiss. I had, however, nothing to fear, for she did not even show much inclination to receive us into her house.

The room devoted to strangers appeared to me to be by far the worst in the presbytery; it was narrow, dirty and offensive. There was, however, no choice about the matter. The Rector had no notion of practising the usual cordial and antique hospitality. Far from it. Before the day was over, I found we had to deal with a blacksmith, a fisherman, a hunter, a carpenter, anything but a clergyman. It must be said in his favor that we had caught him on a weekday; probably he appeared to greater advantage on the Sunday.

These poor priests receive from the Danish government a most ridiculously inadequate salary, and collect one quarter of the tithe of their parish—not more than sixty marks current, or about £3 10s. sterling. Hence the necessity of working to live. In truth, we soon found that our host did not count civility among the cardinal virtues.

My uncle soon became aware of the kind of man he had to deal with. Instead of a worthy and learned scholar, he found a dull, ill-mannered peasant. He therefore resolved to start on his great expedition as soon as possible. He did not care about fatigue, and resolved to spend a few days in the mountains.

The preparations for our departure were made the very next day after our arrival at Stapi; Hans now hired three Icelanders to take the place of the horses, which could no longer carry our luggage. When, however, these worthy islanders had reached the bottom of the crater, they were to go back and leave us to ourselves. This point was settled before they agreed to start.

On this occasion, my uncle partially confided in Hans, the eider-duck hunter, and gave him to understand that it was his intention to continue his exploration of the volcano to the last possible limits.

Hans listened calmly, and then nodded his head. To go there, or elsewhere, to bury himself in the bowels of the earth, or to travel over its summits, was all the same to him! As for me, amused and occupied by the incidents of travel, I had begun to forget the inevitable future; but now I was once more destined to realize the actual state of affairs. What was to be done? Run away? But if I really had intended to leave Professor Hardwigg to his fate, it should have been at Hamburg and not at the foot of Sneffels.

One idea above all others began to trouble me: a very terrible idea, and one calculated to shake the nerves of a man even less sensitive than myself.

"Let us consider the matter," I said to myself. "We are going to ascend the Sneffels mountain. Well and good. We are about to pay a visit to the very bottom of the crater. Good, still. Others have done it and did not perish from that course.

"That, however, is not the whole matter to be considered. If a road does really present itself by which to descend into the dark and subterraneous bowels of Mother Earth, if this thrice unhappy Saknussemm has really told the truth, we shall be most certainly lost in the midst of the labyrinth of subterraneous galleries of the volcano. Now we have no evidence to prove that Sneffels is really extinct. What proof have we that an eruption is not shortly about to take place? Because the monster has slept soundly since 1229, does it follow that he is never to wake?

"If he does wake, what is to become of us?"

These were questions worth thinking about, and upon them I reflected long and deeply. I could not lie down in search of sleep without dreaming of eruptions. The more I thought, the more I objected to be reduced to the state of dross and ashes.

I could stand it no longer; so I determined at last to submit the whole case to my uncle, in the most adroit manner possible, and under the form of some totally irreconcilable hypothesis.

I sought him. I laid before him my fears, and then drew back in order to let him get his passion over at his ease.

"I have been thinking about the matter," he said, in the quietest tone in the world.

What did he mean? Was he at last about to listen to the voice of reason? Did he think of suspending his projects? It was almost too much happiness to be true.

I, however, made no remark. In fact, I was only too anxious not to interrupt him, and allowed him to reflect at his leisure. After some moments he spoke out.

"I have been thinking about the matter," he resumed. "Ever since we have been at Stapi, my mind has been almost solely occupied with the grave question which has been submitted to me by yourself, for nothing would be unwiser or more inconsistent than to act with imprudence."

"I heartily agree with you, my dear uncle," was my somewhat hopeful rejoinder.

"It is now six hundred years since Sneffels has spoken, but though now reduced to a state of utter silence, he may speak again. New volcanic eruptions are always preceded by perfectly well-known phenomena. I have closely examined the inhabitants of this region; I have carefully studied the soil, and I beg to tell you emphatically, my dear Harry, there will be no eruption at present."

As I listened to his positive affirmations, I was stupefied and could say nothing.

"I see you doubt my word," said my uncle; "follow me."

I obeyed mechanically.

Leaving the presbytery, the Professor took a road through an opening in the basaltic rock, which led far away from the sea. We were soon in open country, if we could give such a name to a place all covered with volcanic deposits. The whole land seemed crushed under the weight of enormous stones—of trap, of basalt, of granite, of lava, and of all other volcanic substances.

I could see many spouts of steam rising in the air. These white vapors, called in the Icelandic language "reykir," come from hot water fountains, and indicate by their violence the volcanic activity of the soil. Now the sight of these appeared to justify my apprehension. I was, therefore, all the more surprised and mortified when my uncle thus addressed me.

"You see all this smoke, Harry, my boy?"

"Yes, sir."

"Well, as long as you can see them thus, you have nothing to fear from the volcano."

"How can that be?"

"Be careful to remember this," continued the Professor. "At the approach of an eruption these spouts of vapor redouble their activity—to disappear altogether during the period of volcanic eruption; for the elastic fluids, no longer having the necessary tension, seek refuge in the interior of the crater, instead of escaping through the fissures of the earth. If, then, the steam remains in its normal or habitual state, if their energy does not increase, and if you add to this, the remark, that the wind is not replaced by heavy atmospheric pressure and dead calm, you may be quite sure that there is no fear of any immediate eruption."

"But—"

"Enough, my boy. When Science has sent forth her fiat, it is only to hear and obey."

I came back to the house quite downcast and disappointed. My uncle had completely defeated me with his scientific arguments. Nevertheless, I had still one hope, and that was, when once we were at the bottom of the crater, that it would be impossible in default of a gallery or tunnel, to descend any deeper; and this, despite all the learned Saknussemms in the world.

I passed the whole of the following night with a nightmare on my chest, and, after unheard of miseries and tortures, found myself in the very depths of the earth, from which I was suddenly launched into planetery space, under the form of an eruptive rock!

Next day, June 23d, Hans calmly awaited us outside the presbytery with his two companions loaded with provisions, tools, and instruments. Two iron-shod poles, two guns, and two large game bags were reserved for my uncle and myself. Hans, who was a man who never forgot even the minutest precautions, had added to our baggage a large skin full of water, as an addition to our gourds. This assured us water for eight days.

It was nine o'clock in the morning when we were quite ready. The Rector and his huge wife or servant, I never knew which, stood at the door to see us off. They appeared to be about to inflict on us the usual final kiss of the Icelanders. To our supreme astonishment their adieu took the shape of a formidable bill, in which they even counted the use of the pastoral house, really and truly the most abominable and dirty place I ever was in. The worthy couple cheated and robbed us like a Swiss innkeeper, and made us feel, by the sum we had to pay, the splendors of their hospitality.

My uncle, however, paid without bargaining. A man who had made up his mind to undertake a voyage into the interior of the earth is not the man to haggle over a few miserable rix-dollars.

This important matter settled, Hans gave the signal for departure, and some few moments later we had left Stapi.

12 ... *The Ascent of Mount Sneffels*

THE HUGE VOLCANO which was the first stage of our daring experiment is above five thousand feet high. Sneffels is the termination of a long range of volcanic mountains, of a different character to the system of the island itself. One of its peculiarities is its two huge pointed summits. From whence we started it was impossible to make out the real outlines of the peak against the gray field of sky. All we could distinguish was a vast dome of white, which fell downwards from the head of the giant.

The commencement of the great undertaking filled me with awe. Now that we had actually started, I began to believe in the reality of the undertaking!

Our party formed quite a procession. We walked in single file, preceded by Hans, the imperturbable eider-duck hunter. He calmly led us by narrow paths where two persons could by no possibility walk abreast. Conversation was wholly impossible. We had all the more opportunity to reflect and admire the awful grandeur of the scene around.

Beyond the extraordinary basaltic wall of the fjord of Stapi we found ourselves making our way through fibrous turf, over which grew a scanty vegetation of grass, the residuum of the ancient vegetation of the swampy peninsula. The vast mass of this combustible, the field of which as yet is utterly unexplored, would suffice to warm Iceland for a whole century. This mighty turf pit, measured from the bottom of certain ravines, is often not less than seventy feet deep, and presents to the eye the view of successive layers of black burned-up rocky detritus, separated by thin streaks of porous sandstone.

The grandeur of the spectacle was undoubted, as well as its arid and deserted air.

As a true nephew of the great Professor Hardwigg, and despite my preoccupation and doleful fears of what was to come, I observed with great interest the vast collection of mineralogical curiosities spread out before me in this vast museum of natural history. Looking back to my recent studies, I went over in thought the whole geological history of Iceland.

This extraordinary and curious island must have made its appearance from out of the great world of waters at a comparatively recent date. Like the coral islands of the Pacific, it may, for aught we know, be still rising by slow and imperceptible degrees.

If this really be the case, its origin can be attributed to only one cause—that of the continued action of subterranean fires. This was a happy thought.

If so, if this were true, away with the theories of Sir Humphrey Davy; away with the authority of the parchment of Arne Saknussemm; the wonderful pretensions to discovery on the part of my uncle—and to our journey!

All must end in smoke.

Charmed with the idea, I began more carefully to look about me. A serious study of the soil was necessary to negate or confirm my hypothesis. I took in every item of which I saw, and I began to comprehend the succession of phenomena which had preceded its formation.

Iceland, being absolutely without sedimentary soil, is

77

composed exclusively of volcanic tufa; this is to say, of an agglomeration of stones and rocks of a porous texture. Long before the existence of volcanoes, it was composed of a solid body of massive traprock lifted bodily and slowly out of the sea by the action of the centrifugal force at work in the earth.

The internal fires, however, had not as yet burst their bounds and flooded the exterior cake of Mother Earth with hot and raging lava.

My readers must excuse this brief and somewhat pedantic geological lecture. But it is necessary to the complete understanding of what follows.

At a later period in the world's history, a huge and mighty fissure must, reasoning by analogy, have been dug diagonally from the southwest to the northeast of the island, through which by degrees flowed the volcanic crust. The great and wondrous phenomenon then went on without violence—the outpouring was enormous, and the seething fused matter, ejected from the bowels of the earth, spread slowly and peacefully in the form of vast level plains, or what are called mamelons or mounds.

It was at this epoch that the rocks called feldspars, syenites, and porphyries appeared.

But as a natural consequence of this overflow, the depth of the island increased. It can readily be believed what an enormous quantity of elastic fluids were piled up within its center, when at last it afforded no other openings, after the process of cooling the crust had taken place.

At length a time came when despite the enormous thickness and weight of the upper crust, the mechanical forces of the combustible gases below became so great, that they actually upheaved the weighty back and made for themselves huge and gigantic shafts. Hence the volcanoes which suddenly arose through the upper crust, and next the craters, which burst forth at the summit of these new creations.

It will be seen that the first phenomena in connection with the formation of the island were simply eruptive; to these, however, shortly succeeded the volcanic phenomena.

Through the newly formed openings escaped the marvellous mass of basaltic stones with which the plain we were now crossing was covered. We were trampling our way over heavy rocks of dark gray color, which, while cooling, had been moulded into six-sided prisms. In the "back distance" we could see a number of flattened cones, which formerly were so many fire-vomiting mouths.

After the basaltic eruption was appeased and set at rest, the volcano, the force of which increased with that of the extinct craters, gave free passage to the fiery overflow of lava, and to the mass of cinders and pumice stone, now scattered over the sides of the mountain, like dishevelled hair on the shoulders of a Bacchante.

Here, in a nutshell, I had the whole history of the phenomena from which Iceland arose. All take their rise in the fierce action of interior fires, and to believe that the central mass did not remain in a state of liquid fire, white hot, was simply and purely madness.

This being satisfactorily proved (*q. e. d.*), what insensate folly to pretend to penetrate into the interior of the mighty earth!

This mental lecture delivered to myself while proceeding on a journey did me good. I was quite reassured as to the fate of our enterprise; and therefore went, like a brave soldier mounting a bristling battery, to the assault of old Sneffels.

As we advanced, the road became every moment more difficult. The soil was broken and dangerous.

The rocks broke and gave way under our feet, and we had to be scrupulously careful in order to avoid dangerous and constant falls.

Hans advanced as calmly as if he had been walking over Salisbury Plain; sometimes he would disappear behind huge blocks of stone, and we momentarily lost sight of him. There was a little period of anxiety, and then there was a shrill whistle, just to tell us where to look for him.

Occasionally he would take it into his head to stop to pick up lumps of rock, and silently pile them up into small heaps, *in order that we might not lose our way on our return.*

He had no idea of the journey we were about to undertake.

At all events, the precaution was a good one; though how utterly useless and unnecessary—but I must not anticipate.

Three hours of terrible fatigue, walking incessantly, had only brought us to the foot of the great mountain. This will give some notion of what we had still to undergo.

Suddenly, however, Hans cried a halt—that is, he made signs to that effect—and a summary kind of breakfast was laid out on the lava before us. My uncle, who now was simply Professor Hardwigg, was so eager to advance, that he bolted his food like a greedy clown. This halt for refreshment was also a halt for repose. The Professor was therefore compelled to wait the good pleasure of his imperturbable guide, who did not give the signal for departure for a good hour.

The three Icelanders, who were as taciturn as their comrade, did not say a word; but went on eating and drinking very quietly and soberly.

From this, our first real stage, we began to ascend the slopes of the Sneffels volcano. Its magnificent snowy nightcap, as we began to call it, by an optical delusion very common in mountains, appeared to me to be close at hand; and yet how many long weary hours must elapse before we reached its summit. What unheard-of fatigue must we endure!

The stones on the mountain side, held together by no cement of soil, bound together by no roots or creeping herbs, gave way continually under our feet, and went rushing below into the plains, like a series of small avalanches.

In certain places the sides of this stupendous mountain were at an angle so steep that it was impossible to climb upwards, and we were compelled to get round these obstacles as best we might.

Those who understand Alpine climbing will comprehend our difficulties. Often we were obliged to help each other along by means of our climbing poles.

I must say this for my uncle, that he stuck as close to me as possible. He never lost sight of me, and on many occasions his arm supplied me with firm and solid support. He was strong, wiry, and apparently insensible to fatigue. Another great advantage with him was that he had the innate sentiment of equilibrium, for he never slipped or failed in his steps. The Icelanders, though heavily loaded, climbed with the agility of mountaineers.

Looking up, every now and then, at the height of the great volcano of Sneffels, it appeared to me wholly impossible to reach to the summit on that side; at all events, if the angle of inclination did not speedily change.

Fortunately, after an hour of unheard-of fatigues, and of gymnastic exercises that would have been trying to an acrobat, we came to a vast field of ice, which wholly surrounded the bottom of the cone of the volcano. The natives called it the tablecloth, probably from some such reason as the dwellers in the Cape of Good Hope call their mountain Table Mountain, and their roads Table Bay.

Here, to our mutual surprise, we found an actual flight of stone steps, which wonderfully assisted our ascent. This singular flight of stairs was, like every thing else, volcanic. It had been formed by one of those torrents of stones cast up by the eruptions, and of which the Icelandic name is *stinâ*. If this singular torrent had not been checked in its descent by the peculiar shape of the flanks of the mountain, it would have swept into the sea, and would have formed new islands.

Such as it was, it served us admirably. The abrupt character of the slopes momentarily increased, but these remarkable stone steps, a little less difficult than those of the Egyptian pyramids, were the one simple natural means by which we were enabled to proceed.

About seven in the evening of that day, after having clambered up two thousand of these rough steps, we found ourselves overlooking a kind of spur or projection of the mountain, a sort of buttress upon which the conelike crater, properly so called, leaned for support.

The ocean lay beneath us at a depth of more than three thousand two hundred feet, a grand and mighty spectacle. We had reached the region of eternal snows.

The cold was keen, searching and intense. The wind blew with extraordinary violence. I was utterly exhausted.

My worthy uncle, the Professor, saw clearly that my legs refused further service, and that, in fact, I was utterly exhausted. Despite his hot and feverish impatience, he decided, with a sigh, upon a halt. He called the eider-duck hunter to his side. That worthy, however, shook his head.

"*Ofvanfor,*" was his sole spoken reply.

"It appears," says my uncle with a woe-begone look, "that we must go higher."

He then turned to Hans, and asked him to give some reason for this decisive response.

"*Mistour*," replied the guide.

"*Ja, mistour*," (yes, the mistour,) cried one of the Icelandic guides in a terrified tone.

It was the first time he had spoken.

"What does this mysterious word signify?" I anxiously inquired.

"Look," said my uncle.

I looked down upon the plain below, and I saw a vast, a prodigious volume of pulverized pumice stone, of sand, of dust, rising to the heavens in the form of a mighty waterspout. It resembled the fearful phenomenon of a similar character known to the travellers in the desert of the great Sahara.

The wind was driving it directly toward that side of Sneffels on which we were perched. This opaque veil standing up between us and the sun projected a deep shadow on the flanks of the mountain. If this sandspout broke over us, we must all be infallibly destroyed, crushed in its fearful embraces. This extraordinary phenomenon, very common when the wind shakes the glaciers, and sweeps over the arid plains, is in the Icelandic tongue called *mistour*.

"*Hastigt!*" cried our guide.

Now I certainly knew nothing of Danish, but I thoroughly understood that his gestures were meant to quicken us.

The guide turned rapidly in a direction which would take us to the back of the crater, all the while ascending slightly.

We followed rapidly, despite our excessive fatigue.

A quarter of an hour later Hans paused to enable us to look back. The mighty whirlwind of sand was spreading up the slope of the mountain to the very spot where we had proposed to halt. Huge stones were caught up, cast into the air, and thrown about as during an eruption. We were happily a little out of the direction of the wind, and therefore out of reach of danger. But for the precaution and knowledge of our guide, our dislocated bodies, our crushed and broken limbs, would have been cast to the wind, like dust from some unknown meteor.

Hans, however, did not think it prudent to pass the night on the bare side of the cone. We therefore continued our journey in a zigzag direction. The fifteen hundred feet which remained to be accomplished took us at least five hours. The turnings and windings, the no-thoroughfares, the marches and marches, turned that insignificant distance into at least three leagues. I never felt such misery, fatigue and exhaustion in my life. I was ready to faint from hunger and cold. The rarefied air at the same time painfully acted upon my lungs.

At last, when I thought myself at my last gasp, about eleven at night, it being in that region quite dark, we reached the summit of Mount Sneffels! It was in an awful mood of mind, that, despite my fatigue, before I descended into the crater that was to shelter us for the night, I paused to behold the sun rise at midnight on the very day of its lowest declension, and enjoyed the spectacle of its ghastly pale rays cast upon the isle which lay sleeping at our feet!

I no longer wondered at people travelling all the way from England to Norway, to behold this magical and wondrous spectacle.

13 ... *The Shadow of Scartaris*

OUR SUPPER WAS EATEN with ease and rapidity, after which everybody did the best he could for himself within the hollow of the crater. The bed was hard, the shelter unsatisfactory, the situation painful, lying in the open air, five thousand feet above the level of the sea!

Nevertheless, it has seldom happened to me to sleep so well as I did on that particular night. I did not even dream. So much for the effects of what my uncle called "wholesome fatigue."

Next day, when we awoke under the rays of a bright and glorious sun, we were nearly frozen by the keen air. I left my granite couch, and made one of the party to enjoy a view of the magnificent spectacle which developed itself, panoramalike, at our feet.

I stood upon the lofty summit of Mount Sneffels' southern peak. Thence I was able to obtain a view of the greater part of the island. The optical delusion, common to all lofty heights, raised the shores of the island, while the central portions appeared depressed. It was by no means too great a flight of fancy to believe that a giant picture was stretched out before me. I could see the deep valleys that crossed each other in every direction. I could see precipices looking like sides of wells, lakes that seemed to be changed into ponds that looked like puddles, and rivers that were transformed into petty brooks. To my right were glaciers upon glaciers, and multiplied peaks, topped with light clouds of smoke.

The undulation of these infinite numbers of mountains, whose snowy summits make them look as if covered by foam, recalled to my remembrance the surface of a storm-beaten ocean. If I looked toward the west, the ocean lay before me in all its majestic grandeur; a continuation, as it were, of these fleecy hilltops.

Where the earth ended and the sea began, it was impossible for the eye to distinguish.

I soon felt that strange and mysterious sensation which is awakened in the mind when looking down from lofty hilltops, and now I was able to do so without my feeling of nervousness, having fortunately hardened myself to that kind of sublime contemplation.

I wholly forgot who I was, and where I was. I became intoxicated with a sense of lofty sublimity, without thought of the abysses into which my daring was soon about to plunge me. I was presently, however, brought back to the realities of life by the arrival of the Professor and Hans, who joined me upon the lofty summit of the peak.

My uncle, turning in a westerly direction, pointed out to me a light cloud of vapor, a kind of haze, with a faint outline of land rising out of the waters.

"Greenland!" said he.

"Greenland?" cried I, in reply.

"Yes," continued my uncle, who always when explaining anything spoke as if he were in a Professor's chair. "We are not more than thirty-five leagues distant from that wonderful land. When the great annual break-up of the ice takes place, white bears come over to Iceland, carried by the floating masses of ice from the north. This, however, is a matter of little consequence.

We are now on the summit of the great, the transcendent Sneffels, and here are its two peaks, north and south. Hans will tell you the name by which the people of Iceland call that on which we stand."

My uncle turned to the imperturbable guide, who nodded, and spoke, as usual, one word:—

"*Scartaris*."

My uncle looked at me with a proud and triumphant glance.

"A crater," he said. "You hear?"

I did hear, but I was totally unable to make reply.

The crater of Mount Sneffels represented an inverted cone, the gaping orifice apparently half a mile across; the depth indefinite feet. Conceive what this *hole* must have been like when full of flame and thunder and lightning. The bottom of the funnel-shaped hollow was about five hundred feet in circumference, by which it will be seen that the slope from the summit to the bottom was very gradual, and we were therefore clearly able to get there without much fatigue or difficulty. Involuntarily, I compared this crater to an enormous loaded cannon; and the comparison completely terrified me.

"To descend into the interior of a cannon," I thought to myself, "when perhaps it is loaded, and will go off at the least shock, is the act of a madman."

But there was no longer any opportunity for me to hesitate. Hans, with a perfectly calm and indifferent air, took his usual post at the head of the adventurous little band. I followed without uttering a syllable.

I felt like the lamb led to the slaughter.

In order to render the descent less difficult, Hans took his way down the interior of the cone in rather a zigzag fashion, making, as the sailors say, long tracks to the eastward, followed by equally long ones to the west. It was necessary to walk through the midst of eruptive rocks, some of which, shaken in their balance, went rolling down with thundering clamor to the bottom of the abyss. These continual falls awoke echoes of singular power and effect.

Many portions of the cone consisted of inferior glaciers. Hans, whenever he met with one of these obstacles, advanced with a great show of precaution, sounding the soil with his long iron pole in order to discover fissures and layers of deep soft snow. In many doubtful or dangerous places, it became necessary for us to be tied together by a long rope, in order that should any one of us be unfortunate enough to slip, he would be supported by his companions. This connecting link was doubtless a prudent precaution, but not by any means unattended by danger.

Nevertheless, and despite all the manifold difficulties of the descent, along slopes with which our guide was wholly unacquainted, we made considerable progress without accident. One of our great parcels of rope slipped from one of the Iceland porters, and rushed by a short cut to the bottom of the abyss.

By midday we were at the end of our journey. I looked upwards, and saw only the upper orifice of the cone, which served as a circular frame to a very small portion of the sky—a portion which seemed to me singularly beautiful. Should I ever again gaze on that lovely sunlit sky?

The only exception to this extraordinary landscape was the Peak of Scartaris, which seemed lost in the great void of the heavens.

The bottom of the crater was composed of three separate shafts, through which, during periods of eruption, when Sneffels was in action, the great central furnace sent forth its burning lava and poisonous vapors. Each of these chimneys, or shafts, gaped open-mouthed in our path. I kept as faraway from them as possible, not even venturing to take the faintest peep downwards.

As for the Professor, after a rapid examination of their disposition and characteristics, he became breathless and panting. He ran from one to the other like a delighted schoolboy, gesticulating wildly, and uttering incomprehensible and disjointed phrases in all sorts of languages.

Hans, the guide, and his humbler companions, seated themselves on some piles of lava and looked silently on. They clearly took my uncle for a lunatic; and—waited the result.

Suddenly the Professor uttered a wild, unearthly cry. At first I imagined he had lost his footing, and was falling headlong into one of the yawning gulfs. Nothing of the kind. I saw him, his arms spread out to their widest extent, his legs stretched apart, standing upright before an enormous pedestal, high enough and black enough to bear a gigantic statue of Pluto. His attitude and mien were that of a man utterly stupefied. But his stupefaction was speedily changed to the wildest joy.

"Harry! Harry! come here!" he cried. "Make haste! Wonderful—wonderful!"

Unable to understand what he meant, I turned to obey his commands. Neither Hans nor the other Icelanders moved a step.

"Look!" said the Professor, in something of the manner of the French general pointing out the pyramids to his army.

And fully partaking his stupefaction, if not his joy, I read on the eastern side of the huge block of stone, the same characters, half eaten away by the corrosive action of time, the name, to me a thousand times accursed:—

ᛚᚨᚴᛖ ᛋᛁᛈᚴᚦᚾᛋᛋᛁᚠ

"Arne Saknussemm!" cried my uncle. "Now, unbeliever, do you begin to have faith?"

It was totally impossible for me to answer a single word. I went back to my pile of lava, in a state of silent awe. The evidence was unanswerable, overwhelming!

In a few moments, however, my thoughts were far away, back in my German home, with Gretchen and the old cook. What would I have given for one of my cousin's smiles, for one of the ancient domestic's omelets and for my own feather bed!

How long I remained in this state I know not. All I can say is, that when at last I raised my head from between my hands, there remained at the bottom of the crater only myself, my uncle and Hans. The Icelandic porters had been dismissed, and were now descending the exterior slopes of Mount Sneffels, on their way to Stapi. How heartily did I wish myself with them!

Hans slept tranquilly at the foot of a rock, in a kind of rill of lava, where he had made himself a rough and ready bed. My uncle was walking about the bottom of the crater like a wild beast in a cage. I had no desire, neither had I the strength, to move from my recumbent position. Taking example by the guide, I gave way to a kind of painful somnolency, during which I seemed both to hear and feel continued heavings and shudderings in the mountain.

In this way we passed our first night in the interior of a crater.

Next morning, a gray, cloudy, heavy sky hung like a funeral pall over the summit of the volcanic cone. I did not notice it so much from the obscurity that reigned around us, as from the rage with which my uncle was devoured.

I fully understood the reason, and again a glimpse of hope made my heart leap with joy. I will briefly explain the cause.

Of the three openings which yawned beneath our steps, only one could have been followed by the adventurous Saknussemm. According to the words of the learned Icelander, it was only to be known by that one particular mentioned in the cryptograph that the shadow of Scartaris fell upon it, just touching its mouth in the last days of the month of June.

We were, in fact, to consider the pointed peak as the *stylus* of an immense sundial, the shadow of which pointed on one given day, like the inexorable finger of fate, to the yawning chasm which led into the interior of the earth.

Now, as often happens in these regions, should the sun fail to burst through the clouds, no shadow. Consequently, no chance of discovering the right aperture. We had already reached the 25th of June. If the kindly heavens would only remain densely crowded for six more days, we should have to put off our voyage of discovery for another year, when certainly there would be one person fewer in the party. I already had sufficient of the mad and monstrous enterprise.

It would be utterly impossible to depict the impotent rage of Professor Hardwigg. The day passed away, and not the faintest outline of a shadow could be seen at the bottom of the crater. Hans, the guide, never moved from his place. He must have been curious to know what we were about, if indeed he could believe we were about anything. As for my uncle, he never addressed a word to me. He was nursing his wrath to keep it warm! His eyes fixed on the black and foggy atmosphere, his complexion hideous with suppressed passion. Never had his eyes appeared so fierce, his nose so aquiline, his mouth so hard and firm.

On the 26th no change for the better. A mixture of rain and snow fell during the whole day. Hans very quietly built himself a hut of lava, into which he retired like Diogenes into his tub. I took a malicious delight in watching the thousand little cascades that flowed down the side of the cone, carrying with them at times a stream of stones into the "vasty deep" below.

My uncle was almost frantic: to be sure it was enough to make even a patient man angry. He had reached to a certain extent the goal of his desires, and yet he was likely to be wrecked in port.

But if the heavens and the elements are capable of causing us much pain and sorrow, there are two sides to a medal. And there was reserved for Professor Hardwigg a brilliant and sudden surprise which was to compensate him for all his sufferings.

Next day the sky was still overcast; but on Sunday, the last day but one of the month, with a sudden change of wind and a new moon, there came a change of weather. The sun poured its beaming rays to the very bottom of the crater.

Each hillock, every rock, every stone, every asperity of the soil had its share of the luminous effulgence, and its shadow fell heavily on the soil. Among others, to his insane delight, the shadow of Scartaris was marked and clear, and moved slowly with the radiant star of day.

My uncle moved with it in a state of mental ecstasy.

At twelve o'clock exactly, when the sun had attained its highest altitude for the day, the shadow fell upon the edge of the central pit!

"Here it is," gasped the Professor, in an agony of

joy. "Here it is—we have found it. Forward, my friends, into the interior of the earth."

I looked curiously at Hans to see what reply he would make to this terrific announcement.

"*Forüt,*" said the guide, tranquilly.

"Forward it is," answered my uncle, who was now in the seventh heaven of delight.

When we were quite ready, our watches indicated thirteen minutes past one!

14 ... The Real Journey Commences

OUR REAL JOURNEY had now commenced.

Hitherto our courage and determination had over-come all difficulties. We were fatigued at times; and that was all. Now, unknown and fearful dangers we were about to encounter.

I had not as yet ventured to take a glimpse down the horrible abyss into which in a few minutes more I was about to plunge. The fatal moment had, how-ever, at last arrived. I had still the option of refusing or accepting a share in this foolish and audacious enterprise. But I was ashamed to show more fear than the eider-duck hunter. Hans seemed to accept the difficulties of the journey so tranquilly, with such calm indifference, with such perfect recklessness of all dan-ger, that I actually blushed to appear less of a man than he!

Had I been alone with my uncle, I should certainly have sat down and argued the point fully; but in the presence of the guide I held my tongue. I gave one moment to the thought of my charming cousin, and then I advanced to the mouth of the central shaft.

It measured about a hundred feet in diameter, which made about three hundred in circumference. I leaned over a rock which stood on its edge, and looked down. My hair stood on end, my teeth chattered, my limbs trembled, I seemed utterly to lose my center of gravity, while my head was in a sort of whirl, like that of a drunken man. There is nothing more powerful than this attraction toward an abyss. I was about to fall headlong into the gaping well, when I was drawn back by a firm and powerful hand. It was that of Hans. I had not taken lessons enough at the Vor-Frelser's-Kirk of Copenhagen in the art of looking down from lofty eminences without blinking!

However, few as the minutes were during which I gazed down this tremendous and even wondrous shaft, I had a sufficient glimpse of it to give me some idea of its physical conformation. Its sides, which were almost as perpendicular as those of a well, presented numerous projections which doubtless would assist our descent.

It was a sort of wild and savage staircase, without banister or fence. A rope fastened above, near the surface, would certainly support our weight and enable us to reach the bottom, but how, when we had arrived at its utmost depth, were we to loosen it above? This was, I thought, a question of some importance.

My uncle, however, was one of those men who are nearly always prepared with expedients. He hit upon a very simple method of obviating this difficulty. He unrolled a cord about as thick as my thumb, and at least four hundred feet in length. He allowed about half of it to go down the pit and catch in a hitch over a great block of lava which stood on the edge of the precipice. This done, he threw the second half after the first.

Each of us could now descend by catching the two cords in one hand. When about two hundred feet below, all the explorer had to do was to let go one end and pull away at the other, when the cord would come falling at his feet. In order to go down farther, all that was necessary was to continue the same operation.

This was a very excellent proposition, and, no doubt, a correct one. Going down appeared to me easy enough; it was the coming up again that now occupied my thoughts.

"Now," said my uncle, as soon as he had completed this important preparation, "let us see about the baggage. It must be divided into three separate parcels, and each of us must carry one on his back. I allude to the more important and fragile articles."

My worthy and ingenious uncle did not appear to consider that we came under that denomination.

"Hans," he continued, "you will take charge of the tools and some of the provisions; you, Harry, must take possession of another third of the provisions and of the arms. I will load myself with the rest of the eatables, and with the more delicate instruments."

"But," I exclaimed, "our clothes, this mass of cord and ladders—who will undertake to carry them down?"

"They will go down of themselves."

"And how so?" I asked.

"You shall see."

My uncle was not fond of half measures, nor did he like any thing in the way of hesitation. Giving his orders to Hans, he had the whole of the non-fragile articles made up into one bundle; and the packet, firmly and solidly fastened, was simply pitched over the edge of the gulf.

I heard the moaning of the suddenly displaced air, and the noise of falling stones. My uncle, leaning over the abyss, followed the descent of his luggage with a perfectly self-satisfied air, and did not rise until it had completely disappeared from sight.

"Now then," he cried, "it is our turn."

I put it in good faith to any man of common sense —was it possible to hear this energetic cry without a shudder?

The Professor fastened his case of instruments on his back. Hans took charge of the tools, I of the arms. The descent then commenced in the following order: Hans went first, my uncle followed, and I went last. Our progress was made in profound silence—a silence only troubled by the fall of pieces of rock, which, breaking from the jagged sides, fell with a roar into the depths below

I allowed myself to slide, so to speak, holding frantically on the double cord with one hand and with the other keeping myself off the rocks by the assistance of my iron-shod pole. One idea was all the time impressed upon my brain. I feared that the upper support would fail me. The cord appeared to me far too fragile to bear the weight of three such persons as we were, with our luggage. I made as little use of it as possible, trusting to my own agility, and doing miracles in the way of feats of dexterity and strength upon the projecting shelves and spurs of lava, which my feet seemed to clutch as strongly as my hands.

The guide went first I have said, and when one of the slippery and frail supports broke from under his feet he had recourse to his usual monosyllable way of speaking.

"*Gifakt*—"

"Attention—look out," repeated my uncle.

In about half an hour we reached a kind of small terrace, formed by a fragment of rock projecting some distance from the sides of the shaft.

Hans now began to haul upon the cord on one side only, the other going as quietly upward as the other came down. It fell at last, bringing with it a shower of small stones, lava and dust, a disagreeable kind of rain or hail.

While we were seated on this extraordinary bench I ventured once more to look downwards. With a sigh I discovered that the bottom was still wholly invisible. Were we, then, going direct to the interior of the earth?

The performance with the cord recommenced, and a quarter of an hour later we had reached to the depth of another two hundred feet.

97

I have very strong doubts if the most determined geologist would, during that descent, have studied the nature of the different layers of earth around him. I did not trouble my head much about the matter; whether we were among the combustible carbon, silurians, or primitive soil, I neither knew nor cared to know.

Not so the inveterate Professor. He must have taken notes all the way down, for, at one of our halts, he began a brief lecture.

"The farther we advance," said he, "the greater is my confidence in the result. The disposition of these volcano strata absolutely confirms the theories of Sir Humphrey Davy. We are still within the region of the primordial soil; the soil in which took place the chemical operation of metals becoming inflamed by coming in contact with the air and water. I at once regret the old and now for ever exploded theory of central fire. At all events, we shall soon know the truth."

Such was the everlasting conclusion to which he came. I, however, was very far from being in humor to discuss the matter. I had something else to think of. My silence was taken for consent; and still we continued to go down.

At the expiration of three hours, we were, to all appearance, as far off as ever from the bottom of the well. When I looked upwards, however, I could see that the upper orifice was every minute decreasing in size. The sides of the shaft were getting closer and closer together; we were approaching the regions of eternal night!

And still we continued to descend!

At length, I noticed that when pieces of stone were detached from the sides of this stupendous precipice, they were swallowed up with less noise than before. The final sound was sooner heard. We were approaching the bottom of the abyss!

As I had been very careful to keep account of all the changes of cord which took place, I was able to tell exactly what was the depth we had reached, as well as the time it had taken.

We had shifted the rope twenty-eight times, each operation taking a quarter of an hour, which in all made seven hours. To this had to be added twenty-eight pauses; in all ten hours and a half. We started at one; it was now, therefore, about eleven o'clock at night.

It does not require great knowledge of arithmetic to know that twenty-eight times two hundred feet make five thousand six hundred feet in all (more than an English mile).

While I was making this mental calculation a voice broke the silence. It was the voice of Hans.

"Halt!" he cried.

I checked myself very suddenly, just at the moment when I was about to kick my uncle on the head.

"We have reached the end of our journey," said the worthy Professor, in a satisfied air.

"What, the interior of the earth?" said I, slipping down to his side.

"No, you stupid fellow! but we have reached the bottom of the well."

"And I suppose there is no farther progress to be made?" I hopefully exclaimed.

"Oh, yes; I can dimly see a sort of tunnel, which turns off obliquely to the right. At all events, we must see about that tomorrow. Let us sup now, and seek slumber as best we may."

I thought it time, but made no observations on that point. I was fairly launched on a desperate course, and all I had to do was to go forward hopefully and trustingly.

It was not even now quite dark, the light filtering down in a most extraordinary manner.

We opened the provision bag, ate a frugal supper, and each did his best to find a bed amid the pile of stones, dirt, and lava, which had accumulated for ages at the bottom of the shaft.

I happened to grope out the pile of ropes, ladders, and clothes which we had thrown down; and upon them I stretched myself. After such a day's labor, my rough bed seemed as soft as down!

For a while I lay in a sort of pleasant trance.

Presently, after lying quietly for some minutes, I opened my eyes and looked upwards. As I did so I made out a brilliant little dot, at the extremity of this long, gigantic telescope.

It was a star without scintillating rays. According to my calculations, must be β in the constellation of the Little Bear.

After this little bit of astronomical recreation, I dropped into a sound sleep.

15 ... *We Continue Our Descent*

At eight o'clock the next morning, a faint kind of dawn of day awoke us. The thousand and one prisms of the lava collected the light as it passed, and brought it to us like a shower of sparks.

We were able with ease to see objects around us.

"Well, Harry, my boy," cried the delighted Professor, rubbing his hands together, "what say you now? Did you ever pass a more tranquil night in our house in the Königstrasse? No deafening sounds of cartwheels, no cries of hawkers, no bad language from boatmen or watermen!"

"Well, uncle, we are quiet at the bottom of this well; but to me there is something terrible in this calm."

"Why," said the Professor, hotly, "one would say you were already beginning to be afraid. How will you get on presently? Do you know that, as yet, we have not penetrated one inch into the bowels of the earth?"

"What can you mean, sir?" was my bewildered and astonished reply.

"I mean to say that we have only just reached the soil of the island itself. This long vertical tube, which ends at the bottom of the crater of Sneffels, ceases here just about on a level with the sea."

"Are you sure, sir?"

"Quite sure. Consult the barometer."

It was quite true that the mercury, after rising

gradually in the instrument, as long as our descent was taking place, had stopped precisely at twenty-nine degrees.

"You perceive," said the Professor, "we have as yet only to endure the pressure of air. I am curious to replace the barometer by the manometer."

The barometer, in fact, was about to become useless—as soon as the weight of the air was greater than what was calculated as above the level of the ocean.

"But," said I, "is it not very much to be feared that this ever-increasing pressure may in the end turn out very painful and inconvenient?"

"No," said he. "We shall descend very slowly, and our lungs will be gradually accustomed to breathe compressed air. It is well known that aeronauts have gone so high as to be nearly without air at all; why, then, should we not accustom ourselves to breathe when we have, say, a little too much of it? For myself, I am certain I shall prefer it. Let us not lose a moment. Where is the packet which preceded us in our descent?"

I smilingly pointed it out to my uncle. Hans had not seen it, and believed it caught somewhere above us: "huppe," as he phrased it.

"Now," said my uncle, "let us breakfast, and break fast like people who have a long day's work before them."

Biscuit and dried meat, washed down by some mouthfuls of water flavored with schiedam, was the material of our luxurious meal.

As soon as it was finished, my uncle took from his pocket a notebook destined to be filled by memoranda of our travels. He had already placed his instruments in order, and this was what he wrote:

Monday, July 1st.

Chronometer, 8h. 17m. morning.

Barometer, 29 degrees.

Thermometer, 43 degrees Fahrenheit.

Direction, E. S. E.

This last observation referred to the obscure gallery, and was indicated to us by the compass.

"Now, Harry," cried the Professor, in an enthusiastic tone of voice, "we are truly about to take our first step into the Interior of the Earth; never before visited by man since the first creation of the world. You may consider, therefore, that at this precise moment our travels really commence."

As my uncle made this remark, he took in one hand the Ruhmkorf coil apparatus, which hung round his neck, and with the other he put the electric current into communication with the worm of the lantern. And a bright light at once illumined that dark and gloomy tunnel!

The effect was magical!

Hans, who carried the second apparatus, had it also put into operation. This ingenious application of electricity to practical purposes enabled us to move along by the light of an artificial day, amid even the flow of the most imflammable and combustible gases.

"Forward!" cried my uncle. Each took up his burden. Hans went first, my uncle followed, and I going third, we entered the somber gallery!

Just as we were about to engulf ourselves in this dismal passage, I lifted up my head, and through the tubelike shaft saw that Iceland sky I was never to see again!

Was it the last I should ever see of any sky?

The stream of lava, flowing from the bowels of the earth in 1229, had forced itself a passage through the tunnel. It lined the whole of the inside with its thick and brilliant coating. The electric light added very greatly to the brilliancy of the effect.

The great difficulty of our journey now began. How were we to prevent ourselves from slipping down the steeply inclined plane? Happily some cracks, abrasures

103

of the soil, and other irregularities served the place of steps; and we descended slowly, allowing our heavy luggage to slip on before, at the end of a long cord.

But that which served as steps under our feet, became in other places stalactites. The lava, very porous in certain places, took the form of little round blisters. Crystals of opaque quartz, adorned with limpid drops of natural glass suspended to the roof like lustres, seemed to take fire as we passed beneath them. One would have fancied that the genii of romance were illuminating their underground palaces to receive the sons of men.

"Magnificent, glorious!" I cried, in a moment of involuntary enthusiasm. "What a spectacle, uncle! Do you not admire these variegated shades of lava, which run through a whole series of colors, from reddish brown to pale yellow—by the most insensible degrees? And these crystals—they appear like luminous globes."

"You are beginning to see the charms of travel, Master Harry," cried my uncle. "Wait a bit, until we advance farther. What we have as yet discovered is nothing—onward, my boy, onward!"

It would have been a far more correct and appropriate expression, had he said, "Let us slide," for we were going down an inclined plane with perfect ease. The compass indicated that we were moving in south-easterly direction. The flow of lava had never turned to the right or the left. It had the inflexibility of a straight line.

Nevertheless, to my surprise, we found no perceptible increase in heat. This proved the theories of Humphrey Davy to be founded on truth, and more than once I found myself examining the thermometer in silent astonishment.

Two hours after my departure it only marked 54 degrees Fahrenheit. I had every reason to believe from this that our descent was far more horizontal than

104

vertical. As for discovering the exact depth to which we had attained, nothing could be easier. The Professor, as he advanced, measured the angles of deviation and inclination; but he kept the result of his observations to himself.

About eight o'clock in the evening, my uncle gave the signal for halting. Hans seated himself on the ground. The lamps were hung to fissures in the lava rock. We were now in a large cavern where air was not wanting. On the contrary, it abounded. What could be the cause of this—to what atmospheric agitation could be ascribed this draught? But this was a question which I did not care to discuss just then. Fatigue and hunger made me incapable of reasoning. An unceasing march of seven hours had not been kept up without great exhaustion. I was really and truly worn out, and delighted enough I was to hear the word Halt.

Hans laid out some provisions on a lump of lava, and we each supped with keen relish. One thing, however, caused us great uneasiness—our water reserve was already half exhausted. My uncle had full confidence in finding subterranean resources, but hitherto we had completely failed in so doing. I could not help calling my uncle's attention to the circumstance.

"And you are surprised at this total absence of springs?" he said.

"Doubtless—I am very uneasy on the point. We have certainly not enough water to last us five days."

"Be quite easy on that matter," continued my uncle. "I answer for it we shall find plenty of water—in fact, far more than we shall want."

"But when?"

"When we once get through this crust of lava. How can you expect springs to force their way through these solid stone walls?"

"But what is there to prove that this concrete mass of lava does not extend to the center of the earth? I don't think we have as yet done much in a vertical way."

"What puts that into your head, my boy?" asked my uncle, mildly.

"Well, it appears to me that if we had descended very far below the level of the sea, we should find it rather hotter than we have."

"According to your system," said my uncle; "but what does the thermometer say?"

"Scarcely 15 degrees by Reaumur, which is only an increase of 9 since our departure."

"Well, and what conclusion does that bring you to?" inquired the Professor.

"The deduction I draw from this is very simple. According to the most exact observations, the augmentation of the temperature of the interior of the earth is 1 degree for every hundred feet. But certain local causes may considerably modify this figure. Thus at Yakoust in Siberia, it has been remarked that the heat increases a degree every thirty-six feet. The difference evidently depends on the conductibility of certain rocks. In the neighborhood of an extinct volcano, it has been remarked that the elevation of temperature was only 1 degree on every five-and-twenty feet. Let us, then, go upon this calculation—which is the most favorable—and calculate."

"Calculate away, my boy."

"Nothing easier," said I, pulling out my notebook and pencil. "Nine times one hundred and twenty-five feet make a depth of eleven hundred and twenty-five feet."

"Archimedes could not have spoken more geometrically."

"Well?"

"Well, according to my observations, we are at least ten thousand feet below the level of the sea."

"Can it be possible?"

"Either my calculation is correct, or there is no truth in figures."

The calculations of the Professor were perfectly correct. We were already six thousand feet deeper down in the bowels of the earth than any one had ever been before. The lowest known depth to which man had hitherto penetrated was in the mines of Kitz-Bahl, on the Tyrol, and those of Wuttemburg in Bohemia.

The temperature, which should have been eighty-one, was in this place only fifteen. That was a matter for serious consideration.

16 ... *The Eastern Tunnel*

THE NEXT DAY was Tuesday, the 2nd of July, and at six o'clock in the morning we resumed our journey.

We still continued to follow the gallery of lava, a perfect natural pathway, as easy of descent as some of those inclined planes which, in very old German houses, serve the purpose of staircases. This went on until seventeen minutes past twelve, the precise instant at which we rejoined Hans, who having been somewhat in advance, had suddenly stopped.

"At last," cried my uncle, "we have reached the end of the shaft."

I looked wonderingly about me. We were in the center of four cross paths—somber and narrow tunnels. The question now arose as to which it was wise to take; and this of itself was no small difficulty.

My uncle, who did not wish to appear to have any hesitation about the matter before myself or the guide, at once made up his mind. He pointed quietly to the eastern tunnel; and, without delay, we entered within its gloomy recesses.

Besides, had he entertained any feeling of hesitation, it might have been prolonged indefinitely, for there was no indication by which to determine on a choice. It was absolutely necessary to trust to chance and good fortune!

The descent of this obscure and narrow gallery was very gradual and winding. Sometimes we gazed through a succession of arches, its course very like the aisles of a Gothic cathedral. The great artistic sculptors and builders of the Middle Ages might have here completed their studies with advantage. Many most beautiful and suggestive ideas of architectural beauty would have been discovered by them. After passing through this phase of the cavernous way, we suddenly came, about a mile farther on, upon a square system of arch, adopted by the early Romans, projecting from the solid rock, and keeping up the weight of the roof.

Suddenly we would come upon a series of low subterranean tunnels which looked like beaver holes, or the work of foxes, through whose narrow and winding ways we had literally to crawl!

The heat still remained at quite a supportable degree. With an involuntary shudder, I reflected on what the heat must have been when the volcano of Sneffels was pouring its smoke, flames, and streams of boiling lava—all of which must have come up by the road we were now following. I could imagine the torrents of hot seething stone darting on, bubbling up with accompaniments of smoke, steam, and sulphurous stench!

"Only to think of the consequences," I mused, "if the old volcano were once more to set to work."

I did not communicate these rather unpleasant reflections to my uncle. He not only would not have understood them, but would have been intensely disgusted. His only idea was to go ahead. He walked, he slid, he clambered over piles of fragments, he rolled down heaps of broken lava, with an earnestness and conviction it was impossible not to admire.

At six o'clock in the evening, after a very wearisome journey, but one not so fatiguing as before, we had made six miles toward the southward, but had not gone more than a mile downwards.

My uncle, as usual, gave the signal to halt. We ate

our meal in thoughtful silence, and then retired to sleep.

Our arrangements for the night were very primitive and simple. A travelling rug, in which each rolled himself, was all our bedding. We had no necessity to fear cold or any unpleasant visit. Travellers who bury themselves in the wild and depths of the African desert, who seek profit and pleasure in the forests of the New World, are compelled to take it in turn to watch during the hours of sleep; but in this region of the earth absolute solitude and complete security reigned supreme.

We had nothing to fear either from savages or from wild beasts.

After a night's sweet repose, we awoke fresh and ready for action. There being nothing to detain us, we started on our journey. We continued to burrow through the lava tunnel as before. It was impossible to make out through what soil we were making way. The tunnel, moreover, instead of going down into the bowels of the earth, became absolutely horizontal.

I even thought, after some examination, that we were actually tending upwards. About ten o'clock in the day this state of things became so clear, that finding the change very fatiguing I was obliged to slacken my pace and finally to come to a halt.

"Well," said the Professor, quickly, "what is the matter?"

"The fact is, I am dreadfully tired," was my earnest reply.

"What," cried my uncle, "tired after a three hours' walk, and by so easy a road?"

"Easy enough, I dare say, but very fatiguing."

"But how can that be, when all we have to do is to go downwards?"

"I beg your pardon, sir. For some time I have noticed that we are going upwards."

110

"Upwards!" cried my uncle, shrugging his shoulders; "how can that be?"

"There can be no doubt about it. For the last half hour the slopes have been upward; and if we go on in this way much longer we shall find ourselves back in Iceland."

My uncle shook his head with the air of a man who does not want to be convinced. I tried to continue the conversation. He would not answer me, but once more gave the signal for departure. His silence, I thought, was only caused by concentrated ill temper.

However this might be, I once more took up my load, and boldly and resolutely followed Hans, who was now in advance of my uncle. I did not like to be beaten, or even distanced. I was naturally anxious not to lose sight of my companions. The very idea of being left behind, lost in that terrible labyrinth, made me shiver as with the ague.

Besides, if the ascending path was more arduous and painful to clamber, I had one source of secret consolation and delight. It was to all appearance taking us back to the surface of the earth. That of itself was hopeful. Every step I took confirmed me in my belief, and I began already to build castles in the air in relation to my marriage with my pretty little cousin.

About twelve o'clock there was a great and sudden change in the aspect of the rocky sides of the gallery. I first noticed it from the diminution of the rays of light which cast back the reflection of the lamp. From being coated with shining and resplendent lava, it became living rock. The sides were sloping walls, which sometimes became quite vertical.

We were now in what the geological professors call a state of transition, in the period of Silurian stones, so called because this specimen of early formation is very common in England in the counties formerly inhabited by the Celtic nation known as Silures.

111

"I can see clearly now," I cried. "The sediment from the waters which once covered the whole earth, formed during the second period of its existence these schists and these calcareous rocks. We are turning our backs on the granitic rocks, and are like people from Hamburg who would go to Lübeck by way of Hanover."

I might just as well have kept my observations to myself. My geological enthusiasm got the better, however, of my cooler judgment, and Professor Hardwigg heard my observations.

"What is the matter now?" he said, in a tone of great gravity.

"Well," cried I, "do you not see these different layers of calcareous rocks, and the first indication of slate strata?"

"Well; what then?"

"We have arrived at that period of the world's existence when the first plants and the first animals made their appearance."

"You think so?"

"Yes, look; examine and judge for yourself."

I induced the Professor with some difficulty to cast the light of his lamp on the sides of the long winding gallery. I expected some exclamation to burst from his lips. I was very much mistaken. The worthy Professor never spoke a word.

It was impossible to say whether he understood me or not. Perhaps it was possible that in his pride—my uncle, and a learned Professor—he did not like to own that he was wrong in having chosen the eastern tunnel; or was he determined at any price to go to the end of it? It was quite evident we had left the region of lava, and that the road by which we were going could not take us back to the great crater of Mount Sneffels.

As we went along, I could not help ruminating on the whole question, and asked myself if I did not lay too great a stress on these sudden and peculiar modifications of the earth's crust.

After all, I was very likely to be mistaken; and it was within the range of probability and possibility that we were not making our way through the strata of rocks which I believed I recognized piled on the lower layer of granitic formation.

"At all events, if I am right," I thought to myself, "I must certainly find some remains of primitive plants, and it will be absolutely necessary to give way to such indubitable evidence. Let us have a good search."

I accordingly lost no opportunity of searching, and had not gone more than about a hundred yards, when the evidence I sought for cropped up in the most incontestable manner before my eyes. It was quite natural that I should expect to find these signs, for, during the Silurian period, the seas contained no fewer than fifteen hundred different animal and vegetable species. My feet, so long accustomed to the hard and arid lava soil, suddenly found themselves treading on a kind of soft dust, the remains of plants and shells.

Upon the walls themselves I could clearly make out the outline, as plain as a sun picture, of the fucus and the lycopodes. The worthy and excellent Professor Hardwigg could not of course make any mistake about the matter; but I believe he deliberately closed his eyes, and continued on his way with a firm and unalterable step.

I began to think that he was carrying his obstinacy a great deal too far. I could no longer act with prudence or composure. I stooped on a sudden and picked up an almost perfect shell, which had undoubtedly belonged to some animal very much resembling some of the present day. Having secured the prize, I followed in the wake of my uncle.

"Do you see this?" I said.

"Well," said the Professor, with the most imperturb-

113

able tranquillity, "it is the shell of a crustaceous animal of the extinct order of the trilobites; nothing more, I assure you."

"But," cried I, much troubled at his coolness, "do you draw no conclusion from it?"

"Well, if I may ask, what conclusion do you draw from it yourself?"

"Well, I thought—"

"I know, my boy, what you would say; and you are right, perfectly and incontestably right. We have finally abandoned the crust of lava, and the road by which the lava ascended. It is quite possible that I may have been mistaken, but I shall be unable to discover my error until I get to the end of this gallery."

"You are quite right as far as that is concerned," I replied, "and I should highly approve of your decision, if we had not to fear the greatest of all dangers."

"And what is that?"

"Want of water."

"Well, my dear Harry, it can't be helped. We must put ourselves on rations."

And on he went.

17 ... *Deeper and Deeper* *—The Coal Mine*

IN TRUTH, we were compelled to put ourselves upon rations. Our supply would certainly last not more than three days. I found this out about suppertime. The worst part of the matter was, that in what is called the transition rocks, it was hardly to be expected we should meet with water!

I had read of the horrors of thirst, and I knew that, where we were, a brief trial of its sufferings would put an end to our adventures—and our lives! But it was utterly useless to discuss the matter with my uncle. He would have answered by some axiom from Plato.

During the whole of the next day we proceeded on our journey through this interminable gallery, arch after arch, tunnel after tunnel. We journeyed without exchanging a word. We had become as mute and reticent as Hans, our guide.

The road had no longer an upward tendency; at all events, if it had, it was not to be made out very clearly. Sometimes there could be no doubt that we were going downwards. But this inclination was scarcely to be distinguished, and was by no means reassuring to the Professor, because the character of the strata was in no wise modified, and the transition character of the rocks became more and more marked.

It was a glorious sight to see how the electric light brought out the sparkles in the walls of the calcareous rocks and the old red sandstone. One might have fancied oneself in one of those deep cuttings in Devonshire, which have given their name to this kind of soil. Some magnificent specimens of marble projected from the sides of the gallery; some of an agate gray with white veins of variegated character, others of a yellow spotted color, with red veins; farther off might be seen samples of color in which cherry-tinted seams were to be found in all their brightest shades.

The greater number of these marbles were stamped with the marks of primitive animals. Since the previous evening, nature and creation had made considerable progress. Instead of the rudimentary trilobites, I perceived the remains of a more perfect order. Among others, the fish in which the eye of a geologist has been able to discover the first form of the reptile.

The Devonian seas were inhabited by a vast number of animals of this species, which were deposited in tens of thousands in the rocks of new formation.

It was quite evident to me that we were ascending the scale of animal life, of which man forms the summit. My excellent uncle, the Professor, appeared not to take notice of these warnings. He was determined at any risk to proceed.

He must have been in expectation of one of two things: either that a vertical well was about to open under his feet, and thus allow him to continue his descent, or that some insurmountable obstacle would compel us to stop and go back by the road we had so long travelled. But evening came again, and, to my horror, neither hope was doomed to be realized!

On Friday, after a night when I began to feel the gnawing agony of thirst, and when in consequence appetite decreased, our little band rose and once more followed the turnings and windings, the ascents and descents, of this interminable gallery. All were silent and gloomy. I could see that even my uncle had ventured too far.

After about ten hours of further progress—a progress dull and monotonous to the last degree—I remarked that the reverberation, and reflection of our lamps upon the sides of the tunnel, had singularly diminished. The marble, the schist, the calcareous rocks, the red sandstone, had disappeared, leaving in their places a dark and gloomy wall, somber and without brightness. When we reached a remarkably narrow part of the tunnel, I leaned my left hand against the rock.

When I took my hand away, and happened to glance at it, it was quite black. We had reached the coal strata of the central earth.

"A coal mine!" I cried.

"A coal mine without miners," responded my uncle, a little severely.

"How can we tell?"

"I can tell," replied my uncle, in a sharp and dictatorial tone. "I am perfectly certain that this gallery through successive layers of coal was not cut by the hand of man. But whether it is the work of nature or not, is of little concern to us. The hour for our evening meal has come—let us sup."

Hans, the guide, occupied himself in preparing food. I had come to that point when I could no longer eat. All I cared about were the few drops of water which fell to my share. What I suffered it is useless to record. The guide's gourd, not quite half full, was all that was left for us three!

Having finished their repast, my two companions laid themselves down upon their rugs, and found in sleep a remedy for their fatigue and sufferings. As for me, I could not sleep; I lay counting the hours until morning.

The next morning, Saturday, at six o'clock, we started again. Twenty minutes later we suddenly came upon a vast excavation. From its mighty extent I saw at once that the hand of man could have had nothing to do with this coal mine; the vault above would have

117

fallen in; as it was, it was only held together by some miracle of nature.

This mighty natural cavern was about a hundred feet wide by about a hundred and fifty high. The earth had evidently been cast apart by some violent subterranean commotion. The mass, giving way to some prodigious upheaving of nature, had split in two, leaving the vast gap into which we inhabitants of the earth had penetrated for the first time.

The whole singular history of the coal period was written on those dark and gloomy walls. A geologist would have been able easily to follow the different phases of its formation. The seams of coal were separated by strata of sandstone, a compact clay, which appeared to be crushed down by the weight from above.

. At that period of the world which preceded the secondary epoch, the earth was covered by a coating of enormous and rich vegetation, due to the double action of tropical heat and perpetual humidity. A vast atmospheric cloud of vapor surrounded the earth on all sides, preventing the rays of the sun from ever reaching it.

Hence the conclusion that these intense heats did not arise from this new source of caloric.

Perhaps even the star of day was not quite ready for its brilliant work—to illumine a universe. Climates did not as yet exist, and a level heat pervaded the whole surface of the globe, the same heat existing at the north pole as at the equator.

Whence did it come? From the interior of the earth?

In spite of all the learned theories of Professor Hardwigg, a fierce and vehement fire certainly burned within the entrails of the great spheroid. Its action was felt even to the very topmost crust of the earth; the plants then in existence, being deprived of the vivifying rays of the sun, had neither buds, nor flowers, nor odor, but their roots drew a strong and vigorous life from the burning earth of early days.

There were but few of what may be called trees—only herbaceous plants, immense turfs, biers, mosses, rare families, which, however, in those days were counted by tens of thousands.

It is entirely to this exuberant vegetation that coal owes its origin. The crust of the vast globe still yielded under the influence of the seething, boiling mass, which was forever at work beneath. Hence arose numerous fissures, and continual falling in of the upper earth. The dense mass of plants being beneath the waters, soon formed themselves into vast agglomerations.

Then came about the action of natural chemistry; in the depths of the ocean the vegetable mass at first became turf, then, thanks to the influence of gases and subterranean fermentation, they underwent the complete process of mineralization.

In this manner, in early days, were formed those vast and prodigious layers of coal, which an ever-increasing consumption must utterly use up in about three centuries more, if people do not find some more economic light than gas, and some cheaper motive power than steam.

All these reflections, the memories of my school studies, came to my mind while I gazed upon these mighty accumulations of coal, whose riches, however, are scarcely likely to be ever utilized. The working of these mines could only be carried out at an expense that would never yield a profit.

The matter, however, is scarcely worthy consideration, when coal is scattered over the whole surface of the globe, within a few yards of the upper crust. As I looked at these untouched strata, therefore, I knew they would remain as long as the world lasts.

While we still continued our journey, I alone forgot

the length of the road, by giving myself up wholly to these geological considerations. The temperature continued to be very much the same as while we were travelling amid the lava and the schists. On the other hand, my sense of smell was much affected by a very powerful odor. I immediately knew that the gallery was filled to overflowing with that dangerous gas the miners call firedamp, the explosion of which has caused such fearful and terrible accidents, making a hundred widows and hundreds of orphans in a single hour.

Happily, we were able to illume our progress by means of the Ruhmkorf apparatus. If we had been so rash and imprudent as to explore this gallery, torch in hand, a terrible explosion would have put an end to our travels, simply because no travellers would be left.

Our excursion through this wondrous coal mine in the very bowels of the earth lasted until evening. My uncle was scarcely able to conceal his impatience and dissatisfaction at the road continuing still to advance in a horizontal direction.

The darkness, dense and opaque, a few yards in advance and in the rear, rendered it impossible to make out what was the length of the gallery. For myself, I began to believe that it was simply interminable, and would go on in the same manner for months.

Suddenly, at six o'clock, we stood in front of a wall. To the right, to the left, above, below, nowhere was there any passage. We had reached a spot where the rocks said in unmistakable accents—No Thoroughfare.

I stood stupefied. The guide simply folded his arms. My uncle was silent.

"Well, well, so much the better," cried my uncle, at last; "I now know what we are about. We are decidedly not upon the road followed by Saknussemm. All we have to do is to go back. Let us take one night's good rest, and before three days are over, I promise you we shall have regained the point where the galleries divided."

"Yes, we may, if our strength lasts as long," I cried, in a lamentable voice.

"And why not?"

"Tomorrow, among us three, there will not be a drop of water. It is just gone."

"And your courage with it," said my uncle, speaking in a severe tone.

What could I say? I turned round on my side, and from sheer exhaustion fell into a heavy but troubled sleep. Dreams of water! And I awoke unrefreshed.

I would have bartered a diamond mine for a glass of pure spring water.

18 ... *The Wrong Road!*

NEXT DAY, our departure took place at a very early hour. There was no time for the least delay. According to my account, we had five days' hard work to get back to the place where the galleries divided.

I can never tell all the sufferings we endured upon our return. My uncle bore them like a man who has been in the wrong—that is, with concentrated and suppressed anger; Hans, with all the resignation of his pacific character; and I—I confess that I did nothing but complain and despair. I had no heart for this bad fortune.

But there was one consolation. Defeat at the outset would probably upset the whole journey!

As I had expected from the first, our supply of water gave completely out on our first day's march. Our provision of liquids was reduced to our supply of schiedam; but this horrible—nay, I will say it—this infernal liquor, burnt the throat, and I could not even bear the sight of it. I found the temperature to be stifling. I was paralyzed with fatigue. More than once I was about to fall insensible to the ground. The whole party then halted, and the worthy Icelander and my excellent uncle did their best to console and comfort me. I could, however, plainly see that my uncle was contending painfully against the extreme fatigues of our journey, and the awful torture generated by the absence of water.

At length a time came when I ceased to recollect

anything—when all was one awful, hideous, fantastic dream!

At last, on Tuesday, the ninth of the month of July, after crawling on our hands and knees for many hours, more dead than alive, we reached the point of junction between the galleries. I lay like a log, an inert mass of human flesh on the arid lava soil. It was then ten in the morning.

Hans and my uncle, leaning against the wall, tried to nibble away at some pieces of biscuit, while deep groans and sighs escaped from my scorched and swollen lips. Then I fell off into a kind of deep lethargy.

Presently, I felt my uncle approach and lift me up tenderly in his arms.

"Poor boy," I heard him say, in a tone of deep commiseration.

I was profoundly touched by these words, being by no means accustomed to signs of womanly weakness in the Professor. I caught his trembling hands in mine and gave them a gentle pressure. He allowed me to do so without resistance, looking at me kindly all the time. His eyes were wet with tears.

I then saw him take the gourd which he wore at his side. To my surprise, or rather to my stupefaction, he placed it to my lips.

"Drink, my boy," he said.

Was it possible my ears had not deceived me? Was my uncle mad? I looked at him with, I am sure, quite an idiotic expression. I would not understand him. I too much feared the counteraction of disappointment.

"Drink," he said again.

Had I heard aright? Before, however, I could ask myself the question a second time, a mouthful of water cooled my parched lips and throat—one mouthful, but I do believe it brought me back to life.

I thanked my uncle by clasping my hands. My heart was too full to speak.

123

"Yes," said he, "one mouthful of water, the very last—do you hear, my boy?—the very last! I have taken care of it at the bottom of my bottle as the apple of my eye. Twenty times, a hundred times, I have resisted the fearful desire to drink it. But—no—no, Harry, I saved it for you"

"My dear uncle," I exclaimed, and the big tears rolled down my hot and feverish cheeks.

"Yes, my poor boy, I knew that when you reached this place, this crossroad in the earth, you would fall down half dead, and I saved my last drop of water in order to restore you."

"Thanks," I cried; "thanks from my heart."

As little as my thirst was really quenched, I had nevertheless partially recovered my strength. The contracted muscles of my throat relaxed—and the inflammation of my lips in some measure subsided. At all events, I was able to speak.

"Well," I said, "there can be no doubt now as to what we have to do. Water has utterly failed us; our journey is therefore at an end. Let us return."

While I spoke thus, my uncle evidently avoided my face: he held down his head; his eyes were turned in every possible direction but the right one.

"Yes," I continued, getting excited by my own words, "we must go back to Sneffels. May Heaven give us strength to enable us once more to revisit the light of day. Would that we now stood on the summit of the crater."

"Go back," said my uncle, speaking to himself—"and must it be so?"

"Go back, yes, and without losing a single moment," I vehemently cried.

For some moments there was silence under that dark and gloomy vault.

"So, my dear Harry," said the Professor, in a very

singular tone of voice, "those few drops of water have not sufficed to restore your energy and courage."

"Courage!" I cried.

"I see that you are quite as downcast as before, and still give way to discouragement and despair."

What, then, was the man made of, and what other projects were entering his fertile and audacious brain?

"You are not discouraged, sir!"

"What! give up just as we are on the verge of success?" he cried. "Never, never shall it be said that Professor Hardwigg retreated."

"Then we must make up our minds to perish," I cried, with a helpless sigh.

"No, Harry, my boy; certainly not. Go, leave me; I am very far from desiring your death. Take Hans with you. *I will go on alone.*"

"You ask us to leave you?"

"Leave me, I say. I have undertaken this dangerous and perilous adventure. I will carry it to the end, or I will never return to the surface of Mother Earth. Go, Harry! Once more I say to you—go!"

My uncle, as he spoke, was terribly excited. His voice, which before had been tender, almost womanly, became harsh and menacing. He appeared to be struggling with desperate energy against the impossible. I did not wish to abandon him at the bottom of that abyss, while, on the other hand, the instinct of preservation told me to fly.

Meanwhile, our guide was looking on with profound calmness and indifference. He appeared to be an unconcerned party, and yet he perfectly well knew what was going on between us. Our gestures sufficiently indicated the different roads each wished to follow, and which each tried to influence the other to undertake. But Hans appeared not to take the slightest interest in what was really a question of life and death for us all, but waited quite ready to obey the signal

125

which should say go aloft, or to resume his desperate journey into the interior of the earth.

How then I wished with all my heart and soul that I could make him understand my words. My representations, my sighs and groans, the earnest accents in which I should have spoken, would have convinced that cold, hard nature. Those fearful dangers and perils of which the stolid guide had no idea, I would have pointed them out to him; I would have, as it were, made him see and feel. Between us, we might have convinced the obstinate Professor. If the worst had come to the worst, we could have compelled him to return to the summit of Sneffels.

I quietly approached Hans. I caught his hand in mine. He never moved a muscle. I indicated to him the road to the top of the crater. He remained motionless. My panting form, my haggard countenance, must have indicated the extent of my sufferings. The Icelander gently shook his head and pointed to my uncle.

"*Master*," he said.

The word is Icelandic as well as English.

"The master!" I cried, beside myself with fury. "*Madman!* no—I tell you he is not the master of our lives. We must fly; we must drag him with us! Do you hear me? Do you understand me, I say?"

I have already explained that I held Hans by the arm. I tried to make him rise from his seat. I struggled with him and tried to force him away. My uncle now interposed.

"My good Henry, be calm," he said. "You will obtain nothing from my devoted follower; therefore, listen to what I have to say."

I folded my arms, as well as I could, and looked my uncle full in the face.

"This wretched want of water," he said, "is the sole obstacle to the success of my project. In the entire gallery, composed of lava, schist, and coal, it is true we found not one liquid molecule. It is quite possible that we may be more fortunate in the western tunnel."

My sole reply was to shake my head with an air of incredulity.

"Listen to me to the end," said the Professor, in his well-known lecturing voice. "While you lay yonder, without life or motion, I undertook a reconnoitering journey into the conformation of this other gallery. I have discovered that it goes directly downwards into the bowels of the earth, and in a few hours will take us to the old granitic formation. In this we shall undoubtedly find innumerable springs. The nature of the rock makes this a mathematical certainty, and instinct agrees with logic to say that it is so. Now this is the serious proposition which I have to make to you. When Christopher Columbus asked of his men three days to discover the land of promise, his men, ill, terrified, and hopeless, yet gave him three days—and the New World was discovered. Now I, the Christopher Columbus of this subterranean region, only ask of you one more day. If, when that time is expired, I have not found the water of which we are in search, I swear to you, I will give up my mighty enterprise and return to the earth's surface."

Despite my irritation and despair, I knew how much it cost my uncle to make this proposition, and to hold such conciliatory language. Under the circumstances, what could I do but yield?

"Well," I cried, "let it be as you wish, and may Heaven reward your superhuman energy. But as, unless we discover water, our hours are numbered, let us lose no time, but go ahead."

19 ... *The Western Gallery —A New Route*

OUR DESCENT was now resumed by means of the second gallery. Hans took up his post in front, as usual. We had not gone more than a hundred yards when the Professor carefully examined the walls.

"This is the primitive formation; we are on the right road; onwards is our hope!"

When the whole earth got cool in the first hours of the world's morning, the diminution of the volume of the earth produced a state of dislocation in its upper crust, followed by ruptures, crevasses and fissures. The passage was a fissure of this kind, through which, ages ago, had flowed the eruptive granite. The thousand windings and turnings formed an inextricable labyrinth through the ancient soil.

As we descended, successions of layers composing the primitive soil appeared with the utmost fidelity of detail. Geological science considers this primitive soil as the base of the mineral crust, and it has recognized that it is composed of three different strata or layers, all resting on the immovable rock known as granite.

No mineralogists had ever found themselves placed in such a marvellous position to study nature in all her real and naked beauty. The sounding rod, a mere machine, could not bring to the surface of the earth the objects of value for the study of its internal structure, which we were about to see with our own eyes, to touch with our own hands.

Remember that I am writing this *after* the journey. Across the streak of the rocks, colored by beautiful green tints, wound metallic threads of copper, of manganese, with traces of platinum and gold. I could not help gazing at these riches buried in the entrails of Mother Earth, and of which no man would have the enjoyment to the end of time! These treasures, mighty and inexhaustible, were buried in the morning of the earth's history, at such awful depths that no crowbar or pickaxe will ever drag them from their tomb!

The light of our Ruhmkorf's coil, increased tenfold by the myriad of prismatic masses of rock, sent their jets of fire in every direction, and I could fancy myself travelling through a huge hollow diamond, the rays of which produced myriads of extraordinary effects.

Toward six o'clock, this festival of light began sensibly and visibly to decrease, and soon almost ceased. The sides of the gallery assumed a crystallized tint, with a somber hue; white mica began to commingle more freely with feldspar and quartz, to form what may be called the true rock—the stone which is hard above all, that supports, without being crushed, the four stories of the earth's soil.

We were walled by an immense prison of granite!

It was now eight o'clock, and still there was no sign of water. The sufferings I endured were horrible. My uncle now kept at the head of our little column. Nothing could induce him to stop. I, meanwhile, had but one real thought. My ear was keenly on the watch to catch the sound of a spring. But no pleasant sound of falling water fell upon my listening ear.

But at last the time came when my limbs refused to longer carry me. I contended heroically against the terrible tortures I endured, because I did not wish to compel my uncle to halt. To him I knew this would be the last fatal stroke.

Suddenly I felt a deadly faintness come over me. My eyes could no longer see; my knees shook. I gave one despairing cry—and fell!

"Help, help, I am dying!"

My uncle turned and slowly retraced his steps. He looked at me with folded arms, and then allowed one sentence to escape, in hollow accents, from his lips—

"All is over."

The last thing I saw was a face fearfully distorted with pain and sorrow; and then my eyes closed.

When I again opened them, I saw my companions lying near me, motionless, wrapped in their huge travelling rugs. Were they asleep or dead? For myself, sleep was wholly out of the question. My fainting fit over, I was wakeful as the lark. I suffered too much for sleep to visit my eyelids—the more, that I thought myself sick unto death—dying. The last words spoken by my uncle seemed to be buzzing in my ears—*all is over!* And it was probable that he was right. In the state of prostration to which I was reduced, it was madness to think of ever again seeing the light of day.

Above were miles upon miles of the earth's crust. As I thought of it, I could fancy the whole weight resting on my shoulders. I was crushed, annihilated! and exhausted myself in vain attempts to turn in my granite bed.

Hours upon hours passed away. A profound and terrible silence reigned around us—a silence of the tomb. Nothing could make itself heard through these gigantic walls of granite. The very thought was stupendous.

Presently, despite my apathy, despite the kind of deadly calm into which I was cast, something aroused me. It was a slight but peculiar noise. While I was watching intently, I observed that the tunnel was becoming dark. Then gazing through the dim light that remained, I thought I saw the Icelander taking his departure, lamp in hand.

Why had he acted thus? Did Hans the guide mean to abandon us? My uncle lay fast asleep—or dead. I tried to cry out, and arouse him. My voice, feebly issuing from my parched and fevered lips, found no echo in that fearful place. My throat was dry, my tongue stuck to the roof of my mouth. The obscurity had by this time become intense, and at last even the faint sound of the guide's footsteps was lost in the blank distance. My soul seemed filled with anguish, and death appeared welcome, only let it come quickly.

"Hans is leaving us," I cried. "Hans, Hans, if you are a man, come back."

These words were spoken to myself. They could not be heard aloud. Nevertheless, after the first few moments of terror were over, I was ashamed of my suspicions against a man who hitherto had behaved so admirably. Nothing in his conduct or character justified suspicion. Moreover, a moment's reflection reassured me. His departure could not be a flight. Instead of ascending the gallery, he was going deeper down into the gulf. Had he had any bad design, his way would have been upwards.

This reasoning calmed me a little, and I began to hope!

The good and peaceful and imperturbable Hans would certainly not have arisen from his sleep without some serious and grave motive. Was he bent on a voyage of discovery? During the deep, still silence of the night had he at last heard that sweet murmur about which we were all so anxious?

20 ... *Water, Where Is It?*
A Bitter Disappointment

During a long, long, weary hour, there crossed my wildly delirious brain all sorts of reasons as to what could have aroused our quiet and faithful guide. The most absurd and ridiculous ideas passed through my head, each more impossible than the other. I believe I was either half or wholly mad.

Suddenly, however, there arose, as it were from the depths of the earth, a voice of comfort. It was the sound of footsteps! Hans was returning.

Presently the uncertain light began to shine upon the walls of the passage, and then it came in view far down the sloping tunnel. At length Hans himself appeared.

He approached my uncle, placed his hand upon his shoulder, and gently awakened him. My uncle, as soon as he saw who it was, instantly rose.

"Well!" exclaimed the Professor.

"*Vatten*," said the hunter.

I did not know a single word of the Danish language, and yet by a sort of mysterious instinct I understood what the guide had said.

"Water, water!" I cried, in a wild and frantic tone, clapping my hands, and gesticulating like a madman.

"Water!" murmured my uncle, in a voice of deep emotion and gratitude. "*Hvar?*" (where.)

"*Nedat.*" (below.)

"Where? below!" I understood every word. I had

132

caught the hunter by the hands, and I shook them heartily, while he looked on with perfect calmness.

The preparations for our departure did not take long, and we were soon making a rapid descent into the tunnel.

An hour later we had advanced a thousand yards, and descended two thousand feet.

At this moment I heard an accustomed and well-known sound running along the floors of the granite rock—a kind of dull and sullen roar, like that of a distant waterfall.

During the first half hour of our advance, not finding the discovered spring, my feelings of intense suffering appeared to return. Once more I began to lose all hope. My uncle, however, observing how downhearted I was again becoming, took up the conversation.

"Hans was right," he exclaimed, enthusiastically; "that is the dull roar of a torrent."

"A torrent," I cried, delighted at even hearing the welcome words.

"There's not the slightest doubt about it," he replied: "a subterranean river is flowing beside us."

I made no reply, but hastened on, once more animated by hope. I began not even to feel the deep fatigue which hitherto had overpowered me. The very sound of this glorious murmuring water already refreshed me. We could hear it increasing in volume every moment. The torrent, which for a long time could be heard flowing over our heads, now ran distinctly along the left wall, roaring, rushing, spluttering, and still falling.

Several times I passed my hand across the rock, hoping to find some trace of humidity—of the slightest percolation. Alas! in vain.

Again a half hour passed in the same weary toil. Again we advanced.

It now became evident that the hunter, during his

absence, had not been able to carry his researches any farther. Guided by an instinct peculiar to the dwellers in mountain regions and water finders, he "smelt" the living spring through the rock. Still he had not seen the precious liquid. He had neither quenched his own thirst, nor brought us one drop in his gourd.

Moreover, we soon made the disastrous discovery, that if our progress continued, we should soon be moving away from the torrent, the sound of which gradually diminished. We turned back. Hans halted at the precise spot where the sound of the torrent appeared nearest.

I could bear the suspense and suffering no longer, and seated myself against the wall, behind which I could hear the water seething and effervescing not two feet away. But a solid wall of granite still separated us from it!

Hans looked keenly at me, and, strange enough, for once I thought I saw a smile on his imperturbable face.

He rose from a stone on which he had been seated, and took up the lamp. I could not help rising and following. He moved slowly along the firm and solid granite wall. I watched him with mingled curiosity and eagerness. Presently he halted and placed his ear against the dry stone, moving slowly along and listening with the most extreme care and attention. I understood at once that he was searching for the exact spot where the torrent's roar was most plainly heard. This point he soon found in the lateral wall on the left side, about three feet above the level of the tunnel floor.

I was in a state of intense excitement. I scarcely dared believe what the eider-duck hunter was about to do. It was, however, impossible for a moment more not to both understand and applaud, and even to smother him in my embraces, when I saw him raise the heavy crowbar and commence an attack upon the rock itself.

"Saved," I cried.

"Yes," cried my uncle, even more excited and delighted than myself; "Hans is quite right. Oh, the worthy, excellent man! We should never have thought of such an idea."

And nobody else, I think, would have done so. Such a process, simple as it seemed, would most certainly not have entered our heads. Nothing could be more dangerous than to begin to work with pickaxes in that particular part of the globe. Supposing while he was at work a break-up were to take place, and supposing the torrent once having gained an inch were to take an ell, and come pouring bodily through the broken rock!

Not one of these dangers were chimerical. They were only too real. But at that moment no fear of falling in of roof, or even of inundation, was capable of stopping us. Our thirst was so intense that to quench it we would have dug below the bed of old ocean itself.

Hans went quietly to work, a work which neither my uncle nor I would have undertaken at any price. Our impatience was so great that if he had once begun with pickaxe and crowbar, the rock would soon have split into a hundred fragments. The guide, on the contrary, calm, ready, moderate, wore away the hard rock by little steady blows of his instrument, making no attempt at a larger hole than about six inches. As I stood, I heard, or I thought I heard, the roar of the torrent momentarily increasing in loudness, and at times I almost felt the pleasant sensation of water upon my parched lips.

At the end of what appeared an age, Hans had made a hole which enabled his crowbar to enter two feet into the solid rock. He had been at work exactly an hour. It appeared a dozen. I was getting wild with impatience. My uncle began to think of using more violent measures. I had the greatest difficulty in checking him. He had indeed just got hold of his crowbar when a loud and welcome hiss was heard. Then a stream, or rather jet, of water burst through the wall and came out with such force as to hit the opposite side!

Hans, the guide, who was half upset by the shock, was scarcely able to keep down a cry of pain and grief. I understood his meaning when plunging my hands into the sparkling jet I myself gave a wild and frantic cry. The water was scalding hot!

"Boiling," I cried, in bitter disappointment.

"Well, never mind," said my uncle; "it will soon get cool."

The tunnel began to be filled by clouds of vapor, while a small stream ran way into the interior of the earth. In a short time we had some sufficiently cool to drink. We swallowed it in huge mouthfuls.

Oh, what exalted delight, which rich and incomparable luxury! What was this water? whence did it come? To us what was that? The simple fact was, it was water; and, though still with a tinge of warmth about it, it brought back to the heart that life which, but for it, must surely have faded away. I drank greedily, almost without tasting it.

When, however, I had almost quenched my ravenous thirst, I made a discovery.

"Why it is ferruginous water."

"Most excellent stomachic," replied my uncle, "and highly mineralized. Here is a journey worth twenty to Spa."

"It's very good," I replied.

"I should think so. Water found six miles under ground. There is a peculiarly inky flavor about it, which is by no means disagreeable. Hans may congratulate himself on having made a rare discovery. What do you say, nephew, according to the usual custom of travellers, to naming the stream after him?"

"Good," said I.

And the name of "Hans-bach" was at once agreed upon.

Hans was not a bit more proud after hearing our determination than he was before. After having taken a very small modicum of the welcome refreshment, he had seated himself in a corner with his usual imperturbable gravity.

"Now," said I, "it is not worth while letting this water run to waste."

"What is the use?" replied my uncle; "the source from which this river rises is inexhaustible."

"Never mind," I continued; "let us fill our goatskin and gourds, and then try to stop the opening up."

My advice, after some hesitation, was followed, or attempted to be followed. Hans picked up all the broken pieces of granite he had knocked out, and using some tow he happened to have about him, tried to shut up the fissure he had made in the wall. All he did was to scald his hands. The pressure was too great, and all our attempts were utter failures.

"It is evident," I remarked, "that the upper surface of these springs is situated at a very great height above—as we may fairly infer from the great pressure of the jet."

"That is by no means doubtful," replied my uncle. "If this column of water is about thirty-two thousand feet high, the atmospheric pressure must be something enormous. But a new idea has just struck me."

"And what is that?"

"Why be at so much trouble to close this aperture?"

"Because—"

I hesitated and stammered, having no real reason.

"When our water bottles are empty, we are not at all sure that we shall be able to fill them," observed my uncle.

"I think that is very probable."

137

"Well, then, let this water run. It will, of course, naturally follow in our track, and will serve to guide and refresh us."

"I think the idea a good one," I cried, in reply; "and with this rivulet as a companion, there is no further reason why we should not succeed in our marvellous project."

"Ah, my boy," said the Professor, laughing, "after all, you are coming round."

"More than that, I am now confident of ultimate success. Forward."

"One moment, nephew mine. Let us begin by taking some hours of repose."

I had utterly forgotten that it was night. The chronometer, however, informed me of the fact. Soon we were sufficiently restored and refreshed, and had all fallen into a profound sleep.

21 ... *Under the Ocean*

By THE NEXT DAY we had nearly forgotten our past sufferings. The first sensation I experienced was surprise at not being thirsty, and I actually asked myself the reason. The running stream, which flowed in rippling wavelets at my feet, was the satisfactory reply.

We breakfasted with a good appetite, and then drank our fill of the excellent water. I felt myself quite a new man, ready to go anywhere my uncle chose to lead. I began to think. Why should not a man as seriously convinced as my uncle, succeed, with so excellent a guide as worthy Hans, and so devoted a nephew as myself? These were the brilliant ideas which now invaded my brain. Had the proposition now been made to go back to the summit of Mount Sneffels, I should have declined the offer in a most indignant manner.

But fortunately there was no question of going up. We were about to descend farther into the interior of the earth.

"Let us be moving," I cried, awakening the echoes of the old world.

We resumed our march on Thursday at eight o'clock in the morning. The great granite tunnel going round by sinuous and winding ways, presented every now and then sharp turns, and in fact had the appearance of a labyrinth. Its direction, however, was in general

139

toward the southwest. My uncle made several pauses in order to consult his compass.

The gallery now began to trend downwards in a horizontal direction, with about two inches of fall in every furlong. The murmuring stream flowed quietly at our feet. I could not but compare it to some familiar spirit guiding us through the earth, and I dabbled my fingers in its tepid water, which sang like a naiad as we progressed. My good humor began to assume a mythological character.

As for my uncle, he began to complain of the horizontal character of the road. His route, he found, began to be indefinitely prolonged, instead of "sliding down the celestial ray," according to his expression.

But we had no choice; and as long as our road led toward the center, however little progress we made, there was no reason to complain.

Moreover, from time to time the slopes were much greater; the naiad sang more loudly, and we began to dip downwards in earnest.

As yet, however, I felt no painful sensation. I had not got over the excitement of the discovery of water.

That day and the next we did a considerable amount of horizontal, and relatively very little vertical, travelling.

On Friday evening, the twelfth of July, according to our estimation, we ought to have been thirty leagues to the southwest of Reykjavik, and about two leagues and a half deep. We now received a rather startling surprise.

Under our feet there opened a horrible well. My uncle was so delighted that he actually clapped his hands as he saw how steep and sharp was the descent.

"Ah, ah!" he cried, in rapturous delight; "this will take us a long way. Look at the projections of the rock. Hah!" he exclaimed, "it's a fearful staircase!"

Hans, however, who in all our trouble had never

given up the ropes, took care so to dispose of them as to prevent any accidents. Our descent then began. I dare not call it a perilous descent, for I was already too familiar with that sort of work to look upon it as anything but a very ordinary affair.

This well was a kind of narrow opening in the massive granite, of the kind known as a fissure. The contraction of the terrestrial scaffolding, when it suddenly cooled, had been evidently the cause. If it had ever served in former times as a kind of funnel through which passed the eruptive masses vomited by Sneffels, I was at a loss to explain how it had left no mark. We were, in fact, descending a spiral, something like those winding staircases in use in modern houses.

We were compelled every quarter of an hour or thereabouts to sit down in order to rest our legs. Our calves ached. We then seated ourselves on some projecting rock, with our legs hanging over, and gossiped while we ate a mouthful—drinking still from the pleasantly warm running stream which had not deserted us.

It is scarcely necessary to say that in this curiously shaped fissure the Hansbach had become a cascade to the detriment of its size. It was still, however, sufficient, and more, for our wants. Besides, we knew that as soon as the declivity ceased to be so abrupt, the stream must resume its peaceful course. At this moment it reminded me of my uncle, his impatience and rage, while when it flowed more peacefully, I pictured to myself the placidity of the Icelandic guide.

During the whole of two days, the 13th and 14th of July, we followed the extraordinary spiral staircase of the fissure, penetrating two leagues farther into the crust of the earth, which placed us five leagues below the level of the sea. On the 15th, however, at twelve o'clock in the day, the fissure suddenly assumed a much more gentle slope, still trending in a southeast direction.

The road now became comparatively easy, and at the same time, dreadfully monotonous. It would have been difficult for matters to have turned out otherwise. Our peculiar journey had no chance of being diversified by landscape and scenery. At all events, such was my idea.

At length, on Wednesday, the seventeenth, we were actually seven leagues (twenty-one miles) below the surface of the earth, and fifty leagues distant from the mountain of Sneffels. Though if the truth be told, we were very tired, our health had resisted all suffering, and was in a most satisfactory state. Our traveller's box of medicaments had not even been opened.

My uncle was careful to note every hour the indications of the compass, of the manometer, and of the thermometer, all which he afterwards published in his elaborate philosophical and scientific account of our remarkable voyage. He was therefore able to give an exact relation of the situation. When, therefore, he informed me that we were fifty leagues in a horizontal direction distant from our starting point, I could not suppress a loud exclamation.

"What is the matter now?" cried my uncle.

"Nothing very important; only an idea has entered my head," was my reply.

"Well, out with it, my boy."

"It is my opinion that if your calculations are correct, we are no longer under Iceland."

"Do you think so?"

"We can very easily find out," I replied, pulling out the map and compasses.

"You see," I said, after careful measurement, "that I am not mistaken. We are far beyond Cape Portland; and those fifty leagues to the southwest will take us into the open sea."

"Under the open sea," cried my uncle, rubbing his hands with a delighted air.

"Yes," I cried; "no doubt old ocean flows over our heads."

"Well, my dear boy, what can be more natural? Do you not know that in the neighborhood of Newcastle there are coal mines which have been worked far out under the sea?"

Now my worthy uncle, the Professor, no doubt regarded this discovery as a very simple fact, but to me the idea was by no means a pleasant one. And yet when one came to think the matter over seriously, what mattered it whether the plains and mountains of Iceland were suspended over our devoted heads, or the mighty billows of the Atlantic Ocean? The whole question rested on the solidity of the granite roof above us. However, I soon got used to the idea; for the passage, now level, now running down, and still always to the southeast, kept going deeper and deeper into the profound abysses of Mother Earth.

Three days later, on the twentieth day of July, on a Saturday, we reached a kind of vast grotto. My uncle here paid Hans his usual rix-dollars, and it was decided that the next day should be a day of rest.

22 ... *Sunday Below Ground*

$\mathbf{I}$ AWOKE on Sunday morning without any sense of hurry and bustle attendant on an immediate departure. Though the day to be devoted to repose and reflection was spent under such strange circumstances, and in so wonderful a place, the idea was a pleasant one. Besides, we all began to get used to this kind of existence. I had almost ceased to think of the sun, of the moon, of the stars, of the trees, houses, and towns; in fact, about any terrestrial necessities. In our peculiar position, we were far above such reflections.

The grotto was a vast and magnificent hall. Along its granitic soil the stream flowed placidly and pleasantly. So great a distance was it now from its fiery source, that its water was scarcely lukewarm, and could be drunk without delay or difficulty.

After a frugal breakfast, the Professor made up his mind to devote some hours to putting his notes and calculations in order.

"In the first place," he said, "I have a good many to verify and prove, in order that we may know our exact position. I wish to be able, on our return to the upper regions, to make a map of our journey, a kind of vertical section of the globe, which will be, as it were, the profile of the expedition."

"That would indeed be a curious work, uncle; but can you make your observations with anything like certainty and precision?"

"I can. I have never on one occasion failed to note

with great care the angles and slopes. I am certain as to having made no mistake. Take the compass and examine how she points."

I looked at the instrument with care.

"East one quarter southeast."

"Very good," resumed the Professor, noting the observation, and going through some rapid calculations. "I make out that we have journeyed two hundred and fifty miles from the point of our departure."

"Then the mighty waves of the Atlantic are rolling over our heads?"

"Certainly."

"And at this very moment it is possible that fierce tempests are raging above, and that men and ships are battling against the angry blasts just over our heads?"

"It is quite within the range of possibility," rejoined my uncle, smiling.

"And that whales are playing in shoals, thrashing the bottom of the sea, the roof of our adamantine prison?"

"Be quite at rest on that point; there is no danger of their breaking through. But to return to our calculations. We are to the southeast, two hundred and fifty miles from the base of Sneffels, and, according to my preceding notes, I think we have gone sixteen leagues in a downward direction."

"Sixteen leagues—fifty miles!" I cried.

"I am sure of it."

"But that is the extreme limit allowed by science for the thickness of the earth's crust," I replied, referring to my geological studies.

"I do not contravene that assertion," was his quiet answer.

"And at this stage of our journey, according to all known laws on the increase of heat, there should be here a temperature of *fifteen hundred* degrees of Reaumur."

"There should be, you say, my boy."

"In which case this granite would not exist, but be in a state of fusion."

"But you perceive, my boy, that it is not so, and that facts, as usual, are very stubborn things, overruling all theories."

"I am forced to yield to the evidence of my senses, but I am nevertheless very much surprised."

"What heat does the thermometer really indicate?" continued the philosopher.

"Twenty-seven and six tenths."

"So that science is wrong by fourteen hundred and seventy-four degrees and four tenths. According to which, it is demonstrated that the proportional increase in temperature is an exploded error. Humphrey Davy here shines forth in all his glory. He is right, and I have acted wisely to believe him. Have you any answer to make to this statement?"

Had I chosen to have spoken, I might have said a great deal. I in no way admitted the theory of Humphrey Davy—I still held out for the theory of proportional increase of heat, though I did not feel it.

I was far more willing to allow that this chimney of an extinct volcano was covered by lava of a kind refractory to heat, in fact, a bad conductor, which did not allow the great increase of temperature to percolate through its sides. The hot water jet supported my view of the matter.

But without entering on a long and useless discussion, or seeking for new arguments to controvert my uncle, I contented myself with taking up facts as they were.

"Well, sir, I take for granted that all your calculations are correct; but allow me to draw from them a rigorous and definite conclusion."

"Go on, my boy, have your say," cried my uncle, good-humoredly.

"At the place where we now are, under the latitude

146

of Iceland, the terrestrial depth is about fifteen hundred and eighty-three leagues."

"Fifteen hundred, eighty-three and a quarter."

"Well, suppose we say sixteen hundred in round numbers. Now, out of a voyage of sixteen hundred leagues we have completed sixteen."

"As you say; what then?"

"At the expense of a diagonal journey of no less than eighty-five leagues."

"Exactly."

"We have been twenty days about it."

"Exactly twenty days."

"Now sixteen is the hundredth part of our contemplated expedition. If we go on in this way she shall be two thousand days, that is about five years and a half, going down."

The Professor folded his arms, listened, but did not speak.

"Without counting that if a vertical descent of sixteen leagues costs us a horizontal of eighty-five, we shall have to go about eight thousand leagues to the southeast, and we must therefore come out somewhere in the circumference long before we can hope to reach the center."

"Bother your calculations," cried my uncle, in one of his old rages. "On what basis do they rest? How do you know that this passage does not take us direct to the end we require? Moreover, I have in my favor, fortunately, a precedent. What I have undertaken to do, another has done, and he having succeeded, why should I not be equally successful?"

"I hope, indeed, you will; but still, I suppose I may be allowed to—"

"You are allowed to hold your tongue," cried Professor Hardwigg, "when you talk so unreasonably as this."

I saw at once that the old Professor was still alive in

my uncle, and fearful to rouse his angry passions, I dropped the unpleasant subject.

"Now, then," he explained, "consult the manometer. What does that indicate?"

"A considerable amount of pressure."

"Very good. You see, then, that by descending slowly and by gradually accustoming ourselves to the density of this lower atmosphere, we shall not suffer."

"Well, I suppose not, except it may be a certain amount of pain in the ears," was my rather grim reply.

"That, my dear boy, is nothing, and you will easily get rid of that source of discomfort by bringing the exterior air in communication with the air contained in your lungs."

"Perfectly," said I, for I had quite made up my mind in no wise to contradict my uncle. "I should fancy almost that I should experience a certain amount of satisfaction in making a plunge into this dense atmosphere. Have you taken note of how wonderfully sound is propagated?"

"Of course I have. There can be no doubt that a journey into the interior of the earth would be an excellent cure for deafness."

"But then, uncle," I ventured mildly to observe, "this density will continue to increase."

"Yes, according to a law which, however, is scarcely defined. It is true that the intensity of weight will diminish just in proportion to the depth to which we go. You know very well that it is on the surface of the earth that its action is most powerfully felt, while on the contrary, in the very center of the earth bodies cease to have any weight at all."

"I know that is the case; but as we progress will not the atmosphere finally assume the density of water?"

"I know it; when placed under the pressure of seven hundred and ten atmospheres," cried my uncle, with imperturbable gravity.

"And when we are still lower down?" I asked, with natural anxiety.

"Well, lower down, the density will become even greater still."

"Then how shall we be able to make our way through this atmospheric fog?"

"Well, my worthy nephew, we must ballast ourselves by filling our pockets with stones," said Professor Hardwigg.

"Faith, uncle, you have an answer for everything," was my only reply.

I began to feel that it was unwise in me to go any farther into the wide field of hypotheses, for I should certainly have revived some difficulty, or rather impossibility, that would have enraged the Professor.

It was evident, nevertheless, that the air under a pressure which might be multiplied by thousands of atmospheres, would end by becoming perfectly solid, and that then admitting our bodies resisted the pressure, we should have to stop, in spite of all the reasonings in the world. Facts overcome all arguments.

But I thought it best not to urge this argument. My uncle would simply have quoted the example of Saknussemm. Supposing the learned Icelander's journey ever really to have taken place, there was one simple answer to be made:—

In the sixteenth century, neither the barometer nor the manometer had been invented; how, then, could Saknussemm have been able to discover when he did reach the center of the earth?

This unanswerable and learned objection I, however, kept to myself, and, bracing up my courage, awaited the course of events—little aware of how adventurous yet were to be the incidents of our remarkable journey.

The rest of this day of leisure and repose was spent in calculation and conversation. I made it a point to

149

agree with the Professor in everything; but I envied the perfect indifference of Hans, who, without taking any such trouble about the cause and effect, went blindly onwards wherever destiny chose to lead them.

23 ... Alone

I<small>T MUST IN ALL TRUTH BE CONFESSED</small>, things as yet had gone on well, and I should have acted in bad taste to have complained. If the true medium of our difficulties did not increase, it was within the range of possibility that we might ultimately reach the end of our journey. Then what glory would be ours! I began in the newly aroused ardor of my soul to speak enthusiastically to the Professor. Well, was I serious? The whole state in which we existed was a mystery, and it was impossible to know whether or not I was in earnest.

For several days after our memorable halt, the slopes became more rapid. Some were even of a most frightful character, almost vertical, so that we were forever going down into the solid interior mass. During some days, we actually descended a league and a half, even two leagues, toward the center of the earth. The descents were sufficiently perilous, and while we were engaged in them we learned fully to appreciate the marvellous coolness of our guide Hans. Without him we should have been wholly lost. The grave and impassible Icelander devoted himself to us with the most incomprehensible *sang-froid* and ease; and, thanks to him, many a dangerous pass was got over, where, but for him, we should inevitably have stuck fast.

His silence increased every day. I think that we began to be influenced by this peculiar trait in his character. It is certain that the inanimate objects by

151

which you are surrounded have a direct action on the brain. It must be that a man who shuts himself up between four walls must lose the faculty of associating ideas and words. How many persons condemned to the horrors of solitary confinement have gone mad, simply because the thinking faculties have lain dormant!

During the three weeks that followed our last interesting conversation, there occurred nothing worthy of being especially recorded.

I have, while writing these memoirs, taxed my memory in vain for one incident of travel during this particular period.

But the next event to be related is terrible indeed. Its very memory, even now, makes my soul shudder, and my blood run cold.

It was on the seventh of August. Our constant and successive descents had taken us quite thirty leagues into the interior of the earth, that is to say, that there were above us thirty leagues, nearly a hundred miles, of rocks, and oceans, and continents, and towns, to say nothing of living inhabitants. We were in a south-easterly direction about two hundred leagues from Iceland.

On that memorable day, the tunnel had begun to assume an almost horizontal course.

I was on this occasion walking on in front. My uncle had charge of one of the Ruhmkorf coils, I had possession of the other. By means of its light I was busy examining the different layers of granite. I was completely absorbed in my work.

Suddenly halting and turning round, I found that I was alone!

"Well," thought I to myself, "I have certainly been walking too fast, or else Hans and my uncle have stopped to rest. The best thing I can do is to go back and find them. Luckily, there is very little ascent to tire me."

I accordingly retraced my steps, and while doing so, walked for at least a quarter of an hour. Rather uneasy, I paused and looked eagerly around. Not a living soul. I called aloud. No reply. My voice was lost amid the myriad cavernous echoes it aroused!

I began for the first time to feel seriously uneasy. A cold shiver shook my whole body, and perspiration, chill and terrible, burst upon my skin.

"I must be calm," I said, speaking aloud, as boys whistle to drive away fear. "There can be no doubt that I shall find my companions. There cannot be two roads. It is certain that I was considerably ahead; all I have to do is to go back."

Having come to this determination, I ascended the tunnel for at least half an hour, unable to decide if I had ever seen certain landmarks before. Every now and then I paused to discover if any loud appeal was made to me, well knowing that in that dense and intensified atmosphere I should hear it a long way off. But no. The most extraordinary silence reigned in this immense gallery. Only the echoes of my own footsteps could be heard.

At last I stopped. I could scarcely realize the fact of my isolation. I was quite willing to think that I had made a mistake, but not that I was lost. If I had made a mistake, I might find my way: if lost—I shuddered to think of it.

"Come, come," said I to myself; "since there is only one road, and they must come by it, we shall at last meet. All I have to do is still go upwards. Perhaps, however, not seeing me, and forgetting I was ahead, they may have gone back in search of me. Still, even in this case, if I make haste, I shall get up to them. There can be no doubt about the matter."

But as I spoke these last words aloud, it would have been quite clear to any listener—had there been one —that I was by no means convinced of the fact. More-

153

over, in order to associate together these simple ideas
and to reunite them under the form of reasoning, required some time. I could not all at once bring my
brain to think.

Then another dread doubt fell upon my soul. After
all, was I ahead? Of course I was. Hans was no doubt
following behind, preceded by my uncle. I perfectly
recollected his having stopped for a moment to strap
his baggage on his shoulder. I now remembered this
trifling detail. It was, I believed, just at that very
moment that I had determined to continue my route.

"Again," thought I, reasoning as calmly as was possible, "there is another sure means of not losing my
way, a thread to guide me through the labyrinthine
subterraneous retreat, one which I had forgotten—my
faithful river."

This course of reasoning roused my drooping spirits,
and I resolved to resume my journey without further
delay. No time was to be lost.

It was at this moment that I had reason to bless the
thoughtfulness of my uncle when he refused to allow
the eider hunter to close the orifices of the hot spring,
—that small fissure in the great mass of granite. This
beneficent spring, after having saved us from thirst
during so many days, would now enable me to regain
the right road.

Having come to this mental decision, I made up my
mind before I started upwards that ablution would
certainly do me a great deal of good.

I stopped to plunge my hands and forehead in the
pleasant water of the Hansbach stream, blessing its
presence as a certain consolation.

Conceive my horror and stupefaction!—I was treading
a hard, dusty, shingly road of granite. The stream on
which I reckoned had wholly disappeared!

24 ... Lost!

No words in any human language can depict my utter despair. I was literally buried alive; with no other expectation before me but to die in all the slow, horrible torture of hunger and thirst.

Mechanically I crawled about, feeling the dry and arid rock. Never, to my fancy, had I ever felt any thing so dry.

But, I frantically asked myself, how had I lost the course of the flowing stream? There could be no doubt it had ceased to flow in the gallery in which I now was. Now I began to understand the cause of the strange silence which prevailed when last I tried if any appeal from my companions might perchance reach my ear.

It so happened that when I first took an imprudent step in the wrong direction, I did not perceive the absence of the all-important stream.

It was now quite evident that when we halted another tunnel must have received the waters of the little torrent, and that I had unconsciously entered a different gallery. To what unknown depths had my companions gone? Where was I?

How to get back! Clue or landmark there was absolutely none! My feet left no signs on the granite and shingle. My brain throbbed with agony as I tried to discover the solution of this terrible problem. My situation, after all sophistry and reflection, had finally to be summed up in three awful words—

Lost! lost!! LOST!!!

Lost at a depth which, to my finite understanding, appeared to be immeasurable.

These thirty leagues of the crust of the earth weighed upon my shoulders like the globe on the shoulders of Atlas. I felt myself crushed by the awful weight. It was indeed a position to drive the sanest man to madness!

I tried to bring my thoughts back to the things of the world so long forgotten. It was with the greatest difficulty that I succeeded in doing so. Hamburg, the house on the Königstrasse, my dear cousin Gretchen —all that world which had before vanished like a shadow floated before my now vivid imagination.

There they were before me, but how unreal! Under the influence of a terrible hallucination I saw the whole incidents of our journey pass before me like the scenes of a panorama. The ship and its inmates, Iceland, M. Fridriksson, and the great summit of Mount Sneffels! I said to myself that if in my position I retained the most faint and shadowy outline of a hope, it would be a sure sign of approaching delirium. It were better to give way wholly to despair!

In fact, did I but reason with calmness and philosophy, what human power was there in existence able to take me back to the surface of the earth, and ready, too, to split asunder, to rend in twain, those huge and mighty vaults which stand above my head? Who could enable me to find my road, and regain my companions?

Insensate folly and madness to entertain even a shadow of hope!

"O uncle!" was my despairing cry.

This was the only word of reproach which came to my lips; for I thoroughly understood how deeply and sorrowfully the worthy Professor would regret my loss, and how in his turn he would patiently seek for me.

When I at last began to resign myself to the fact that no further aid was to be expected from man, and knowing that I was utterly powerless to do anything for my own salvation, I kneeled with earnest fervor and asked assistance from Heaven. The remembrance of my innocent childhood, the memory of my mother, known only in my infancy, came welling forth from my heart. I had recourse to prayer. And little as I had right to be remembered by Him whom I had forgotten in the hour of prosperity, and whom I so tardily invoked, I prayed earnestly and sincerely.

This renewal of my youthful faith brought about a much greater amount of calm, and I was enabled to concentrate all my strength and intelligence on the terrible realities of my unprecedented situation.

I had about me that which I had at first wholly forgotten—three days' provisions. Moreover, my water bottle was quite full. Nevertheless, the one thing which it was impossible to do was to remain alone. Try to find my companions I must, at any price. But which course should I take? Should I go upwards, or again descend? Doubtless it was right to retrace my steps in an upward direction.

By doing this with care and coolness, I must reach the point where I had turned away from the rippling stream. I must find the fatal bifurcation or fork. Once at this spot, once the river at my feet, I could, at all events, regain the awful crater of Mount Sneffels. Why had I not thought of this before? This, at last, was a reasonable hope of safety. The most important thing, then, to do was to discover the bed of the Hansbach.

After a slight meal and a draught of water, I rose like a giant refreshed. Leaning heavily on my pole, I began the ascent of the gallery. The slope was very rapid and rather difficult. But I advanced hopefully and carefully, like a man who at last is making his

157

way out of a forest, and knows there is only one road to follow.

During one whole hour nothing happened to check my progress. As I advanced I tried to recollect the shape of the tunnel, to recall to my memory certain projections of rocks, to persuade myself that I had followed certain winding routes before. But no one particular sign could I bring to mind, and I was soon forced to allow that this gallery would never take me back to the point at which I had separated myself from my companions. It was absolutely without issue—a mere blind alley in the earth.

The moment at length came when, facing the solid rock, I knew my fate, and fell inanimate on the arid floor!

To describe the horrible state of despair and fear into which I then fell, would now be vain and impossible. My last hope, the courage which had sustained me, drooped before the sight of this pitiless granite rock!

Lost in a vast labyrinth, the sinuosities of which spread in every direction, without guide, clue or compass, it was a vain and useless task to attempt flight. All that remained to me was to lie down and die. To lie down and die the most cruel and horrible of deaths!

In my state of mind, the idea came into my head that one day perhaps, when my fossil bones were found, their discovery so far below the level of the earth might give rise to solemn and interesting scientific discussions.

I tried to cry aloud, but hoarse, hollow and inarticulate sounds alone could make themselves heard through my parched lips. I literally panted for breath.

In the midst of all these horrible sources of anguish and despair, a new horror took possession of my soul. My lamp, by falling down, had got out of order. I had no means of repairing it. Its light was already becoming paler and paler, and soon would expire.

With a strange sense of resignation and despair, I watched the luminous current in the coil getting less and less. A procession of shadows moved flashing along the granite wall. I scarcely dared to lower my eyelids, fearing to lose the last spark of this fugitive light. Every instant it seemed to me that it was about to vanish and to leave me forever—in utter darkness!

At last, one final trembling flame remained in the lamp; I followed it with all my power of vision, I gasped for breath; I concentrated upon it all the power of my soul, as upon the last scintillation of light I was ever destined to see: and then I was to be lost for ever in Cimmerian and tenebrous shades.

A wild and plaintive cry escaped my lips. On earth during the most profound and comparatively complete darkness, light never allows a complete destruction and extinction of its power. Light is so diffuse, so subtle, that it permeates everywhere, and whatever little may remain, the retina of the eye will succeed in finding it. In this place nothing—not the faintest ray of light. It amazed me!

My head was now wholly lost. I raised my arms, trying the effects of the feeling in getting against the cold stone wall. It was painful in the extreme. Madness must have taken possession of me. I knew not what I did. I began to run, to fly, rushing at haphazard in this inextricable labyrinth, always going downwards, running wildly underneath the terrestrial crust like an inhabitant of the subterranean furnaces, screaming, roaring, howling, until bruised by the pointed rocks, falling and picking myself up all covered with blood, seeking madly to drink the blood which dripped from my torn features, mad because this blood only trickled over my face, and watching always for this horrid wall which ever presented to me the fearful obstacle against which I could not dash my head.

159

Where was I going? It was impossible to say. I was perfectly ignorant of the matter.

Several hours passed in this way. After a long time, having utterly exhausted my strength, I fell a heavy inert mass along the side of the tunnel, and lost all consciousness of existence!

25 ... *The Whispering Gallery*

WHEN AT LAST I came back to a sense of life and being, my face was wet; but wet as I soon knew with tears. How long this state of insensibility lasted, it is quite impossible for me now to say. I had no means left to me of taking any account of time. Never, since the creation of the world, had such a solitude as mine existed. I was completely abandoned.

After my fall I lost much blood. I felt myself flooded with the life-giving liquid. My first sensation was perhaps a natural one. Why was I not dead? Because I was alive, there was something left to do. I tried to make up my mind to think no longer. As far as I was able, I drove away all ideas, and utterly overcome by pain and grief, I crouched against the granite wall.

I just commenced to feel the fainting coming on again, and the sensation that this was the last struggle before complete annihilation, when, on a sudden, a violent uproar reached my ears. It had some resemblance to the prolonged rumbling voice of thunder, and I clearly distinguished sonorous voices, lost one after the other, in the distant depths of the gulf.

Whence came this noise? Naturally, it was to be supposed from new phenomena which were taking place in the bosom of the solid mass of Mother Earth! The explosion of some gaseous vapors, or the fall of some solid, of the granitic or other rock.

Again I listened with deep attention. I was extremely anxious to hear if this strange and inexplicable sound was likely to be renewed! A whole quarter of an hour elapsed in painful expectation. Deep and solemn silence reigned in the tunnel. So still that I could hear the beatings of my own heart! I waited, waited, waited with a strange kind of hopefulness.

Suddenly my ear, which leant accidentally against the wall, appeared to catch, as it were, the faintest echo of a sound. I thought that I heard vague, incoherent and distant voices. I quivered all over with excitement and hope!

"It must be hallucination," I cried. "It cannot be! It is not true!"

But no! By listening more attentively, I really did convince myself that what I heard was truly the sound of human voices. To make any meaning out of the sound, however, was beyond my power. I was too weak even to hear distinctly. Still it was a positive fact that someone was speaking. Of that I was quite certain.

There was a moment of fear. A dread fell upon my soul that it might be my own words brought back to me by a distant echo. Perhaps without knowing it, I might have been crying aloud. I resolutely closed my lips, and once more placed my ear to the huge granite wall.

Yes, for certain. It was in truth the sound of human voices.

I now by the exercise of great determination dragged myself along the sides of the cavern, until I reached a point where I could hear more distinctly. But though I could detect the sound, I could only make out uncertain, strange and incomprehensible words. They reached my ear as if they had been spoken in a low tone—murmured, as it were, afar off.

At last, I made out the word *förlorad*, repeated several times in a tone betokening great mental anguish and sorrow.

What could this word mean, and who was speaking

it? It must be either my uncle or the guide Hans! If, therefore, I could hear them, they must surely be able to hear me.

"Help!" I cried, at the top of my voice. "Help, I am dying!"

I then listened with scarcely a breath; I panted for the slightest sound in the darkness—a cry, a sigh, a question! But silence reigned supreme. No answer came! In this way some minutes passed. A whole flood of ideas flashed through my mind. I began to fear that my voice, weakened by sickness and suffering, could not reach my companions who were in search of me.

"It must be them," I cried; "what other men can by possibility be buried a hundred miles below the level of the earth?"

The mere supposition was preposterous.

I began, therefore, to listen again with the most breathless attention. As I moved my ears along the side of the place I was in, I found a mathematical point, as it were, where the voices appeared to attain their maximum of intensity. The word *förlorad* again distinctly reached my ear. Then came again that rolling noise like thunder which had awakened me out of torpor.

"I begin to understand," I said to myself, after some little time devoted to reflection; "it is not through the solid mass that the sound reaches my ears. The walls of my cavernous retreat are of solid granite, and the most fearful explosion would not make uproar enough to penetrate them. The sound must come along the gallery itself. The place I was in must possess some peculiar acoustic properties of its own."

Again I listened; and this time—yes, this time—I heard my name distinctly pronounced: cast, as it were, into space.

It was my uncle the Professor who was speaking. He was in conversation with the guide, and the word which

163

had so often reached my ears, *förlorad*, was a Danish expression.

Then I understood it all. In order to make myself heard, I too must speak as it were along the side of the gallery, which would carry the sound of my voice just as the wire carries the electric fluid from point to point.

But there was no time to lose. If my companions were only to remove a few feet from where they stood, the acoustic effect would be over, my Whispering Gallery would be destroyed. I again therefore crawled toward the wall, and said as clearly and distinctly as I could:—

"Uncle Hardwigg."

I then awaited a reply.

Sound does not possess the property of travelling with such extreme rapidity. Besides, the density of the air at that depth from light and motion was very far from adding to the rapidity of circulation. Several seconds elapsed, which to my excited imagination appeared ages; and these words reached my eager ears, and moved my wildly beating heart:

"Harry, my boy, is that you?"

A short delay between question and answer.

"Yes—yes."

"Where are you?"

"Lost!"

"And your lamp?"

"Out."

"But the guiding stream?"

"Is lost."

"Keep your courage, Harry. We will do our best."

"One moment, my uncle," I cried; "I have no longer strength to answer your questions. But—for Heaven's sake—do you—continue—to speak—to me!"

Absolute silence I felt would be annihilation.

"Keep up your courage," said my uncle. "As you

are so weak, do not speak. We have been searching for you in all directions, both by going upwards and downwards in the gallery. My dear boy, I had begun to give over all hope, and you can never know what bitter tears of sorrow and regret I have shed. At last, supposing you to be still on the road beside the Hansbach, we again descended, firing off guns as signals. Now, however, that we have found you, and that our voices reach each other, it may be a long time before we actually meet. We are conversing by means of some extraordinary acoustic arrangement of the labyrinth. But do not despair, my dear boy. It is something gained even to hear each other."

While he was speaking, my brain was at work reflecting. A certain undefined hope, vague and shapeless as yet, made my heart beat wildly. In the first place, it was absolutely necessary for me to know one thing. I once more, therefore, leaned my head against the wall, which I almost touched with my lips, and again spoke.

"Uncle."

"My boy," was his ready answer.

"It is of the utmost consequence that we should know how far we are asunder."

"That is not difficult."

"You have your chronometer at hand?" I asked.

"Certainly."

"Well, take it into your hand. Pronounce my name, noting exactly the second at which you speak. I will reply as soon as I hear your words—and you will then note exactly the moment at which my reply reaches you."

"Very good; and the meantime between my question and your answer will be the time occupied by my voice in reaching you."

"That is exactly what I mean, uncle," was my eager reply.

"Are you ready?"

"Yes."

"Well, make ready; I am about to pronounce your name," said the Professor.

I applied my ear close to the sides of the cavernous gallery, and as soon as the word Harry reached my ear, I turned round, and placing my lips to the wall, repeated the sound.

"Forty seconds," said my uncle. "There has elapsed forty seconds between the two words. The sound, therefore, takes twenty seconds to ascend. Now, allowing a thousand and twenty feet for every second, we have twenty thousand four hundred feet—a league and a half and one eighth."

These words fell on my soul like a kind of death-knell.

"A league and a half," I muttered, in a low and despairing voice.

"It shall be got over, my boy," cried my uncle, in a cheery tone; "depend on us."

"But do you know whether to ascend or descend?" I asked, faintly enough.

"We have to descend, and I will tell you why. You have reached a vast open space, a kind of bare cross-road, from which galleries diverge in every direction. That in which you are now lying must necessarily bring you to this point, for it appears that all these mighty fissures, these fractures of the globe's interior, radiate from the vast cavern which we at this moment occupy. Rouse yourself, then; have courage and continue your route. Walk, if you can; if not, drag yourself along—slide, if nothing else is possible. The slope must be rather rapid, and you will find strong arms to receive you at the end of your journey. Make a start, like a good fellow."

These words served to rouse some kind of courage in my sinking frame.

"Farewell for the present, good uncle; I am about to take my departure. As soon as I start, our voices will cease to commingle. Farewell, then, until we meet again."

"Adieu, Harry—until we say Welcome." Such were the last words which reached my anxious ears, before I commenced my weary and almost hopeless journey.

This wonderful and surprising conversation which took place through the vast mass of the earth's labyrinth, these words exchanged, the speakers being about five miles apart, ended with hopeful and pleasant expressions. I breathed one more prayer to Heaven, I sent up words of thanksgiving, believing in my inmost heart that He had led me to the only place where the voices of my friends could reach my ears.

This apparently astounding acoustic mystery is easily explainable by simple natural laws; it arose from the conductibility of the rock. There are many instances of this singular propagation of sound which are not perceptible in its less mediate positions. In the interior gallery of St. Paul's, and amid the curious caverns in Sicily, these phenomena are observable. The most marvellous of them all is known as the Ear of Dionysius.

These memories of the past, of my early reading and studies, came fresh to my thoughts. Moreover, I began to reason that if my uncle and I could communicate at so great a distance, no serious obstacle could exist between us. All I had to do was to follow the direction whence the sound had reached me; and, logically putting it, I must reach him if my strength did not fail.

I accordingly rose to my feet. I soon found, however, that I could not walk; that I must drag myself along. The slope, as I expected, was very rapid; but I allowed myself to slip down.

Soon the rapidity of the descent began to assume

frightful proportions, and menaced a fearful fall. I clutched at the sides; I grasped at projections of rocks; I threw myself backwards.

All in vain. My weakness was so great I could do nothing to save myself.

Suddenly earth failed me.

I was first launched into a dark and gloomy void. I then struck against the projecting asperities of a vertical gallery, a perfect well. My head bounded against a pointed rock, and I lost all knowledge of existence. As far as I was concerned, death had claimed me for his own.

26 ... *A Rapid Recovery*

WHEN I RETURNED to the consciousness of existence, I found myself surrounded by a kind of semi-obscurity, lying on some thick and soft coverlets. My uncle was watching—his eyes fixed intently on my countenance, a grave expression on his face, a tear in his eye. At the first sigh which struggled from my bosom, he took hold of my hand. When he saw my eyes open and fix themselves upon his, he uttered a loud cry of joy.

"He lives! he lives!"

"Yes, my good uncle," I whispered.

"My dear boy," continued the grim Professor, clasping me to his heart, "you are saved!"

I was deeply and unaffectedly touched by the tone in which these words were uttered, and even more by the kindly care which accompanied them. The Professor, however, was one of those men who must be severely tried in order to induce any display of affection or gentle emotion. At this moment our friend Hans, the guide, joined us. He saw my hand in that of my uncle; and I venture to say that, taciturn as he was, his eyes beamed with lively satisfaction.

"*God-dag,*" he said.

"Good-day, Hans, good day," I replied, in as hearty a tone as I could assume. "And now, uncle, that we are together, tell me where we are. I have lost all idea of our position, as of everything else."

169

"Tomorrow, Harry; tomorrow," he replied. "Today you are far too weak. Your head is surrounded with bandages and poultices that must not be touched. Sleep, my boy; sleep, and tomorrow you will know all that you require."

"But," I cried, "let me know what o'clock it is, what day it is?"

"It is now eleven o'clock at night, and this is once more Sunday. It is now the eleventh of the month of August. And I distinctly prohibit you from asking any more questions until the twelfth of the same."

I was, if the truth were told, very weak indeed, and my eyes soon closed involuntarily. I did require a good night's rest, and I went off reflecting at the last moment that my perilous adventure in the interior of the earth, in total darkness, had lasted four days!

On the morning of the next day, at my awakening, I began to look around me. My sleeping place, made of all our travelling bedding, was in a charming grotto, adorned with magnificent stalagmites, glittering in all the colors of the rainbow, the floor of soft and silvery sand.

A dim obscurity prevailed. No torch, no lamp, was lighted, and yet certain unexplained beams of light penetrated from without, and made their way through the opening of the beautiful grotto.

I, moreover, heard a vague and indefinite murmur, like the ebb and flow of waves upon a strand, and sometimes I verily believed I could hear the sighing of the wind.

I began to believe that, instead of being awake, I must be dreaming. Surely my brain had not been affected by my fall, and all that occurred during the last twenty-four hours was not the frenzied visions of madness? And yet after some reflection, a trial of my faculties, I came to the conclusion that I could not be mistaken. Eyes and ears could not surely both deceive me.

170

"It is a ray of the blessed daylight," I said to myself, "which has penetrated through some mighty fissure in the rocks. But what is the meaning of this murmur of waves, this unmistakable moaning of the salt sea billows? I can hear, too, plainly enough, the whistling of the wind. But can I be altogether mistaken? If my uncle, during my illness, has but carried me back to the surface of the earth! Has he, on my account, given up his wondrous expedition, or in some strange manner has it come to an end?"

I was puzzling my brain over these and other questions when the Professor joined me.

"Good-day, Harry," he cried, in a joyous tone. "I fancy you are quite well."

"I am very much better," I replied, actually sitting up in my bed.

"I knew that would be the end of it, as you slept both soundly and tranquilly. Hans and I have each taken turn to watch, and every hour we have seen visible signs of amelioration."

"You must be right, uncle," was my reply, "for I feel as if I could do justice to any meal you could put before me. I am really hungry."

"You shall eat, my boy, you shall eat. The fever has left you. Our excellent friend Hans has rubbed your wounds and bruises with I know not what ointment, of which the Icelanders alone possess the secret. And they have healed your bruises in the most marvellous manner. Ah, he's a wise fellow, is Master Hans."

While he was speaking, my uncle was placing before me several articles of food, which, despite his earnest injunctions, I readily devoured. As soon as the first rage of hunger was appeased, I overwhelmed him with questions, to which he now no longer hesitated to give answers.

I then learned, for the first time, that my providential fall had brought me to the bottom of an almost perpendicular gallery. As I came down, amidst a perfect shower of stones, the least of which falling on me would have crushed me to death, they came to the conclusion that I had carried with me an entire dislocated rock. Riding, as it were, on this terrible chariot, I was cast headlong into my uncle's arms. And into them I fell, insensible and covered with blood.

"It is indeed a miracle," was the Professor's final remark, "that you were not killed a thousand times over. But let us take care not to separate; for surely we should risk never meeting again."

"Let us take care never again to separate."

These words fell with a sort of chill upon my heart. The journey, then, was not over. I looked at my uncle with surprise and astonishment. My uncle, after an instant's examination of my countenance, said:

"What is the matter, Harry?"

"I want to ask you a very serious question. You say that I am all right in health?"

"Certainly you are."

"And all my limbs are sound and capable of new exertion?" I asked.

"Most undoubtedly."

"But what about my head?" was my next anxious question.

"Well, your head, except that you have one or two contusions, is exactly where it ought to be—on your shoulders," said my uncle, laughing.

"Well, my own opinion is that my head is not exactly right. In fact, I believe myself slightly delirious."

"What makes you think so?"

"I will explain why I fancy I have lost my senses," I cried. "Have we not returned to the surface of Mother Earth?"

"Certainly not."

"Then truly I must be mad, for do I not see the light of day? do I not hear the whistling of the wind?

172

and can I not distinguish the wash of a great sea?"

"And that is all that makes you uneasy?" said my uncle, with a smile.

"Can you explain?"

"I will not make any attempt to explain; for the whole matter is utterly inexplicable. But you shall see and judge for yourself. You will then find that geological science is as yet in its infancy, and that we are doomed to enlighten the world."

"Let us advance, then," I cried, eagerly, no longer able to restrain my curiosity.

"Wait a moment, my dear Harry," he responded; "you must take precautions after your illness before going into the open air."

"The open air?"

"Yes, my boy. I have to warn you that the wind is rather violent, and I have no wish for you to expose yourself without necessary precautions."

"But I beg to assure you that I am perfectly recovered from my illness."

"Have just a little patience, my boy. A relapse would be inconvenient to all parties. We have no time to lose, as our approaching sea voyage may be of long duration."

"Sea voyage?" I cried, more bewildered than ever.

"Yes. You must take another day's rest, and we shall be ready to go on board by tomorrow," replied my uncle, with a peculiar smile.

Go on board! The words utterly astonished me.

Go on board—what and how? Had we come upon a river, a lake? had we discovered some inland sea? Was a vessel lying at anchor in some part of the interior of the earth?

My curiosity was worked up to the very highest pitch. My uncle made vain attempts to restrain me. When at last, however, he discovered that my feverish impatience would do more harm than good, and that

173

the satisfaction of my wishes could alone restore me to a calm state of mind, he gave way.

I dressed myself rapidly, and then taking the precaution to please my uncle, of wrapping myself in one of the coverlets, I rushed out of the grotto.

27 ... *The Central Sea*

AT FIRST I saw absolutely nothing. My eyes, wholly unused to the effulgence of light, could not bear the sudden brightness; and I was compelled to close them. When I was able to reopen them, I stood still, far more stupefied than astonished. Not all the wildest effects of my imagination could have conjured up such a scene!

"The sea—the sea," I cried.

"Yes," replied my uncle, in a tone of pardonable pride; "the Central Sea. No future navigator will deny the fact of my having discovered it; and hence of acquiring a right of giving it a name."

It was quite true. A vast, limitless expanse of water, the end of a lake if not an ocean, spread before us, until it was lost in the distance. The shore, which was very much indented, consisted of a beautiful soft golden sand, mixed with small shells, the long deserted home of some of the creatures of a past age. The waves broke incessantly, and with a peculiarly sonorous murmur—to be found in underground localities. A slight frothy flake arose as the wind blew along the pellucid water; and many a dash of spray was blown into my face. The mighty superstructure of rock which rose above to an inconceivable height left only a narrow opening, but where we stood, there was a large margin of strand. On all sides were capes and promontories and enormous cliffs, partially worn by the eternal break-

175

ing of the waves, through countless ages! And as I gazed from side to side, the mighty rocks faded away like a fleecy film of cloud.

It was in reality an ocean, with all the usual characteristics of an inland sea, only horribly wild—so rigid, cold and savage.

One thing startled and puzzled me greatly. How was it that I was able to look upon that vast sheet of water, instead of being plunged in utter darkness? The vast landscape before me was lit up like day. But there was wanting the dazzling brilliancy, the splendid irradiation of the sun; the pale cold illumination of the moon; the brightness of the stars. The illuminating power in this subterraneous region, from its trembling and flickering character, its clear dry whiteness, the very slight elevation of its temperature, its great superiority to that of the moon, was evidently electric; something in the nature of the aurora borealis, only that its phenomena were constant, and able to light up the whole of the ocean cavern.

The tremendous vault above our heads, the sky, so to speak, appeared to be composed of a conglomeration of nebulous vapors, in constant motion. I should originally have supposed, that under such an atmospheric pressure as must exist in that place, the evaporation of water could not really take place, and yet from the action of some physical law, which escaped my memory, there were heavy and dense clouds rolling along that mighty vault, partially concealing the roof. Electric currents produced astonishing play of light and shade in the distance, especially around the heavier clouds. Deep shadows were cast beneath, and then suddenly, between two clouds, there would come a ray of unusual beauty and remarkable intensity. And yet it was not like the sun, for it gave no heat.

The effect was sad and excruciatingly melancholy. Instead of a noble firmament of blue, studded with stars, there was above me a heavy roof of granite, which seemed to crush me.

Gazing around, I began to think of the theory of the English captain, who compared the earth to a vast hollow sphere in the interior of which the air is retained in a luminous state by means of atmospheric pressure, while two stars, Pluto and Proserpine, circled there in their mysterious orbits. After all, suppose the old fellow was right!

In truth, we were imprisoned, bound, as it were, in a vast excavation. Its width was impossible to make out; the shore, on either hand, widening rapidly until lost to sight; while its length was equally uncertain. A haze on the distant horizon bounded our view. As to its height, we could see that it must be many miles to the roof. Looking upward, it was impossible to discover where the stupendous roof began. The lowest of the clouds must have been floating at an elevation of two thousand yards, a height greater than that of terrestrial vapors, which circumstance was doubtless owing to the extreme density of the air.

I use the word cavern in order to give an idea of the place. I cannot describe its awful grandeur; human language fails to convey an idea of its savage sublimity. Whether this singular vacuum had or had not been caused by the sudden cooling of the earth when in a state of fusion, I could not say. I had read of most wonderful and gigantic caverns—but none in any way like this.

The great grotto of Guachara, in Colombia, visited by the learned Humboldt; the vast and partially explored Mammoth Cave in Kentucky; what were these holes in the earth to that in which I stood in speechless admiration! with its vapory clouds, its electric light, and the mighty ocean slumbering in its bosom! Imagination, not description, can alone give an idea of the splendor and vastness of the cave.

I gazed at these marvels in profound silence. Words were utterly wanting to indicate the sensations of wonder I experienced. It seemed, as I stood upon that mysterious shore, as if I were some wandering inhabitant of a distant planet, present for the first time at the spectacle of some terrestrial phenomena belonging to another existence. To give body and existence to such new sensations would have required the coinage of new words—and here my feeble brain found itself wholly at fault. I looked on, I thought, I reflected, I admired, in a state of stupefaction not altogether unmingled with fear!

The unexpected spectacle restored some color to my pallid cheeks. I seemed to be actually getting better under the influence of this novelty. Moreover, the vivacity of the dense atmosphere reanimated my body by inflating my lungs with unaccustomed oxygen.

It will be readily conceived that after an imprisonment of forty-seven days, in a dark and miserable tunnel, it was with infinite delight that I breathed this saline air. It was like the genial, reviving influence of the salt sea waves.

My uncle had already got over the first surprise. With the Latin poet Horace, his idea was that—

> "Not to admire is all the art I know,
> To make man happy and to keep him so."

"Well," he said, after giving me time thoroughly to appreciate the marvels of this underground sea, "do you feel strong enough to walk up and down?"

"Certainly," was my ready answer. "Nothing would give me greater pleasure."

"Well, then, my boy," he said, "lean on my arm, and we will stroll along the beach."

I accepted his offer eagerly, and we began to walk along the shores of this extraordinary lake. To our left were abrupt rocks, piled one upon the other—a stupendous Titanic pile. Down their sides leapt innumerable cascades, which at last, becoming limpid and murmuring streams, were lost in the waters of the lake. Light vapors, which rose here and there, and floated in fleecy clouds from rock to rock, indicated hot springs, which also poured their superfluity into the vast reservoir at our feet.

Among them I recognized our old and faithful stream, the Hansbach, which, lost in that wild basin, seemed as if it had been flowing since the creation of the world.

"We shall miss our excellent friend," I remarked, with a deep sigh.

"Bah!" said my uncle, testily, "what matters it? That or another, it is all the same."

I thought the remark ungrateful, and felt almost inclined to say so; but I forebore.

At this moment my attention was attracted by an unexpected spectacle. After we had gone about five hundred yards, we suddenly turned a steep promontory, and found ourselves close to a lofty forest! It consisted of straight trunks with tufted tops, in shape like parasols. The air seemed to have no effect upon these trees, which in spite of a tolerable breeze, remained as still and motionless as if they had been petrified.

I hastened forward. I could find no name for these singular formations. Did they not belong to the two thousand and more known trees? or were we to make the discovery of a new growth? By no means. When we at last reached the forest, and stood beneath the trees, my surprise gave way to admiration.

In truth, I was simply in the presence of a very ordinary product of the earth, of singular and gigantic proportions. My uncle unhesitatingly called them by their real names.

"It is only," he said, in his coolest manner, "a forest of mushrooms."

On close examination I found that he was not mistaken. Judge of the development attained by this product of damp, hot soils. I had heard that the *lycoperdon giganteum* reaches nine feet in circumference, but here were white mushrooms, nearly forty feet high, and with tops of equal dimensions. They grew in countless thousands; the light could not make its way through their massive substance, and beneath them reigned a gloomy and mystic darkness.

Still I wished to go forward. The cold in the shades of this singular forest was intense. For nearly an hour we wandered about in this darkness visible. At length we left the spot, and once more returned to the shores of the lake, to light and comparative warmth.

But the amazing vegetation of subterraneous land was not confined to gigantic mushrooms. New wonders awaited us at every step. We had not gone many hundred yards, when we came upon a mighty group of other trees, with discolored leaves, the common humble trees of Mother Earth, of an exorbitant and phenomenal size: lycopodes a hundred feet high; flowering ferns as tall as pines; gigantic grasses!

"Astonishing, magnificent, splendid!" cried my uncle. "Here we have before us the whole flora of the second period of the world, that of transition. Behold the humble plants of our gardens, which in the first ages of the world were mighty trees. Look around you, my dear Harry. No botanist ever before gazed on such a sight!"

My uncle's enthusiasm, always a little more than was required, was now excusable.

"You are right, uncle," I remarked. "Providence appears to have designed the preservation in this vast and mysterious hothouse of antediluvian plants, to prove the sagacity of learned men in figuring them so marvellously on paper."

"Well said, my boy, very well said; it is indeed a mighty hothouse; but you would also be within the bounds of reason and common sense if you also added —a vast menagerie."

I looked rather anxiously around. If the animals were as exaggerated as the plants, the matter would certainly be serious.

"A menagerie?"

"Doubtless. Look at the dust we are treading under foot; behold the bones with which the whole soil of the seashore is covered—"

"Bones," I replied; "yes, certainly; the bones of antediluvian animals."

I stooped down as I spoke, and picked up one or two singular remains, relics of a bygone age. It was easy to give a name to these gigantic bones, in some instances as big as trunks of trees.

"Here is, clearly, the lower jawbone of a mastodon," I cried, almost as warmly and enthusiastically as my uncle. "Here are the molars of the dinotherium; here is a leg bone which belonged to the megatherium. You are right, uncle; it is indeed a menagerie, for the mighty animals to which these bones once belonged have lived and died on the shores of this subterranean sea, under the shadow of these plants. Look, yonder are whole skeletons; and yet—"

"And yet, nephew?" said my uncle, noticing that I suddenly came to a full stop.

"I do not understand the presence of such beasts in granite caverns, however vast and prodigious," was my reply.

"Why not?" said my uncle, with very much of his old professional impatience.

"Because it is well known that animal life only existed on earth during the secondary period, when the

181

sedimentary soil was formed by the alluviums, and thus replaced the hot and burning rocks of the primitive age."

"I have listened to you earnestly and with patience, Harry, and I have a simple and clear answer to your objections: and that is, that this itself is a sedimentary soil."

"How can that be at such enormous depth from the surface of the earth?"

"The fact can be explained both simply and geologically. At a certain period, the earth consisted only of an elastic crust, liable to alternative upward and downward movements in virtue of the law of attraction. It is very probable that many a landslip took place in those days, and that large portions of sedimentary soil were cast into huge and mighty chasms."

"Quite possible," I dryly remarked. "But, uncle, if these antediluvian animals formerly lived in these subterraneous regions, what more likely that one of these huge monsters may at this moment be concealed behind one of yonder mighty rocks."

As I spoke, I looked keenly around, examining with care every point of the horizon; but nothing alive appeared to exist on these deserted shores.

I now felt rather fatigued, and told my uncle so. The walk and excitement were too much for me in my weak state. I therefore seated myself at the end of a promontory, at the foot of which the waves broke in incessant rolls. I looked around a bay formed by projections of vast granitic rocks. At the extreme end was a little port protected by huge pyramids of stones. A brig and three or four schooners might have lain there with perfect ease. So natural did it seem, that every minute my imagination induced me to expect a vessel coming out under all sail and making for the open sea, under the influence of a warm southerly breeze.

But the fantastic illusion never lasted more than a

minute. We were the only living creatures in this sub-terranean world!

During certain periods there was an utter cessation of wind, when a silence deeper, more terrible than the silence of the desert, fell upon these solitary and arid rocks, and seemed to hang like a leaden weight upon the waters of this singular ocean. I sought, amid the awful stillness, to penetrate through the distant fog, to tear down the veil which concealed the mysterious distance. What unspoken words were murmured by my trembling lips! What questions did I wish to ask and did not! Where did this sea end? To what did it lead? Should we ever be able to examine its distant shores?

But my uncle had no doubts about the matter. He was convinced that our enterprise would in the end be successful. For my part, I was in a state of painful indecision—I desired to embark on the journey and to succeed, and still I feared the result.

After we had passed an hour or more in silent contemplation of the wondrous spectacle, we rose and went down toward the bank on our way to the grotto, which I was not sorry to gain. After a slight repast, I sought refuge in slumber, and at length, after many and tedious struggles, sleep came over my weary eyes.

28 ... *Launching the Raft*

On the morning of the next day, to my great surprise, I awoke completely restored. I thought a bath would be delightful after my long illness and sufferings. So, soon after rising, I went and plunged into the waters of this new Mediterranean. The bath was cool, fresh and invigorating.

I came back to breakfast with an excellent appetite. Hans, our worthy guide, thoroughly understood how to cook such eatables as we were able to provide; he had both fire and water at discretion, so that he was enabled slightly to vary the weary monotony of our ordinary repast.

Our morning meal was like a capital English breakfast, with coffee by way of a windup. And never had this delicious beverage been so welcome and refreshing.

My uncle had sufficient regard for my state of health not to interrupt me in the enjoyment of the meal, but he was evidently delighted when I had finished.

"Now then," said he, "come with me. It is the height of the tide, and I am anxious to study its curious phenomena."

"What!" I cried, rising in astonishment, "did you say the tide, uncle?"

"Certainly I did."

"You do not mean to say," I replied, in a tone of

respectful doubt, "that the influence of the sun and moon is felt here below."

"And pray why not? Are not all bodies influenced by the law of universal attraction? Why should this vast underground sea be exempt from the general law, the rule of the universe? Besides, there is nothing like that which is proved and demonstrated. Despite the great atmospheric pressure down here, you will notice that this inland sea rises and falls with as much regularity as the Atlantic itself."

As my uncle spoke, we reached the sandy shore, and saw and heard the waves breaking monotonously on the beach. They were evidently rising.

"This is truly the flood," I cried, looking at the water at my feet.

"Yes, my excellent nephew," replied my uncle, rubbing his hands with the gusto of a philosopher, "and you see by these several streaks of foam that the tide rises at least ten or twelve feet."

"It is indeed marvellous."

"By no means," he responded; "on the contrary, it is quite natural."

"It may appear so in your eyes, my dear uncle," was my reply, "but the whole phenomena of the place appear to me to partake of the marvellous. It is almost impossible to believe that which I see. Who, in his wildest dreams, could have imagined that beneath the crust of our earth there could exist a real ocean, with ebbing and flowing tides, with its changes of winds, and even its storms? I for one should have laughed the suggestion to scorn."

"But, Harry, my boy, why not?" inquired my uncle, with a pitying smile. "Is there any physical reason in opposition to it?"

"Well, if we give up the great theory of the central heat of the earth, I certainly can offer no reasons why anything should be looked upon as impossible."

"Then you will own," he added, "that the system of Sir Humphrey Davy is wholly justified by what we have seen?"

"I allow that it is, and that point once granted, I certainly can see no reason for doubting the existence of seas and other wonders, even countries, in the interior of the globe."

"That is so, but of course these varied countries are uninhabited?"

"Well, I grant that it is more likely than not; still, I do not see why this sea should not have given shelter to some species of unknown fish."

"Hitherto we have not discovered any, and the probabilities are rather against our ever doing so," observed the Professor.

I was losing my skepticism in the presence of these wonders.

"Well, I am determined to solve the question. It is my intention to try my luck with my fishing line and hook."

"Certainly; make the experiment," said my uncle, pleased with my enthusiasm. "While we are about it, it will certainly be only proper to discover all the secrets of this extraordinary region."

"But, after all, where are we now?" I asked. "All this time I have quite forgotten to ask you a question, which, doubtless, your philosophical instruments have long since answered."

"Well," replied the Professor, "examining the situation from only one point of view, we are now distant three hundred and fifty leagues from Iceland."

"So much?" was my exclamation.

"I have gone over the matter several times, and am sure not to have made a mistake of five hundred yards," replied my uncle, positively.

"And as to the direction—are we still going to the southeast?"

"Yes, with a western declination of nineteen degrees, forty-two minutes, just as it is above. As for the inclination, I have discovered a very curious fact."

"What may that be, uncle? Your information interests me."

"Why, that the needle, instead of dipping toward the pole as it does on earth, in the northern hemisphere has an upward tendency."

"This proves," I cried, "that the great point of magnetic attraction lies somewhere between the surface of the earth and the spot we have succeeded in reaching."

"Exactly, my observant nephew," exclaimed my uncle, elated and delighted; "and it is quite probable that if we succeed in getting toward the polar regions —somewhere near the seventy-third degree of latitude, where Sir James Ross discovered the magnetic pole, we shall behold the needle point directly upward. We have, therefore, discovered by analogy that this great center of attraction is not situated at a very great depth."

"Well," said I, rather surprised, "this discovery will astonish experimental philosophers. It was never suspected."

"Science, great, mighty, and in the end unerring," replied my uncle, dogmatically, "science has fallen into many errors—errors which have been fortunate and useful, rather than otherwise, for they have been the steppingstones to truth."

After some further discussion, I turned to another matter.

"Have you any idea of the depth we have reached?"

"We are now," continued the Professor, "exactly thirty-five leagues—above a hundred miles—down into the interior of the earth."

"So," said I, after measuring the distance on the map, "we are now beneath the Scottish Highlands, and have over our heads the lofty Grampian hills."

"You are quite right," said the Professor, laughing; "it sounds very alarming, the weight being heavy, but the vault which supports this vast mass of earth and rock, is solid and safe—the mighty Architect of the Universe has constructed it of solid materials. Man, even in his highest flights of vivid and poetic imagination, never thought of such things! What are the finest arches of our bridges, what the vaulted roofs of our cathedrals, to that mighty dome above us, and beneath which floats an ocean with its storms and calms and tides!"

"I admire it all as much as you can, uncle, and have no fear that our granite sky will fall upon our heads. But now that we have discussed matters of science and discovery, what are your future intentions? Are you not thinking of getting back to the surface of our beautiful earth?"

This was said more as a feeler, than with any hope of success.

"Go back, nephew," cried my uncle in a tone of alarm; "you are not surely thinking of anything so absurd or cowardly. No, my intention is to advance and continue our journey. We have as yet been singularly fortunate, and henceforth I hope we shall be more so."

"But," said I, "how are we to cross yonder liquid plain?"

"It is not my intention to leap into it head foremost, or even to swim across it, like Leander over the Hellespont. But as oceans are, after all, only great lakes, inasmuch as they are surrounded by land, so does it stand to reason that this central sea is circumscribed by granite surroundings."

"Doubtless," was my natural reply.

"Well, then, do you not think that when once we reach the other end, we shall find some means of continuing our journey?"

"Probably; but what extent do you allow to this internal ocean?"

"Well, I should fancy it to extend about forty or fifty leagues, more or less."

"But even supposing this approximation to be a correct one—what then?" I asked.

"My dear boy, we have no time for further discussion. We shall embark tomorrow."

I looked around with surprise and incredulity. I could see nothing in the shape of boat or vessel.

"What!" I cried. "We are about to launch out upon an unknown sea; and where, if I may ask, is the vessel to carry us?"

"Well, my dear boy, it will not be exactly what you would call a vessel. For the present we must be content with a good and solid raft."

"A raft," I cried, incredulously; "but down here a raft is as impossible of construction as a vessel—and I am at a loss to imagine—"

"My good Harry, if you were to listen instead of talking so much, you would hear," said my uncle, waxing a little impatient.

"I should hear?"

"Yes—certain knocks with the hammer, which Hans is now employing to make the raft. He has been at work for many hours."

"Making a raft?"

"Yes."

"But where has he found trees suitable for such a construction?"

"He found the trees already to his hand. Come, and you shall see our excellent guide at work."

More and more amazed at what I heard and saw, I followed my uncle like one in a dream.

After a walk of about a quarter of an hour, I saw Hans at work on the other side of the promontory which formed our natural port. A few minutes more and I was beside him. To my great surprise, on the sandy shore lay a half-finished raft. It was made from beams of a very peculiar wood, and a great number of limbs, joints, boughs, and pieces lay about, sufficient to have constructed a fleet of ships and boats.

I turned to my uncle, silent with astonishment and awe.

"Where did all this wood come from?" I cried. "What wood is it?"

"Well, there is pine wood, fir, and the palms of the northern regions, mineralized by the action of the sea," he replied, sententiously.

"Can it be possible?"

"Yes," said the learned Professor; "what you see is called fossil wood."

"But then," cried I, after reflecting for a moment, "like the lignites, it must be as hard and as heavy as iron, and therefore will certainly not float."

"Sometimes that is the case. Many of these woods have become true anthracites, but others again, like those you see before you, have only undergone one phase of fossil transformation. But there is no proof like demonstration," added my uncle, picking one or two of these precious waifs, and casting them into the sea.

The piece of wood, after having disappeared for a moment, came to the surface, and floated about with the oscillation produced by wind and tide.

"Are you convinced?" said my uncle, with a self-satisfied smile.

"I am convinced," I cried, "that what I see is incredible."

The fact was that my journey into the interior of the earth was rapidly changing all preconceived notions, and day by day preparing me for the marvellous.

I should not have been surprised to have seen a fleet of native canoes afloat upon that silent sea.

The very next evening, thanks to the industry and ability of Hans, the raft was finished. It was about ten feet long and five feet wide. The beams, bound together with stout ropes, were solid and firm, and, once launched by our united efforts, the improvised vessel floated tranquilly upon the waters of what the Professor had well named the Central Sea.

29 ... *On the Waters* *—A Raft Voyage*

On the 15th of August we were up betimes. There was no time to be lost. We now had to inaugurate a new kind of locomotion, which would have the advantage of being rapid and not fatiguing.

A mast, made of two pieces of wood fastened together to give additional strength, a yard made from another one, the sail a linen sheet from our bed. We were fortunately in no want of cordage, and the whole on trial appeared solid and seaworthy.

At six o'clock in the morning, when the eager and enthusiastic Professor gave the signal to embark, the victuals, the luggage, all our instruments, our weapons, and a goodly supply of sweet water, which we had collected from springs in the rocks, were placed on the raft.

Hans had, with considerable ingenuity, contrived a rudder, which enabled him to guide the floating apparatus with ease. He took the tiller, as a matter of course. The worthy man was as good a sailor as he was a guide and duck hunter. I then let go the painter which held us to the shore, the sail was brought to the wind, and we made a rapid offing.

Our sea voyage had at length commenced; and once more we were making for distant and unknown regions.

Just as we were about to leave the little port where the raft had been constructed, my uncle, who was very strong as to geographic nomenclature, wanted to give it a name, and, among others, suggested mine.

"Well," said I, "before you decide, I have another to propose."

"Well; out with it."

"I should like to call it Gretchen. Port Gretchen will sound very well on our future map."

"Well, then, Port Gretchen let it be," said the Professor.

And thus it was that the memory of my dear girl was attached to our adventurous and memorable expedition.

When we left the shore the wind was blowing from the northward and eastward. We went directly before the wind at a much greater speed than might have been expected from a raft. The dense layers of atmosphere at that depth had great propelling power, and acted upon the sail with considerable force.

At the end of an hour, my uncle, who had been taking careful observations, was enabled to judge of the rapidity with which we moved. It was far beyond anything seen in the upper world.

"If," he said, "we continue to advance at our present rate, we shall have travelled at least thirty leagues in twenty-four hours. With a mere raft this is an almost incredible velocity."

I certainly was surprised, and without making any reply, went forward upon the raft. Already the northern shore was fading away on the edge of the horizon. The two shores appeared to separate more and more, leaving a wide and open space for our departure. Before me I could see nothing but the vast and apparently limitless sea, upon which we floated, the only living objects in sight.

Huge and dark clouds cast their gray shadows below, shadows which seemed to crush that colorless and sullen water by their weight. Anything more suggestive of gloom and of regions of nether darkness I never beheld. Silvery rays of electric light, reflected here and there upon some small spots of water, brought up luminous sparkles in the long wake of our cumbrous bark. Presently we were wholly out of sight of land; not a vestige could be seen, nor any indication of where we were going. So still and motionless did we seem, without any distant point to fix our eyes on, that but for the phosphoric light at the wake of the raft I should have fancied that we were still and motionless.

But I knew that we were advancing at a very rapid rate.

About twelve o'clock in the day, vast collections of seaweed were discovered surrounding us on all sides. I was aware of the extraordinary vegetative power of these plants, which have been known to creep along the bottom of the great ocean, and stop the advance of large ships. But never were seaweeds seen so gigantic and wonderful as those of the Central Sea. I could well imagine how, seen at a distance, tossing and heaving on the summit of the billows, the long lines of algae have been taken for living things, and thus have been the fertile sources of the belief in sea serpents.

Our raft swept past great specimens of fucus, or sea wrack, from three to four thousand feet in length, immense, incredibly long, looking like snakes that stretched out far beyond our horizon. It afforded me great amusement to gaze on their variegated ribbon-like endless lengths. Hour after hour passed without our coming to the termination of these floating weeds. If my astonishment increased, my patience was well-nigh exhausted.

What natural force could possibly have produced such abnormal and extraordinary plants? What must have been the aspect of the globe, during the first centuries of its formation, when under the combined

194

action of heat and humidity, the vegetable kingdom occupied its vast surface, to the exclusion of everything else?

These were considerations of never-ending interest for the geologist and the philosopher.

All this while we were advancing on our journey; and at length night came; but, as I had remarked the evening before, the luminous state of the atmosphere was in nothing diminished. Whatever was the cause, it was a phenomenon upon the duration of which we could calculate with certainty.

As soon as our supper had been disposed of and some little speculative conversation indulged in, I stretched myself at the foot of the mast, and presently went to sleep.

Hans remained motionless at the tiller, allowing the raft to rise and fall on the waves. The wind being aft, and the sail square, all he had to do was to keep his oar in the center.

Ever since we had taken our departure from the newly named Port Gretchen, my worthy uncle had directed me to keep a regular log of our day's navigation, with instructions to put down even the most minute particulars, every interesting and curious phenomenon, the direction of the wind, our rate of sailing, the distance we went; in a word, every incident of our extraordinary voyage.

From our log, therefore, I tell the story of our voyage on the Central Sea.

Friday, August 16th. A steady breeze from the northwest. Raft progressing with extreme rapidity, and going perfectly straight. Coast still dimly visible about thirty leagues to leeward. Nothing to be seen beyond the horizon in front. The extraordinary intensity of the light neither increases nor diminishes. It is singularly stationary. The weather remarkably fine; that is to say, the clouds have ascended very high, and are light and fleecy, and surrounded by an atmosphere resembling silver in fusion.

Thermometer plus 32 degrees centigrade.

About twelve o'clock in the day, our guide Hans, having prepared and baited a hook, cast his line into the subterranean waters. The bait he used was a small piece of meat, by means of which he concealed his hook. Anxious as I was, I was for a long time doomed to disappointment. Were these waters supplied with fish, or not. That was the important question. No, was my decided answer. Then there came a sudden and rather hard tug. Hans coolly drew it in, and with it a fish which struggled violently to escape.

"A fish," cried my uncle, putting on his spectacles to examine it.

"It is a sturgeon!" I cried. "Certainly a small sturgeon."

The Professor examined the fish carefully, noting every characteristic; and he did not coincide in my opinion. The fish had a flat head, round body, and the lower extremities covered with bony scales; its mouth was wholly without teeth, the pectoral fins, which were highly developed, sprouted direct from the body, which, properly speaking, had no tail. The animal certainly belonged to the order in which naturalists class the sturgeon, but it differed from that fish in many essential particulars.

My uncle, after all, was not mistaken. After a long and patient examination, he said:—

"This fish, my dear boy, belongs to a family which has been extinct for ages, and of which no trace has ever been found on earth, except fossil remains in the Devonian strata."

"You do not mean to say," I cried, "that we have captured a live specimen of a fish belonging to the primitive stock that existed before the deluge?"

"We have," said the Professor, who all this time was

continuing his observations; "and you may see by careful examination that these fossil fish have no identity with existing species. To hold in one's hand, therefore, a living specimen of the order is enough to make a naturalist happy for life."

"But," cried I, "to what family does it belong?"

"To the order of Ganoides—an order of fish having angular scales, covered with bright enamel—forming one of the family of the Cephalaspides, of the genus—"

"Well, sir," I remarked, as I noticed my uncle hesitated to conclude.

"To the Genus Pterychtis—yes, I am certain of it. Still, though I am confident of the correctness of my surmise, this fish offers to our notice a remarkable peculiarity, never known to exist in any other fish but those which are the natives of subterranean waters, wells, lakes, caverns, and such like hidden pools."

"And what may that be?"

"It is blind."

"Blind!" I cried, much surprised.

"Not only blind," continued the Professor, "but absolutely without organs of sight."

I now examined our discovery for myself. It was singular, to be sure, but it was really a fact. This, however, might be a solitary instance, I suggested. The hook was baited again and once more thrown into the water. This subterranean ocean must have been tolerably well supplied with fish, for in two hours we took a large number of Pterychtis, as well as other fish belonging to another supposed extinct family, the Dipterides (a genus of fish furnished with two fins only, whence the name), though my uncle could not class it exactly. All, without exception, however, were blind. This unexpected capture enabled us to renew our stock of provisions in a very satisfactory way.

We were now convinced that this subterranean sea

contained only fish known to us as fossil specimens, and fish and reptiles alike were all the more perfect the farther back they dated their origin.

We began to hope that we should find some of those Saurians which science has succeeded in reconstructing from bits of bone or cartilage.

I took up the telescope and carefully examined the horizon, looked over the whole sea; it was utterly and entirely deserted. Doubtless we were still too near the coast.

After an examination of the ocean, I looked upward, toward the strange and mysterious sky. Why should not one of the birds, reconstructed by the immortal Cuvier, flap his stupendous wings aloft in the dull strata of subterranean air? It would, of course, find quite sufficient food from the fish in the sea. I gazed for some time upon the void above. It was as silent and as deserted as the shores we had but lately left.

Nevertheless, though I could neither see nor discover anything, my imagination carried me away into wild hypotheses. I was in a kind of waking dream. I thought I saw on the surface of the water those enormous antediluvian turtles as big as floating islands. Upon those dull and somber shores passed a spectral row of the mammifers of early days, the great Leptotherium found in the cavernous hollow of the Brazilian hills, the Mesicotherium, a native of the glacial regions of Siberia.

Farther on, the pachydermatous, Lophrodon, that gigantic tapir, which concealed itself behind rocks, ready to do battle for its prey with the Anoplotherium, a singular animal partaking of the nature of the rhinoceros, the horse, the hippopotamus and the camel.

There was the giant mastodon, twisting and turning his horrid trunk, with which he crushed the rocks of the shore to powder, while the Megatherium, his back raised like a cat in a passion, his enormous claws stretched out, dug into the earth for food, at the same time that he awoke the sonorous echoes of the whole place with his terrible roar.

Higher up still, the first monkey ever seen on the face of the globe clambered, gambolling and playing up the granite hills. Still farther away, ran the Pterodactyl, with the winged hand, gliding, or rather sailing, through the dense and compressed air like a huge bat.

Above all, near the leaden granitic sky, were immense birds, more powerful than the casoar, giants to the ostrich, which spread their mighty wings and fluttered against the huge stone vault of the inland sea.

I thought, such was the effect of my imagination, that I saw this whole tribe of antediluvian creatures. I carried myself back to far ages, long before man existed —when, in fact, the earth was in too perfect a state for him to live upon it.

My dream was of countless ages before the existence of man. The mammifers first disappeared, then the mighty birds, then the reptiles of the secondary period, presently the fish, the crustacea, the molluscs, and finally the vertebrata. The zoophytes of the period of transition in their turn sank into annihilation.

The whole panorama of the world's life before the historic period seemed to be born over again, and mine was the only human heart that beat in this unpeopled world! There were no more seasons; there were no more climates; the natural heat of the world increased unceasingly, and neutralized that of the great radiant Sun.

Vegetation was exaggerated in an extraordinary manner. I passed like a shadow in the midst of brushwood as lofty as the giant trees of California, and trod under foot the moist and humid soil, reeking with a rank and varied vegetation.

I leaned against the huge columnlike trunks of giant
199

trees, to which those of Canada were as ferns. Whole ages passed, hundreds upon hundreds of years were concentrated into a single day.

Next, unrolled before me like a panorama, came the great and wondrous series of terrestrial transformations. Plants disappeared; the granitic rocks lost all trace of solidity; the liquid state was suddenly substituted for that which had before existed. This was caused by intense heat acting on the organic matter of the earth. The waters flowed over the whole surface of the globe; they boiled; they were volatilized, or turned into vapor; a kind of steam-cloud wrapped the whole earth, the globe itself becoming at last nothing but one huge sphere of gas, indescribable in color, between white heat and red, as big and as brilliant as the sun.

In the very center of this prodigious mass, fourteen hundred thousand times as large as our globe, I was whirled round in space, and brought into close conjunction with the planets. My body was subtilized, or rather became volatile, and commingled in a state of atomic vapor with the prodigious clouds, which rushed forward like a mighty comet into infinite space!

What an extraordinary dream! Where would it finally take me? My feverish hand began to write down the marvellous details—details more like the imaginings of a lunatic than anything sober and real. I had during this period of hallucination forgotten everything—the Professor, the guide, and the raft on which we were floating. My mind was in a state of semioblivion.

"What is the matter, Harry?" said my uncle, suddenly.

My eyes, which were wide opened like those of a somnambulist, were fixed upon him, but I did not see him, nor could I clearly make out anything around me.

"Take care, my boy," again cried my uncle; "you will fall into the sea."

As he uttered these words, I felt myself seized on the other side by the firm hand of our devoted guide. Had it not been for the presence of mind of Hans, I must infallibly have fallen into the waves and been drowned.

"Have you gone mad?" cried my uncle, shaking me on the other side.

"What—what is the matter?" I said at last, coming to myself.

"Are you ill, Harry?" continued the Professor, in an anxious tone.

"No—no; but I have had an extraordinary dream. It, however, has passed away. All now seems well," I added, looking around me with strangely puzzled eyes.

"All right," said my uncle; "a beautiful breeze, a splendid sea. We are going along at a rapid rate, and if I am not out in my calculations we shall soon see land. I shall not be sorry to exchange the narrow limits of our raft for the mysterious strand of the subterranean ocean."

As my uncle uttered these words, I rose and carefully scanned the horizon. But the line of water was still confounded with the lowering clouds that hung aloft, and in the distance appeared to touch the edge of the water.

30 ... *Terrific Saurian Combat*

SATURDAY, August 17th. The sea still retains its uniform monotony. The same leaden hue, the same eternal glare from above. No indication of land being in sight. The horizon appears to retreat before us more and more as we advance.

My head, still dull and heavy from the effects of my extraordinary dream, which I cannot as yet banish from my mind.

The Professor, who has not dreamed, is, however, in one of his morose and unaccountable humors. Spends his time in scanning the horizon, at every point of the compass. His telescope is raised every moment to his eyes, and when he finds nothing to give any clue to our whereabouts, he assumes a Napoleonic attitude and walks anxiously.

I remarked that my uncle, the Professor, had a strong tendency to resume his old impatient character, and I could not but make a note of the disagreeable circumstance in my journal. I saw clearly that it had required all the influence of my danger and suffering to extract from him one scintillation of humane feeling. Now that I was quite recovered, his original nature had conquered and obtained the upper hand.

And, after all, what had he to be angry and annoyed about now more than at any other time? Was not the journey being accomplished under the most favorable circumstances? Was not the raft progressing with the most marvellous rapidity?

What, then, could be the matter? After one or two preliminary hems, I determined to inquire.

"You seem uneasy, uncle," said I, when for about the hundredth time he put down his telescope and walked up and down muttering to himself.

"No, I am not uneasy," he replied, in a dry, harsh tone; "by no means."

"Perhaps I should have said impatient," I replied, softening the force of my remark.

"Enough to make me so, I think."

"And yet we are advancing at a rate seldom attained by a raft," I remarked.

"What matters that?" cried my uncle. "I am not vexed at the rate we go at, but I am annoyed to find the sea so much vaster than I expected."

I then recollected that the Professor, before our departure, had estimated the length of this subterranean ocean as at most about thirty leagues. Now we had travelled at least over thrice that distance without discovering any trace of the distant shore. I began to understand my uncle's anger.

"We are not going down," suddenly exclaimed the Professor. "We are not progressing with our great discoveries. All this is utter loss of time. After all, I did not come from home to undertake a party of pleasure. This voyage on a raft over a pond annoys and wearies me."

He called this adventurous journey a party of pleasure, and this great inland sea a pond!

"But," argued I, "if we have followed the route indicated by the great Saknussemm, we can not be going far wrong."

"'That is the question,' as the great immortal Shakespeare has it. Are we following the route indicated by that wondrous sage? Did Saknussemm ever fall in

203

with this great sheet of water? If he did, did he cross it? I begin to fear that the rivulet we adopted for a guide has led us wrong."

"In any case, we can never regret having come thus far. It is worth the whole journey to have enjoyed this magnificent spectacle—it is something to have seen."

"I care nothing about seeing, nor about magnificent spectacles. I came down into the interior of the earth with an object, and that object I mean to attain. Don't talk to me about admiring scenery, or any other sentimental trash."

After this I thought it well to hold my tongue, and allow the Professor to bite his lips until the blood came, without further remark.

At six o'clock in the evening, our matter-of-fact guide, Hans, asked for his week's salary, and receiving his rix-dollars, put them carefully in his pocket. He was perfectly contented and satisfied.

Sunday, August 18th. Nothing new to record. The same weather as before. The wind has a slight tendency to freshen up, with signs of an approaching gale. When I awoke, my first observation was in regard to the intensity of the light. I kept on fearing, day after day, that the extraordinary electric phenomena should become first obscured, and then go wholly out, leaving us in total darkness. Nothing, however, of the kind occurs. The shadow of the raft, its mast and sails, is clearly distinguished on the surface of the water.

This wondrous sea is, after all, infinite in its extent. It must be quite as wide as the Mediterranean, or perhaps even as the great Atlantic Ocean. Why, after all, should it not be so?

My uncle has on more than one occasion tried deep sea soundings. He tied the cross of one of our heaviest crowbars to the extremity of a cord, which he allowed to run out to the extent of two hundred fathoms. We had the greatest difficulty in hoisting in our novel kind of lead.

When the crowbar was finally dragged on board, Hans called my attention to some singular marks upon its surface. The piece of iron looked as if it had been crushed between two very hard substances.

I looked at our worthy guide with an inquiring glance.

"*Tänder*," said he.

Of course I was at a loss to understand. I turned round toward my uncle, absorbed in gloomy reflections. I had little wish to disturb him from his reverie. I accordingly turned once more toward our worthy Icelander.

Hans very quietly and significantly opened his mouth once or twice, as if in the act of biting, and in this way made me understand his meaning.

"Teeth!" cried I, with stupefaction, as I examined the bar of iron with more attention.

Yes. There can be no doubt about the matter. The indentations on the bar of iron are the marks of teeth! What jaws must the owner of such molars be possessed of! Have we, then, come upon a monster of unknown species, which still exists within the vast waste of waters—a monster more voracious than a shark, more terrible and bulky than the whale. I am unable to withdraw my eyes from the bar of iron, actually half crushed!

Is, then, my dream about to come true—a dread and terrible reality?

All day my thoughts were bent upon these speculations, and my imagination scarcely regained a degree of calmness and power of reflection until after a sleep of many hours.

This day, as on other Sundays, we observed as a day of rest and pious meditation.

Monday, August 19th. I have been trying to realize

from memory the particular instincts of those ante-diluvian animals of the secondary period, which succeeding to the mollusca, to the crustacea, and to the fish, preceded the appearance of the race of mammifers. The generation of reptiles then reigned supreme upon the earth. These hideous monsters ruled everything in the seas of the secondary period, which formed the strata of which the Jura mountains are composed. Nature has endowed them with perfect organization. What a gigantic structure was theirs; what vast and prodigious strength they possessed!

The existing Saurians, which include all such reptiles as lizards, crocodiles, and alligators, even the largest and most formidable of their class, are but feeble imitations of their mighty sires, the animals of ages long ago. If there were giants in the days of old, there were also gigantic animals.

I shuddered as I evolved from my mind the idea and recollection of these awful monsters. No eye of man had seen them in the flesh. They took their walks abroad upon the face of the earth thousands of ages before man came into existence, and their fossile bones, discovered in the limestone, have allowed us to reconstruct them anatomically, and thus to get some faint idea of their colossal formation.

I recollect once seeing in the great Museum of Hamburg the skeleton of one of these wonderful Saurians. It measured no less than thirty feet from the nose to the tail. Am I, then, an inhabitant of the earth of the present day, destined to find myself face to face with a representative of this antediluvian family? I can scarcely believe it possible; can hardly believe it true. And yet these marks of powerful teeth upon the bar of iron! can there be a doubt from their shape that the bite is the bite of a crocodile?

My eyes stared wildly and with terror upon the subterranean sea. Every moment I expect one of these monsters to rise from the vast cavernous depths.

I fancy that the worthy Professor in some measure shares my notions, if not in my fears, for, after an attentive examination of the crowbar, he cast his eyes rapidly over the mighty and mysterious ocean.

"What could possess him to leave the land!" I thought; "as if the depth of this water was of any importance to us. No doubt he has disturbed some terrible monster in his watery home, and perhaps we may pay dearly for our temerity."

Anxious to be prepared for the worst, I examined our weapons, and saw that they were in a fit state for use. My uncle looked on at me and nodded his head approvingly. He, too, has noticed what we have to fear.

Already the uplifting of the waters on the surface indicates that something is in motion below. The danger approaches. It comes nearer and nearer. It behooves us to be on the watch.

Tuesday, August 20th. Evening came at last, the hour when the desire to sleep caused our eyelids to be heavy. Night there is not, properly speaking, in this place, any more than there is in summer in the arctic regions. Hans, however, is immovable at the rudder. When he snatches a moment of rest I really cannot say. I take advantage of his vigilance to take some little repose.

But two hours after, I was awakened from a heavy sleep by an awful shock. The raft appeared to have struck upon a sunken rock. It was lifted right out of the water by some wondrous and mysterious power, and then started off twenty fathoms distant.

"Eh, what is it?" cried my uncle, starting up. "Are we shipwrecked, or what?"

Hans raised his hand and pointed to where, about two hundred yards off, a huge black mass was moving up and down. I looked with awe. My worst fears were realized.

"It is a colossal monster!" I cried, clasping my hands.

"Yes," cried the agitated Professor, "and there yonder is a huge sea lizard of terrible size and shape."

"And farther on behold a prodigious crocodile. Look at his hideous jaws, and that row of monstrous teeth. Ha! he has gone."

"A whale! a whale!" shouted the Professor. "I can see her enormous fins. See, see, how she blows air and water!"

Two liquid columns rose to a vast height above the level of the sea, into which they fell with a terrific crash, waking up the echoes of that awful place. We stood still—surprised, stupefied, terror-stricken at the sight of this group of fearful marine monsters, more hideous in the reality than in my dream. They were of supernatural dimensions; the very smallest of the whole party could with ease have crushed our raft and ourselves with a single bite.

Hans, seizing the rudder which had flown out of his hand, puts it hard aweather in order to escape from such dangerous vicinity; but no sooner does he do so, than he finds he is flying from Scylla to Charybdis. To leeward is a turtle about forty feet wide, and a serpent quite as long, with an enormous and hideous head peering from out the waters.

Look which way we will, it is impossible for us to fly. The fearful reptiles advanced upon us; they turned and twisted about the raft with awful rapidity. They formed around our devoted vessel a series of concentric circles. I took up my rifle in desperation. But what effect can a rifle ball produce upon the armor scales with which the bodies of these horrid monsters are covered?

We remain still and dumb from utter horror. They

advance upon us, nearer and nearer. Our fate appears certain, fearful and terrible. On one side the mighty crocodile; on the other the great sea serpent. The rest of the fearful crowd of marine prodigies have plunged beneath the briny waves and disappeared!

I am about at all risks to fire, and try the effect of a shot. Hans, the guide, however, interfered by a sign to check me. The two hideous and ravenous monsters passed within fifty fathoms of the raft, and then made a rush at one another, their fury and rage preventing them from seeing us.

The combat commenced. We distinctly made out every action of the two hideous monsters.

But to my excited imagination the other animals appeared about to take part in the fierce and deadly struggle—the monster, the whale, the lizard, and the turtle. I distinctly saw them every moment. I pointed them out to the Icelander. But he only shook his head.

"*Tva*," he said.

"What—'two' only does he say? Surely he is mistaken," I cried, in a tone of wonder.

"He is quite right," replied my uncle, coolly and philosophically, examining the terrible duel with his telescope, and speaking as if he were in a lecture room.

"How can that be?"

"Yes, it is so. The first of these hideous monsters has the snout of a porpoise, the head of a lizard, the teeth of a crocodile; and it is this that has deceived us. It is the most fearful of all antediluvian reptiles, the world-renowned Ichthyosaurus, or Great Fish Lizard."

"And the other?"

"The other is a monstrous serpent, concealed under the hard vaulted shell of the turtle, the terrible enemy of its fearful rival, the Plesiosaurus, or Sea Crocodile."

Hans was quite right. The two monsters, only, disturbed the surface of the sea!

At last have mortal eyes gazed upon two reptiles of the great primitive ocean! I see the flaming red eyes of the Ichthyosaurus, each as big, or bigger, than a man's head. Nature, in its infinite wisdom, has gifted this wondrous marine animal with an optical apparatus of extreme power, capable of resisting the pressure of the heavy layers of water which rolled over him in the depth of the ocean where he usually fed. It has by some authors truly been called the whale of the Saurian race, for it is as big and quick in its motions as our king of the seas. This one measures not less than a hundred feet in length, and I can form some idea of his girth when I see him lift his prodigious tail out of the waters. His jaw is of awful size and strength, and, according to the best informed naturalists, it does not contain less than a hundred and eighty-two teeth.

The other was the mighty Plesiosaurus, a serpent with a cylindrical trunk, with a short, stumpy tail, with fins like a bank of oars in a Roman galley.

Its whole body covered by a carapace, or shell, and its neck, as flexible as that of a swan, rose more than thirty feet above the waves, a tower of animated flesh!

These animals attacked one another with inconceivable fury. Such a combat was never *seen* before by mortal eyes, and to us, who did see it, it appeared more like the phantasmagoric creation of a dream than anything else. They raised mountains of water, which dashed in spray over the raft, already tossed to and fro by the waves. Twenty times we seemed on the point of being upset and hurled headlong into the waves. Hideous hisses appeared to shake the gloomy granite roof of that mighty cavern—hisses which carried terror to our hearts. The awful combatants held each other in a tight embrace. I could not make out one from the other. Still the combat could not last forever; and woe unto us, whichsoever became the victor.

One hour, two hours, three hours passed away, without any decisive result. The struggle continued with the same deadly tenacity, but without apparent result. The deadly opponents now approached, now drew away from the raft. Once or twice we fancied they were about to leave us altogether, but, instead of that, they came nearer and nearer.

We crouched on the raft, ready to fire at them at a moment's notice, poor as the prospect of hurting or terrifying them was. Still we were determined not to perish without a struggle.

Suddenly the Ichthyosaurus and the Plesiosaurus disappeared beneath the waves, leaving behind them a maelstrom in the midst of the sea. We were very nearly drawn down by the indraught of the water!

Several minutes elapsed before anything was again seen. Was this wonderful combat to end in the depths of the ocean? Was the last act of this terrible drama to take place without spectators?

It was impossible for us to say.

Suddenly, at no great distance from us, an enormous mass rises out of the waters—the head of the great Plesiosaurus. The terrible monster is now wounded unto death. I can see nothing now of his enormous body. All that could be distinguished was his serpent-like neck, which he twisted and curled in all the agonies of death. Now he struck the waters with it as if it had been a gigantic whip, and then again wriggled like a worm cut in two. The water was spurted up to a great distance in all directions. A great portion of it swept over our raft and nearly blinded us. But soon the end of the beast approached nearer and nearer; his movements slackened visibly; his contortions almost ceased; and at last, the body of the mighty snake lay an inert, dead mass on the surface of the now calm and placid waters.

As for the Ichthyosaurus, has he gone down to his mighty cavern under the sea to rest, or will he reappear to destroy us?

This question remained unanswered. And we had breathing time.

31 ... *The Sea Monster*

WEDNESDAY, August 21st. Fortunately the wind, which at the present blows with great violence, has allowed us to escape from the scene of the unparalleled and extraordinary struggle. Hans, with his usual imperturbable calm, remained at the helm. My uncle, who for a short time had been withdrawn from his absorbing reverie by the novel incidents of this sea fight, fell back again apparently into a brown study. All this time, however, his eyes were fixed impatiently on the widespread ocean.

Our voyage now became monotonous and uniform. Dull as it has become, I have no desire to have it broken by any repetition of the perils and adventures of yesterday.

Thursday, August 22nd. The wind is now N. N. E., and blows very irregularly. It has changed to fitful gusts. The temperature is exceedingly high. We are now progressing at the average rate of about ten miles and a half per hour.

About twelve o'clock, a distant sound as of thunder fell upon our ears. I make a note of the fact without even venturing a suggestion as to its cause. It was one continued roar, as of a sea falling over mighty rocks.

"Far off in the distance," said the Professor, dogmatically, "there is some rock or some island against which the sea, lashed to fury by the wind, is breaking violently."

Hans, without saying a word, clambered to the top of the mast, but could make out nothing. The ocean was level in every direction as far as the eye could reach.

Three hours passed away without any sign to indicate what might be before us. The sound began to assume that of a mighty cataract.

I expressed my opinion on this point strongly to my uncle. He merely shook his head. I, however, am strongly impressed by a conviction that I am not wrong. Are we advancing toward some mighty waterfall which shall cast us into the abyss? Probably this mode of descending into the abyss may be agreeable to the Professor, because it would be something like the vertical descent he is so eager to make. I entertain a very different opinion.

Whatever be the truth, it is certain that not many leagues distant there must be some very extraordinary phenomenon, for as we advance the roar becomes something mighty and stupendous. Is it in the water, or in the air?

I cast hasty glances aloft at the suspended vapors, and I seek to penetrate their mighty depths. But the vault above is tranquil. The clouds, which are now elevated to the very summit, appear utterly still and motionless, and completely lost in the irradiation of electric light. It is necessary, therefore, to seek for the cause of this phenomenon elsewhere.

I examine the horizon, now perfectly calm, pure, and free from all haze. Its aspect still remains unchanged. But if this awful noise proceeds from a cataract—if, so to speak in plain English, this vast interior ocean is precipitated into a lower basin—if these tremendous roars are produced by the noise of falling waters, the current would increase in activity, and its increasing swiftness would give me some idea of the extent of the peril with which we are

214

menaced. I consult the current. It simply does not exist: there is no such thing. An empty bottle cast into the water lies to leeward without motion.

About four o'clock Hans rises, clambers up the mast and reaches the truck itself. From this elevated position his looks are cast around. They take in a vast circumference of the ocean.

At last, his eyes remain fixed. His face expresses no astonishment, but his eyes slightly dilate.

"He has seen something, at last," cried my uncle.

"I think so," I replied.

Hans came down, stood beside us, and pointed with his right hand to the south.

"*Der nere,*" he said.

"There," replied my uncle.

And, seizing his telescope, he looked at it with great attention for about a minute, which to me appeared an age. I knew not what to think or expect.

"Yes, yes," he cried, in a tone of considerable surprise, "there it is."

"What?" I asked.

"A tremendous spurt of water rising out of the waves."

"Some other marine monster," I cried, already alarmed.

"Perhaps."

"Then let us steer more to the westward, for we know what we have to expect from antediluvian animals," was my eager reply.

"Go ahead," said my uncle.

I turned toward Hans. Hans was at the tiller steering with his usual imperturbable calm.

Nevertheless, if from the distance which separated us from this creature, a distance which must be estimated at not less than a dozen leagues, and this spurting of water proceeded from the pranks of some antediluvian animal, his dimensions must be some-

215

thing preternatural. To fly is, therefore, the course to be suggested by ordinary prudence. But we have not come into that part of the world to be prudent. Such is my uncle's determination.

We, accordingly, continued to advance. The nearer we come, the loftier is the spouting water. What monster can fill himself with such huge volumes of water, and then unceasingly spout them out in such lofty jets!

At eight o'clock in the evening, reckoning as above ground where there is day and night, we are not more than two leagues from the mighty beast. Its long, black, enormous, mountainous body lies on the top of the water like an island. But then, sailors have been said to have gone ashore on sleeping whales, mistaking them for land. Is it illusion, or is it fear? Its length cannot be less than a thousand fathoms. What, then, is this cetaceous monster, of which no Cuvier ever thought?

It is quite motionless, and presents the appearance of sleep. The sea seems unable to lift him upwards; it is rather the waves which break on his huge and gigantic frame. The waterspout, rising to a height of five hundred feet, breaks in spray with a dull, sullen roar.

We advance, like senseless lunatics, toward this mighty mass.

I honestly confess that I was abjectly afraid. I declared that I would go no farther. I threatened in my terror to cut the sheet of the sail. I attacked the Professor with considerable acrimony, calling him foolhardy, mad, I know not what. He made no answer.

Suddenly the imperturbable Hans once more pointed his finger toward the menacing object.

"*Holme!*"

"An island!" cried my uncle.

216

"An island!" I replied, shrugging my shoulders at this poor attempt at deception.

"Of course it is," cried my uncle, bursting into a loud and joyous laugh.

"But the waterspout?"

"Geyser," said Hans.

"Yes, of course, a geyser," replied my uncle, still laughing, "a geyser like those common in Iceland. Jets like this are the great wonders of the country."

At first I would not allow that I had been so grossly deceived. What could be more ridiculous than to have taken an island for a marine monster? But, kick as one may, one must yield to evidence, and I was finally convinced of my error. It was nothing, after all, but a natural phenomenon.

As we approached nearer and nearer, the dimensions of the liquid sheaf of waters became truly grand and stupendous. The island had, at a distance, presented the appearance of an enormous whale, whose head rose high above the waters. The geyser, a word the Icelanders pronounce geysir, and which signifies fury, rose majestically from its summit. Dull detonations are heard every now and then, and the enormous jet, taken, as it were, with sudden fury, shakes its plume of vapor, and bounds into the first layer of the clouds. It is alone. Neither spurts of vapor nor hot springs surround it, and the whole volcanic power of that region is concentrated in one sublime column. The rays of electric light mix with this dazzling sheaf, every drop as it falls assuming the prismatic colors of the rainbow.

"Let us go on shore," said the Professor, after some minutes of silence.

It is necessary, however, to take great precaution, in order to avoid the weight of falling waters, which would cause the raft to founder in an instant. Hans, however, steers admirably, and brings us to the other extremity of the island.

I was the first to leap on the rock. My uncle followed, while the eider-duck hunter remained still, like a man above any childish sources of astonishment. We are now walking on granite mixed with silicious sandstone; the soil shivered under our feet like the sides of boilers in which overheated stream is forcibly confined. It is burning. We soon came in sight of the little central basin from which rose the geyser. I plunged a thermometer into the water which ran bubbling from the center, and it marked a heat of a hundred and sixty-three degrees!

This water, therefore, came from some place where the heat was intense. This was singularly in contradiction with the theories of Professor Hardwigg. I could not help telling him my opinion on the subject.

"Well," said he, sharply, "and what does this prove against my doctrine?"

"Nothing," replied I, dryly, seeing that I was running my head against a foregone conclusion.

Nevertheless, I am compelled to confess that until now we have been most remarkably fortunate, and that this voyage is being accomplished in most favorable conditions of temperature; but it appears evident, in fact, certain, that we shall sooner or later arrive at one of those regions where the central heat will reach its utmost limits, and will go far beyond all the possible gradations of thermometers.

Visions of the Hades of the ancients, believed to be in the center of the earth, floated through my imagination.

We shall, however, see what we shall see. That is the Professor's favorite phrase now. Having christened the volcanic island by the name of his nephew, the leader of the expedition turned away and gave the signal for embarkation.

218

I stood still, however, for some minutes, gazing upon the magnificent geyser. I soon was able to perceive that the upward tendency of the water was irregular; now it diminished in intensity, and then suddenly it regained new vigor, which I attributed to the variation of the pressure of the accumulated vapors in its reservoir.

At last we took our departure, going carefully round the projecting and rather dangerous rocks of the southern side. Hans had taken advantage of this brief halt to repair the raft. Not before it was required.

Before we took our final departure from the island, however, I made some observations to calculate the distance we had gone over, and I put them down in my journal. Since we left Port Gretchen, we had travelled two hundred and seventy leagues—more than eight hundred miles—on this great inland sea; we were, therefore, six hundred and twenty leagues from Iceland, and exactly under England.

32 ... *The Battle of the Elements*

FRIDAY, August 23rd. This morning the magnificent geyser had wholly disappeared. The wind had freshened up, and we were fast leaving the neighborhood of Harry's Island. Even the roaring sound of the mighty column was lost to the ear.

The weather, if, under the circumstances, we may use such an expression, is about to change very suddenly. The atmosphere is being gradually loaded with vapors, which carry with them the electricity formed by the constant evaporation of the saline waters; the clouds are slowly but sensibly falling toward the sea, and are assuming a dark olive texture; the electric rays can scarcely pierce through the opaque curtain which has fallen like a drop scene before this wondrous theatre, on the stage of which another and terrible drama is soon to be enacted. This time it is no fight of animals; it is the fearful battle of the elements.

I feel that I am very peculiarly influenced, as all creatures are on land when a deluge is about to take place.

The cumuli, a perfectly oval kind of cloud, piled upon the south, presented a most awful and sinister appearance with the pitiless aspect often seen before a storm. The air is extremely heavy; the sea is comparatively calm.

In the distance, the clouds have assumed the appearance of enormous balls of cotton, or rather pods, piled one above the other in picturesque confusion. By degrees, they appear to swell out, break, and gain in number what they lose in grandeur; their heaviness is so great that they are unable to lift themselves from the horizon; but under the influence of the upper currents of air, they are gradually broken up, become much darker, and then present the appearance of one single layer of a formidable character; now and then a lighter cloud, still lit up from above, rebounds upon this gray carpet, and is lost in the opaque mass.

There can be no doubt that the entire atmosphere is saturated with electric fluid; I am myself wholly impregnated; my hairs literally stand on end, as if under the influence of a galvanic battery. If one of my companions ventured to touch me, I think he would receive rather a violent and unpleasant shock.

About ten o'clock in the morning, the symptoms of the storm became more thorough and decisive; the wind appeared to soften down as if to take breath for a renewed attack; the vast funereal pall above us looked like a huge bag—like the cave of Æolus, in which the storm was collecting its forces for the attack.

I tried all I could not to believe in the menacing signs of the sky, and yet I could not avoid saying, as it were, involuntarily:

"I believe we are going to have bad weather."

The Professor made me no answer. He was in a horrible, in a destestable humor to see the ocean stretching interminably before his eyes. On hearing my words he simply shrugged his shoulders.

"We shall have a tremendous storm," I said again, pointing to the horizon. "These clouds are falling lower and lower upon the sea, as if to crush it."

A great silence prevailed. The wind wholly ceased. Nature assumed a dead calm, and ceased to breathe. Upon the mast, where I noticed a sort of slight *ignis*

221

fatuus, the sail hangs in loose, heavy folds. The raft is motionless in the midst of a dark, heavy sea—without undulation, without motion. It is as still as glass. But as we are making no progress, what is the use of keeping up the sail, which may be the cause of our perdition if the tempest should suddenly strike us without warning.

"Let us lower the sail," I said; "it is only an act of common prudence."

"No—no," cried my uncle, in an exasperated tone, "a hundred times, no. Let the wind strike us and do its worst, let the storm sweep us away where it will— only let me see the glimmer of some coast, of some rocky cliffs, even if they dash our raft into a thousand pieces. No! keep up the sail, no matter what happens."

These words were scarcely uttered, when the southern horizon underwent a sudden and violent change. The long accumulated vapors were resolved into water, and the air required to fill up the void produced became a wild and raging tempest.

It came from the most distant corners of the mighty cavern. It raged from every point of the compass. It roared; it yelled; it shrieked with glee as of demons let loose. The darkness increased and became indeed darkness visible.

The raft rose and fell with the storm, and bounded over the waves. My uncle was cast headlong upon the deck. I with great difficulty dragged myself toward him. He was holding on with might and main to the end of a cable, and appeared to gaze with pleasure and delight at the spectacle of the unchained elements.

Hans never moved a muscle. His long hair driven hither and thither by the tempest, and scattered wildly over his motionless face, gave him a most extraordinary appearance, for every single hair was illuminated by little sparkling sprigs.

His countenance presents the extraordinary appearance of an antediluvian man, a true contemporary of the Negatherium.

Still the mast holds good against the storm. The sail spreads out and fills like a soap bubble about to burst. The raft rushes on at a pace impossible to estimate, but still less swiftly than the body of water displaced beneath it, the rapidity of which may be seen by the lines which fly right and left in the wake.

"The sail, the sail!" I cried, making a trumpet of my hands, and then endeavoring to lower it.

"Let it alone!" said my uncle, more exasperated than ever.

"*Nej*," said Hans, gently shaking his head.

Nevertheless, the rain formed a roaring cataract before this horizon of which we were in search, and to which we were rushing like madmen.

But before this wilderness of waters reached us, the mighty veil of cloud was torn in twain; the sea began to foam wildly; and the electricity, produced by some vast and extraordinary chemical action in the upper layer of cloud, is brought into play. To the fearful claps of thunder are added dazzling flashes of lightning, such as I had never seen. The flashes crossed one another, hurled from every side; while the thunder came pealing like an echo. The mass of vapor becomes incandescent; the hailstones which strike the metal of our boots and our weapons are actually luminous; the waves as they rise appear to be fire-eating monsters, beneath which seethes an intense fire, their crests surmounted by combs of flame.

My eyes are dazzled, blinded by the intensity of light, my ears are deafened by the awful roar of the elements. I am compelled to hold onto the mast, which bends like a reed beneath the violence of the storm, to which none ever before seen by mariners bore any resemblance.

223

* * *

Here my travelling notes become very incomplete, loose and vague. I have only been able to make out one or two fugitive observations, jotted down in a mere mechanical way. But even their brevity, even their obscurity, show the emotions which overcame me.

* * *

Sunday, August 25th. Where have we got to? In what region are we wandering? We are still carried forward with inconceivable rapidity.

The night has been fearful, something not to be described. The storm shows no signs of cessation. We exist in the midst of an uproar which has no name. The detonations as of artillery are incessant. Our ears literally bleed. We are unable to exchange a word, or hear each other speak.

The lightning never ceases to flash for a single instant. I can see the zigzags, after a rapid dart, strike the arched roof of this mightiest of mighty vaults. If it were to give way and fall upon us! Other lightnings plunge their forked streaks in every direction, and take the form of globes of fire, which explode like bombshells over a beleaguered city. The general crash and roar do not apparently increase; it has already gone far beyond what human ear can appreciate. If all the powder magazines in the world were to explode together, it would be impossible for us to hear worse noise.

There is a constant emission of light from the storm clouds; the electric matter is incessantly released; evidently the gaseous principles of the air are out of order; innumerable columns of water rush up like waterspouts, and fall back upon the surface of the ocean in foam.

Whither are we going? My uncle still lies at full length upon the raft, without speaking, without taking any note of time.

The heat increases. I look at the thermometer; to my surprise it indicates—*the exact figure is here rubbed out in my manuscript.*

Monday, August 26th. This terrible storm will never end. Why should not this state of the atmosphere, so dense and murky, once modified, again remain definitive?

We are utterly broken and harassed by fatigue. Hans remains just as usual. The raft runs to the southeast invariably. We have now already run two hundred leagues from the newly discovered island.

About twelve o'clock the storm became worse than ever. We are obliged now to fasten every bit of cargo tightly on the deck of the raft, or everything would be swept away. We tie ourselves to the mast, each man lashing the other. The waves drive over us, so that several times we are actually under water.

We had been under the painful necessity of abstaining from speech for three days and three nights. We opened our mouths, we moved our lips, but no sound came. Even when we placed our mouths to each other's ears it was the same.

The wind carried the voice away.

My uncle once contrived to get his head close to mine after several almost vain endeavors. He appeared to my nearly exhausted senses to articulate some word. I had a notion, more from intuition than anything else, that he said to me, "we are lost."

I took out my notebook, from which under the most desperate circumstances I never parted, and wrote a few words as legibly as I could.

"Take in sail."

With a deep sigh he nodded his head and acquiesced.

His head had scarcely time to fall back in the position from which he had momentarily raised it, than a disc, or ball of fire, appeared on the very edge of the raft, our devoted, our doomed craft. The mast and sail are carried away bodily, and I see them swept away to a prodigious height like a kite.

We were frozen, actually shivered, with terror. The ball of fire, half white, half azure colored, about the size of a ten-inch bombshell, moved along, turning with prodigious rapidity to leeward of the storm. It ran about here, there and everywhere; it clambered up one of the bulwarks of the raft, it leaped upon the sack of provisions, and then finally descended lightly, fell like a football and landed on our powder barrel.

Horrible situation. An explosion of course was now inevitable.

By Heaven's mercy it is not so.

The dazzling disc moves on one side, it approaches Hans, who looked at it with singular fixity; then it approached my uncle, who cast himself on his knees to avoid it; it came toward me as I stood pale and shuddering in the dazzling light and heat; it pirouetted round my feet, which I endeavored to withdraw.

An odor of nitrous gas filled the whole air; it penetrated to the throat, to the lungs. I felt ready to choke.

Why is it that I cannot withdraw my feet? Are they riveted to the flooring of the raft?

No.

The fall of the electric globe has turned all the iron on board into lodestones—the instruments, the tools, the arms, are clanging together with awful and horrible noise; the nails of my heavy boots adhere closely to the plate of iron incrustated in the wood. I cannot withdraw my foot.

It is the old story over again of the mountain of adamant.

At last, by a violent and almost superhuman effort, I tear it away just as the ball, which is still executing its gyratory motions, is about to run round it and drag me with it—if—

Oh, what intense stupendous light! The globe of fire bursts—we are enveloped in cascades of living fire, which flood the space around with luminous matter.

Then all went out and darkness once more fell upon the deep! I had just time to see my uncle once more cast apparently senseless on the flooring of the raft, Hans at the helm, "spitting fire" under the influence of the electricity which seemed to have gone through him.

Whither are we going? I ask, and echo answers, Whither?

Tuesday, August 27th. I have just come out of a long fainting fit. The awful and hideous storm still continues; the lightning has increased in vividness, and pours out its fiery wrath like a brood of serpents let loose in the atmosphere.

Are we still upon the sea? Yes, and being carried along with incredible velocity.

We have passed under England, under the Channel, under France, probably under the whole extent of Europe.

* * *

Another awful clamor in the distance. This time it is certain that the sea is breaking upon the rocks at no great distance. Then—

33 ... *Our Route Reversed*

HERE ENDS what I call My Journal of our voyage on board the raft, which journal was happily saved from the wreck. I proceed with my narrative as I did before I commenced my daily notes.

What happened when the terrible shock took place, when the raft was cast upon the rocky shore, it would be impossible for me now to say. I felt myself precipitated violently into the boiling waves, and if I escaped from a certain and cruel death, it was wholly owing to the determination of the faithful Hans, who, clutching me by the arm, saved me from the yawning abyss.

The courageous Icelander then carried me in his powerful arms far out of the reach of the waves, and laid me down upon a burning expanse of sand, where I found myself some time afterwards in the company of my uncle, the Professor.

Then he quietly returned toward the fatal rocks, against which the furious waves were beating, in order to save any stray waifs from the wreck. This man was always practical and thoughtful. I could not utter a word; I was quite overcome with emotion; my whole body was broken and bruised with fatigue; it took hours before I was anything like myself.

Meanwhile there fell a fearful deluge of rain, drenching us to the skin. Its very violence, however, proclaimed the approaching end of the storm. Some overhanging rocks afforded us a slight protection from the torrents.

Under this shelter Hans prepared some food, which, however, I was unable to touch; and exhausted by the three weary days and nights of watching, we fell into a deep and painful sleep. My dreams were fearful; but at last exhausted Nature asserted her supremacy, and I slumbered.

Next day when I awoke, the change was magical. The weather was magnificent. Air and sea, as if by mutual consent, had regained their serenity. Every trace of the storm, even the faintest, had disappeared. I was saluted on my awakening by the first joyous tones I had heard from the Professor for many a day. His gayety, indeed, was something terrible.

"Well, my lad," he cried, rubbing his hands together, "have you slept soundly?"

Might it not have been supposed that we were in the old house of the Königsstrasse, that I had just come down quietly to my breakfast, and that my marriage with Gretchen was to take place that very day? My uncle's coolness was exasperating.

Alas, considering how the tempest had driven us in an easterly direction, we had passed under the whole of Germany, under the city of Hamburg where I had been so happy, under the very street which contained all I loved and cared for in the world.

It was a positive fact that I was only separated from her by a distance of forty leagues. But these forty leagues were of hard, impenetrable granite!

All these dreary and miserable reflections passed through my mind before I attempted to answer my uncle's question.

"Why, what is the matter?" he cried. "Can not you say whether you have slept well or not?"

"I have slept very well," was my reply; "but every

bone in my body aches. I suppose that will lead to nothing."

"Nothing at all, my boy. It is only the result of the fatigue of the last few days; that is all."

"You appear, if I may be allowed to say so, to be very jolly this morning," I said.

"Delighted, my dear boy, delighted. Was never happier in my life. We have at last reached the wished-for port."

"The end of our expedition?" cried I, in a tone of considerable surprise.

"No, but to the confines of that sea which I began to fear would never end, but go round the whole world. We will now tranquilly resume our journey by land, and once again endeavor to dive into the center of the earth."

"My dear uncle," I began, in a hesitating kind of way, "allow me to ask you one question."

"Certainly, Harry; a dozen, if you think proper."

"One will suffice. How about getting back?" I asked.

"How about getting back? What a question to ask! We have not as yet reached the end of our journey."

"I know that. All I want to know is, how you propose we shall manage the return voyage?"

"In the most simple manner in the world," said the imperturbable Professor. "Once we reach the exact center of this sphere, either we shall find a new road by which to ascend to the surface, or we shall simply turn round and go back by the way we came. I have every reason to believe that while we are travelling forward, it will not close behind us."

"Then one of the first matters to see to will be to repair the raft," was my rather melancholy response.

"Of course. We must attend to that, above all things," continued the Professor.

"Then comes the all-important question of provisions," I urged. "Have we anything like enough left to enable us to accomplish such great, such amazing designs as you contemplate carrying out?"

"I have seen into the matter, and my answer is in the affirmative. Hans is a very clever fellow, and I have reason to believe that he has saved the greater part of the cargo. But the best way to satisfy your scruples is to come and judge for yourself."

Saying which, he led the way out of the kind of open grotto in which we had taken shelter. I had almost begun to hope that which I should rather have feared, and this was the impossibility of such a shipwreck leaving even the slightest signs of what it had carried as freight. I was, however, thoroughly mistaken.

As soon as I reached the shores of this inland sea, I found Hans standing gravely in the midst of a large number of things laid out in complete order. My uncle wrung his hands with deep and silent gratitude. His heart was too full for speech.

This man, whose superhuman devotion to his employers I not only never saw surpassed, nor even equalled, had been hard at work all the time we slept, and at the risk of his life had succeeded in saving the most precious articles of our cargo.

Of course, under the circumstances, we necessarily experienced several severe losses. Our weapons had wholly vanished. But experience had taught us to do without them. The provision of powder, had, however, remained intact, after having narrowly escaped blowing us all to atoms in the storm.

"Well," said the Professor, who was now ready to make the best of everything, "as we have no guns, all we have to do is to give up all idea of hunting."

"Yes, my dear sir, we can do without them; but what about all our instruments?"

"Here is the manometer, the most useful of all, and which I gladly accept in lieu of the rest. With it alone

I can calculate the depth as we proceed; by its means alone I shall be able to decide when we have reached the center of the earth. Ha, ha! but for this little instrument we might make a mistake, and run the risk of coming out at the antipodes!"

All this was said amidst bursts of unnatural laughter.

"But the compass," I cried; "without that what can we do?"

"Here it is, safe and sound!" he cried, with real joy. "Ah, ah, and here we have the chronometer and the thermometers. Hans the hunter is indeed an invaluable man!"

It was impossible to deny this fact. As far as the nautical and other instruments were concerned, nothing was wanting. Then on further examination, I found ladders, cords, pickaxes, crowbars, and shovels, all scattered about on the shore.

There was, however, finally the most important question of all, and that was, provisions.

"But what are we to do for food?" I asked.

"Let us see to the commissariat department," replied my uncle, gravely.

The boxes which contained our supply of food for the voyage were placed in a row along the strand, and were in a capital state of preservation; the sea had in every case respected their contents, and to sum up in one sentence, taking into consideration biscuits, salt meat, schiedam and dried fish, we could still calculate on having about four months' supply, if used with prudence and caution.

"Four months," cried the sanguine Professor, in high glee; "then we shall have plenty of time both to go and to come, and with what remains I undertake to give a grand dinner to my colleagues of the Johanneum."

I sighed. I should by this time have used myself to

the temperament of my uncle, and yet this man astonished me more and more every day. He was the greatest human enigma I ever had known.

"Now," said he, "before we do anything else, we must lay in a stock of fresh water. The rain has fallen in abundance, and filled the hollows of the granite. There is a rich supply of water, and we have no fear of suffering from thirst, which in our circumstances is of the last importance. As for the raft, I shall recommend Hans to repair it to the best of all his abilities; though I have every reason to believe we shall not require it again."

"How is that?" I cried, more amazed than ever at my uncle's style of reasoning.

"I have an idea, my dear boy; it is none other than this simple fact: we shall not come out by the same opening as that by which we entered."

I began to look at my uncle with vague suspicion. An idea had more than once taken possession of me; and this was that he was going mad. And yet, little did I think how true and prophetic his words were doomed to be.

"And now," he said, "having seen to all these matters of detail, to breakfast."

I followed him to a sort of projecting cape, after he had given his last instructions to our guide. In this original position, with dried meat, biscuit, and a delicious cup of tea, we made a satisfactory meal; I may say one of the most welcome and pleasant I ever remember. Exhaustion, the keen atmosphere, the state of calm after so much agitation, all contributed to give me an excellent appetite. Indeed, it contributed very much to producing a pleasant and cheerful state of mind.

While breakfast was in hand, and between the sips of warm tea, I asked my uncle if he had any idea of how he now stood in relation to the world above.

233

"For my part," I added; "I think it will be rather difficult to determine."

"Well, if we were compelled to fix the exact spot," said my uncle, "it might be difficult, since during the three days of that awful tempest I could keep no account either of the quickness of our pace, or of the direction in which the raft was going. Still, we will endeavor to approximate to the truth. We shall not, I believe, be so very far out."

"Well, if I recollect rightly," I replied, "our last observation was made at the Geyser Island."

"Harry's Island, my boy! Harry's Island. Do not decline the honor of having named it; given your name to an island discovered by us, the first human beings who trod it since the creation of the world!"

"Let it be so, then. At Harry's Island we had already gone over two hundred and seventy miles of sea, and we were, I believe, about six hundred leagues, more or less, from Iceland."

"Good. I am glad to see that you remember so well. Let us start from that point, and let us count four days of storm, during which our rate of travelling must have been very great. I should say that our velocity must have been about eighty leagues to the twenty-four hours."

I agreed that I thought this a fair calculation. There were, then, three hundred leagues to be added to the grand total.

"Yes, and the Central Sea must extend at least six hundred leagues from side to side. Do you know, my boy Harry, that we have discovered an inland lake larger than the Mediterranean?"

"Certainly; and we only know of its extent in one way. It may be hundreds of miles in length."

"Very likely."

"Then," said I, after calculating for some minutes, "if

your previsions are right, we are at this moment exactly under the Mediterranean itself."

"Do you think so?"

"Yes, I am almost certain of it. Are we not nine hundred leagues distant from the Reykjavik?"

"That is perfectly true, and a famous bit of road we have travelled, my boy. But why we should be under the Mediterranean more than under Turkey or the Atlantic Ocean, can only be known when we are sure of not having deviated from our course; and of this we know nothing."

"I do not think we were driven very far from our course: the wind appears to me to have been always about the same. My opinion is that this shore must be situated to the southeast of Port Gretchen."

"Good—I hope so. It will, however, be easy to decide the matter by taking the bearings from our departure by means of the compass. Come along, and we will consult that invaluable invention."

The Professor now walked eagerly in the direction of the rock where the indefatigable Hans had placed the instruments in safety. My uncle was gay and light-hearted; he rubbed his hands, and assumed all sorts of attitudes. He was to all appearance once more a young man. Since I had known him never had he been so amiable and pleasant. I followed him, rather curious to know whether I had made any mistake in my estimation of our position.

As soon as we had reached the rock, my uncle took the compass, placed it horizontally before him, and looked keenly at the needle.

As he had at first shaken it to give it vivacity, it oscillated considerably, and then slowly assumed its right position under the influence of the magnetic power.

The Professor bent his eyes curiously over the wondrous instrument. A violent start immediately showed the extent of his emotion.

He closed his eyes, rubbed them, and took another and a keener survey.

Then he turned slowly round to me, stupefaction depicted on his countenance.

"What is the matter?" said I, beginning to be alarmed.

He could not speak. He was too overwhelmed for words. He simply pointed to the instrument.

I examined it eagerly, according to his mute directions, and a loud cry of surprise escaped my lips. The needle of the compass pointed due north, in the direction we expected was the south!

It pointed to the shore instead of to the high seas.

I shook the compass; I examined it with a curious and anxious eye. It was in a state of perfection. No blemish in any way explained the phenomenon. Whatever position we forced the needle into, it returned invariably to the same unexpected point.

It was useless to attempt to conceal from ourselves the fatal truth.

There could be no doubt about it, unwelcome as was the fact, that during the tempest there had been a sudden slant of wind, of which we had been unable to take any account, and thus the raft had carried us back to the shores we had left, apparently forever, so many days before!

34 ... *A Voyage of Discovery*

IT WOULD BE altogether impossible for me to give
any idea of the utter astonishment which overcame
the Professor on making this extraordinary discovery.
Amazement, incredulity, and rage were blended in
such a way as to alarm me.

During the whole course of my life I had never
seen a man at first so chapfallen; and then so furiously
indignant.

The terrible fatigues of our sea voyage, the fearful
dangers we had passed through, had all, all, gone
for nothing. We had to begin them all over again.

Instead of progressing, as we fondly expected, during a voyage of so many days, we had retreated.
Every hour of our expedition on the raft had been so
much lost time!

Presently, however, the indomitable energy of my
uncle overcame every other consideration.

"So," he said, between his set teeth, "fatality will
play me these terrible tricks. The elements themselves
conspire to overwhelm me with mortification. Air, fire,
and water combine their united efforts to oppose my
passage. Well, they shall see what the earnest will
of a determined man can do. I will not yield, I will
not retreat even one inch; and we shall see who
shall triumph in this great contest—man or nature."

Standing upright on a rock, irritated and menacing,
Professor Hardwigg, like the ferocious Ajax, seemed to

237

defy the fates. I, however, took upon myself to interfere, and to impose some sort of check upon such insensate enthusiasm.

"Listen to me, uncle," I said, in a firm but temperate tone of voice, "there must be some limit to ambition here below. It is utterly useless to struggle against the impossible. Pray listen to reason. We are utterly unprepared for a sea voyage; it is simple madness to think of performing a journey of five hundred leagues upon a wretched pile of beams, with a counterpane for a sail, a paltry stick for a mast, and a tempest to contend with. As we are totally incapable of steering our frail craft, we shall become the mere plaything of the storm, and it is acting the part of madmen if we, a second time, run any risk upon this dangerous and treacherous Central Sea."

These are only a few of the reasons and arguments I put together—reasons and arguments which to me appeared unanswerable. I was allowed to go on without interruption for about ten minutes. The explanation to this I soon discovered. The Professor was not even listening, and did not hear a word of all my eloquence.

"To the raft!" he cried, in a hoarse voice, when I paused for a reply.

Such was the result of my strenuous effort to resist his iron will. I tried again; I begged and implored him; I got into a passion; but I had to deal with a will more determined than my own. I seemed to feel like the waves which fought and battled against the huge mass of granite at our feet, which had smiled grimly for so many ages at their puny efforts.

Hans, meanwhile, without taking part in our discussion, had been repairing the raft. One would have supposed that he instinctively guessed at the further projects of my uncle.

By means of some fragments of cordage, he had again made the raft seaworthy.

While I had been speaking he had hoisted a new mast and sail, the latter already fluttering and waving in the breeze.

The worthy Professor spoke a few words to our imperturbable guide, who immediately began to put our baggage on board, and to prepare for our departure. The atmosphere was now tolerably clear and pure, and the northeast wind blew steadily and serenely. It appeared likely to last for some time.

What, then, could I do? Could I undertake to resist the iron will of two men? It was simply impossible; if even I could have hoped for the support of Hans. This, however, was out of the question. It appeared to me that the Icelander had set aside all personal will and identity. He was a picture of abnegation.

I could hope for nothing from one so infatuated with and devoted to his master. All I could do, therefore, was to swim with the stream.

In a mood of stolid and sullen resignation, I was about to take my accustomed place on the raft, when my uncle placed his hand upon my shoulder.

"There is no hurry, my boy," he said, "we shall not start until tomorrow."

I looked the picture of resignation to the dire will of fate.

"Under the circumstances," he said, "I ought to neglect no precautions. As fate has cast me upon these shores, I shall not leave without having completely examined them."

In order to understand this remark, I must explain that though we had been driven back to the northern shore, we had landed at a very different spot from that which had been our starting point.

Port Gretchen must, we calculated, be very much to the westward. Nothing, therefore, was more natural

239

and reasonable than that we should reconnoiter this new shore upon which we had so unexpectedly landed.

"Let us go on a journey of discovery," I cried.

And leaving Hans to his important operation, we started on our expedition. The distance between the foreshore at high water and the foot of the rocks was considerable. It would take about half an hour's walking to get from one to the other.

As we trudged along, our feet crushed innumerable shells of every shape and size—once the dwelling place of animals of every period of creation.

I particularly noticed some enormous shells—carapaces (turtle and tortoise species) the diameter of which exceeded fifteen feet.

They had in past ages belonged to those gigantic Glyptodons of the Pliocene period, of which the modern turtle is but a minute specimen. In addition, the whole soil was covered by a vast quantity of stony relics having the appearance of flints worn by the action of the waves, and lying in successive layers one above the other. I came to the conclusion that in past ages the sea must have covered the whole district. Upon the scattered rocks, now lying far beyond its reach, the mighty waves of ages had left evident marks of their passage.

On reflection, this appeared to me partially to explain the existence of this remarkable ocean, forty leagues below the surface of the earth's crust. According to my new, and perhaps fanciful, theory, this liquid mass must be gradually lost in the deep bowels of the earth. I had also no doubt that this mysterious sea was fed by infiltration of the ocean above, through imperceptible fissures.

Nevertheless, it was impossible not to admit that these fissures must now be nearly choked up, for if not, the cavern, or rather the immense and stupendous reservoir, would have been completely filled in a short space of time. Perhaps even this water, having to contend against the accumulated subterraneous fires of the interior of the earth, had become partially vaporized. Hence the explanation of those heavy clouds suspended over our heads, and the superabundant display of that electricity which occasioned such terrible storms in this deep and cavernous sea.

This lucid explanation of the phenomena we had witnessed appeared to me quite satisfactory. However great and mighty the marvels of nature may seem to us, they are always to be explained by physical reasons. Everything is subordinate to some great law of nature.

It now appeared clear that we were walking upon a kind of sedimentary soil, formed like all the soils of that period, so frequent on the surface of the globe, by the subsidence of the waters. The Professor, who was now in his element, carefully examined every rocky fissure. Let him only find an opening and it directly became important to him to examine its depth.

For a whole mile we followed the windings of the Central Sea, when suddenly an important change took place in the aspect of the soil. It seemed to have been rudely cast up, convulsionized, as it were, by a violent upheaving of the lower strata. In many places, hollows here, and hillocks there, attested great dislocations at some other period of the terrestrial mass.

We advanced with great difficulty over the broken masses of granite mixed with flint, quartz and alluvial deposits, when a large field, more even than a field, a plain of bones, appeared suddenly before our eyes! It looked like an immense cemetery, where generation after generation had mingled their mortal dust.

Lofty barrows of early remains rose at intervals. They undulated away to the limits of the distant horizon and were lost in a thick brown fog.

241

On that spot, some three square miles in extent, was accumulated the whole history of animal life—scarcely one creature upon the comparatively modern soil of the upper and inhabited world had there existed.

Nevertheless, we were drawn forward by an all-absorbing and impatient curiosity. Our feet crushed with a dry and crackling sound the remains of those prehistoric fossils, for which the museums of great cities quarrel, even when they obtain only rare and curious morsels. A thousand such naturalists as Cuvier would not have sufficed to recompose the skeletons of the organic beings which lay in this magnificent osseous collection.

I was utterly confounded. My uncle stood for some minutes with his arms raised on high toward the thick granite vault which served us for a sky. His mouth was wide open; his eyes sparkled wildly behind his spectacles (which he had fortunately saved), his head bobbed up and down and from side to side, while his whole attitude and mien expressed unbounded astonishment.

He stood in the presence of an endless, wondrous and inexhaustibly rich collection of antediluvian monsters, piled up for his own private and peculiar satisfaction.

Fancy an enthusiastic lover of books carried suddenly into the very midst of the famous library of Alexandria burned by the sacrilegious Omar, and which some miracle had restored to its pristine splendor! Such was something of the state of mind in which Uncle Hardwigg was now placed.

For some time he stood thus, literally aghast at the magnitude of his discovery.

But it was even a greater excitement when, darting wildly over this mass of organic dust, he caught up a naked skull and addressed me in a quivering voice—

"Harry, my boy—Harry—this is a human head!"

"A human head, uncle!" I said, no less amazed and stupefied than himself.

"Yes, nephew. Ah! Mr. Milne-Edwards—ah! Mr. De Quatrefages, why are you not here where I am—I, Professor Hardwigg!"

35 ... *Discovery upon Discovery*

I N ORDER fully to understand the exclamation made by my uncle, and his allusions to these illustrious and learned men, it will be necessary to enter into certain explanations in regard to a circumstance of the highest importance to palæontology or the science of fossil life, which had taken place a short time before our departure from the upper regions of the earth.

On the 28th of March, 1863, some navigators under the direction of M. Boucher de Perthes were at work in the great quarries of Moulin-Quignon, near Abbeville, in the department of the Somme, in France. While at work, they unexpectedly came upon a human jawbone buried fourteen feet below the surface of the soil. It was the first fossil of the kind that had ever been brought to the light of day. Near this unexpected human relic were found stone hatchets and carved flints, colored and clothed by time in one uniform brilliant tint of verdigris.

The report of this extraordinary and unexpected discovery spread not only all over France, but over England and Germany. Many learned men belonging to various scientific bodies, and noteworthy among others, Messrs. Milne-Edwards and De Quatrefages, took the affair very much to heart, demonstrated the incontestable authenticity of the bone in question, and became—to use the phrase then recognized in England—the most ardent supporters of the "jawbone question."

To the eminent geologists of the United Kingdom who looked upon the fact as certain—Messrs. Falconer, Buck, Carpenter and others—were soon united the learned men of Germany, and among those in the first rank, the most eager, the most enthusiastic, was my worthy uncle, Professor Hardwigg.

The authenticity of a human fossil of the Quaternary period seemed then to be incontestably demonstrated, and even to be admitted by the most sceptical.

This system or theory, call it what you will, had, it is true, a bitter adversary in M. Elie de Beaumont. This learned man, who holds such a high place in the scientific world, holds that the soil of Moulin-Quignon does not belong to the diluvium, but to a much less ancient strata, and, in accordance with Cuvier in this respect, he would by no means admit that the human species was contemporary with the animals of the Quaternary epoch. My worthy uncle, Professor Hardwigg, in concert with the great majority of geologists, had held firm, had disputed, discussed, and finally, after considerable talking and writing, M. Elie de Beaumont had been pretty well left alone in his opinions.

We were familiar with all the details of this discussion, but were far from being aware then that since our departure the matter had entered upon a new phase. Other similar jawbones, though belonging to individuals of varied types and very different natures, had been found in the movable gray sands of certain grottoes in France, Switzerland, and Belgium; together with arms, utensils, tools, bones of children, of men in the prime of life, and of old men. The existence of men in the Quaternary period became, therefore, more positive every day.

But this was far from being all. New remains, dug up from the Pliocene or Tertiary deposits, had enabled the more farseeing or audacious among learned men to assign even a far greater degree of antiquity to the human race. These remains, it is true, were not those of men; that is, were not the bones of men, but objects decidedly having served the human race, shinbones, thighbones of fossil animals, regularly scooped out, and in fact sculptured—bearing the unmistakable signs of human handiwork.

By means of these wondrous and unexpected discoveries, man ascended endless centuries in the scale of time; he, in fact, preceded the mastodon; became the contemporary of the *elephas meridionalis*—the southern elephant; acquired an antiquity of over a hundred thousand years—since that is the date given by the most eminent geologists to the Pliocene period of the earth. Such was then the state of palæontologic science, and what we moreover knew sufficed to explain our attitude before this great cemetery of the plains of the Hardwigg Ocean.

It will now be easy to understand the Professor's mingled astonishment and joy when, on advancing about twenty yards, he found himself in the presence of, I may say face to face with, a specimen of the human race actually belonging to the Quaternary period!

It was indeed a human skull, perfectly recognizable. Had a soil of very peculiar nature, like that of the cemetery of St. Michel at Bordeaux, preserved it during countless ages? This was the question I asked myself, but which I was wholly unable to answer. But this head with stretched and parchmenty skin, with the teeth whole, the hair abundant, was before our eyes as in life!

I stood mute, almost paralyzed with wonder and awe before this dread apparition of another age. My uncle, who on almost every occasion was a great talker, remained for a time completely dumbfounded. He was too full of emotion for speech to be possible. After a while, however, he raised up the body to which the skull belonged. We stood it on end. It seemed, to our excited imaginations, to look at us with its terrible hollow eyes.

After some minutes of silence, the man was vanquished by the Professor. Human instincts succumbed to scientific pride and exultation. Professor Hardwigg, carried away by his enthusiasm, forgot all the circumstances of our journey, the extraordinary position in which we were placed, the immense cavern which stretched faraway over our heads. There can be no doubt that he thought himself at the Institution addressing his attentive pupils, for he put on his most doctorial style, waved his hand, and began—

"Gentlemen, I have the honor on this auspicious occasion to present to you a man of the Quaternary period of our globe. Many learned men have denied his very existence, while other able persons, perhaps of even higher authority, have affirmed their belief in the reality of his life. If the St. Thomases of palæontology were present, they would reverentially touch him with their fingers and believe in his existence, thus acknowledging their obstinate heresy. I know that science should be careful in relation to all discoveries of this nature. I am not without having heard of the many Barnums and other quacks who have made a trade of such like pretended discoveries. I have, of course, heard of the discovery of the kneebones of Ajax, of the pretended finding of the body of Orestes by the Spartiates, and of the body of Asterius, ten spans long, fifteen feet—of which we read in Pausanias.

"I have read everything in relation to the skeleton of Trapani, discovered in the fourteenth century, and which many persons chose to regard as that of Polyphemus, and the history of the giant dug up during the sixteenth century in the environs of Palmyra. You are as well aware as I am, gentlemen, of the existence of the celebrated analysis made near Lucerne, in 1577, of the great bones which the celebrated Doctor Felix Plater declared belonged to a giant about nineteen feet high. I have devoured all the treatises of Cassanion, and all those memoirs, pamphlets, speeches, and replies, published in reference to the skeleton of Teutobochus, king of the Cimbri, the invader of Gaul, dug out of a gravel pit in Dauphiny, in 1613. In the eighteenth century I should have denied, with Peter Campet, the existence of the pre-Adamites of Scheuchzer. I have had in my hands the writing called Gigans"—

Here my uncle was afflicted by the natural infirmity which prevented him from pronouncing difficult words in public. It was not exactly stuttering, but a strange sort of constitutional hesitation.

"The writing named Gigans"—he repeated.

He, however, could get no further.

"*Giganteo*"—

Impossible! The unfortunate word would not come out. There would have been great laughter at the Institution, had the mistake happened there.

"Gigantosteology!" at last exclaimed Professor Hardwigg, between two savage growls.

Having got over his difficulty, and getting more and more excited—

"Yes, gentlemen, I am well acquainted with all these matters, and know, also, that Cuvier and Blumenbach fully recognized in these bones, the undeniable remains of mammoths of the Quaternary period. But after what we now see, to allow a doubt is to insult scientific inquiry. There is the body; you can see it; you can touch it. It is not a skeleton, it is a complete and uninjured body, preserved with an anthropological object."

I did not attempt to controvert this singular and astounding assertion.

"If I could but wash this corpse in a solution of sul-

248

phuric acid," continued my uncle, "I would undertake to remove all the earthy particles, and these resplendent shells, which are incrusted all over this body. But I am without this precious dissolving medium. Nevertheless, such as it is, this body will tell its own history."

Here the Professor held up the fossil body, and exhibited it with rare dexterity. No professional showman could have shown more activity.

"As on examination you will see," my uncle continued, "it is only about six feet in length, which is a long way from the pretended giants of early days. As to the particular race to which it belonged, it is incontestably Caucasian. It is of the white race, that is, of our own. The skull of this fossil being is a perfect ovoid without any remarkable or prominent development of the cheekbones, and without any projection of the jaw. It presents no indication of the prognathism which modifies the facial angle. Measure the angle for yourselves, and you will find that it is just ninety degrees. But I will advance still farther on the road of inquiry and deduction, and I dare venture to say that this human sample or specimen belongs to the Japhetic family, which spread over the world from India to the uttermost limits of western Europe. There is no occasion, gentlemen, to smile at my remarks."

Of course nobody smiled. But the excellent Professor was so accustomed to beaming countenances at his lectures, that he believed he saw all his audience laughing during the delivery of his learned dissertation.

"Yes," he continued, with renewed animation, "this is a fossil man, a contemporary of the mastodons, with the bones of which this whole amphitheater is covered. But if I am called on to explain how he came to this place, how these various strata by which he is covered have fallen into this vast cavity, I can undertake to give you no explanation. Doubtless, if we carry ourselves back to the Quaternary epoch, we shall find that great and mighty convulsions took place in the crust of the earth; the continually cooling operation, through which the earth had to pass, produced fissures, landslips, and chasms, through which a large portion of the earth made its way. I come to no absolute conclusion, but there is the man, surrounded by the works of his hands, his hatchets, and his carved flints, which belong to the stony period; and the only rational supposition is, that, like myself, he visited the center of the earth as a travelling tourist, a pioneer of science. At all events, there can be no doubt of his great age, and of his being one of the oldest race of human beings."

The Professor with these words ceased his oration, and I burst forth into loud and "unanimous" applause. Besides, after all, my uncle was right. Much more learned men than his nephew would have found it rather hard to refute his facts and arguments.

Another circumstance soon presented itself. This fossilized body was not the only one in this vast plain of bones—the cemetery of an extinct world. Other bodies were found, as we trod the dusty plain, and my uncle was able to choose the most marvellous of these specimens in order to convince the most incredulous.

In truth, it was a surprising spectacle, the successive remains of generations and generations of men and animals confounded together in one vast cemetery. But a great question now presented itself to our notice, and one we were actually afraid to contemplate in all its bearings.

Had these once animated beings been buried so far beneath the soil by some tremendous convulsion of nature, after they had been earth to earth and ashes to ashes, or had they lived here below, in this subterranean world, under this factitious sky, born, married, and given in marriage, and dying at last, just like ordinary inhabitants of the earth?

Up to the present moment, marine monsters, fish, and such like animals, had alone been seen alive!

The question which rendered us rather uneasy, was a pertinent one. Were any of these men of the abyss wandering about the deserted shores of this wondrous sea of the center of the earth?

This was a question which rendered me very uneasy and uncomfortable. How, should they really be in existence, would they receive us men from above?

36 ... *What Is It?*

For a long and weary hour we tramped over this great bed of bones. We advanced regardless of everything, drawn on by ardent curiosity. What other marvels did this great cavern contain—what other wondrous treasures for the scientific man? My eyes were quite prepared for any number of surprises, my imagination lived in expectation of something new and wonderful.

The borders of the great Central Ocean had for some time disappeared behind the hills that were scattered over the ground occupied by the plain of bones. The imprudent and enthusiastic Professor, who did not care whether he lost himself or not, hurried me forward. We advanced silently, bathed in waves of electric fluid.

By reason of a phenomenon which I cannot explain, and thanks to its extreme diffusion, now complete, the light illumined equally the sides of every hill and rock. Its seat appeared to be nowhere, in no determined force, and produced no shade whatever.

The appearance presented was that of a tropical country at midday in summer—in the midst of the equatorial regions and under the vertical rays of the sun.

All signs of vapor had disappeared. The rocks, the distant mountains, some confused masses of far-off forests, assumed a weird and mysterious aspect under this equal distribution of the luminous fluid!

We resembled, to a certain extent, the mysterious

personage in one of Hoffmann's fantastic tales—the man who lost his shadow.

After we had walked about a mile farther, we came to the edge of a vast forest, not, however, one of the vast mushroom forests we had discovered near Port Gretchen.

It was the glorious and wild vegetation of the Tertiary period, in all its superb magnificence. Huge palms, of a species now unknown, superb palmacites —a genus of fossil palms from the coal formation— pines, yews, cypress, and conifers or cone-bearing trees, the whole bound together by an inextricable and complicated mass of creeping plants.

A beautiful carpet of mosses and ferns grew beneath the trees. Pleasant brooks murmured beneath umbrageous boughs, little worthy of this name, for no shade did they give. Upon their borders grew small treelike shrubs, such as are seen in the hot countries on our own inhabited globe.

The one thing wanted to these plants, these shrubs, these trees—was color! Forever deprived of the vivifying warmth of the sun, they were vapid and colorless. All shade was lost in one uniform tint, of a brown and faded character. The leaves were wholly devoid of verdure, and the flowers, so numerous during the Tertiary period which gave them birth, were without color and without perfume, something like paper discolored by long exposure to the atmosphere.

My uncle ventured beneath the gigantic groves. I followed him, though not without a certain amount of apprehension. Since nature had shown herself capable of producing such stupendous vegetable productions, why might we not meet with mammals (animals with breasts) as large, and therefore dangerous.

I particularly remarked, in the clearings left by trees that had fallen and been partially consumed by time, many leguminous (beanlike) shrubs, such as the maple and other eatable trees, dear to ruminating animals. Then there appeared confounded together and intermixed, the trees of such varied lands, specimens of the vegetation of every part of the globe; there was the oak near the palm tree, the Australian eucalyptus, an interesting class of the order *Myrtaceæ*—leaning against the tall Norwegian pine, the poplar of the north, mixing its branches with those of the New Zealand kauris. It was enough to drive the most ingenious classifier of the upper regions out of his mind, and to upset all his received ideas about botany.

Suddenly I stopped short and restrained my uncle.

The extreme diffuseness of the light enabled me to see the smallest objects in the distant copses. I thought I saw—no, I really did see with my own eyes—immense, gigantic animals moving about under the mighty trees. Yes, they were truly gigantic animals, a whole herd of mastodons, not fossils, but living, and exactly like those discovered in 1801, on the marshy banks of the great Ohio, in North America.

Yes, I could see these enormous elephants, whose trunks were tearing down large boughs, and working in and out the trees like a legion of serpents. I could hear the sounds of the mighty tusks uprooting huge trees!

The boughs crackled, and the whole masses of leaves and green branches went down the capacious throats of these terrible monsters!

That wondrous dream, when I saw the ante-historical times revivified, when the Tertiary and Quaternary periods passed before me, was now realized!

And there we were alone, far down in the bowels of the earth, at the mercy of its ferocious inhabitants!

My uncle paused, full of wonder and astonishment.

"Come," he said at last, when his first surprise was over, "come along, my boy, and let us see them nearer."

"No," replied I, restraining his efforts to drag me forward, "we are wholly without arms. What should we do in the midst of that flock of gigantic quadrupeds? Come away, uncle, I implore you. No human creature can with impunity brave the ferocious anger of these monsters."

"No human creature," said my uncle, suddenly lowering his voice to a mysterious whisper, "you are mistaken, my dear Henry. Look! look yonder! It seems to me that I behold a human being—a being like ourselves—a man!"

I looked, shrugging my shoulders, decided to push incredulity to its very last limits. But whatever might have been my wish, I was compelled to yield to the weight of ocular demonstration.

Yes—not more than a quarter of a mile off, leaning against the trunk of an enormous tree, was a human being—a Proteus of these subterranean regions, a new son of Neptune keeping this innumerable herd of mastodons.

Immanis pecoris custos, immanis ipse!—The keeper of gigantic cattle, himself a giant!

Yes—it was no longer a fossil whose corpse we had raised from the ground in the great cemetery, but a giant capable of guiding and driving these prodigious monsters. His height was above twelve feet. His head, as big as the head of a buffalo, was lost in a mane of matted hair. It was indeed a huge mane, like those which belonged to the elephants of the earlier ages of the world.

In his hand was a branch of a tree, which served as a crook for this antediluvian shepherd.

We remained profoundly still, speechless with surprise.

But we might at any moment be seen by him. Nothing remained for us but instant flight.

"Come, come!" I cried, dragging my uncle along;

255

and, for the first time, he made no resistance to my wishes.

A quarter of an hour later we were faraway from that terrible monster!

Now that I think of the matter calmly, and that I reflect upon it dispassionately; now that months, years, have passed since this strange and unnatural adventure befell us—what am I to think, what am I to believe?

No, it is utterly impossible! Our ears must have deceived us, and our eyes have cheated us! we have not seen what we believed we had seen. No human being could by any possibility have existed in that subterranean world! No generation of men could inhabit the lower caverns of the globe without taking note of those who peopled the surface, without communication with them. It was folly, folly, folly! nothing else!

I am rather inclined to admit the existence of some animal resembling in structure the human race—of some monkey of the first geological epochs, like that discovered by M. Lartet in the ossiferous deposit of Sansan.

But this animal, or being, whichsoever it was, surpassed in height all things known to modern science. Never mind. However unlikely it may be, it might have been a monkey—but a man, a living man, and with him a whole generation of gigantic animals, buried in the entrails of the earth—it was too monstrous to be believed!

37 ... *The Mysterious Dagger*

During this time, we had left the bright and transparent forest far behind us. We were mute with astonishment, overcome by a kind of feeling which was next door to apathy. We kept running in spite of ourselves. It was a perfect flight, which resembled one of those horrible sensations we sometimes meet with in our dreams.

Instinctively we made our way toward the Central Sea, and I cannot now tell what wild thoughts passed through my mind, nor of what follies I might have been guilty, but for a very serious preoccupation which brought me back to practical life.

Though I was aware that we were treading on a soil quite new to us, I, however, every now and then noticed certain aggregations of rock, the shape of which forcibly reminded me of those near Port Gretchen.

This confirmed, moreover, the indications of the compass and our extraordinary and unlooked-for, as well as involuntary, return to the north of this great Central Sea. It was so like our starting point that I could scarcely doubt the reality of our position. Streams and cascades fell in hundreds over the numerous projections of the rocks.

I actually thought I could see our faithful and monotonous Hans and the wonderful grotto in which I had come back to life after my tremendous fall.

Then, as we advanced still farther, the position of the cliffs, the appearance of a stream, the unexpected profile of a rock, threw me again into a state of bewildering doubt.

After some time, I explained my state of mental indecision to my uncle. He confessed to a similar feeling of hesitation. He was totally unable to make up his mind in the midst of this extraordinary but uniform panorama.

"There can be no doubt," I insisted, "that we have not landed exactly at the place whence we took our first departure; but the tempest has brought us above our starting point. I think, therefore, that if we follow the coast we shall once more find Port Gretchen."

"In that case," cried my uncle, "it is useless to continue our exploration. The very best thing we can do is to make our way back to the raft. Are you quite sure, Harry, that you are not mistaken?"

"It is difficult," was my reply, "to come to any decision, for all these rocks are exactly alike. There is no marked difference between them. At the same time, the impression on my mind is that I recognize the promontory at the foot of which our worthy Hans constructed the raft. We are, I am nearly convinced, near the little port: if this be not it," I added carefully examining a creek which appeared singularly familiar to my mind.

"My dear Harry—if this were the case, we should find traces of our own footsteps, some signs of our passage; and I can really see nothing to indicate our having passed this way."

"But I see something," I cried, in an impetuous tone of voice, as I rushed forward and eagerly picked up something which shone in the sand under my feet.

"What is it?" cried the astonished and bewildered Professor.

"This," was my reply.

And I handed to my startled relative a rusty dagger, of singular shape.

"What made you bring with you so useless a weapon?" he exclaimed. "It was needlessly hampering yourself."

"I bring it?—it is quite new to me. I never saw it before—are you sure it is not out of your collection?"

"Not that I know of," said the Professor, puzzled. "I have no recollection of the circumstance. It was never my property."

"This is very extraordinary," I said, musing over the novel and singular incident.

"Not at all. There is a very simple explanation, Harry. The Icelanders are known to keep up the use of these antiquated weapons, and this must have belonged to Hans, who has let it fall without knowing it."

I shook my head. That dagger had never been in the possession of the pacific and taciturn Hans. I knew him and his habits too well.

"Then what can it be—unless it be the weapon of some antediluvian warrior," I continued, "of some living man, a contemporary of that mighty shepherd from whom we have just escaped? But no—mystery upon mystery—this is no weapon of the Stony epoch, nor even of the Bronze period. It is made of excellent steel"—

Ere I could finish my sentence, my uncle stopped me short from entering upon a whole train of theories, and spake in his most cold and decided tone of voice.

"Calm yourself, my dear boy, and endeavor to use your reason. This weapon, upon which we have fallen so unexpectedly, is a true *dague*, one of those worn by gentlemen in their belts during the sixteenth century. Its use was to give the *coup de grâce*, the final blow, to the foe who would not surrender. It is clearly of Spanish workmanship. It belongs neither to you, nor

259

to me, nor the eider-down hunter, nor to any of the living beings who may still exist so marvellously in the interior of the earth."

"What can you mean, uncle?" I said, now lost in a host of surmises.

"Look closely at it," he continued; "these jagged edges were never made by the resistance of human blood and bone. The blade is covered with a regular coating of iron-mould and rust, which is not a day old, not a year old, not a century old, but much more"—

The Professor began to get quite excited, according to custom, and was allowing himself to be carried away by his fertile imagination. I could have said something. He stopped me.

"Harry," he cried, "we are now on the verge of a great discovery. This blade of a dagger you have so marvellously discovered, after being abandoned upon the sand for more than a hundred, two hundred, even three hundred years, has been indented by some one endeavoring to carve an inscription on these rocks."

"But this poniard never got here of itself," I exclaimed, "it could not have twisted itself. Some one, therefore, must have preceded us upon the shores of this extraordinary sea."

"Yes, a man."

"But what man has been sufficiently desperate to do such a thing?"

"A man who has somewhere written his name with this very dagger—a man who has endeavored once more to indicate the right road to the interior of the earth. Let us look around, my boy. You know not the importance of your singular and happy discovery."

Prodigiously interested, we walked along the wall of rock, examining the smallest fissures, which might finally expand into the much wished for gully or shaft.

We at last reached a spot where the shore became

extremely narrow. The sea almost bathed the foot of the rocks, which were here very lofty and steep. There was scarcely a path wider than two yards at any point. At last, under a huge overhanging rock, we discovered the entrance of a dark and gloomy tunnel.

There, on a square tablet of granite, which had been smoothed by rubbing it with another stone, we could see two mysterious, and much worn, letters, the two initials of the bold and extraordinary traveller who had preceded us on our adventurous journey.

$$ \cdot \, \text{ᚼ} \cdot \text{ᛁ} \cdot $$

"A.S.," cried my uncle. "You see I was right. Arne Saknussemm, always Arne Saknussemm!"

38 ... *No Outlet*
—Blasting the Rock

Ever since the commencement of our marvellous journey, I had experienced many surprises, had suffered from many illusions. I thought that I was case-hardened against all surprises, and could neither see nor hear anything to amaze me again.

I was like a man who, having been round the world, finds himself wholly blasé and proof against the marvellous.

When, however, I saw these two letters, which had been engraven three hundred years before, I stood fixed in an attitude of mute surprise.

Not only was there the signature of the learned and enterprising alchemist written in the rock, but I held in my hand the very identical instrument with which he had laboriously engraved it.

It was impossible, without showing an amount of incredulity scarcely becoming a sane man, to deny the existence of the traveller, and the reality of that voyage which I believed all along to have been a myth—the mystification of some fertile brain.

While these reflections were passing through my mind, my uncle, the Professor, gave way to an access of feverish and poetical excitement.

"Wonderful and glorious genius, great Saknussemm," he cried, "you have left no stone unturned, no resource omitted, to show to other mortals the way into the interior of our mighty globe, and your fellow creatures can find the trail left by your illustrious footsteps, three hundred years ago, at the bottom of these obscure subterranean abodes. You have been careful to secure for others the contemplation of these wonders and marvels of creation. Your name engraved at every important stage of your glorious journey leads the hopeful traveller direct to the great and mighty discovery to which you devoted such energy and courage. The audacious traveller, who shall follow your footsteps to the last, will doubtless find your initials engraved with your own hand upon the center of the earth. *I* will be that audacious traveller—*I*, too, will sign my name upon the very same spot, upon the central granite stone of this wondrous work of the Creator. But in justice to your devotion, to your courage, and to your being the first to indicate the road, let this Cape, seen by you upon the shores of this sea discovered by you, be called of all time, Cape Saknussemm."

This is what I heard, and I began to be roused to the pitch of enthusiasm indicated by those words. A fierce excitement roused me. I forgot everything. The dangers of the voyage, and the perils of the return journey, were now as nothing!

What another man had done in ages past, could, I felt, be done again; I was determined to do it myself, and now nothing that man had accomplished appeared to me impossible.

"Forward—forward," I cried in a burst of genuine and hearty enthusiasm.

I had already started in the direction of the somber and gloomy gallery, when the Professor stopped me; he, the man so rash and hasty, he, the man so easily roused to the highest pitch of enthusiasm, checked me, and asked me to be patient and show more calmness.

"Let us return to our good friend, Hans," he said;

"we will then bring the raft down to this place."

I must say that though I at once yielded to my uncle's request, it was not without dissatisfaction, and I hastened along the rocks of that wonderful coast.

"Do you know, my dear uncle," I said, as we walked along, "that we have been singularly helped by a concurrence of circumstances, right up to this very moment."

"So you begin to see it, do you, Harry?" said the Professor, with a smile.

"Doubtless," I responded, "and strangely enough, even the tempest has been the means of putting us on the right road. Blessings on the tempest! It brought us safely back to the very spot from which fine weather would have driven us forever. Supposing we had succeeded in reaching the southern and distant shores of this extraordinary sea, what would have become of us? The name of Saknussemm would never have appeared to us, and at this moment we should have been cast away upon an inhospitable coast, probably without an outlet."

"Yes, Harry, my boy, there is certainly something providential in that wandering at the mercy of wind and waves toward the south: we have come back exactly north; and what is better still, we fall upon this great discovery of Cape Saknussemm. I mean to say, that it is more than surprising; there is something in it which is far beyond my comprehension. The coincidence is unheard-of, marvellous!"

"What matter! It is not our duty to explain facts, but to make the best possible use of them."

"Doubtless, my boy; but if you will allow me"—said the really delighted Professor.

"Excuse me, sir, but I see exactly how it will be; we shall take the northern route; we shall pass under the northern regions of Europe, under Sweden, under Russia, under Siberia, and who knows where—instead of burying ourselves under the burning plains and deserts of Africa, or beneath the mighty waves of the ocean; and that is all, at this stage of our journey, that I care to know. Let us advance, and Heaven will be our guide!"

"Yes, Harry, you are right, quite right; all is for the best. Let us abandon this horizontal sea, which could never have led to anything satisfactory. We shall descend, descend, and everlastingly descend. Do you know, my dear boy, that to reach the interior of the earth we have only five thousand miles to travel!"

"Bah!" I cried, carried away by a burst of enthusiasm, "the distance is scarcely worth speaking about. The thing is to make a start."

My wild, mad, and incoherent speeches continued until we rejoined our patient and phlegmatic guide. All was, we found, prepared for an immediate departure. There was not a single parcel but what was in its proper place. We all took up our posts on the raft, and the sail being hoisted, Hans received his directions, and guided the frail bark toward Cape Saknussemm, as we had definitely named it.

The wind was very unfavorable to a craft that was unable to sail close to the wind. It was constructed to go before the blast. We were continually reduced to pushing ourselves forward by means of poles. On several occasions the rocks ran far out into deep water, and we were compelled to make a long round. At last, after three long and weary hours of navigation, that is to say, about six o'clock in the evening, we found a place at which we could land.

I jumped on shore first. In my present state of excitement and enthusiasm, I was always first. My uncle and the Icelander followed. The voyage from the port to this point of the sea had by no means calmed me. It had rather produced the opposite effect. I even proposed to burn our vessel, that is to destroy our raft, in order to completely cut off our retreat. But my uncle sternly opposed this wild project. I began to think him particularly lukewarm and unenthusiastic.

"At any rate, my dear uncle," I said, "let us start without delay."

"Yes, my boy, I am quite as eager to do so as you can be. But, in the first place, let us examine this mysterious gallery, in order to find if we shall need to prepare and mend our ladders."

My uncle now began to see to the efficiency of our Ruhmkorff's coil, which would doubtless soon be needed; the raft, securely fastened to a rock, was left alone. Moreover, the opening into the new gallery was not twenty paces distant from the spot. Our little troop, with myself at the head, advanced.

The orifice, which was almost circular, presented a diameter of about five feet; the somber tunnel was cut in the living rock, and coated on the inside by the different material which had once passed through it in a state of fusion. The lower part was about level with the water, so that we were able to penetrate to the interior without difficulty.

We followed an almost horizontal direction; when, at the end of about a dozen paces, our farther advance was checked by the interposition of an enormous block of granite rock.

"Accursed stone!" I cried, furiously, on perceiving that we were stopped by what seemed an insurmountable obstacle.

In vain we looked to the right, in vain we looked to the left; in vain examined it above and below. There existed no passage, no sign of any other tunnel. I experienced the most bitter and painful disappointment. So enraged was I that I would not admit the reality of any obstacle. I stooped to my knees; I looked under the mass of stone. No hole, no interstice. I then looked above. The same barrier of granite! Hans, with the lamp, examined the sides of the tunnel in every direction. But all in vain! It was necessary to renounce all hope of passing through.

I had seated myself upon the ground. My uncle walked angrily and hopelessly up and down. He was evidently desperate.

"But," I cried, after some moments' thought, "what about Arne Saknussemm?"

"You are right," replied my uncle, "he can never have been checked by a lump of rock."

"No—ten thousand times no," I cried, with extreme vivacity. "This huge lump of rock, in consequence of some singular concussion, or process, one of those magnetic phenomena which have so often shaken the terrestrial crust, has in some unexpected way closed up the passage. Many and many years have passed away since the return of Saknussemm, and the fall of this huge block of granite. Is it not quite evident that this gallery was formerly the outlet for the pent-up lava in the interior of the earth, and that these eruptive matters then circulated freely? Look at these recent fissures in the granite roof; it is evidently formed of pieces of enormous stone, placed here as if by the hand of a giant, who had worked to make a strong and substantial arch. One day, after an unusually strong shock, the vast rock which stands in our way, and which was doubtless the key of a kind of arch, fell through to a level with the soil and has barred our farther progress. We are right, then, in thinking that this is an unexpected obstacle, with which Saknussemm did not meet; and if we do not upset it in some way, we are unworthy of following in the footsteps of the great discoverer; and incapable of finding our way to the Center of the Earth!"

In this wild way I addressed my uncle. The zeal of the Professor, his earnest longing for success, had become part and parcel of my being. I wholly forgot the past; I utterly despised the future. Nothing existed for me upon the surface of this spheroid in the bosom of which I was ingulfed, no towns, no country, no Hamburg, no Königstrasse, not even my poor Gretchen, who by this time would believe me utterly lost in the interior of the earth!

"Well," cried my uncle, roused to enthusiasm by my words, "let us go to work with pickaxes, with crowbars, with anything that comes to hand—but down with these terrible walls."

"It is far too tough and too big to be destroyed by a pickaxe or crowbar," I replied.

"What then?"

"As I said, it is useless to think of overcoming such a difficulty by means of ordinary tools."

"What then?"

"What else but gunpowder, a subterranean mine? Let us blow up the obstacle that stands in our way."

"Gunpowder!"

"Yes; all we have to do is to get rid of this paltry obstacle."

"To work, Hans, to work!" cried the Professor.

The Icelander went back to the raft, and soon returned with a huge crowbar, with which he began to dig a hole in the rock, which was to serve as a mine. It was by no means a slight task. It was necessary for our purpose to make a cavity large enough to hold fifty pounds of fulminating gun cotton, the expansive power of which is four times as great as those of ordinary gunpowder.

I had now roused myself to an almost miraculous state of excitement. While Hans was at work, I actively assisted my uncle to prepare a long wick, made from damp gunpowder, the mass of which we finally enclosed in a bag of linen.

"We are bound to go through," I cried, enthusiastically.

"We are bound to go through," responded the Professor, tapping me on the back.

At midnight, our work as miners was completely finished; the charge of fulminating cotton was thrust into the hollow, and the match, which we had made of considerable length, was ready.

A spark was now sufficient to ignite this formidable engine, and to blow the rock to atoms!

"We will now rest until tomorrow."

It was absolutely necessary to resign myself to my fate, and to consent to wait for the explosion for six weary hours!

39 ... The Explosion and Its Results

THE NEXT DAY, which was the twenty-ninth of
August, was a date celebrated in our wondrous,
subterranean journey.

I never think of it even now, but I shudder with
horror. My heart beats wildly at the very memory of
that awful day.

From this time forward, our reason, our judgment,
our human ingenuity have nothing to do with the
course of events. We are about to become the plaything of the great phenomena of the earth!

At six o'clock we were all up and ready. The
dreaded moment was arriving when we were about to
seek an opening into the interior of the earth by means
of gunpowder. What would be the consequence of
breaking through the crust of the earth?

I begged that it might be my duty to set fire to
the mine. I looked upon it as an honor. This task once
performed, I could rejoin my friends upon the raft,
which had not been unloaded. As soon as we were all
ready, we were to sail away to some distance to avoid
the consequences of the explosion, the effect of which
would certainly not be concentrated in the interior of
the earth.

The slow match we calculated to burn for about
ten minutes, more or less, before it reached the chamber
in which the great body of powder was confined. I
should therefore have plenty of time to reach the raft
and put off to a safe distance.

I prepared to execute my self-allotted task—not, it must be confessed, without considerable emotion.

After a hearty repast, my uncle and the hunter-guide embarked on board the raft, while I remained alone upon the desolate shore.

I was provided with a lantern which was to enable me to set fire to the wick of the infernal machine.

"Go, my boy," said my uncle, "and Heaven be with you. But come back as soon as you can. I shall be all impatience."

"Be easy on that matter," I replied. "There is no fear of my delaying on the road."

Having said this, I advanced toward the opening of the somber gallery. My heart beat wildly. I opened my lantern and seized the extremity of the wick.

The Professor, who was looking on, held his chronometer in his hand.

"Are you ready?" cried he.

"Quite ready."

"Well, then, fire away!"

I hastened to put the light to the wick, which crackled and sparkled, hissing and spitting like a serpent; then, running as fast as I could, I returned to the shore.

"Get on board my lad, and you, Hans, shove off," cried my uncle.

By a vigorous application of his pole Hans sent us flying over the water. The raft was quite twenty fathoms distant.

It was a moment of palpitating interest, of deep anxiety. My uncle, the Professor, never took his eyes off the chronometer.

"Only five minutes more," he said in a low tone, "only four, only three."

My pulse went a hundred to the minute. I could hear my heart beating.

271

"Only two, one! Now, then, mountains of granite, crumble beneath the power of man!"

What happened after that? As to the terrific roar of the explosion, I do not think I heard it. But the form of the rocks completely changed in my eyes—they seemed to be drawn aside like a curtain. I saw a fathomless, a bottomless abyss, which yawned beneath the turgid waves. The sea, which seemed suddenly to have gone mad, then became one great mountainous mass, upon the top of which the raft rose perpendicularly.

We were all thrown down. In less than a second the light gave place to the most profound obscurity. Then I felt all solid support give way not to my feet, but to the raft itself. I thought it was going bodily down a tremendous well. I tried to speak, to question my uncle. Nothing could be heard but the roaring of the mighty waves. We clung together in utter silence.

Despite the awful darkness, despite the noise, the surprise, the emotion, I thoroughly understood what had happened.

Beyond the rock which had been blown up, there existed a mighty abyss. The explosion had caused a kind of earthquake in this soil, broken by fissures and rents. The gulf, thus suddenly thrown open, was about to swallow the inland sea, which, transformed into a mighty torrent, was dragging us with it.

Only one idea filled my mind. We were utterly and completely lost!

One hour, two hours—what more I cannot say, passed in this manner. We sat close together, elbow touching elbow, knee touching knee! We held one another's hands not to be thrown off the raft. We were subjected to the most violent shocks, whenever our sole dependence, a frail wooden raft, struck against the rocky sides of the channel. Fortunately for us, these concussions became less and less frequent, which made me fancy that the gallery was getting wider and wider. There could be now no doubt that we had chanced upon the road once followed by Saknussemm, but instead of going down in a proper manner, we had, through our own imprudence, drawn a whole sea with us!

These ideas presented themselves to my mind in a very vague and obscure manner. I felt rather than reasoned. I put my ideas together only confusedly, while spinning along like a man going down a waterfall. To judge by the air which, as it were, whipped my face, we must have been rushing at a perfectly lightning rate.

To attempt under these circumstances to light a torch was simply impossible, and the last remains of our electric machine, of our Ruhmkorf's coil, had been destroyed during the fearful explosion.

I was therefore very much confused to see at last a bright light shining close to me. The calm countenance of the guide seemed to gleam upon me. The clever and patient hunter had succeeded in lighting the lantern; and though, in the keen and thorough draught, the flame flickered and vacillated and was nearly put out, it served partially to dissipate the awful obscurity.

The gallery into which we had entered was very wide. I was, therefore, quite right in that part of my conjecture. The insufficient light did not allow us to see both of the walls at the same time. The slope of waters, which was carrying us away, was far greater than that of the most rapid river of America. The whole surface of the stream seemed to be composed of liquid arrows, darted forward with extreme violence and power. I can give no idea of the impression it made upon me.

The raft, at times, caught in certain whirlpools, and rushed forward, yet turned on itself all the time. How it did not upset I shall never be able to understand.

When it approached the sides of the gallery, I took care to throw upon them the light of the lantern, and I was able to judge of the rapidity of motion by looking at the projecting masses of rock, which as soon as seen were again invisible. So rapid was our progress that points of rock, at a considerable distance one from the other, appeared like portions of transverse lines, which enclosed us in a kind of net, like that of a line of telegraphic wires.

I believe we were now going at a rate of not less than a hundred miles an hour.

My uncle and I looked at one another with wild and haggard eyes; we clung convulsively to the stump of the mast, which at the moment when the catastrophe took place, had snapped short off. We turned our backs as much as possible to the wind, in order not to be stifled by a rapidity of motion which nothing human could face and live.

And still the long monotonous hours went on. The situation did not change in the least, though a discovery I suddenly made seemed to complicate it very much.

When we had slightly recovered our equilibrium, I proceeded to examine our cargo. I then made the unsatisfactory discovery that the greater part of it had utterly disappeared.

I became alarmed, and determined to discover what were our resources. My heart beat at the idea, but it was absolutely necessary to know on what we had to depend. With this view, I took the lantern and looked around.

Of all our former collection of nautical and philosophical instruments there remained only the chronometer and the compass. The ladders and ropes were reduced to a small piece of rope fastened to the stump of the mast. Not a pickaxe, not a crowbar, not a hammer, and, far worse than all, no food—not enough for one day!

This discovery was a prelude to a certain and horrible death.

Seated gloomily on the raft, clasping the stump of the mast mechanically, I thought of all I had read as to sufferings from starvation.

I remembered everything that history had taught me on the subject, and I shuddered at the remembrance of the agonies to be endured.

Maddened at the prospects of enduring the miseries of starvation, I persuaded myself that I must be mistaken. I examined the cracks in the raft; I poked between the joints and beams; I examined every possible hole and corner. The result was—simply nothing!

Our stock of provisions consisted of nothing but a piece of dry meat and some soaked and half-mouldy biscuits.

I gazed around me scared and frightened. I could not understand the awful truth. And yet of what consequence was it in regard to any new danger? Supposing that we had had provisions for months, and even for years, how could we ever get out of the awful abyss into which we were being hurled by the irresistible torrent we had let loose?

Why should we trouble ourselves about the sufferings and tortures to be endured from hunger, when death stared us in the face under so many other swifter and perhaps even more horrid forms?

It was very doubtful, under the circumstances in which we were placed, if we should have time to die of inanition.

But the human frame is singularly constituted.

I knew not how it was; but, from some singular hallucination of the mind, I forgot the real, serious and immediate danger to which we were exposed, to think of the menaces of the future, which appeared before us in all their naked terror. Besides, after all, suggested Hope, perhaps we might finally escape the fury of the raging torrent, and once more revisit the glimpses of the moon, on the surface of our beautiful Mother Earth.

How was it to be done? I had not the remotest idea. Where were we to come out? No matter, so that we did.

One chance in a thousand is always a chance, while death from hunger gave us not even the faintest glimpse of hope. It left to the imagination nothing but blank horror, without the faintest chance of escape!

I had the greatest mind to reveal all to my uncle, to explain to him the extraordinary and wretched position to which we were reduced, in order that, between the two, we might make a calculation as to the exact space of time which remained for us to live.

It was, it appeared to me, the only thing to be done. But I had the courage to hold my tongue, to gnaw at my entrails like the Spartan boy. I wished to leave him all his coolness.

At this moment, the light of the lantern slowly fell, and at last went out.

The wick had wholly burnt to an end. The obscurity became absolute. It was no longer possible to see through the impenetrable darkness! There was one torch left, but it was impossible to keep it alight. Then, like a child, I shut my eyes, that I might not see the darkness.

After a great lapse of time, the rapidity of our journey increased. I could feel it by the rush of air upon my face. The slope of the waters was excessive. I began to feel that we were no longer going down a slope; we were falling. I felt as one does in a dream, going down bodily—falling; falling; falling!

I felt that the hands of my uncle and Hans were vigorously clasping my arms.

Suddenly, after a lapse of time scarcely appreciable, I felt something like a shock. The raft had not struck a hard body, but had suddenly been checked in its course. A waterspout, a liquid column of water fell upon us. I felt suffocating. I was being drowned.

Still the sudden inundation did not last. In a few seconds I felt myself once more able to breathe. My uncle and Hans pressed my arms, and the raft carried us all three away.

40 ... *The Ape Gigans*

I**T IS DIFFICULT** for me to determine what was the real time, but I should suppose, by after calculation, that it must have been ten at night.

I lay in a stupor, a half dream, during which I saw visions of astounding character. Monsters of the deep were side by side with the mighty elephantine shepherd. Gigantic fish and animals seemed to form strange conjunctions.

The raft took a sudden turn, whirled round; entered another tunnel; this time illumined in a most singular manner. The roof was formed of porous stalactite, through which a moonlit vapor appeared to pass, casting its brilliant light upon our gaunt and haggard figures. The light increased as we advanced, while the roof ascended; until at last, we were once more in a kind of water cavern, the lofty dome of which disappeared in a luminous cloud.

A rugged cavern of small extent appeared to offer a halting place to our weary bodies.

My uncle and the guide moved as men in a dream. I was afraid to waken them, knowing the danger of such a sudden start. I seated myself beside them to watch.

As I did so, I became aware of something moving in the distance, which at once fascinated my eyes. It was floating, apparently, upon the surface of the water, advancing by means of what at first appeared paddles.

I looked with glaring eyes. One glance told me that it was something monstrous.

But what?

It was the great *Shark Crocodile* of the early writers on geology. About the size of an ordinary whale, with hideous jaws and two gigantic eyes, it advanced, its eyes fixed on me with terrible sternness. Some indefinite warning told me that it had marked me for its own.

I attempted to rise—to escape, no matter where, but my knees shook under me; my limbs trembled violently; I almost lost my senses. And still the mighty monster advanced. My uncle and the guide made no effort to save themselves.

With a strange noise, like none other I had ever heard, the beast came on. His jaws were at least seven feet apart, and his distended mouth looked large enough to have swallowed a boatful of men.

We were about ten feet distant, when I discovered that much as his body resembled that of a crocodile, his mouth was wholly that of a shark.

His twofold nature now became apparent. To snatch us up at a mouthful it was necessary for him to turn on his back, which motion necessarily caused his legs to kick up helplessly in the air.

I actually laughed even in the very jaws of death!

But next minute, with a wild cry, I darted away into the interior of the cavern, leaving my unhappy comrades to their fate! This cavern was deep and dreary. After about a hundred yards, I paused and looked around.

The whole floor, composed of sand and malachite, was strewn with bones, freshly gnawed bones of reptiles and fish, with a mixture of mammalia. My very soul grew sick as my body shuddered with horror. I had truly, according to the old proverb, fallen out of the frying pan into the fire. Some beast larger and more ferocious even than the Shark-Crocodile inhabited this den.

What could I do? The mouth of the cave was guarded by one ferocious monster, the interior was inhabited by something too hideous to contemplate. Flight was impossible!

Only one resource remained, and that was to find some small hiding place to which the fearful denizens of the cavern could not penetrate. I gazed wildly around, and at last discovered a fissure in the rock, to which I rushed in the hope of recovering my scattered senses.

Crouching down, I waited shivering as in an ague fit. No man is brave in presence of an earthquake, or a bursting boiler, or an exploding torpedo. I could not be expected to feel much courage in the presence of the fearful fate that appeared to await me.

An hour passed. I heard all the time a strange rumbling outside the cave.

What was the fate of my unhappy companions? It was impossible for me to pause to inquire. My own wretched existence was all I could think of.

Suddenly a groaning, as of fifty bears in a fight, fell upon my ears—hisses, spitting, moaning, hideous to hear—and then I saw—

Never, were ages to pass over my head, shall I forget the horrible apparition.

It was the Ape Gigans!

Fourteen feet high, covered with coarse hair, of a blackish brown, the hair on the arms, from the shoulder to the elbow joints, pointing downwards, while that from the wrist to the elbow pointed upwards, it advanced. Its arms were as long as its body, while its legs were prodigious. It had thick, long, and sharply pointed teeth—like a mammoth saw.

It struck its breast as it came on smelling and sniffing, reminding me of the stories we read in our early childhood of giants who ate the flesh of men and little boys!

Suddenly it stopped. My heart beat wildly, for I was conscious that, somehow or other, the fearful monster had smelt me out and was peering about with his hideous eyes to try and discover my whereabouts.

My reading, which as a rule is a blessing, but which on this occasion, seemed momentarily to prove a curse, told me the real truth. It was the Ape Gigans, the Antediluvian Gorilla.

Yes! This awful monster, confined by good fortune to the interior of the earth, was the progenitor of the hideous monster of Africa.

He glared wildly about, seeking something—doubtless myself. I gave myself up for lost. No hope of safety or escape seemed to remain.

At this moment, just as my eyes appeared to close in death, there came a strange noise from the entrance of the cave; and turning, the Gorilla evidently recognized some enemy more worthy his prodigious size and strength. It was the huge Shark-Crocodile, which perhaps having disposed of my friends, was coming in search of further prey.

The Gorilla placed himself on the defensive, and clutching a bone some seven or eight feet in length, a perfect club, aimed a deadly blow at the hideous beast, which reared upwards and fell with all its weight upon its adversary.

A terrible combat, the details of which it is impossible to give, now ensued. The struggle was awful and ferocious. I, however, did not wait to witness the result. Regarding myself as the object of contention, I determined to remove from the presence of the victor. I slid down from my hiding place, reached the ground, and gliding against the wall, strove to gain the open mouth of the cavern.

But I had not taken many steps when the fearful

clamor ceased to be followed by a mumbling and groaning which appeared to be indicative of victory.

I looked back and saw the huge ape, gory with blood, coming after me with glaring eyes, with dilated nostrils that gave forth two columns of heated vapor. I could feel his hot and fetid breath on my neck; and with a horrid jump—awoke from my nightmare sleep.

Yes—it was all a dream. I was still on the raft with my uncle and the guide.

The relief was not instantaneous, for under the influence of the hideous nightmare my senses had become numbed. After a while, however, my feelings were tranquillized. The first of my perceptions which returned in full force was that of hearing. I listened with acute and attentive ears. All was still as death. All I comprehended was silence. To the roaring of the waters, which had filled the gallery with awful reverberations, succeeded perfect peace.

After some little time my uncle spoke, in a low and scarcely audible tone—

"Harry, boy, where are you?"

"I am here," was my faint rejoinder.

"Well don't you see what has happened? We are going upwards."

"My dear uncle, what can you mean?" was my half-delirious reply.

"Yes, I tell you we are ascending rapidly. Our downward journey is quite checked."

I held out my hand, and, after some little difficulty, succeeded in touching the wall. My hand was in an instant covered with blood. The skin was torn from the flesh. We were ascending with extraordinary rapidity.

"The torch—the torch!" cried the Professor wildly. "It must be lighted."

Hans, the guide, after many vain efforts, at last succeeded in lighting it, and the flame having now nothing to prevent its burning, shed a tolerably clear light. We were enabled to form an idea of the truth.

"It is just as I thought," said my uncle, after a moment or two of silent attention. "We are in a narrow well about four fathoms square. The waters of the great inland sea, having reached the bottom of the gulf, are now forcing themselves up the mighty shaft. As a natural consequence, we are being cast up on the summit of the waters."

"That I can see," was my lugubrious reply, "but where will this shaft end, and to what fall are we likely to be exposed?"

"Of that I am as ignorant as yourself. All I know is, that we should be prepared for the worst. We are going up at a fearfully rapid rate. As far as I can judge, we are ascending at the rate of two fathoms a second, or a hundred and twenty fathoms a minute, or rather more than three and a half leagues an hour. At this rate, our fate will soon be a matter of certainty."

"No doubt of it," was my reply. "The great concern I have now, however, is to know whether this shaft has any issue. It may end in a granite roof—in which case we shall be suffocated by compressed air, or dashed to atoms against the top. I fancy, already, that the air is beginning to be close and condensed. I have a difficulty in breathing."

This might be fancy, or it might be the effect of our rapid motion, but I certainly felt a great oppression of the chest.

"Harry," said the Professor, "I do believe that the situation is to a certain extent desperate. There remain, however, many chances of ultimate safety, and I have, in my own mind, been revolving them over during your heavy but agitated sleep. I have come to this logical conclusion—whereas we may at any moment perish, so at any moment we may be saved! We need, therefore, prepare ourselves for whatever

283

may turn up in the great chapter of accidents."

"But what would you have us do?" I cried. "Are we not utterly helpless?"

"No! While there is life there is hope. At all events, there is one thing we can do—eat, and thus obtain strength to face victory or death."

As he spoke, I looked at my uncle with a haggard glance. I had put off the fatal communication as long as possible. It was now forced upon me, and I must tell him the truth. Still I hesitated.

"Eat," I said, in a deprecating tone as if there were no hurry.

"Yes, and at once. I feel like a starving prisoner," he said, rubbing his yellow and shivering hands together.

And, turning round to the guide, he spoke some hearty, cheering words, as I judged from his tone, in Danish. Hans shook his head in a terribly significant manner. I tried to look unconcerned.

"What!" cried the Professor. "You do not mean to say that all our provisions are lost?"

"Yes," was my lowly spoken reply, as I held out something in my hand, "this morsel of dried meat is all that remains for us three."

My uncle gazed at me as if he could not fully appreciate the meaning of my words. The blow seemed to stun him by its severity. I allowed him to reflect for some moments.

"Well," said I, after a short pause, "what do you think now? Is there any chance of our escaping from our horrible subterranean dangers? Are we not doomed to perish in the great hollows of the Center of the Earth?"

But my pertinent questions brought no answer. My uncle either heard me not, or appeared not to do so.

And in this way a whole hour passed. Neither of us cared to speak. For myself, I began to feel the most fearful and devouring hunger. My companions, doubtless, felt the same horrible tortures, but neither of them would touch the wretched morsel of meat that remained. It lay there, a last remnant of all our great preparations for the mad and senseless journey!

I looked back, with wonderment, to my own folly. Fully was I aware that, despite his enthusiasm, and the ever-to-be-hated scroll of Saknussemm, my uncle should never have started on his perilous voyage. What memories of the happy past, what previsions of the horrible future, now filled my brain!

41 ... *Hunger*

HUNGER, prolonged, is temporary madness!

The brain is at work without its required food, and the most fantastic notions fill the mind. Hitherto I had never known what hunger really meant. I was likely to understand it now.

And yet, three months before I could tell my terrible story of starvation, as I thought it. As a boy I used to make frequent excursions in the neighborhood of the Professor's house.

My uncle always acted on system, and he believed that, in addition to the day of rest and worship, there should be a day of recreation. In consequence, I was always free to do as I liked on a Wednesday.

Now, as I had a notion to combine the useful and the agreeable, my favorite pastime was birds' nesting. I had one of the best collections of eggs in all the town. They were classified, and under glass cases.

There was a certain wood, which, by rising at early morn, and taking the cheap train, I could reach at eleven in the morning. Here I would botanize or geologize at my will. My uncle was always glad of specimens for his herbarium, and stones to examine. When I had filled my wallet, I proceeded to search for nests.

After about two hours of hard work, I, one day, sat down by a stream to eat my humble but copious lunch. How the remembrance of the spiced sausage, the wheaten loaf, and the beer made my mouth water now! I would have given every prospect of worldly wealth for such a meal. But to my story.

While seated thus at my leisure, I looked up at the ruins of an old castle, at no great distance. It was the remains of an historical dwelling, ivy-clad, and now falling to pieces.

While looking, I saw two eagles circling about the summit of a lofty tower. I soon became satisfied that there was a nest. Now, in all my collection, I wanted eggs of the native eagle and the large owl.

My mind was made up. I would reach the summit of that tower, or perish in the attempt. I went nearer, and surveyed the ruins. The old staircase, years before, had fallen in. The outer walls were, however, intact. There was no chance that way, unless I looked to the ivy solely for support. This was, as I soon found out, futile.

There remained the chimney, which still went up to the top, and had once served to carry off the smoke from every story of the tower.

Up this I determined to venture. It was narrow, rough, and therefore the more easily climbed. I took off my coat and crept into the chimney. Looking up, I saw a small, light opening, proclaiming the summit of the chimney.

Up—up I went, for some time using my hands and knees, after the fashion of a chimney sweep. It was slow work, but, there being continual projections, the task was comparatively easy. In this way, I reached halfway. The chimney now became narrower. The atmosphere was close, and, at last, to end the matter, I stuck fast. I could ascend no higher.

There could be no doubt of this, and there remained no resource but to descend, and give up my glorious prey in despair. I yielded to fate and endeavored to descend. But I could not move. Some unseen and mysterious obstacle intervened and stopped me. In an instant the full horror of my situation seized me.

I was unable to move either way, and was doomed to a terrible and horrible death, that of starvation. In a boy's mind, however, there is an extraordinary amount of elasticity and hope, and I began to think of all sorts of plans to escape my gloomy fate.

In the first place, I required no food just at present, having had an excellent meal, and was therefore allowed time for reflection. My first thought was to try and move the mortar with my hand. Had I possessed a knife, something might have been done, but that useful instrument I had left in my coat pocket.

I soon found that all efforts of this kind were vain and useless, and that all I could hope to do was to wriggle downwards.

But though I jerked and struggled, and strove to turn, it was all in vain. I could not move an inch, one way or the other. And time flew rapidly. My early rising probably contributed to the fact that I felt sleepy, and gradually gave way to the sensation of drowsiness.

I slept, and awoke in darkness, ravenously hungry.

Night had come, and still I could not move. I was tight bound, and did not succeed in changing my position an inch. I groaned aloud. Never since the days of my happy childhood, when it was a hardship to go from meal to meal without eating, had I really experienced hunger. The sensation was as novel as it was painful. I began now to lose my head and to scream and cry out in my agony. Something appeared, startled by my noise. It was a harmless lizard, but it appeared to me a loathsome reptile. Again I made the old ruins resound with my cries, and finally so exhausted myself that I fainted.

How long I lay in a kind of trance or sleep I cannot say, but when again I recovered consciousness it was day. How ill I felt, how hunger still gnawed at me, it would be hard to say. I was too weak to scream now, far too weak to struggle.

Suddenly I was startled by a roar.

"Are you there, Harry?" said the voice of my uncle. "Are you there, my boy?"

I could only faintly respond, but I also made a desperate effort to turn. Some mortar fell. To this I owed my being discovered. When the search took place, it was easily seen that mortar and small pieces of stone had recently fallen from above. Hence my uncle's cry.

"Be calm," he cried, "if we pull down the whole ruin, you shall be saved."

They were delicious words, but I had little hope.

Soon however, about a quarter of an hour later, I heard a voice *above me*, at one of the upper fireplaces.

"Are you below or above?"

"Below," was my reply.

In an instant a basket was lowered with milk, a biscuit, and an egg. My uncle was fearful to be too ready with his supply of food. I drank the milk first, for thirst had nearly deadened hunger. I then, much refreshed, ate my bread and hard egg.

They were now at work at the wall. I could hear a pickaxe. Wishing to escape all danger from this terrible weapon I made a desperate struggle, and the belt, which surrounded my waist and which had been hitched on a stone, gave way. I was free, and only escaped falling down by a rapid motion of my hands and knees.

In ten minutes more I was in my uncle's arms, after being two days and nights in that horrible prison. My occasional delirium prevented me from counting time.

I was weeks recovering from that awful starvation adventure: and yet what was that to the hideous sufferings I now endured?

After dreaming for some time, and thinking of this and other matters, I once more looked around me. We were still ascending with fearful rapidity. Every now and then the air appeared to check our respiration as it does that of aëronauts when the ascension of the balloon is too rapid. But if they feel a degree of cold in proportion to the elevation they attain in the atmosphere, we experienced quite a contrary effect. The heat began to increase in a most threatening and exceptional manner. I cannot tell exactly the mean, but I think it must have reached 122 degrees of Fahrenheit.

What was the meaning of this extraordinary change in the temperature? As far as we had hitherto gone, facts had proved the theories of Davy and of Lidenbrock to be correct. Until now, all the peculiar conditions of refractory rocks, of electricity, of magnetism, had modified the general laws of nature, and had created for us a moderate temperature; for the theory of the central fire remained, in my eyes, the only explainable one.

Were we, then, going to reach a position in which these phenomena were to be carried out in all their rigor, and in which the heat would reduce the rocks to a state of fusion?

Such was my not unnatural fear, and I did not conceal the fact from my uncle. My way of doing so might be cold and heartless, but I could not help it.

"If we are not drowned, or smashed into pancakes, and if we do not die of starvation, we had the satisfaction of knowing that we must be burned alive."

My uncle, in presence of this brusque attack, simply shrugged his shoulders, and resumed his reflections—whatever they might be.

An hour passed away, and except that there was a slight increase in the temperature no incident modified the situation. My uncle at last, of his own accord, broke silence.

"Well, Henry, my boy," he said, in a cheerful way, "we must make up our minds."

"Make up our minds to what?" I asked, in considerable surprise.

"Well—to something. We must at whatever risk recruit our physical strength. If we make the fatal mistake of husbanding our little remnant of food, we may probably prolong our wretched existence a few hours—but we shall remain weak to the end."

"Yes," I growled, "to the end. That, however, will not keep us long waiting."

"Well, only let a chance of safety present itself—only allow that a moment of action be necessary—where shall we find the means of action if we allow ourselves to be reduced to physical weakness by inanition?"

"When this piece of meat is devoured, uncle, what hope will there remain unto us?"

"None, my dear Harry, none. But will it do you any good to devour it with your eyes? You appear to me to reason like one without will or decision, like a being without energy."

"Then," cried I, exasperated to a degree which is scarcely to be explained, "you do not mean to tell me —that you—that you—have not lost all hope."

"Certainly not," replied the Professor, with consummate coolness.

"You mean to tell me, uncle, that we shall get out of this monstrous subterranean shaft?"

"While there is life there is hope. I beg to assert, Harry, that as long as a man's heart beats, as long as a man's flesh quivers, I do not allow that a being gifted with thought and will can allow himself to despair."

What a nerve! The man placed in a position like that we occupied must have been very brave to speak like this.

"Well," I cried, "what do you mean to do?"

291

"Eat what remains of the food we have in our hands; let us swallow the last crumb. It will be, Heaven willing, our last repast. Well, never mind—instead of being exhausted skeletons, we shall be men."

"True," muttered I in a despairing tone, "let us take our fill."

"We must," replied my uncle, with a deep sigh, "call it what you will."

My uncle took a piece of the meat that remained, and some crusts of biscuit which had escaped the wreck. He divided the whole into three parts.

Each had one pound of food to last him as long as he remained in the interior of the earth.

Each now acted in accordance with his own private character.

My uncle, the Professor, ate greedily, but evidently without appetite, eating simply from some mechanical motion. I put the food inside my lips, and hungry as I was, chewed my morsel without pleasure, and without satisfaction.

Hans the guide, just as if he had been eider-down hunting, swallowed every mouthful, as though it were a usual affair. He looked like a man equally prepared to enjoy superfluity or total want.

Hans, in all probability, was no more used to starvation than ourselves, but his hardy Icelandic nature had prepared him for many sufferings. As long as he received his three rix-dollars every Saturday night, he was prepared for anything.

The fact was, Hans never troubled himself about much except his money. He had undertaken to serve a certain man at so much per week, and no matter what evils befell his employer or himself, he never found fault or grumbled, so long as his wages were duly paid.

Suddenly my uncle roused himself. He had seen a smile on the face of our guide. I could not make it out.

"What is the matter?" said my uncle.

"Schiedam," said the guide, producing a bottle of this precious fluid.

We drank. My uncle and myself will own to our dying day that hence we derived strength to exist until the last bitter moment. That precious bottle of Hollands was in reality only half full; but, under the circumstances, it was nectar.

It took some minutes for myself and my uncle to form a decided opinion on the subject. The worthy Professor swallowed about half a pint and did not seem able to drink any more.

"*Fortrafflig*," said Hans, swallowing nearly all that was left.

"Excellent—very good," said my uncle, with as much gusto as if he had just left the steps of the club at Hamburg.

I had begun to feel as if there had been one gleam of hope. Now all thought of the future vanished!

We had consumed our last ounce of food, and it was five o'clock in the morning!

42 ... The Volcanic Shaft

MAN'S CONSTITUTION is so peculiar, that his health is purely a negative matter. No sooner is the rage of hunger appeased, than it becomes difficult to comprehend the meaning of starvation. It is only when you suffer that you really understand.

As to anyone who has not endured privation having any notion of the matter, it is simply absurd.

With us, after a long fast, some mouthfuls of bread and meat, a little mouldy biscuit and salt beef triumphed over all our previous gloomy and saturnine thoughts.

Nevertheless, after this repast each gave way to his own reflections. I wondered what were those of Hans —the man of the extreme north, who was yet gifted with the fatalistic resignation of Oriental character. But the utmost stretch of the imagination would not allow me to realize the truth. As for my individual self, my thoughts had ceased to be anything but memories of the past, and were all connected with that upper world which I never should have left. I saw it all now, the beautiful house in the Königstrasse, my poor Gretchen, the good Martha; they all passed before my mind like visions of the past. Every time any of the lugubrious groanings which were to be distinguished in the hollows around fell upon my ears, I fancied I heard the distant murmur of the great cities above my head.

As for my uncle, always thinking of his science, he

examined the nature of the shaft by means of a torch. He closely examined the different strata one above the other, in order to recognize his situation by geological theory. This calculation, or rather this estimation, could by no means be anything but approximate. But a learned man, a philosopher, is nothing if not a philosopher, when he keeps his ideas calm and collected; and certainly the Professor possessed this quality to perfection.

I heard him, as I sat in silence, murmuring words of geological science. As I understood his object and his meaning, I could not but interest myself despite my preoccupation in that terrible hour.

"Eruptive granite," he said to himself. "We are still in the primitive epoch. But we are going up—going up, still going up. But who knows? Who knows?"

Then he still hoped. He felt along the vertical sides of the shaft with his hand, and some few minutes later, he would go on again in the following style—

"This is gneiss. This is mocashites—silicious mineral. Good again; this is the epoch of transition, at all events, we are close to them—and then, and then"—

What could the Professor mean? Could he, by any conceivable means, measure the thickness of the crust of the earth suspended above our heads? Did he possess any possible means of making any approximation to this calculation? No.

The manometer was wanting, and no summary estimation could take the place of it.

And yet, as we progressed, the temperature increased in the most extraordinary degree, and I began to feel as if I were bathed in a hot and burning atmosphere. Never before had I felt anything like it. I could only compare it to the hot vapor from an iron foundry, when the liquid iron is in a state of ebullition and runs over. By degrees, and one after the other, Hans, my uncle, and myself had taken off our coats and waistcoats. They were unbearable. Even the slightest garment was not only uncomfortable, but the cause of extreme suffering.

"Are we ascending to a living fire?" I cried; when, to my horror and astonishment, the heat became greater than before. "No, no," said my uncle, "it is simply impossible, quite impossible."

"And yet," said I, touching the side of the shaft with my naked hand, "this wall is literally burning."

At this moment, feeling as I did that the sides of this extraordinary wall were red hot, I plunged my hands into the water to cool them. I drew them back with a cry of despair.

"The water is boiling!" I cried.

My uncle, the Professor, made no reply other than a gesture of rage and despair.

Something very like the truth had probably struck his imagination.

But I could take no share in either what was going on, or in his speculations. An invincible dread had taken possession of my brain and soul. I could only look forward to an immediate catastrophe, such a catastrophe as not even the most vivid imagination could have thought of. An idea, at first vague and uncertain, was gradually being changed into certainty.

I tremulously rejected it at first, but it forced itself upon me by degrees with extreme obstinacy. It was so terrible an idea that I scarcely dared to whisper it to myself.

And yet all the while certain, and as it were, involuntary observations determined my convictions. By the doubtful glare of the torch, I could make out some singular changes in the granitic strata; a strange and terrible phenomenon was about to be produced, in which electricity played a part.

Then this boiling water, this terrible and excessive

heat? I determined as a last resource to examine the compass.

The compass had gone mad!

Yes, wholly stark staring mad. The needle jumped from pole to pole with sudden and surprising jerks, ran round, or as it is said, boxed the compass, and then ran suddenly back again as if it had the vertigo.

I was aware that, according to the best acknowledged theories, it was a received notion that the mineral crust of the globe is never, and never has been, in a state of complete repose.

The modifications caused by the decomposition of internal matter, the agitation consequent on the flowing of extensive liquid currents, the excessive action of magnetism which tends to shake it incessantly, at a time when even the multitudinous beings on its surface do not suspect the seething process to be going on.

Still this phenomenon would not have alarmed me alone; it would not have aroused in my mind a terrible, an awful idea.

But other facts could not allow my self-delusion to last.

Terrible detonations, like Heaven's artillery, began to multiply themselves with fearful intensity. I could only compare them with the noise made by hundreds of heavily laden chariots being madly driven over a stone pavement. It was a continuous roll of heavy thunder.

And then the mad compass, shaken by the wild electric phenomena, confirmed me in my rapidly formed opinion. The mineral crust was about to burst, the heavy granite masses were about to rejoin, the fissure was about to close, the void was about to be filled up, and we poor atoms to be crushed in its awful embrace!

"Uncle, uncle!" I cried. "We are wholly, irretrievably lost!"

"What, then, my young friend, is your new cause of

297

terror and alarm?" he said, in his calmest manner. "What fear you now?"

"What do I fear now!" I cried, in fierce and angry tones. "Do you not see that the walls of the shaft are in motion? do you not see that the solid granite masses are cracking? do you not feel the terrible, torrid heat? do you not observe the awful boiling water on which we float? Do you not remark this mad needle? every sign and portent of an awful earthquake?"

My uncle coolly shook his head.

"An earthquake," he replied, in the most calm and provoking tone.

"Yes."

"My nephew, I tell you that you are utterly mistaken," he continued.

"Do you not, can you not, recognize all the well-known symptoms"—

"Of an earthquake? By no means. I am expecting something far more important."

"My brain is strained beyond endurance—what, what do you mean?" I cried.

"An eruption, Harry."

"An eruption," I gasped. "We are, then, in the volcanic shaft of a crater in full action and vigor."

"I have every reason to think so," said the Professor in a smiling tone, "and I beg to tell you that it is the most fortunate thing that could happen to us."

The most fortunate thing! Had my uncle really and truly gone mad? What did he mean by these awful words—what did he mean by this terrible calm, this solemn smile?

"What!" cried I, in the height of my exasperation, "we are on the way to an eruption, are we? Fatality has cast us into a well of burning and boiling lava, of rocks on fire, of boiling water, in a word, filled with every kind of eruptive matter? We are about to be expelled, thrown up, vomited, spit out of the interior of the earth, in common with huge blocks of granite, with showers of cinders and scoriae, in a wild whirlwind of flame, and you say—the most fortunate thing which could happen to us."

"Yes," replied the Professor, looking at me calmly from under his spectacles, "it is the only chance which remains to us of ever escaping from the interior of the earth to the light of day."

It is quite impossible that I can put on paper the thousand strange, wild thoughts which followed this extraordinary announcement.

But my uncle was right, quite right, and never had he appeared to me so audacious and so convinced as when he looked me calmly in the face and spoke of the chances of an eruption—of our being cast upon Mother Earth once more through the gaping crater of a volcano!

Nevertheless, while we were speaking we were still ascending; we passed the whole night going up, or to speak more scientifically, in an ascensional motion. The fearful noise redoubled; I was ready to suffocate. I seriously believed that my last hour was approaching, and yet, so strange is imagination, all I thought of was some childish hypothesis or other. In such circumstances you do not choose your own thoughts. They overcome you.

It was quite evident that we were being cast upwards by eruptive matter; under the raft there was a mass of boiling water, and under this was a heaving mass of lava, and an aggregate of rocks which on reaching the summit of the water would be dispersed in every direction.

That we were inside the chimney of a volcano there could no longer be the shadow of a doubt. Nothing more terrible could be conceived!

But on this occasion, instead of Sneffels, an old and extinct volcano, we were inside a mountain of fire in full activity. Several times I found myself asking, what mountain was it, and on what part of the world we should be shot out. As if it were of any consequence!

In the northern regions, there could be no reasonable doubt about that. Before it went decidedly mad, the compass had never made the slightest mistake. From the cape of Saknussemm, we had been swept away to the northward many hundreds of leagues. Now the question was, were we once more under Iceland— should we be belched forth on to the earth through the crater of Mount Hecla, or should we reappear through one of the other seven fire-funnels of the island? Taking in my mental vision a radius of five hundred leagues to the westward, I could see under this parallel only the little-known volcanoes of the north-west coast of America.

To the east one only existed somewhere about the eightieth degree of latitude, the Esk, upon the island of Jean Mayen, not far from the frozen regions of Spitzbergen.

It was not craters that were wanting, and many of them were big enough to vomit a whole army; all I wished to know was the particular one toward which we were making with such fearful velocity.

I often think now of my folly: as if I should ever have expected to escape!

Toward morning, the ascending motion became greater and greater. If the degree of heat increased instead of decreasing, as we approached the surface of the earth, it was simply because the causes were local and wholly due to volcanic influence. Our very style of locomotion left in my mind no doubt upon the subject. An enormous force, a force of some hundreds of combined atmospheres produced by vapors accumulated and long compressed in the interior of the earth, were hoisting us upwards with irresistible power.

But though we were approaching the light of day, to

what fearful dangers were we about to be exposed?

Instant death appeared the only fate which we could expect or contemplate.

Soon a dim, sepulchral light penetrated the vertical gallery, which became wider and wider. I could make out to the right and left long dark corridors like immense tunnels, from which awful and horrid vapors poured out. Tongues of fire, sparkling and crackling, appeared about to lick us up.

The hour had come!

"Look, uncle, look!" I cried.

"Well, what you see are the great sulphurous flames. Nothing more common in connection with an eruption."

"But if they lap us round!" I angrily replied.

"They will not lap us round," was his quiet and serene answer.

"But it will be all the same in the end if they stifle us," I cried.

"We shall not be stifled. The gallery is rapidly becoming wider and wider, and if it be necessary, we will presently leave the raft and take refuge in some fissure in the rock."

"But the water, the water, which is continually ascending?" I despairingly replied.

"There is no longer any water, Harry," he answered, "but a kind of lava paste, which is heaving us up, in company with itself, to the mouth of the crater."

In truth, the liquid column of water had wholly disappeared to give place to dense masses of boiling eruptive matter. The temperature was becoming utterly insupportable, and a thermometer exposed to this atmosphere would have marked between 189 and 190 degrees Fahrenheit.

Perspiration rushed from every pore. But for the extraordinary rapidity of our ascent we should have been stifled.

Nevertheless, the Professor did not carry out his

301

proposition of abandoning the raft; and he did quite wisely. Those few ill-joined beams offered, anyway, a solid surface—a support which elsewhere must have utterly failed us.

Toward eight o'clock in the morning a new incident startled us. The ascensional movement suddenly ceased. The raft became still and motionless.

"What is the matter now?" I said, querulously, very much startled by this change.

"A simple halt," replied my uncle.

"Is the eruption about to fail?" I asked.

"I hope not."

Without making any reply, I rose. I tried to look around me. Perhaps the raft, checked by some projecting rock, opposed a momentary resistance to the eruptive mass. In this case, it was absolutely necessary to release it as quickly as possible.

Nothing of the kind had occurred. The column of cinders, of scoriae, of broken rocks and earth, had wholly ceased to ascend.

"I tell you, uncle, that the eruption has stopped," was my oracular decision.

"Ah," said my uncle, "you think so, my boy. You are wrong. Do not be in the least alarmed; this sudden moment of calm will not last long, be assured. It has already endured five minutes, and before we are many minutes older we shall be continuing our journey to the mouth of the crater."

All the time he was speaking the Professor continued to consult his chronometer, and he was probably right in his prognostics. Soon the raft resumed its motion, in a very rapid and disorderly way, which lasted two minutes or thereabout; and then again it stopped as suddenly as before.

"Good," said my uncle, observing the hour, "in ten minutes we shall start again."

"In ten minutes?"

"Yes—precisely. We have to do with a volcano, the eruption of which is intermittent. We are compelled to breathe just as it does."

Nothing could be more true. At the exact minute he had indicated, we were again launched on high with extreme rapidity. Not to be cast off the raft, it was necessary to hold onto the beams. Then the hoist again ceased.

Many times since have I thought of this singular phenomenon without being able to find for it any satisfactory explanation. Nevertheless, it appeared quite clear to me, that we were not in the principal chimney of the volcano, but in an accessory conduit, where we felt the counter shock of the great and principal tunnel filled by burning lava.

It is impossible for me to say how many times this maneuver was repeated. All that I can remember is, that on every ascensional motion, we were hoisted up with ever-increasing velocity, as if we had been launched from a huge projectile. During the sudden halts we were nearly stifled; during the moments of projection the hot air took away our breath.

I thought for a moment of the voluptuous joy of suddenly finding myself in the hyperborean regions with the cold 30 degrees below zero!

My exalted imagination pictured to itself the vast snowy plains of the arctic regions, and I was impatient to roll myself on the icy carpet of the North Pole.

By degrees my head, utterly overcome by a series of violent emotions, began to give way to hallucination. I was delirious. Had it not been for the powerful arms of Hans the guide, I should have broken my head against the granite masses of the shaft.

I have, in consequence, kept no account of what followed for many hours. I have a vague and confused remembrance of continual detonations, of the shaking of the huge granitic mass, and of the raft going round like a spinning top. It floated on the stream of hot lava, amidst a falling cloud of cinders. The huge flames, roaring, wrapped us around.

A storm of wind which appeared to be cast forth from an immense ventilator roused up the interior fires of the earth. It was a hot incandescent blast.

At last I saw the figure of Hans as if enveloped in the huge halo of burning blaze, and no other sense remained to me but that sinister dread which the condemned victim may be supposed to feel when led to the mouth of a cannon, at the supreme moment when the shot is fired and his limbs are dispersed into empty space.

43 ... *Daylight at Last*

WHEN I OPENED MY EYES I felt the hand of the guide clutching me firmly by the belt. With his other hand he supported my uncle. I was not grievously wounded, but bruised all over in the most remarkable manner.

After a moment I looked around, and found that I was lying down on the slope of a mountain not two yards from a yawning gulf into which I should have fallen had I made the slightest false step. Hans had saved me from death, while I rolled insensible on the flanks of the crater.

"Where are we?" dreamily asked my uncle, who literally appeared to be disgusted at having returned to earth.

The eider-down hunter simply shrugged his shoulders as a mark of total ignorance.

"In Iceland?" said I, not positively but interrogatively.

"*Nej*," said Hans.

"How do you mean?" cried the Professor. "No—what are your reasons?"

"Hans is wrong," said I, rising.

After all the innumerable surprises of this journey, a yet more singular one was reserved to us. I expected to see a cone covered by snow, by extensive and widespread glaciers, in the midst of the arid deserts of the extreme northern regions, beneath the full rays of a polar sky, beyond the highest latitudes.

But contrary to all our expectations, I, my uncle, and the Icelander, were cast upon the slope of a mountain calcined by the burning rays of a sun which was literally baking us with its fires.

I could not believe my eyes, but the actual heat which affected my body allowed me no chance of doubting. We came out of the crater half naked, and the radiant star from which we had asked nothing for two months, was good enough to be prodigal to us of light and warmth—a light and warmth we could easily have dispensed with.

When our eyes were accustomed to the light we had lost sight of so long, I used them to rectify the errors of my imagination. Whatever happened, we should have been at Spitzbergen, and I was in no humor to yield to anything but the most absolute proof.

After some delay, the Professor spoke.

"Hem!" he said, in a hesitating kind of way, "it really does not look like Iceland."

"But supposing it were the island of Jean Mayen?" I ventured to observe.

"Not in the least, my boy. This is not one of the volcanoes of the north, with its hills of granite and its crown of snow."

"Nevertheless"—

"Look, look, my boy," said the Professor, as dogmatically as usual.

Right above our heads, at a great height, opened the crater of a volcano from which escaped, from one quarter of an hour to the other, with a very loud explosion, a lofty jet of flame mingled with pumice stone, cinders, and lava. I could feel the convulsions of nature in the mountain, which breathed like a huge whale, throwing up from time to time fire and air through its enormous vents.

Below, and floating along a slope of considerable angularity, the stream of eruptive matter spread away to

306

a depth which did not give the volcano a height of three hundred fathoms.

Its base disappeared in a perfect forest of green trees, among which I perceived olives, fig trees, and vines loaded with rich grapes.

Certainly this was not the ordinary aspect of the arctic regions. About that there could not be the slightest doubt.

When the eye was satisfied at its glimpse of this verdant expanse, it fell upon the waters of a lovely sea or beautiful lake, which made of this enchanted land an island of not many leagues in extent.

On the side of the rising sun was to be seen a little port, crowded with houses, and near which the boats and vessels of peculiar build were floating upon azure waves.

Beyond, groups of islands rose above the liquid plain, so numerous and close together as to resemble a vast beehive.

Toward the setting sun, some distant shores were to be made out on the edge of the horizon. Some presented the appearance of blue mountains of harmonious conformation; upon others, much more distant, there appeared a prodigiously lofty cone, above the summit of which hung dark and heavy clouds.

Toward the north, an immense expanse of water sparkled beneath the solar rays, occasionally allowing the extremity of a mast or the convexity of a sail bellying to the wind, to be seen.

The unexpected character of such a scene added an hundredfold to its marvellous beauties.

"Where can we be?" I asked, speaking in a low and solemn voice.

Hans shut his eyes with an air of indifference, and my uncle looked on without clearly understanding.

"Whatever this mountain may be," he said, at last, "I must confess it is rather warm. The explosions do

307

not leave off, and I do not think it is worth while to have left the interior of a volcano and remain here to receive a huge piece of rock upon one's head. Let us carefully descend the mountain and discover the real state of the case. To confess the truth, I am dying of hunger and thirst."

Decidedly the Professor was no longer a truly reflective character. For myself, forgetting all my necessities, ignoring my fatigues and sufferings, I should have remained still for several hours longer—but it was necessary to follow my companions.

The slope of the volcano was very steep and slippery; we slid over piles of ashes, avoiding the streams of hot lava which glided about like fiery serpents. Still, while we were advancing, I spoke with extreme volubility, for my imagination was too full not to explode in words.

"We are in Asia!" I exclaimed. "We are on the coast of India, in the great Malay islands, in the center of Oceania. We have crossed the one half of the globe to come out right at the antipodes of Europe!"

"But the compass!" exclaimed my uncle. "Explain that to me!"

"Yes—the compass," I said, with considerable hesitation. "I grant that is a difficulty. According to it, we have always been going northward."

"Then it lied."

"Hem—to say it lied is rather a harsh word," was my answer.

"Then we are at the North Pole"—

"The pole—no—well—well, I give it up," was my reply.

The plain truth was, that there was no explanation possible. I could make nothing of it.

And all the while we were approaching this beautiful verdure, hunger and thirst tormented me fearfully. Happily, after two long hours' march, a beautiful country spread out before us, covered by olives, pomegranates, and vines, which appeared to belong to anybody and everybody.

In the state of destitution into which we had fallen, we were not particular to a grape.

What delight it was to press these delicious fruits to our lips, and to bite at grapes and pomegranates fresh from the vine. Not far off, near some fresh and mossy grass, under the delicious shade of some trees, I discovered a spring of fresh water, into which we voluptuously laved our faces, hands, and feet.

While we were all giving way to the delights of new-found pleasures, a little child appeared between two tufted olive trees.

"Ah," cried I, "an inhabitant of this happy country."

The little fellow was poorly dressed, weak and suffering, and appeared terribly alarmed at our appearance. Half naked, with tangled, matted and ragged beards, we did look supremely ill-favored; and unless the country was a bandit land, we were not unlikely to alarm the inhabitants!

Just as the boy was about to take to his heels, Hans ran after him, and brought him back, despite his cries and kicks.

My uncle tried to look as gentle as possible, and then spoke in German.

"What is the name of this mountain, my friend?"

The child made no reply.

"Good," said my uncle, with a very positive air of conviction, "we are not in Germany."

He then made the same demand in English, of which language he was an excellent scholar.

The child shook its head and made no reply. I began to be considerably puzzled.

"Is he dumb?" cried the Professor, who was rather proud of his polyglot knowledge of languages, and making the same demand in French.

309

The boy only stared in his face.

"I must perforce try him in Italian," said my uncle, with a shrug.

"*Dove noi siamo?*"

"Yes, tell me where we are?" I added, impatiently and eagerly.

Again the boy remained silent.

"My fine fellow, do you or do you not mean to speak?" cried my uncle, who began to get angry. He shook him, and spoke another dialect of the Italian language.

"*Come si noma questa isola?*"—what is the name of this island?

"Stromboli," replied the rickety little shepherd, dashing away from Hans and disappearing in the olive groves.

We thought little enough about him.

Stromboli! What effect on the imagination did these few words produce! We were in the center of the Mediterranean; amidst the Eastern archipelago of mythological memory; in the ancient Strongylos, where Æolus kept the wind and the tempest chained up. And those blue mountains, which rose toward the rising of the sun, were the mountains of Calabria.

And that mighty volcano which rose on the southern horizon was Etna, the fierce and celebrated Etna!

"Stromboli! Stromboli!" I repeated to myself.

My uncle played a regular accompaniment to my gestures and words. We were singing together like an ancient chorus.

Ah—what a journey—what a marvellous and extraordinary journey! Here we had entered the earth by one volcano, and we had come out by another. And this other was situated more than twelve hundred leagues from Sneffels, from that drear country of

Iceland cast away on the confines of the earth. The wondrous chances of this expedition had transported us to the most harmonious and beautiful of earthly lands. We had abandoned the region of eternal snows for that of infinite verdure, and had left over our heads the gray fog of the icy regions to come back to the azure sky of Sicily!

After a delicious repast of fruits and fresh water, we again continued our journey in order to reach the port of Stromboli. To say how we had reached the island would scarcely have been prudent. The superstitious character of the Italians would have been at work, and we would have been called demons vomited from the infernal regions. It was therefore necessary to pass for humble and unfortunate shipwrecked travellers. It was certainly less striking and romantic, but it was decidedly safer.

As we advanced, I could hear my worthy uncle muttering to himself—

"But the compass. The compass most certainly marked north. This is a fact I cannot explain in any way."

"Well, the fact is," said I, with an air of disdain, "we must not explain anything. It will be much more easy."

"I should like to see a professor of the Johanneum Institution, who is unable to explain a cosmic phenomenon—it would indeed be strange."

And, speaking thus, my uncle, half naked, his leathern purse round his loins, and his spectacles upon his nose, became once more the terrible Professor of mineralogy.

An hour after leaving the wood of olives, we reached the fort of San Vicenza, where Hans demanded the price of his thirteenth week of service. My uncle paid him, with very many warm shakes of the hand.

At that moment, if he did not indeed quite share our natural emotion, he allowed his feelings so far to give

311

way as to indulge in an extraordinary expression for him.

With the tips of two fingers he gently pressed our hands and smiled.

44 ... *The Journey Ended*

THIS IS THE FINAL CONCLUSION of a narrative which will be probably disbelieved even by people who are astonished at nothing. I am, however, armed at all points against human incredulity.

We were kindly received by the Strombolite fishermen, who treated us as shipwrecked travellers. They gave us clothes and food. After a delay of forty-eight hours, on the 31st of September a little vessel took us to Messina, where a few days of delightful and complete repose restored us to ourselves.

On the fourth of October, we embarked in the Volturus, one of the postal packets of the Imperial Messagerie of France; and three days later we landed at Marseilles, having no other care on our minds but that of our precious but erratic compass. This inexplicable circumstance tormented me terribly. On the 9th of October, in the evening, we reached Hamburg.

What was the astonishment of Martha, what the joy of Gretchen! I will not attempt to define it.

"Now then, Harry, that you really are a hero," she said, "there is no reason why you should ever leave me again."

I looked at her. She was weeping tears of joy.

I leave it to be imagined if the return of Professor Hardwigg made or did not make a sensation in Hamburg. Thanks to the indiscretion of Martha, the news

313

of his departure for the Interior of the Earth had been spread over the whole world.

No one would believe it—and when they saw him come back in safety they believed it all the less.

But the presence of Hans and many stray scraps of information by degrees modified public opinion.

Then my uncle became a great man, and I the nephew of a great man; which, at all events, is something. Hamburg gave a festival in our honor. A public meeting of the Johanneum Institution was held, at which the Professor related the whole story of his adventures, omitting only the facts in connection with the compass.

That same day he deposited in the archives of the town the document he had found written by Saknussemm, and he expressed his great regret that circumstances stronger than his will did not allow him to follow the Icelandic traveller's track into the very Center of the Earth. He was modest in his glory, but his reputation only increased.

So much honor necessarily created for him many envious enemies. Of course they existed; and as his theories, supported by certain facts, contradicted the system of science upon the question of central heat, he maintained his own views both with pen and speech against the learned of every country. Although I still believe in the theory of central heat, I confess that certain circumstances, hitherto very ill defined, may modify the laws of such natural phenomena.

At the moment when these questions were being discussed with interest, my uncle received a rude shock—one that he felt very much. Hans, despite everything he could say to the contrary, quitted Hamburg; the man to whom we owed so much would not allow us to pay our deep debt of gratitude. He was taken with nostalgia, a love for his Icelandic home.

"*Farvel*," said he, one day, and with this one short

314

word of adieu, he started for Reykjavik, which he soon reached in safety.

We were deeply attached to our brave eider-duck hunter. His absence will never cause him to be forgotten by those whose lives he saved, and I hope, at some not distant day, to see him again.

To conclude, I may say that our journey into the Interior of the Earth created an enormous sensation throughout the civilized world. It was translated and printed in many languages. All the leading journals published extracts from it, which were commentated, discussed, attacked, and supported with equal animation by those who believed in its episodes, and by those who were utterly incredulous.

Wonderful! My uncle enjoyed during his lifetime all the glory he deserved; and he was even offered a large sum of money, by Mr. Barnum, to exhibit himself in the United States; while I am credibly informed by a traveller that he is to be seen in waxwork at Madame Tussaud's!

But one care preyed upon his mind, a care which rendered him very unhappy. One fact remained inexplicable—that of the compass. For a learned man to be baffled by such an inexplicable phenomenon was very aggravating. But Heaven was merciful, and in the end my uncle was happy.

One day, while he put some minerals belonging to his collection in order, I fell upon the famous compass and examined it keenly.

For six months it had lain unnoticed and untouched.

I looked at it with curiosity, which soon became surprise. I gave a loud cry. The Professor, who was at hand, soon joined me.

"What is the matter?" he cried.

"The compass!"

"What then?"

315

"Why, its needle points to the south and not to the north."

"My dear boy, you must be dreaming."

"I am not dreaming. See, the poles are changed."

"Changed!"

My uncle put on his spectacles, examined the instrument, and leaped for joy, shaking the whole house.

A clear light fell upon our minds.

"Here it is!" he cried, as soon as he had recovered the use of his speech. "After we had once passed Cape Saknussemm, the needle of this compass pointed to the southward instead of northward."

"Evidently."

"Our error is now easily explained. But to what phenomenon do we owe this alteration in the needle?"

"Nothing more simple."

"Explain yourself, my boy. I am on thorns."

"During the storm, upon the Central Sea, the ball of fire which made a magnet of the iron in our raft, turned our compass topsy-turvy."

"Ah!" cried the Professor, with a loud and ringing laugh. "It was a trick of that inexplicable electricity."

From that hour my uncle was the happiest of learned men, and I the happiest of ordinary mortals. For my pretty Virland girl, abdicating her position as ward, took her place in the house in King Street (Königstrasse) in the double quality of niece and wife.

We need scarcely mention that her uncle was the illustrious Professor Hardwigg, corresponding member of all the scientific, geographical, mineralogical and geological societies of the five quarters of the globe.